CLARKESWORLD

YEAR NINE - VOLUME TWO

CLARKESWORLD
YEAR NINE - VOLUME TWO

EDITED BY NEIL CLARKE & SEAN WALLACE

WYRM PUBLISHING

CLARKESWORLD: YEAR NINE VOLUME TWO

For more information, contact Wyrm Publishing:
wyrmpublishing@gmail.com

ISBN: 978-1-64236-002-8 (trade paperback)
ISBN: 978-1-64236-001-1 (ebook)

Visit Clarkesworld Magazine at:
clarkesworldmagazine.com

Table of Contents

Introduction
NEIL CLARKE

Clarkesworld's ninth year marks the first time our annual fiction output was too large for just one book. This anthology closes out the set and includes stories from our April 2015 through September 2015 issues. While many exciting things happened in the first half of the year—our 100th issue, the launch of our translation project, and our first Hugo winner—the second half brought with it its fair share too.

Opening and closing this book are, "The Empress in Her Glory" by Robert Reed—a finalist for the WSFA Small Press Award—and "Today, I am Paul" by Martin L. Shoemaker—the winner of that award. Over the years, many *Clarkesworld* stories had been finalists, but this was our first win and it was my pleasure to accept the award on Martin's behalf. (Unfortunately, neither of us thought to open the speech with "Today, I am Martin.") Martin's story was also a Nebula finalist alongside "When Your Child Strays from God" by Sam J. Miller and, a story from the previous volume, "Cat Pictures Please" by Naomi Kritzer.

While publishing Chinese science fiction continued to be the focus of our relationship with Storycom International, our original Kickstarter funding to launch the project exceeded expectations and allowed us to establish a small fund for translations from other parts of the world. The first of those was "An Evolutionary Myth," a South Korean story written by Bo-young Kim and translated by Gord Sellar—a name you may recognize from his stories in *Clarkesworld* and elsewhere—and Jihyun Park. Efforts to bring more of the world to our readers and listeners is something we're passionate about and the endeavor has become an important part of our vision for the future.

And while not a part of these anthologies, I've always considered each issue's cover art to be a standalone story in picture form. Over the years, several of those covers have go on to be selected as finalists for the Chesley Award by the Association of Science Fiction and Fantasy Artists (ASFA). Covers from year nine—and a small portion of year ten—earned ASFA recognition in the form of a nomination and Chesley Award win for Best Art Director. Maybe someday we'll be able to publish an art book to feature some of the best covers our artists have produced over the years. I've always thought it would be a fun project to tackle.

As a reminder, each story in this anthology can be listened to directly on our website, so please join us there for the audio version, some SF/F related non-fiction, and creative ways to help support the magazine as we continue to grow.

Enough with the history lesson though. It's time to let the stories speak for themselves.

Neil Clarke
June 3, 2018

The Empress in Her Glory
ROBERT REED

Fruits ripen and worlds ripen.

If not taken at the right moment, any ripe prize falls from its tree and rots away, and nothing is gained.

That was how They looked at the situation.

Call them "alien." The word isn't ridiculous, yet by the same token, no label does justice to their origins or far-reaching powers. And after four and a half billion years of slow, often irregular growth, the Earth was deemed ripe. In the parlance of universal laws, that little orb had grown just soft enough and sweet enough. That's why They came. That's why an ordinary day in late June came and left again, and in those hours, by invasive and ephemeral means, every aspect of human existence was conquered.

The new rulers were few, less than a hundred, but they were an experienced, well-practiced partnership. Avoiding sloppiness and haste, they followed their occupation with months of careful study. This was a new colony, one realm among ten thousand thousand scattered about the galaxy, and their first job was to understand the world's nature. Out of that collection of meat and history, failure and divine promise, they had to select one good leader—a human face and mind to be entrusted with the administration of what was theirs.

At fifty-eight, Adrianne Hammer ruled an empire of cubicles and computers as well as an impressive stockpile of Folgers Classic Roast. She was sharp-minded and quietly demanding of her seven-person staff. Weighing data from multiple sources, she was paid to make honest, unsentimental guesses about the future. Economic growth and downturns were predicted. The odds of storms and plagues and various medical breakthroughs had to be rendered as numbers. Hers was one minuscule department inside a major insurance conglomerate, but while other departments often duplicated their work, Adrianne and her team were unusually competent. Which is to say that the eight of them were correct a little more often than their competitors.

She was a widow. People who barely knew Adrianne knew that much. Her husband had struggled for a year against liver cancer. His prognosis was poor but never hopeless, and he might have survived. There were good reasons for optimism. But the man must have been too terrified to face his difficult future. One morning, Adrianne kissed him before driving to work, and the man subsequently drank half a bottle of quality wine and then jabbed a pistol under his fleshy chin.

As a rule, humans enjoy tragedies that involve others. They also believe suffering lends depth to the afflicted. Years after the event, co-workers still spoke about the police coming to deliver the awful news. It happened to be a rainy day. The poor lady was sitting alone in the cafeteria. The officers sat in front her and beside her, speaking slowly, and she seemed to hear them. But shock and pain must have left her numb. With a flat, unemotional voice, she asked, "Where did it happen?" Her husband shot himself at home. "But what room?" Inside the home office. "Who found him?" A delivery man looked through the window, called it in. She nodded, eyes narrowing. "Which gun?" she demanded. "And how bad is the mess?"

That's when a bystander took hold of her hands, urging Adrianne to shut her eyes for a moment, to collect her wits.

She had one child, a grown boy already living in a distant state. Husband and son were the only people pictured on her work desk, and in keeping with a spirit of relentless honesty, neither photograph was flattering. The dead Mr. Hammer sported a beefy, rounded face dominated by an alcoholic's bright nose. The son was an ugly fellow needing a comb and a smile. People on Adrianne's staff knew about her life. She wasn't particularly secretive, no. But there was a persistent story, popular in the other departments and divisions, that she was a cat lady. Didn't she look the part? Except Adrianne didn't keep any pets, and she didn't suffer from mothering urges, and despite some very confident rumors, she also didn't quilt or garden or ride cruise ships. She wasn't unattractive, and so acquaintances imagined male friends. But except for a few dinner dates and a couple change of sheets, she never dated. Men and romance were difficulties best left behind. Alone inside the tidy, cat-free house, Mrs. Hammer filled her private hours with activities that mirrored her official job, She stood before a tall desk, in the same office where her husband killed himself. To her, the world was one giant and splendid puzzle, and like the best puzzles, it was built out of simple repeating pieces. Her passion was to search the Internet for odd papers and unexplored pools of data, reading everything interesting as slowly and carefully as she could, and when she was ready—but only when ready—she would weave conclusions that were often a little more true than every other half-mad opinion on the Web.

Adrianne Hammer was a blogger.

Regularity. Reliability. Those were qualities she demanded of herself, and her tiny audience had always appreciated the results. She posted every Sunday, and the only postings missed were because of one bout of swine flu, and before that, her husband's messy suicide. Thousands of people had her tools and intellect, or they had better. But brilliance likes to be focused. The average genius wants to fall in love with some narrow cause, a topic that generates passion and that she can master better than anyone else. And the most powerful minds often ended up being driven by the rawest, most predictable emotions.

But this human didn't suffer from a narrow focus.

In fifteen years, that lifelong Republican had successfully predicted elections and civil wars as well as giving shrewd warnings about which stable nations would fail to rule effectively. She warned her readers about stock bubbles and the diminishing stocks of easy petroleum. China was on the precipice of ten environmental disasters. Russia was a rotted husk. She studied SARS and MERS and then successfully predicted the onset of GORS. Climate change was a growing maelstrom worth visiting every couple months, and with a perpetually reasoned tone, she warned her careless species to watch out for even more serious hazards. Comet impacts. Solar flares. Nuclear war between small players and firestorms born from mistakes made in North Dakota.

In one popular posting, she wrote about the Singularity. "I can only guess when the day comes, but self-aware computers are inevitable. In fact, synthetic intelligence is more likely today than it was yesterday. And it's a little more plausible this afternoon than it was just this morning."

At the heart of every posting was the inescapable truth: The future was chaos smothered inside more chaos. Even at her best, Adrianne cautioned that no marriage of learning and insight can envision what comes in another ten years, or in some cases, in another ten seconds.

Yet even the most difficult, disorganized race had to have its winner.

And Adrianne Hammer was among of the quickest of the best.

The invisible lords made her one candidate among twenty-three. Each human was secretly examined, every life measured against an assortment of ideals. Adrianne was fifth on the list, and she wouldn't have climbed any higher. But her son called her at home one evening. Intoxicated, plainly furious, the young man began by telling his mother that she was a bloodless bitch, unloving and ugly.

Adrianne reacted with a soft sigh, shaking her head.

The son's rapid prattle continued, insults scattered through recollections from childhood. Old slights and embarrassments were recounted. One cold, wicked parent had destroyed the young man's future. Didn't she see the crimes? Didn't she understand what a miserable mess she had made of his little life?

Once and then again, she said her son's name. Quietly, but not softly.

The tirade finally broke. Then he muttered, "Dad."

She nodded, apparently unsurprised by the conversation's turn.

"Yes," she said.

"You should have known," the young man said. "Of all people, you should have seen it coming. Why didn't you sense what he was planning?"

"Because he didn't give clues."

"Dad didn't have to kill himself," her son said. "He wasn't that sick."

She said, "Honey, he was very ill. And that doesn't matter now."

"It does matter."

"Not after the gunshot," she said. "That's why people kill themselves. One action, and everything else is inconsequential."

Both stopped talking.

Forty seconds passed.

"I wasn't there," her son complained.

"Nobody was."

"Poor Dad was alone."

"We're all alone, honey."

By a thousand means, the Earth's new owners studied the woman's pain. They watched the candidate open her mouth and close it again. They measured her breathing, her heart. The electricity running along her wet neurons. They even tried to read her thoughts, which was difficult with most humans and quite impossible with this specimen.

To their minds, opacity was a noble quality.

"After he shot himself," her son began.

"I know."

"At the funeral—"

"I remember."

"You were angry at him. Because he used the .357. Because he aimed up and made a mess in the ceiling, and you'd have to find someone to come pull out the bones and make patches and then paint. That's why you were angry with him."

"I wasn't angry," she said.

"Yes you were."

"No, I was reasonable frustrated," she said. "You're always the furious one."

"Don't fucking say that."

Eyes narrowed. Adrianne fell silent.

Her pulse was slow, regular.

"You see everything, Mom. You should have predicted this."

Just then, Adrianne's heart rate elevated. Slightly.

"You could have taken precautions," he said.

"It was my mistake," she agreed. "I underestimated your father's fears, and overestimated his aversion to violence."

Her son sobbed.

Honesty was easy for the woman. "I always assumed your father would drink himself to death," she said. "Which perhaps was how he made himself sick in the first place."

"Listen to yourself."

"I always do."

"You don't care. You make an awful mistake like that, and it's nothing to you."

"One error among thousands," she pointed out.

The young man said nothing.

Adrianne's pulse had returned to normal.

"Do you miss him, Mom?"

She said nothing, apparently giving the problem some thought. "I miss you," she said at last.

Her son broke the connection.

Adrianne set the phone down on the desk, and after a sigh and seven seconds of introspection, she glanced up at the patched, repainted ceiling. Then she returned to work, crafting a long, tightly reasoned blog about thorium reactors, their blessings and why they were coming too late to the discussion.

Those watching came to one enduring conclusion: This was an exceptionally tough-minded, determined beast.

Which was why a month later, without warnings or the barest explanations, an obscure blogger was given complete control over the secretly conquered world.

At work and at home, Adrianne wielded tools that she didn't understand. The web crawlers and other bots gathered data and then filtered it for her eyes. But even the most competent expert wouldn't have noticed the unique bots added to her account. That small event happened early on a Saturday morning. Waking at ten after five, as usual, she discovered e-mails and classified reports from mainland China. Asking for origin reports, the new software told reasonable lies about failures to encrypt and a nameless hacker who must have let her cleverness sit exposed for too long.

This week's blog was supposed to focus on a renewed US space program.

Not anymore.

Adrianne read and reread the translations, slept five hours, and finished her research on Sunday morning. The blog was written in two hours, which was quick for her. Instead of railguns, she described the secret fissures inside the Three Gorges Dam and how the Chinese government was doing nothing of significance, nervously hoping that their wildest worries would prove without merit.

At the moment of publication, the empress had 709 scattered followers.

Sunday evening was unremarkable, and the next two days were pleasant enough. Wednesday seemed to offer more of the same. A courtyard was adjacent to the cafeteria. Adrianne sat in the shadows, eating a peanut butter sandwich and small apple and then two Girl Scout cookies bought from a colleague's daughter. Thin Mints. Arguably the finest cookie in the history of humankind.

"How bad?" a bypasser asked.

"They still don't know," his companion said.

"How many people live downstream?"

"Millions."

The men were past, gone. The final cookie was half eaten. That very calm woman took a moment to examine her tooth marks in the bright black chocolate. Then she finished the cookie and the last of her low fat milk, and she disposed of the trash and used the restroom, returning to her station two minutes before one o'clock.

Every monitor in the office showed the Chinese flood. The giant dam didn't just split open. It had failed catastrophically, dissolving into rubble and a wall of filthy black water that was slashing through the nightbound countryside, and it wouldn't stop flowing until wreckage was washing up on American shores.

That portion of the future was easy to predict.

Other parts were less certain.

Most humans would have been traumatized, and many would have mentioned their brilliance or dumb luck. But no, Adrianne had a project to shepherd along.

Her department was trying to calculate the likely changes in life spans in the Western world. Insurance companies never stopped making these assessments. Until now, she had been enjoying a productive week, discovering speculative works in places that normally didn't share ideas, including several interesting reports about a small start-up in France working with anti-aging drugs.

Adrianne was the only person in the office who had found the anti-aging references. Which was bothersome. Her staff was badly distracted, but she sent one of her boys chasing the French story, expecting and even hoping that he would follow the crumbs to the same destination.

But he didn't, no.

"I'm not finding anything, ma'am. Where am I supposed to look?"

Adrianne drove home as usual. The evening news was filled with videos of cities being gutted, churning waters filled with animal corpses and human corpses. She stayed awake past midnight, just after a light-water reactor and various storage facilities were inundated. The disaster had reached a new level of appalling. By five o'clock the next morning, her time, martial law had been imposed across China, and there were rumors of a major shake-up in Beijing.

The Chinese civil war remained weeks in the future.

Arriving late to work, Adrianne found one of her boys standing beside her desk. He smiled nervously. The young man looked happy yet uncertain, rocking from foot to foot. His voice cracked when he said, "Hello," and then he laughed at his obvious terror.

"What's wrong?" she asked.

Her voice broke. Just a little, in places only she could hear.

The man tried laughing again. But he couldn't make himself. "I don't read it a lot," he confessed.

"Read what?" she asked.

"Your blog." He sighed. "But I did see something . . . I don't know . . . it's been a couple years. And you were right."

"Was I?"

"China. It was ripe for environmental disaster."

At that moment, Adrianne would have been hard-pressed to write any coherent opinions about Chinese futures. The flood was enormous, but good things might come from this. Sometimes chaos supplied the fuel to make meaningful changes, destroying corruption, ensuring stability for hundreds of millions of survivors.

"You were right," he repeated.

Finally, she saw what was obvious. "You didn't read my last article. Did you?"

"No, ma'am, I'm sorry. Like I said, I don't get to it much."

Adrianne felt sick.

"Why? Should I become a follower?" He was nearly a boy, years younger than her son. "I'll read it right now. How's that?"

"No," she said.

Loudly, almost shouting.

He blinked. "Okay. You're right. Work first."

Adrianne's hope was to cross the day, to finish these hours and escape back home and then make some accommodations to this very unlikely coincidence. But the peace only lasted until ten in the morning. People from other departments began to stop outside the office. Familiar, nameless faces came to look at the slender woman with the neat gray hair and out-of-fashion glasses. With caution and nervous wonder, they stared, and then she would glance up and they would retreat. Then one bold lawyer asked how she could be so right about this goddamn mess. And suddenly her own people were demanding explanations. Adrianne had no choice but some species of honesty, and then nobody was working. Everyone inside her office and throughout the complex began to read and reread a few thousand words predicting the century's largest disaster.

Adrianne took her lunch home and called in sick.

By evening, with the help of two cocktails, she checked her blog. The comments went on and on, many in Chinese. And she had just under fourteen thousand followers, the number rising every time she refreshed.

Someone had fed her the information.

That was the first and still obvious explanation. She kept imagining the Chinese dissident, crafty and out of reach, and with that bit of false-knowledge in hand, Adrianne wrote her next blog—a careful piece using bits of new research. With words and tidy graphs, she reminded her readers that hydrocarbons were common, both in the world and across the universe. But being common didn't matter. Most of the world's oil was too expensive to lift out of the ground, and what could be lifted was often too expensive to refine, and the energy gained at the day's end was approaching the grim fulcrum where the modern world couldn't afford to pay its bills.

The topic was familiar. She had investigated peak oil many times. But she had more followers now, a lot of new heads to absorb her thinking, and that's why she wrote the piece, expecting that a few of her readers would appreciate and maybe even welcome her calm logic.

Fifty-eight years of life gives a person experience with insults and curses. But what surprised Adrianne was the intimacy of the threats—violent words coupled with images from people who didn't simply doubt her numbers and good sense, but who wanted to come her house just so they could cut off her head, to claim it as a trophy they would nail to their truck hoods or use in ways far worse than that.

She slept badly for a week. And while awake, every stranger deserved small anxieties.

Yet nothing evil ever came to her door, and everything that was good proved to be excellent. Adrianne's staff rallied around her. Unfit men in their thirties and forties acted as unofficial bodyguards, and without fanfare, the youngest member of her staff—a girl in her mid-twenties—broke company rules by bringing both a Taser and pepper spray into the office.

That next Sunday, Adrianne published a brief, dense blog about magneto-inertial fusion engines—the best means for opening up the solar system. And inside the piece, she included schematics plucked from what looked like a NASA website.

Her followers had reached eighty thousand.

The rocket blog was followed by a long, complicated piece about increasing lifespans and why that was a damnable trend. Long-term environmental successes would never be possible if too many bodies were prepared to live comfortably in the increasingly overheated world.

By then, her followers' comments had dropped by half, insults by one third, and she had the carefully plotted data to prove it.

By then, the Chinese civil war was underway, and feeling invested in that particular horror, Adrianne suggested a solution. Like an innoculate into a sick body, she proposed that one of the peripheral Chinese enclaves could supply a new paradigm. Taiwan was offered, then dismissed. Too much history. Hong Kong had its potentials, but it didn't have the necessary freedom of motion. So instead she voted for the distant and very wealthy city-state of Singapore. Its authoritarian leaders and billionaires were Chinese by heritage. They could broker deals and supply guidance that wouldn't end the strife today, but in another couple years, perhaps with only fifty million dead from war and famine, some new normalcy could be established.

Adrianne's final Monday at work was pleasantly forgettable.

Actuarial adventures.

Lunch.

More adventures.

Plus one long meeting.

Then home and a light dinner, one drink and idle reading, and bed.

On Monday, Ghawar was the greatest oil field on the Earth. But early Tuesday, Adrianne's time, a series of prolonged earthquakes rolled across northern Saudi Arabia. By Wednesday morning, virtually every oil well in the region had seized up and died. The spot market for crude was driving towards three hundred dollars. An initial explanation, full of panic and half-informed conjecture, blamed the greedy Saudis. An ocean of oil had been removed from the Ghawar field, and the strata must have been pushed too hard. Despite sound geologic evidence that this was impossible, an entire region had slumped, and the world was several million barrels short of oil today and tomorrow, and always.

By Wednesday evening, the Prime Minister of Singapore was opening public talks with three of the main combatants inside China.

Thursday morning saw a news conference from France. An upstart medical firm was going to sell expensive compounds that could only be described as elixirs, and lifespans would soon triple.

But the blogger at the heart of it remained surprisingly unnoticed. Only half a dozen news crews sat on the street outside Adrianne's home. With her phone off and drapes closed, it was possible to believe that her life hadn't changed. Then came Friday morning, and a team of MIT engineers announced that the design for a novel rocket propulsion system, posted on a small blog, was not from any governmental database. Or commercial database. Nor any other reasonable source. Yet A. Hammer's documents contained quite a few interesting features, some invoking the newest ideas about energy in the universe, and it might be possible to build a prototype star-drive within the next five years.

By then, the world was plunging into its Grand Depression.

But those financial horrors were augmented by promises of endless life and easy commutes to the other worlds.

The raging chaos had a center—one quiet woman barely known a month ago.

Adrianne escaped her house through the back gate, taking a cab to work. Nobody in her office was pretending to work. They watched the news together, the door left mostly closed. A manager and two security people arrived before lunch, and Adrianne was ushered into the largest conference room. Every important person in the corporation had gathered to stare at her. Several of them remembered to thank her for her long service. Then the CFO offered her a worried smile and a substantial buyout.

Everybody adored her work, but she was too much of a distraction.

Twenty million followers were just the beginning. Adrianne was going to have advertising revenues flowing from her blog, and she had her buyout package, plus savings and numerous offers of cash for appearances on news networks and talk shows. With those prospects and a numbed resolve, she began the long walk back to her office and the cubicle, ready to wish her people the best before heading off into this unforeseen life.

But stepping through the door, an idea took hold.

Seven others watched the old lady make coffee for everyone. The Folgers was brewing, and she sat with her back to her desk, in a pose they had never seen before. She didn't look regal or even particularly confident. No, nothing was special in her appearance, save for the weariness of great events, and they felt sorry for the lady, even while wondering which of them would end up in charge. She looked at each face. Then she gave the carpet a long stare. Somebody thought to pour coffee into eight mugs and everyone had their share and there was sitting and more silence, except out in the hallway where someone had slipped indoors. A supporter or an enemy: The invader's goals were never known. Security noticed the interloper and tackled her, and when the screaming was finished, Adrianne looked up at the ceiling. Quietly, soberly, she said, "There's no reasonable set of factors that can make this possible. What's happening. To me and to the world. I don't know why, but I seem to have a pipeline to things I don't understand."

Nobody could disagree with that assessment.

Then she surprised them, saying, "If somebody has to wield this kind of influence, why not me?"

It was the first inkling that their boss saw the potential.

"But I need a staff," she said. "A well-paid, familiar group of people who know me well enough not to take offense when I'm lost in work."

The girl with the Taser said, "Oh. You want to hire us."

"And later, others," Adrianne admitted. "But you're my nucleus."

Every head nodded.

There. It was agreed. They would leave work together, after tendering their resignations.

"Nothing about this is reasonable," Adrianne continued. "But this world is built on unreasonable coincidences. Until we understand what's happening, I'm going to be the Empress of Everything. And for as long as I have the job, I should at least try to do my best."

Her house was abandoned. There was no choice in the matter. Adrianne lived for three days on the Taser girl's sofa, writing a sharp blog delineating recent history and her apparent, surprising hold on some form of cosmic power or blunt magic. Whatever this was. Her hostess suggested adding a little personal noise to the piece. "So people think they know you." But it was Adrianne who gave the post its signature moment. Mentioning the horrors of liver cancer, she added a quick request for people to send a few dollars to one of several appropriate agencies. And by the time she slipped out of the girl's apartment, nearly a hundred million dollars had appeared in the welcoming coffers. With a flood of unexpected gifts choking the blogger's PayPal account too.

That next week was spent in anonymous hotel rooms, talking strategy, giving possibilities flesh and shadow. Her people did their best to keep the media at bay, scaring off senators and business leaders as well. And they also found a recently constructed, never occupied warehouse complex, far from the city but close to highways and a high-grade optical cable that could be secured.

Only the president was given access to the world's boss. There were three long, very exhausting conversations. The last talk was a face-to-face session. Adrianne was touring the warehouse, preparing to sign a long-term lease on the facility and a power commitment from an adjacent windmill farm. A security firm still needed to be hired, and her team was interviewing remodelers. Apartments would be installed in back, and because nobody knew where this madness would lead, plans were being drawn up for a school and playground for children, a swimming pool for everyone, and a bar for the ruling class.

In those two phone conversation, the president tried charm. But charm had proved useless. Ready to unleash stronger tactics, his helicopters landed on the empty parking lot. Flanked by high-ranking civilians and officers in dress uniforms, he met the empress in the front office. With a careful blending of rage and authority, he defined his level of scorn. Adrianne listened silently. Then he invited his aides to talk about various legal actions that might be appropriate. She interrupted with a raised hand, which amusingly was enough to stop every voice. Everyone stared at her. "Which laws have I broken? I would very much like to know," she said. Then the ranking general outlined what his people would do if faced with a dangerous power trying to usurp the nation's security. "Except that sounds like war," was her response. "And I don't approve of war. If I can find the words, I intend to make every army in the world obsolete."

That brought a chill, and more rage.

Sensing failure, the president returned to charm.

"You're a registered Republican," he pointed out. "I'm assuming you voted for me."

"No," she said. "I've never voted for national candidates."

"But you do vote, correct?"

"Only for local candidates. Bond issues. I have a tiny but real chance of making an impact. But I can't pretend to have a role in presidential races."

The man needed to pause, giving himself a chance to recalculate.

"Come over here, sir. If you would."

He joined her beside a laptop.

"I've been working on a new blog. In fact, I intend to publish in the next few minutes."

Some prior briefing came to mind. "It's Saturday. I was told that you put these things out on Sundays."

"Except I don't have a normal job anymore. And with the change of fates, I think I need to embrace a more ambitious schedule. Which makes this is a good day to begin."

Keys were pressed. The unpublished text appeared.

Stepping back, she said, "Read the piece, if you wish. Sir."

The blog spoke about the dangers inherent in the aging nuclear fleets. Adrianne was arguing that the only wise course was to put the weapons to bed, today if possible. But she was afraid that people wouldn't change their natures until they received a good clear warning. So at the end of the piece, she had written, "I want to see one of their swords pull itself out of its scabbard."

The president hadn't finished reading the piece.

"Lady, what are you talking about?" he asked.

She didn't answer. Her heart pounding, she clicked the publish button and stepped back. "I don't understand what's happened to me," she said, quietly but not quietly. "I can make guesses. I doubt if anyone can decipher what's true, not in the short-term. But there are clues. If you look hard. With the Three Gorges and the stardrive, I was fed information of something already happening. Which is one phenomena. But I wrote about oil. On my own. And whatever this power is, it needed time to make preparations before the quake struck, before we started this overdue collapse into economic ruin.

"Sir, I have a sense," she said. "My very strong intuition is that simple directions are more likely to lead to immediate effects.

"Consider this blog a test. Both of us need to know. What marvels do I have in this hand?"

Moments later, an alarm sounded.

An Air Force general turned away, muttering into a sat-phone.

Voices spoke of "the football."

"It's ours and it's launched," someone cried out.

The president looked ill, looked simple, his face drained of blood and most of its life. He glared at Adrianne. He stared numbly at his own hands. And then someone said, "No, the missile broke apart after launching. It's down. It over."

Adrianne turned to her people.

Winked.

Then looking at the visitors, she said, "I have six blogs written. They're waiting on servers around the world. If anything unseemingly happens to me or to any of my people, those pieces get published automatically. And you don't want those ideas getting loose on the world. Believe me."

They believed, at least enough to retreat.

Then the Taser girl asked, "Is that right? Six blogs waiting to kill the world?"

The Empress didn't seem to hear the questions. She seemed intrigued by the details in the her own tiny hand. Then to the hand, in that calm dry voice, she said, "By tomorrow, there will be. Now let's get to work."

Eventually she would be known as Adrianne the First. But in those early years, she was the Hammer, a respected and feared and often scorned entity sitting in a warehouse in the bleakest bowels of Ohio. She appeared on television when she wanted, which was rare. Her speeches and occasional interviews proved nothing except that she was no public speaker. And where the lowliest princess—some creature born with a good name and small inheritance—would have carried her head high, Adrianne became more and more like she had always been. Chilled. Collected. Long of thought, careful with words. Not the smartest person in a room, but the entity most likely to see exactly what was happening and what the next step needed to be.

During her brief, busy reign, she oversaw a thousand projects. Not every initiative was a success. Some were close to disasters, in fact. Urging Egypt and Jordan to annex the Palestine enclaves proved horrific, and her plan for paying the Jewish populations to emigrate to Canada was only a little more productive. But approaching her mid-sixties, Adrianne saw lifespans expanding and the first eight flights of the infamous Hammer Drive. Words carrying her name triggered changes in tax codes worldwide. Small, tidy rebellions began and ended with her words, various authoritarian regimes swept away, and she was better than anyone else when it came to picking the most deserving winners. And more importantly, she was very quick to admit errors and change paths.

No, the lady wasn't loved, but that didn't stop people from building temples in her honor.

Her rational mind was the largest force among many, but the public talked about her magic for saving lives that she had never noticed.

Her stoic personality never failed. Early on, she told her core group that she was an agent in a very mysterious game. Aliens, machines, or demons from some unmapped dimension: Explanations were numerous and useless and why bother? But she accepted that she was too old to benefit from the new elixirs, and even if she lived a million years, she was still human. In other words, she was going to run out of good advice.

"Ten or twelve years from now," she guessed.

She was wrong by a factor of two.

A very good guess, in other words.

On an ordinary Wednesday, she published a small blog about the desperate need for rain in northern Mexico. It was one of the little gifts that she gave to single places, and she didn't expect instantaneous results. But that same day, in Capetown, a half Zulu and half Boer fellow published plans for a machine that would suck carbon dioxide out of the atmosphere—a simple and quick device powered by sunlight and the earth's heat.

His machine was authentic.

Her rain never fell.

She retired, but not without some difficulties. Within a week, this woman who cared nothing for pomp and spectacle had little to fill her time, and perhaps that's why she ended up in a serious depression. Returning to her old house, she drank. She slept too much. And then she didn't sleep at all, weeping for no reason.

The tumor was discovered three months after she became an ordinary citizen.

Surgery was a possibility, but with the likelihood of significant brain damage. She refused. Radiation and various forms of chemo would be stopgaps, prolonging life by weeks at most. She considered and decided otherwise. On their own initiative, three of her original team flew to Capetown, attempting to meet with the new emperor. Their plan was to argue for a special blog, perhaps a call for a new cancer-fighting agent. The right words written in the proper order, not unlike a magical chant, might lead researchers to find a miracle hiding inside some little tropical plant. But the emperor refused to see them, much less consider their request. And hearing about the trip and the verdict, Adrianne sighed, saying, "Wisdom and kindness. They're not the same word spelled with different letters."

There was still money in the coffers.

Doctors and cooks and maids and more doctors arrived and then left the house again, following complicated schedules.

And the original seven disciples took up residence in the nearby houses, complete with spouses and kids and at least one mistress.

Adrianne left her doors unlocked.

Her balance wasn't worth trusting anymore, and she hated the chore of seeing who was calling.

One day, a boy from another neighborhood invited himself inside that famous house. He was curious what brain cancer looked like. It looked like an ordinary old lady sitting before a small desk, watching a thousand solar panels opening like giant flowers on someone's desert. It looked like a dull thing to watch, and he said so.

The woman turned slowly, looking at him and then looking back at the monitor.

"What are you doing here?" he asked.

"Sitting," she said. And she began to laugh, one hand touching the back of her skull. He thought she was strange and left.

She didn't notice her solitude.

Then another boy said, "You should lock your doors."

Adrianne turned to discover what she assumed was the first boy. Except he had grown up in the last few moments. Grown up and grown heavy too, and his hair had left him and then come back again. The new hair was paler and thicker than natural, which was common with these treatments.

Thirty years had passed in an instant.

This was a very interesting disease, she thought.

But no, that face wasn't the same face, even with the added decades. She almost remembered the face and its name. But then with a hurt tone, the new visitor said, "I'm your son. I've come to see you."

That seemed enough reason to stand.

The legs proved strong, at least for the moment.

"I heard the news," her son said.

"There's always news," she said. "What are you talking about?"

"Your health," he said.

"Is there something I don't know?"

"Oh, Mother." The man blinked, shrinking down a bit.

"You mean this growth." She tapped her head and laughed again. Twice in one day. She was practically a giddy little girl. "Yes, it's going to kill me. But probably not today."

The conversation stopped altogether.

Casting for words, she fell into cliches. "How is your life, son?"

"Well," he said, happy for the prodding. "I'm doing well. Sober three years, and very rich."

"Are you?"

"Exceptionally rich, thanks to you."

"Sober, I meant."

But the man with the fresh hair didn't want to dwell on old weaknesses. "It's amazing what people give you, particularly when they learn that your mother controls the world and everyone on it."

Honest thoughts came to Adrianne.

She worked hard, and her mouth remained closed.

The man was wearing both fine clothes and a smug smile, and he was watching her. But his thoughts were on the move. Feeling strong enough, he stopped smiling. "This is where he killed himself. Isn't it?"

She said nothing.

He looked at the ceiling. Then he stepped past her, touching the desk. The earlier desk was gone, too big and too bloody for the room that she had wanted. Maybe he didn't remember the original furniture. She refused to clear up these matters. What she wanted was to be left alone . . .

But this was her only child.

Mindless, uncaring pressure on neurons. Pressure bringing emotion. Is that where this sudden trickle of tears was coming from?

Her son didn't notice.

Again, the smug, rich-man's smile.

"I was sorry when you lost the job," he confessed.

"Were you?"

"But it's all right," he said. "Our relationship is still valuable."

"Is it?" she asked, wiping one wet eye.

"You often talk to our overlords," he said.

"I don't," she said.

"But they don't know that. And I'm very convincing."

She approached the office door. Wanting something. To send him away, or flee for herself?

The awful man kept talking.

"In fact, I'll sometimes claim that I can talk to them too. The powers in charge. Not so much that I have to prove anything. But you know, it's crazy what smart people believe, if you give them any excuse."

She gasped.

Her son blinked, straightening his back.

"Help me," she said. "Would you do me one enormous favor?"

He nodded.

"Wait," she said.

Waiting was an easy favor, easily accomplished.

She returned with the handgun and bullets, and his first reaction was to warn, "Guns are illegal now. You made it so."

"I did," she agreed. "Maybe somebody should arrest me."

He watched her load one chamber.

"Now," she said. "Kill me."

"What?"

"That's the favor. I'm sick. I'm going to get sicker and die horribly. But according to euthanasia laws—my wise laws—I can implore another person to end my suffering by whatever means I want."

"Mother . . . !"

"And I don't want to do the chore myself. So if you would." She shoved the gun into his hands, aiming the barrel at her chest. Then, as if having second thoughts, she said, "No, wait. Let me sit, and we can catch the bullet and the spray with pillows. I'll get my pillows out of the bedroom."

"Mother, no!"

The heavy man dropped the gun and ran away.

The disturbance was finished.

Alone, Adrianne unloaded the one bullet, placing the weaponry into a closet. And exhausted, she sat at the desk, watching a live view from a probe launched last month and already halfway to Neptune.

Time passed.

And someone else came to visit.

The first boy was back, an older sister holding his hand.

"This is her," he said with conviction. "That's our Empress."

Adrianne didn't have the legs to stand. That's why their faces were at the same level when she said, "Yes, it's your empress. Sitting in her glory."

She laughed hard.

The children laughed with her, to be friendly.

Touching her head once more, she said, "The monster inside my head. It's pushing at the best nerves."

They stopped.

"A talent for comedy," she said, her laugh growing dark and slow. "That's what the gods give you, if they want to be kind, right before you die."

Postcards From Monster Island
EMILY DEVENPORT

Sometimes people ask me, "Why didn't you run?"

"Because I had the Martian Death Flu," I tell them.

They look at me funny because they've seen the footage of people clogging the roads, and the subways and trains, desperate to get out of town the day *he* waded ashore. I wasn't in that crowd. I was flat on my back in my studio apartment, blitzed out of my mind with medicine. Two of my cats slept on top of me and my dog was snoring beside us when the whole building began to shake. Some of my books fell off their shelves, and I could hear the dishes clattering in their cupboards. I thought it was an earthquake. I considered dragging myself out of bed and crouching in a doorway.

That impulse didn't make it past the notion stage. I couldn't even muster the ambition to be worried as more books tumbled off my shelves and the windows rattled. I only managed a little curiosity when I noticed that the shaking was a side effect of slow, ponderous *BOOM*s, spaced like colossal footsteps. If the Statue of Liberty took a walk through town, she might make noises like that.

Wow, I thought. *This is the weirdest fever dream I've ever had.* And then I fell asleep again.

All night long I felt the tremors and heard the sirens. Once I awoke to a sound like ten foghorns going off at once. The cry was challenging, yet—oddly lonesome. That was the only time during the night when I believed something might really be going on. I thought I should at least *try* to get up. And then I passed out.

When the bombs started to drop, I pried my eyes open and squinted at the window. Morning light was trying to penetrate the dust and debris floating in the air. It wasn't making much headway.

Any normal person would have been thinking about evacuating the scene by that point. But the Martian Death Flu, though not actually from Mars, made me feel anything but normal. For one thing, when I sat up, the room started to spin. For another, my pets let me know in no uncertain terms that they were hungry. Plus my dog needed to potty.

I had to answer my own call of nature first. Halfway to the bathroom, I decided I'd better crawl if I really wanted to get there. Afterward I took more medicine, my head pounding in tune with the bombs going off outside.

The war sounded like it might be about a mile away. My apartment shook more than it had during the night, yet everything was still pretty much intact. My pets didn't like the noise, but they seemed more worried about their stomachs, so I staggered out of the bathroom and fixed their bowls.

I could barely hold myself upright long enough to do it. Once my dog had eaten, she reminded me that I needed to do something more challenging. I managed to get her collar attached and find the pooper-scooper. Then it was out into the cold, cruel world.

We passed one of my neighbors in the hall: Mr. Abé. He operated an African-clothing shop on our street. As the *BOOMs* and *RAT-TAT-TATs* shook our building, I lurched back and forth across the hall, and Mr. Abé gracefully sidestepped me.

"Sorry," I rasped.

"I hope you feel better soon, Miss Herrmann," he said. "Terrible racket, isn't it?"

"Yeah," I managed, before Peachy almost pulled me off my feet. She had her priorities, and she would tolerate no delay.

Under the circumstances it was crazy to get into the elevator, but I knew I wouldn't make it down the stairs. I don't remember how we got outside from there, but we ended up in the alley behind our building. Peachy did her business cautiously, but not as nervously as I expected she would. She stopped from time to time and perked her ears at the sounds of battle. She sniffed out her favorite spots, and I pooper-scooped. Then she pulled me back toward the alley door, and I took a moment to be grateful she wasn't going to insist on walkies. The way I was feeling, it would have been more like draggies.

Just before we got through the door, that foghorn cry sounded again. It was much louder without the walls of our well-constructed building to muffle it. Both Peachy and I were extremely impressed. Instead of loneliness, this time I heard a note of exasperation.

Peachy trotted through the door and I stumbled after her. I don't remember how I got rid of the poop I had scooped, but I can only hope I did the right thing with it. I made it back up to our floor and into our little apartment.

I *really* wanted to fall into bed. I also wanted to throw up. But I made myself grab my phone, and I also snagged the remote. All four of the cats were on the bed by then, but they made room for me once they realized I was about to fall on them.

For several moments I just lay there, the remote and phone still clutched in my hands, my stomach and my head competing for Most Amazingly Wretched Body Part. I waited until I was fairly sure I wasn't going to throw up, and then I dialed the first of my three jobs.

They were part-time jobs, the best I could find with my new bachelor's degree in library science, and I juggled them to keep myself afloat. Only one of them paid for sick time, so I had planned to dose myself with the medicine and stagger in to work, regardless of how horrible I felt. That plan had wilted in the painful (and extremely filtered) light of day. I speed-dialed the morning job.

An operator told me the number was no longer in service. I got the same message for the afternoon job. The number for the evening job didn't even connect with a recording; it just made horrible noises.

I gave up on the phone. "Guess what, gang," I croaked. "I don't have to go to work—ever again."

My building shook, the dishes rattled, and another book fell off the shelf. I should have been worried, possibly even depressed to lose my livelihood. Yet somehow I felt relieved. I knew it wasn't a rational reaction, but I couldn't help it.

I pointed the remote at the TV and pushed the ON button.

I didn't have to surf for a news channel. The story was on all of them. I hadn't seen that kind of coverage since 9/11 (though I was in the 4th grade at the time, and spent most of my time watching the Cartoon Channel, so maybe I wasn't an authority on that). Talking heads babbled about the giant creature who had waded ashore, and the bombs that didn't seem to do anything but annoy it, and the pollution and/or nuclear waste that had probably created it, and the wreckage that used to be our city, and the conference with the president that was supposed to happen any minute (but never did on that night)—and on the bottom of the screen scrolled the words: SCIENTISTS BAFFLED BY BEHEMOTH.

It was hard to get a good look at him with all the smoke, fire, tracers, exploding debris, etc. But I could see bits and pieces. He was colossal (apparently they felt *behemoth* was easier to spell). He sometimes stood on two legs, sometimes on four, and I couldn't help comparing him to a giant lemur—except that he had a thick tail that he used to bash things.

Another not-so-lemur-ish characteristic was his hide. Instead of fur, he had these triangular, rocky scales that seemed impervious to everything they hurled at him. No missiles could penetrate that hide. And some of them were *really big* missiles.

They did no damage to Behemoth. But they did plenty of damage to our city. Just when I thought they would wise up and stop with the bombs, a troops of marines jumped out of an airplane and parachuted onto him. They bounced off too. When they landed, the ones who didn't get tangled in their parachutes launched grenades at him. He turned and walked away from them, toppling several buildings that had been damaged by the bombs.

"This just in," said the reporter, who sounded like he might OD on the excitement. "All troops are being withdrawn. Readings on the geiger counters are spiking. The creature seems to be generating dangerous levels of radiation."

That didn't sound good. But no one had anything very smart to add, and amazingly, the behemoth story began to suffer from the same problem every other big news story seems to have: endless rehashing of theories and footage, without anything new or intelligent to offer.

I passed out again while waiting for clarification on the radiation thing. It sounded pretty bad, and it also sounded like a good reason to clear out, assuming I could find a way to wrangle four cats and a dog. And my dizzy, flu-bedeviled ass. To where, I couldn't imagine. Because no shelter was going to take my pets; I had heard about what happened to the pets in New Orleans after that hurricane.

Maybe the radiation wouldn't reach my part of the city . . .

A few hours later I woke to hear someone on the TV saying that Behemoth wasn't radioactive *all* the time, just when a lot of missiles had been fired at him. Like maybe it was a defense mechanism or something. But then they started that old rehash again, and I stopped listening. The only thing that made my ears perk up was a rumor that another giant creature had been spotted over our city, this one in the clouds.

Yes, that was the Cloud Squid. She showed up inside a thunder storm. The rain thrashed us so long, parts of the city flooded. It did clean most of the smoke and debris out of the air, though. You've got to look on the bright side.

The bright side was pretty easy for me to see. Because thanks to Behemoth, I wouldn't have to drag my half-dead carcass out of bed and go to work anytime soon. Sadly, it was that simple. I wondered if I might qualify for some kind of hazard pay, or even radiation disability. When I passed out again, I dreamed I was taking selfies of my new, glow-in-the-dark face, and I kept having to do it over because I couldn't quite seem to capture the pretty colors of my triangular scales.

When I woke up, my neighbor Frida stood looking down at me. "Bernadette—are you still alive?" she wondered.

This was an ironic question, considering that Frida, who actually did look like Frida Khalo when she wasn't in Santa Muerta drag, had painted her face to look like a flowery Dia de los Muertos skull. The effect was quite gorgeous, but it looked as if Death herself had paid me a visit. Death carrying a container of chicken soup. Accompanied by a pet ferret on a leash.

"Maybe," I croaked. I sounded even worse than the last time I had tried to communicate, but I felt better. Not great, but there was a definite improvement; my head wasn't spinning and my stomach had settled. The chicken soup smelled good.

"Can you sit up?" asked Frida. "I'll fix you a bowl of this soup and then take Peachy for her walk."

"You really are a saint, Miss Muerta." I pushed myself into a sitting position and watched her putter in the kitchen. Frankenferret sat on the foot of the bed, ignoring and being ignored by the cats while she socialized with Peachy, her best walkies buddy. Frida took Peachy out every day while I was at work, and in return she had a key to my place and unlimited borrowing privileges to my extensive library.

Frida is an artist who specializes in skeleton/calavera images, though her repertoire is much broader, including murals for businesses and private homes and illustrations for children's books. She is a *successful* artist, which in this day and age means that she barely makes a living and has to rent a studio in our odd little building. But she is living La Vida Loca, and her soup is good. She dished up a bowl and put it on a tray, then waited with her hands on her hips until she was sure I could get it down and keep it there.

"I investigated the water tank on our roof," she informed me. "I worried there might be gunk in there because of all the smoke and debris from the explosions. You know what I found?"

I swallowed a spoonful of soup and guessed, "Gunk?"

"Nope. Pure rainwater. The cleanest water I've ever seen. I have a theory about why, but I'm going to do some investigation when I take these rascals on their walk."

"Okay."

Frida herded Peachy and Frankenferret out the door and I reached for the remote. No bombs were going off, so I thought I'd better turn on the TV and find out where things stood.

Once again, the Creature Crisis dominated all stations, but now it was the Cloud Squid they couldn't get enough of. I watched some very entertaining footage of her evading air force jets and attack helicopters. Every time they fired something at her she darted away, leading them on quite a merry chase. What was *not* so entertaining was the destruction they caused when their missiles hit what was left of the city. So they weren't making any more headway against the Cloud Squid than they had against Behemoth. And I learned something else from the news ticker scrolling across the bottom of the TV screen:

DANGER ZONE HAS BEEN CLOSED . . . NO ONE ALLOWED IN OR OUT DUE TO RADIATION THREAT . . .

Closed. Yet I still had electricity, cable, water—all the important stuff. This would make life easier, as long as it lasted. Now that the Danger Zone was closed, I couldn't leave even if I wanted to, so that simplified things. But if they were isolating us, did that mean they might drop a bomb on us? I mean a *really big bomb*? As in nuclear? Since we were already kind of radioactive sometimes?

I tried to reassure myself that they would have the common sense to realize the radiation from nuclear bombs would travel, along with dust and debris that would cause a nuclear winter. I tried and tried. And tried.

I gave that up and surfed the channels on the TV, until I found a story that was unfolding in real time. The Cloud Squid and Behemoth had discovered each other.

"It looks as though we're about to see a battle *royale* between those two monsters." The reporter was trying to sound worried, but instead he sounded like this would be the coolest thing ever.

The Cloud Squid eased herself into the airspace over Behemoth, moving almost shyly. She hovered over him, her limbs opening like the petals of a flower. He gazed up, his mouth open, revealing rows of teeth that looked like stalactites (and stalagmites).

Damn, I thought. I didn't want to see them fight. They were both beautiful in their odd ways. But then something amazing happened.

The Cloud Squid began to flash with color. I remembered the idea of bioluminescence: cephalopods communicating with each other using light and color. It was a glorious sight. Behemoth seemed to think so too, from the way he gazed at her.

And then another amazing thing happened. Behemoth's hide began to flash with color too. And why would the giant lemur with the rocky skin have bioluminescence? Beats me (though he did come out of the sea).

They flashed colors at each other for maybe twenty minutes. Reporters chattered, baffled by the scene, yet feeling compelled to make inane comments anyway. They were still hoping for a fight, but that wasn't going to happen. The two creatures stopped flashing colors, and then the Cloud Squid drifted away with her rainstorm. Behemoth sat in the rubble he had been collecting and gazed at the news cameras, and if to say, *What do you think of that?*

Reporters dutifully started their rehash cycle. After another half hour of that, I turned off the set. I was about to drift off to sleep again when Frida came in with Peachy and Frankenferret.

"Our branch of the subway line is intact," said Frida. "And as far as I can tell, so are the cables that provide our internet and electricity. If you were willing to walk, you could get from here to the edge of the Danger Zone, but you'd have to cross some flooded parts up to your chest, maybe even up to your neck."

"Are you planning to leave?" I asked.

She looked surprised. "No way. They'd have to drag me out of here."

I felt happy to hear that. I doubted anyone else would bring me chicken soup. "So—did you see anyone down there?"

"Nope. Something better." She pulled her iPad out of her backpack and called up a picture file. "I found another creature."

The picture she showed me was murky. There was very little light in the tunnel, and the water level was high enough to hide a lot of stuff. But right in the middle of it all, a face grinned at me. "It looks like a friendly dog," I said. "A giant—happy—water dog."

"He acts like one, too," said Frida, calling up more pictures. "You can't see from these pics, but he's about the size of a school bus. It's hard to tell how many legs he has, because the number seems to change—see?" She selected a picture where he seemed to have five limbs, and then another where he might have only three, though in both of them he seemed to have a vaguely tail-shaped appendage. "I call him Mega Whatsis. Sometimes he seems to be solid, but other times he's kind of gelatinous. Here's a short video I took on my iPad."

My stomach stirred uneasily at the thought of looking at something that was *sometimes kind of gelatinous,* but when I watched Mega Whatsis in the video, I saw a creature who moved confidently, even joyously, both in and out of the water. "Cool!"

"He's smart," said Frida. "Watch this next part."

Frida's hand appeared in the bottom edge of the picture. She held a cookie out to Mega Whatsis. His colossal head filled the frame until all I could see was a giant nostril sniffing the cookie. He delicately maneuvered the cookie into his mouth, using his rubbery lips, then pulled back for a moment and contemplated the taste, his happy face shifting into thoughtful lines. After another minute, he produced the cookie intact and nudged it back into Frida's hand.

"It was dry," said Frida. "No creature slobber on it."

"Wow. Peachy couldn't do that."

Frida pulled up some more pictures on the laptop. "I expected the water down there to be full of waste and toxins. But it was more like natural creek water."

I remembered what she had said about our water tank. "You think Mega Whatsis cleaned *our* water? Is that what you went down to investigate?"

She nodded. "But I don't think it was him. He likes to stay underground. And *his* water has mud and silt in it." She closed the picture files and put her pad back into its case. "I'm not telling anyone about this. If those jerks go down there to shoot bombs at Mega Whatsis, they'll cut off our supply route. And he's a big sweetheart, there's no reason to hurt him."

I decided to keep the radiation argument to myself for the time being. After all, *I* didn't have a geiger counter.

Frida undid Peachy's leash and patted her head. "She's already gone potty. I'll see you tomorrow."

"Thanks," I said.

After Frida had left, I surfed the TV stations, looking for evidence that anyone besides Frida knew about Mega Whatsis. I didn't find any—now they were full of politicians arguing about whether or not any more money ought to be spent trying to kill Behemoth and the Cloud Squid. They couldn't agree on that any more than they could agree on other stuff, so I drifted off to sleep again.

Sometime later, I approached wakefulness like a swimmer floating toward a bright surface. I couldn't quite open my eyes, but I felt one of the cats lying across my stomach. I petted it, enjoying the velvety feel of its fur and its plump, warm body. I heard purring, but didn't feel it vibrating in the body I was stroking.

And the fur felt too short. *Way* too short. Almost like you would expect the fur of a seal to be. I opened my eyes and saw the fat thing stretched across me. It tapered to a narrow tip that was lazily curling to and fro like a cat's tail. It widened as it crossed my body and continued off the bed, onto the floor, and out the window, most of which was blocked by its bulk.

It was a tentacle.

Two things occurred to me then. The first was that you don't expect a tentacle to be warm and fuzzy. The second was that the Cloud Squid was probably going to drag me through the window and eat me.

I lay there frozen, waiting for the Squid to make her move. When she ate me, who would take care of Peachy? Who would take care of Sheba, and Buster, and Thugly, and Jingle Monster (four more pets than I had officially declared in my lease agreement)? Would she eat them too? Jingle was grooming the tentacle as if it were another cat. Peachy had rested her head on top of it, and she was snoring again.

I'm not sure how long I lay there arguing with myself. But it was the Cloud Squid who resolved the situation. She used the tip of her tentacle like a hand and gently moved Peachy's head onto the bed. Then she patted each of the cats and the dog, and slipped away out the window.

I stayed frozen for a few more moments, but I couldn't resist the urge to look out the window to see where she had gone. I poked my head into mild morning air and the clean smell of recent rain. I saw the tentacle slipping back over the top of the roof. But why was she on the roof?

The water tank, I thought. *She's the one who put the rainwater in there . . .*

After all, she moved around in a rain cloud. Maybe the rainwater was a pleasant side effect to one of her visitations. Whatever the reason, I didn't feel like I wanted to lie in bed anymore. And I was sick of trying to get information out of the stupid talking-heads TV. Instead, I headed for my computer.

I logged onto Facebook. I wasn't surprised to see that rumors about our creatures dominated the feed. What *did* surprise me was that there were still plenty of posts about politics, religion, status reports of how people's diets were going, and pictures of funny cats. Once I got used to that, I composed my own status report and posted it.

To everyone who lives outside the Danger Zone, I said. *Please stop bombing us. Don't send any more troops. And please don't let them drop an atomic bomb. Stop attacking, period! You're doing more damage than good.*

Once I had posted that, and tweeted an abbreviated version, I got an idea. I logged onto Google Blogger and created a blog called *Postcards From Monster Island.* It was just a template, but I thought maybe I could get Frida to send me some picture files. As I was plotting and scheming over all this, I realized something.

I felt better. I could breathe. I wasn't dizzy. My head didn't hurt. I was snarf-free. And my stomach was no longer my mortal enemy.

So I fed the beasties and took Peachy out for her business. Once we were outside, we even did a little walkies. But our world looked very different now.

A sort of mountain range had grown between my street and Behemoth's battle zone. It seemed to consist of a combination of ruined buildings and actual rock. Hardly anyone was on the street, which looked largely untouched by the destruction. The temperature was mild, flowers bloomed in pots and window boxes, cooking smells tempted my starved palate, and most of the odd little shops were open, though there could be very few customers these days. The air still had that freshly washed smell, and breezes blew along the new corridor that had been created by Behemoth's Makeshift Mountains.

Call me weird, but I thought it was an improvement. The noise of traffic was gone too, though I would still hear Behemoth moving big things around, with thuds and groans as stuff fell into place. He didn't trumpet any challenges, but grumbled to himself, as if thinking aloud. Peachy perked her ears, seeming to understand every word. She even replied a few times.

Once she felt satisfied in every possible way, we came back inside and walked through the empty halls of our building. I wondered how many residents had evacuated. There weren't that many of us in the first place, maybe around ten people. Our bottom floor had been converted into shops (or maybe the top floors had been converted into apartments, I wasn't sure). We saw our super just once a month, though he did a good job with repairs. And he had put up bulletin boards next to the elevators, so I saw the note:

MEETING AT HOUDINI'S, UNIT 3C, 1:00 P.M. PLEASE COME AND
DISCUSS THE CREATURE SITUATION

The numbering in our building was as eccentric as the residents, so Apartment 3C was on the 2nd floor. The door stood open—someone had stuck a sign on it with an arrow pointing inside.

I pushed the door open further and saw Mr. Abé across the room. He waved from a wingback chair, where he nursed a cup of coffee. As I hesitated on the threshold, Houdini poked his tattooed head around the corner from his kitchen. "Come on in," he said, with the voice of a carney barker.

Houdini had a magician's name, but his true passion was the classic sideshow. He honored that tradition with the tattoos that covered him from head to toe, and he split his time between his circus memorabilia shop and a variety of sword-swallowing, fire-eating, knife-juggling gigs. His apartment was dominated by his personal collection, but everything was lovingly displayed, not jumbled together.

Over his couch hung a giant poster featuring all of the lions and tigers in the Barnum & Bailey Circus. Beneath the leaping cats sat Beetle, whose specialty was mounting insects for collectors and museums, and his partner Poe, who did professional skeleton articulation. Both held plates with orange scones made by Oskar, who perched on one arm of the couch, sipping a cup of mint tea. Oscar owned a bakery, and seeing the scones reminded me that my stomach was back to normal.

The gathering was completed by Frida, who fussed at the computer with her occasional boyfriend, Gee, who was a buyer for the Museum of Weird Stuff.

"So . . ." I took account of my neighbors. "We're the ones who stayed. Somehow, that doesn't surprise me."

Oskar sipped his tea. "Running seemed like a hysterical reaction," he said. "Like lemmings jumping off a cliff."

"Yes," agreed Mr. Abé. "I've lived through much worse conflicts. And I can tell you from personal experience that refugee camps are not necessarily better than war zones."

If you were wondering why two normal guys like Mr. Abé and Oskar would be friends with a tattooed knife juggler, a skull-faced artist, the Bug Guy, the Skeleton Guy, Mr. Weird Stuff, and Crazy Cat/Library Girl, I can only say that Mr. Abé's remark about refugee camps might explain why he's willing to look past the surface and put up with our eccentricities. And as for Oskar, baker *par excellence,* he's a very nice fellow with a flaw that was well tolerated in Germany, but is decidedly odd in the U.S. Oskar looks like Uncle Fester from *The Addams Family.* He smiles like him, too.

Houdini snagged a chair for me and for himself. "So here's why I called the meeting." His tone was so commanding, even Frida and Gee stopped surfing. "For all intents and purposes, we are now in the Danger Zone. We are stuck here, and we're the ones getting hurt by the bombs and stuff. We have to start telling the outside world what we want."

"Won't they just ignore us?" asked Beetle, around a bit of scone.

"Maybe not," I said. "We're what passes for experts now."

Mr. Abé raised an eyebrow. "Interesting. How did we pull that off?"

But Poe was nodding enthusiastically. "No, we are! I've been tweeting about it. I got the president's office to talk to me—can you believe it?"

"Good." Houdini waved a hand at Poe as if he were one of his side show performers, and he wanted everyone to step right up. "Because the biggest problem we've got is not the creatures. It's the idiots in Congress who want to drop an A-bomb on us. The only thing we've got going for us is that the president is commander in chief, and he thinks it won't work."

"But what will he think when he finds out we've got *three* creatures now?" I worried.

"There are more than three," said Gee. "I think there may be as many as seven in our city alone. *So far.* Look at the pictures we took."

Frida tapped the screen to show us action shots. "They're all doing stuff, but none of them are attacking people. See? There are people in all of these shots—some of them taking pics like we were doing, so it won't be long until the outside world finds out."

"Ah, but *what* are the creatures doing, Miss Muerta? That's what we need to prove."

Gee pushed a lock of his blue hair out of his face. "All we have is theories about most of them right now—except for Behemoth. Frida thinks he's an artist."

That remark provoked a conspicuous silence. But Frida was undaunted. "You notice he's been piling debris up? Well, he's fusing it together in particular ways. Look . . ." She found the video she wanted and hit play. We watched Behemoth shove debris into piles, then look at it critically. He rearranged things a bit, then pondered it again. When he felt satisfied, he stretched out on the pile and his underside began to glow.

When he stepped away from it, the result was an oddly pleasing amalgam of cityscape and mountain range. I had never seen anything quite like it.

"He's an artist," said Frida, with the reverence most people reserve for guys like Michelangelo.

"And I think that's why radiation levels keep spiking and then falling off. That's how he's melting stuff together."

"All well and good," Oskar said. "But that will only make people angry when we tell them. They think Behemoth is a monster, like from the movies. They see that he's giant, he waded ashore and destroyed the city. We know the military did most of that, but that will leave egg on the faces of the politicians and the generals. They will despise us if we point that out."

I heard him, but something that was unfolding on Frida's screen snared my attention. "Hey—is that footage you guys took?"

"No," said Gee. "That's from YouTube; someone took it with their cell phone the night Behemoth came ashore."

Behemoth was walking through the city, away from planes that shot missiles at him. An elevated train line stretched across his path; the train was stranded, and full of people. It looked like Behemoth was going to walk right into them, so people were screaming, trying to climb out windows. Then Behemoth paused, pivoted just as another missile was fired at him, and the bridge started to collapse.

"Wait a minute," I said. "Did you see that? Can you go back and play it again?"

He replayed the segment, then froze it at the crucial moment.

"Wow," said Frida. "Did I just see that?"

We watched the segment again.

"We've got to blitz social media with this clip," said Frida. "I've seen the early part of the footage, but they keep cutting out the end. A lot of people probably haven't seen the whole thing!"

"And there's something else we have to do," I said. "If we want to make them believe that we're experts, and they should listen to us, we need to work on our bona fides."

"But how?" wondered Houdini.

I pointed to the image on the screen. "We need to make contact with Behemoth."

Our trip into the Makeshift Mountains made me wonder if Behemoth and the other creatures were having some positive effect on us after all. It was a challenging climb (though a few parts of Behemoth's construct still had functioning elevators), yet I was able to troop alongside the others, despite the fact that I had just been very sick. We let Frida and Gee lead the way, since they were the youngest, and since they had also made several forays into those mountains.

For over two hours we wormed our way through mountain passages, walked single file along ridges, climbed in and out of shattered windows and across rooftops and balconies. We could hear Behemoth doing his work. We knew we were close.

"My friends," Oskar warned, "we hope Behemoth will not hurt us, but what if we're wrong? What if all those bombs and grenades have taught him to hate us?"

I didn't have an answer to that, and by then I realized I wasn't nearly as scared as I should have been. I just wanted to find Behemoth, I wasn't even thinking about *how* we should contact him. But we had to do it if we wanted a future. We were bound together with him, for better or worse.

We climbed several rows of steps, some from old structures and some newly formed, until we reached a lookout point. As we made our way around an outcrop on the pinnacle, we came face-to-face with Behemoth. He stood in the valley on the other side of the peak, not more than one hundred yards away from us—a distance he could have crossed in just a few steps. His head was almost level with us.

Those great, golden eyes rolled in our direction and focused on us.

"Oops," I said.

Yet I didn't turn to run back down the path. None of us did. And it wasn't just because we couldn't have gotten away. Those eyes saw us, and we stared back at them, but it wasn't an exchange between predator and prey. We, the Oddballs of the City, recognized Behemoth, the Oddball of the World.

We had seen it in that footage when he bumped into the elevated train. The cars began to topple from the track. Behemoth reached out and grabbed the train as it was going down. Once he had it settled more or less on *terra firma,* he shielded the people from the missiles until they could get out and flee the scene. One guy with a cell phone had caught that moment, and no one said anything about it. But we saw it. And now we were looking him right in his gigantic eyes.

Behemoth opened his mouth and emitted that cry we had heard so often in the last few days. There was no mistaking what he meant by it. I think he tempered it for us, it was gentler. It was still full of loneliness. But a new note had entered that symphony. To me, it sounded like hope.

"What should we do?" wondered Frida.

Without discussing it, we all waved at Behemoth. His ears perked. His pupils expanded, as if he were drinking in the sight. He sighed, and settled down to contemplate us further.

We sat down and ate the lunch Oskar and Houdini had packed for us, where Behemoth could see us. When we had finished, Oskar said, "I can sit with him for a few hours. You guys go home and rest up."

"I'll spell you after that," offered Frida.

And so it went. For the next few days, one of us was always where Behemoth could see us. Once we had established that habit with him, more of the creatures began to come into the open. We waved at them. Cloud Squid waved back with all her tentacles. Mega Whatsis grinned and wagged his vaguely tail-shaped appendage.

But that's not all we were doing. We started blitzing social media with our posts and pictures.

"Stop attacking!" we pleaded. "We've reached an accord with the creatures. We can manage them."

When outraged people demanded to know just where they were going to rebuild the centers of commerce and culture that had once dominated our city, we pointed out that it would be a hundred times more expensive to rebuild that stuff than it would be to build new centers of commerce somewhere else. In response, we got a lot of flack from trolls. "Do the math!" we pleaded.

Just when we thought no one was listening, the trolling stopped. And the talking heads on TV stopped speculating whether more marines were going to jump out of planes so they could bounce off Behemoth's teflon hide. Instead, the government started to drop emergency supplies for us along the Neutral Zone. And that's when I got an email from the president.

We'll make sure you have electricity and water, he promised. *We'll keep the food and medicine coming, too. Your debts have been settled, and you won't be paying rent anymore. In return, all that we ask is that you keep managing the creatures. Keep them peaceful. Can you do that?*

Yes, I replied, though I felt a little guilty about claiming credit for what seemed more like good luck.

On the other hand, it might be something more than that. It might be the fact that even when the city seemed to be coming down around us, we didn't want to leave. The more people outside lost hope, the more we gained it. They wanted to throw bombs at Behemoth, we wanted to sit down and have lunch with him. That counted for something.

So—you remember that footage of all the people pouring out of the city the day Behemoth came ashore? Now a lot of people want to come back. Not to live—to see the creatures. So we started Danger Zone Tours. We take selected visitors to multiple stops, including the shops of Mr. Abé, Houdini, and Gee, to Oskar's bakery and Frida's gallery, Beetle's exhibit and Poe's museum, and to lots of other odd places that have sprung up. We've all got some extra cash on the side now.

We take them to see the creatures, too. Ten of them have come out into the open, so far. Mega Whatsis is the usual favorite (though he still doesn't like cookies).

The last stop on the tour is a spot where people can see Behemoth. When he looks our way, we all wave. People love that. It's the kind of reverence you would expect to see for whales breaking the surface next to a Greenpeace boat. When our visitors leave us, they talk about how glad they are the creatures showed up to teach us the error of our ways, that we were poisoning our world.

I agree that Nature has a reason for everything it does. If people who live outside of Monster Island think the creatures appeared because we abused the Earth, I won't try to tell them otherwise. Maybe they'll behave more responsibly. But I think there's another reason.

Last night, I went to sit with Behemoth, and the two of us gazed at the stars. We've done that a lot, lately. Now that the Danger Zone is dark at night, we can see the Milky Way. Behemoth usually ponders the sky with a combination of wonder and inquiry, but last night was different. Last night, he watched with a vigilance that put me on edge. When Oskar came to spell me at midnight, I didn't leave. The two of us studied the heavens alongside Behemoth.

Then one of the stars glowed brighter. It glowed so bright, I realized it wasn't a star. It moved closer; I could see other lights on it. Behemoth stood to his full height, a low rumble sounding deep within his chest. The lights began to flash at him in patterns.

Behemoth's eyes glowed red, his brows clashed together like thunderclouds, and he fixed that bright light in the sky with his vigilant glare, opened his mouth, and sucked a colossal lungful of air for one of his fog-horn blasts.

This time his cry had no trace of loneliness in it. I wouldn't even call it a cry. This was a full-throated roar, so loud the farthest stars must have heard it. This was the sound of challenge, the promise of doom to anyone who would threaten our world.

The light flashed white-hot, then streaked across the sky and away from Earth.

"Was that what I think it was?" Oskar asked, warily.

"Yep," I agreed. "A UFO. I think Behemoth scared it away."

The creatures aren't here to destroy us. They're not even here to rebuke us for our destructive ways. They're here to defend us.

"The Creature War isn't over," I told Oskar. "This is the war that is yet to be fought."

Oskar settled down for his vigil. "Better tell the others what you saw."

I climbed back down through the Makeshift Mountains and walked up my street in our remade city, past all the odd shops, new and old, that defined the true character of the Danger Zone, until I arrived home to tend my beasties and compose a letter to the president.

Loving Grace

ERICA L. SATIFKA

When Marybeth's number comes up in the employment lottery, Chase goes with her to her orientation, but they won't let him inside the operating theater.

Chase and Marybeth had watched the videos together on YouTube, though, so he knows what she's in for. Two small holes are drilled at the temples. That's where the wires go in. The intestines they put in a bucket for easy drainage. No muss, no fuss. All other parts are distributed around the cubicle, either hung on thick hooks or slid into drawers for safekeeping.

"You'll wait for me?" she asks via speakerphone, right before they download her into the drone.

"Of course," Chase answers. His stomach still roils from the surgery clips.

The Employment Bureau sends him a holo of Marybeth, to replace what they've taken away. Every night since she left, Chase sits on the couch with the holo next to him. It has slight corporeality. When it pats his thigh, the touch feels like a kitten's paw. "Can you get me some ice cream, honey?"

He doesn't feed it ice cream. He doesn't make eye contact with it, even though it looks just like his wife. Marybeth's amateur charcoal drawings line the mantle above the television, a reminder he can't bring himself to stash away.

When things get bad, he takes a walk around the neighborhood.

And when things get *really* bad, he goes to see the storyteller.

"Gather around the fire," says the storyteller. The two dozen people collected in the parking lot of the old strip mall edge in closer to the wizened old man, their ties and linen skirts nearly brushing the coals. The storefronts are empty sockets, their gaudy paint peeling and faded. "Let me tell you a story."

Chase hangs around the back, near an old fiberglass statue of a lumberjack once used to sell maple syrup. He can barely hear the storyteller's words above the crackling of the fire and the humming of the drones overhead. He looks up at the drones. He thinks about Marybeth.

"This is a tale about an ant," continues the storyteller. He paces the parking lot, his wooden cane thumping like a heartbeat. "She was a very good ant, and knew her place in the colony. She was born to fill a role and she filled that role with great competency. The ant loved her queen. One day, the little ant's mound filled with a thick green smoke. The ant felt herself *changed*. She couldn't lift a piece of food ten times her size anymore. She couldn't quite march in line with the other ants. And she began to have doubts about the queen."

Chase has heard this story before, except it used to be about a bee. Regardless, he listens. It's better than returning to the sparse apartment with the holo in it.

"The little ant, she thought and thought. 'Why am I thinking this way?' the little ant pondered. And then the little ant realized what the problem was. She was *thinking*."

Chase looks up, up. The drones aren't recruiting now, but they still drift in a river of lights above him, rear thrusters twinkling like eyes. So many eyes.

"The little ant had a choice to make. She was free of her programming, but her epiphany made her realize that she had only a short time left to live. Armed with that fateful knowledge, she departed the colony she'd been sheltered in for such a long time—all of her tiny life—and went to see the world."

Chase lights a joint and lets himself relax. The night air is so cool. A brisk wind picks up, letting the embers of the fire scatter. He rests his spine on the lumberjack's shin and stretches his feet out. He feels very far away from the apartment at times like this.

"The little ant was free! She was so happy. She picked her way along, paying no attention to the scent trails left by her sisters. She knew that only a few days' walk away there was a great city full of food. Maybe there were other ants out there who had been touched by the green gas. They would understand.

"Then a hiker stepped on the little ant and ground her into dust."

When full automation made human employment superfluous, the first reaction was panic. Pink slips fell like confetti. Even Chase had protested against the coming of the machines at first, though Marybeth hadn't.

"It's a paradigm shift," she'd said. "Relax, Chase. It's the way things were meant to be. Machines can do things better than we *ever* could."

The early days of the Shift were a time of great upheaval, as people who'd spent their whole lives working suddenly found themselves without a job, a purpose. The solution was drastic: a complete social safety net, and a draft. Every day, a few people were called for employment, targeted by the drones that also swept the city clean, monitored crime, and performed chit drops. Stretches of employment varied from a few months to a few years.

You'll come back, the Employment Bureau said. *Everyone will come back. We count on it.* Chase knows nobody who has returned, but that doesn't prove anything.

The draft wasn't *needed,* not exactly. The drones ran on their own, filling all necessary roles with machine intelligence alone. But you couldn't just give people something for nothing. Not in *this* country. People liked to feel useful.

Marybeth and the others were the wetware. They gave the drones that special human touch. That flash of recognition you felt when a drone faced you across a parking lot: human eyes. The gentle way they'd scold you for dropping your litter on the sidewalk before they picked it up: human voice. The Employment Bureau said it was a good thing to be uploaded into a drone. That it was everyone's patriotic duty.

One by one, Chase's neighbors file out of their boarded-over apartment buildings dressed in their best business casual, waiting for the drones. He doesn't want to look at the others, their faces frozen in rictuses of fear, so he drops his eyes to the squeaky-clean sidewalk. A stalk of fennel pokes through the asphalt, reaching toward the cuffs of his rumpled trousers. He doesn't look up, not even when one of his neighbors screams. *Especially* not when she screams.

It might be an hour later, or it might be fifteen minutes. But every day, there's a palpable sense of relief as the passed-over people realize they haven't been taken.

Some, the ones who still find themselves purposeless, are upset. Most are not.

Chase thinks of organs in drawers, and of the holo on his tattered couch. Then he takes a deep breath and heads to the coffee shop. The pink-haired barista places his order when he comes in. He's a regular.

"Slow day?" he asks. The barista is the only person he knows who has a job doing anything except running a drone. A child of privilege, she inherited this place, and runs it more as a lark than anything else. The shop's walls are lined with posters advertising music festivals and political protests, all of them over a decade old. He wonders how many places like this still remain, places run by human operators instead of machines. Probably not very many.

"Sandy was taken last night."

"Last *night*?" The employment drones never show up at night. The barista has to be mistaken.

The barista shrugs. "Guess they're expanding into the night shift."

Chase's veins run cold. "Are you sure it was the drones?"

"Her girlfriend got the holo this morning." The barista shakes her head. "Terrible."

"But . . . " Chase's throat begins to close up. Knives of fear cut into his skin, slicing him up. Destroying him.

"I wouldn't worry too much about it," the barista says, obviously trying to make Chase feel better.

It's too late. Chase is already worried about it. He slaps down his chits on the scratched tile counter, sucks down the foul-tasting coffee, and sprints to his apartment. He doesn't look up.

"This is the story of the bird who laid golden eggs," says the storyteller. From his vantage point outside the sacred semicircle, Chase leans in to listen, though he's heard this one before.

I've heard them all before, Chase thinks. But he misses Marybeth, and the holo's still creeping him out, six months after it arrived on his doorstep.

"The bird wasn't unhappy to be owned. She knew that her shining eggs, though worthless to her, brought great joy to the prince of the kingdom. The bird's power made her unusual, she knew, and she was quite willing to forego the garden outside the barred window of her cage to bring delight to the prince and his kingdom. All was well for many years."

The storyteller takes a swig of water from the mason jar at his side. He smacks his lips.

"Then came a day when the prince brought in the royal scientists to study the bird. They made copies of her DNA and inserted them into other birds. The bird that laid golden eggs was no larger than a wren, you see, and even ten of her eggs could make only one small crown, even when melted down. They started with a chicken, then an eagle, then finally worked their way up to an ostrich. For a while, the little bird was even happier! She was no longer alone, and though the aviary was now crowded with many different species of gold-laying birds, not all of whom got along, her life was much less dull than it was before. She was so grateful to the prince."

Chase makes eye contact with a young woman illuminated by the soft moonlight. Her jacket is shredded on one side and her hair is lank and dirty, but she smiles at him warmly. He smiles back.

"For a few years," the storyteller says, "things remained as they were. The little bird, and all the other gold-laying birds, got along as well as they could. The eagle still sometimes pestered the little bird, but even the eagle knew that they all had a job to do. Then, one day, the royal scientists unveiled their greatest creation ever! They handed a jewel-encrusted box to the prince.

" 'What is this contraption?' said the prince.

" 'It's a replicator, a grand replicator. With this box, you can produce all the gold you could ever want. You don't need the birds anymore. You can set them free.'

"The prince paused. He looked at the aviary. The birds had never known life outside their cage. Could they be trusted to be free? Would they even want that? He thought for seven days and seven nights, as the grand replicator passed out brick after brick of solid gold, forged from nothing at all."

Chase inches closer to the woman, drawn like a magnet to her, though he doesn't know why. His breath catches in his throat. On a night like this he feels so lonely he can't even think straight.

"At the end of a week of intense deliberation, the prince threw the key to the birdcage from the top of the tallest tower in the kingdom. There was no need to tell the birds about the grand replicator. They were only birds, after all."

The following Monday, Chase sees the woman from the park in the automated grocery store. She's wearing a dress with a large stain on the front and one kitten heel. Her other foot has twigs between the toes.

Just go talk to her, he thinks. *You'll regret it if you don't.* Chase runs a hand through his own greasy hair and nonchalantly bumps her cart with his own.

"Hey," he says, "nice shoe."

She looks at her bare foot. "I don't get my chits for two weeks. Their products aren't as good as they think they are."

Chase has noticed that too. "We met last night. But I don't remember your name."

Her eyes dart around. The storyteller's sermons aren't illegal, exactly—freedom of assembly and all—but it's still not considered patriotic to attend. "Victoria," she says, holding out a hand.

"Chase." They shake.

She looks in his cart. It's a typical bachelor's spread: crackers, Velveeta, microbrew. None of it is real, all of it made, packaged, and delivered by drones. "I've seen you there before."

"I go sometimes. It's something to do."

"Yeah, it's nice to go out when they can't get you."

Chase doesn't tell her what the barista told him, about the recruitment drones expanding into the night shift. It probably isn't true, and anyway, *he* was still going out at night. "There's another one tonight. Would you like to go with me?"

Her forehead scrunches up, the gears working. Finally, she smiles. "I wonder which one he'll tell this time. The one about the ant or the one about the leopard?"

Chase laughs a little too forcefully. "He doesn't really have a lot of range, does he?"

It's the one about the ant, so instead of listening, Chase and Victoria sneak behind the lumberjack and pass a beer back and forth. It isn't until the off-service drone overhead lights up its rear thruster that he sees a pale line of skin encircling her brown finger.

"You were married?"

"He offered himself up, oh, four years ago. After they instituted the program."

Chase frowns. "*Offered* himself?"

"He said it was his patriotic duty to ensure full employment, even after the Shift. We had a huge fight because I wouldn't go. He called me lazy. I suppose I am."

"And your skin isn't back to normal after four years?"

"The ring was an implant. I had to go to a doctor to remove it." She holds out her hand, fingers splayed. "True love forever."

Her curly hair glistens in the dronelight. She's pretty, though nothing like Marybeth. *No,* he thinks, *stop it. You're married.*

"My wife is there," Chase blurts out. "In a cube. She didn't volunteer, they just took her."

Victoria places her hands over his. "I could tell."

"She'll be back someday."

She stares at him hard, her dark eyes like glassy rocks. "Has anyone ever come back from employment, Chase?"

"Just because we haven't seen them return—"

"No. They don't come back. I'm sorry."

Over by the fire, the storyteller wraps up his yarn. The listeners stand and stretch. Chase and Victoria get up, link hands, and walk to Chase's apartment.

He can tell the holo isn't happy, but he doesn't even care.

Chase leads Victoria through the worn doorway of his coffee shop. The barista quirks one pierced eyebrow at their entwined hands, then makes a kissy face at him.

"Stop it," he says, though he can't even pretend to frown.

Victoria's gaze flickers around the cramped, colorful room. The coffee shop is like a time capsule, Chase realizes, a glimpse into the aging barista's pre-Shift life. Chase can barely remember these not-so-long-ago times, and that depresses the hell out of him.

"Let's go to the shore," he says, "Just the two of us."

"We can't go far. We have to be here in case we're drafted."

Drafted for a job that we're not really needed for, he thinks. *Sent to be carved up and shoved into drawers, never to return.* He still can't believe that, even if he's acting as though it's true. "We could go out to the coast on Friday afternoon, camp for two days, and be back in time for the next draft." Saturdays and Sundays were always free, a vestige of the pre-Shift weekly routine.

"Supposed to be nice out there," says the barista as she wipes down the countertop the old-fashioned way, with a rag.

Victoria only has to think for a moment. "Yes. Let's do it."

The barista sighs and folds her hands into the shape of a heart. Chase throws an empty sweetener packet at her. "Go back to work."

They all laugh at that.

The holo pouts as Chase packs a duffel bag with his least-scuffed casual wear. "It's another woman, isn't it?"

It's not talking about Victoria. It can't form any memories. He lies anyway. "No, it's not. And you don't exist anymore, sweetheart."

It pauses, then repeats the same line in the same stilted tone.

Chase doesn't have time for this. He has only a scant forty-eight hours in the country with Victoria, away from the drones, away from the holo. He throws an extra set of socks into his bag and zips it up. "Don't touch anything while I'm gone."

He knows it's not sentient. He knows it's not Marybeth. Her body is in the drawers of her cubicle and her mind is in a drone. It still hurts when the holo locks itself in the bathroom and turns on the tap.

The doorbell rings. Victoria.

She locks eyes with the holo, then glances at Marybeth's sketches. The blood runs to Chase's ears, and before Victoria can ask any questions he takes her bag and throws it over his shoulder with his own.

"It's a good likeness," Victoria says, but Chase doesn't ask if she means the holo or his charcoal image.

The path to the nearest transit station is littered with all the nervous people thronging the sidewalks, taking their daily constitutionals to nowhere. For the first time in ages, Chase feels no desire to look at the drone-flecked sky. It feels like freedom.

"After you," he says, dropping two chits into the turnstile.

The drones kept the light rail running, even after the Shift, so Chase and Victoria take it all the way to the end of the line. The burbland stretches out forever, its abandoned houses like diseased teeth in a gaping maw. Nobody can afford to live so far away from the lottery, except a handful of off-gridders testing the patience of the Employment Bureau. Chase had grown up in such a suburb, near a different city. He looks over at Victoria.

"What are you thinking about?"

"You. The ocean. I don't know." She yawns, and it turns into a smile.

Chase puts an arm around her. There's nothing more to say.

Brakes screech as the train pulls into the station. They'll have to walk the rest of the way to the sea. Chase helps boost the barefoot Victoria over a guardrail.

His hands become slick with the watery blood from her heel. She must have scratched it somewhere.

I should have bought her new shoes with my extra chits, he thinks. *Too late now.*

"It doesn't hurt," she says, though he hasn't even asked her, and he knows she's lying.

"Not too much longer."

"I think I can hear the ocean from here." Another lie, but Chase can forgive it. He wants it to be true too. They walk down the stretch of highway hand in hand, and he feels only a small pang of guilt at that, a tiny knot that rests at the bottom of his chest.

When the heat makes the asphalt below them into a hot griddle, he and Victoria set up a picnic on the median strip. The not-cheese and ersatz crackers taste terrible, but they gobble them all down anyway.

"What was your husband like?"

She frowns. "A serious man. Lived for his work. He was an investment banker. No need for them after the Shift. I think a part of him died when it happened. Before, he didn't come home until ten most nights. Now he doesn't come home at all."

"Marybeth was the opposite. She loved her freedom, loved the drones for freeing her from something that was pointless. She was an artist." Chase shakes his head. "It should have been me."

"Don't say that." Victoria removes a strand of hair from Chase's eyes.

It's true, he thinks.

The sun is below the horizon when they finally make it to the coast. Chase scouts a rickety shack half-buried under the white sand. There's a mattress there, with not too many spiders on it, and the springs scream as they collapse onto the thin foam. Victoria falls asleep right away, but Chase lingers for a few minutes, enjoying the feel of her supple body against his.

Not a holo, he thinks. *Never a holo.*

They're playing in the ice-cold water when a drone passes by, but it's Sunday, so they don't have to worry. *Probably maintenance,* Chase thinks, *tidying up the beach that nobody ever visits.*

He's naked as a buzzard's head. So is Victoria, her clothes stacked neatly near a dune. Her feet are still raw and bleeding, but she claims the salinity of the ocean helps.

They're safe. But when the drone nears, they still hold their breath, waiting for it to pass by. It's a little one, no larger than a toaster, and it's heading straight for Victoria.

Please, Chase thinks, *no.*

The small maintenance drone reaches out two feelers and strokes her cheeks. It digs its claws into the brown rings of her hair. It beeps one, twice. Victoria trembles.

"Get away!" Chase yells. He splashes through the shallow water and thumps the drone on its side with his fist. "Go!" *Please.*

The drone turns. It whirs. It squares its glittering optical sensors with Chase's eyes, and within the glass bubbles of the sensors he can see a miniature version of himself staring back at him. He feels a moment of sickening recognition before the drone speeds away.

No. It can't be her. Chase shakes his head, letting the insane thought pass.

Victoria collects her clothes. "We should go. We'll be late."

They retrace their steps along the highway. Chase doesn't tell her what he saw, or what he *thinks* he saw. He doesn't say much at all.

When they finally get back to the station, the light rail is running a major delay. They're late for the draft.

Chase doesn't see Victoria the next day, or the day after that. Thursday is a storyteller day, and so he goes to the abandoned strip mall. He knows there must be some grave consequence for skipping the draft, but it hasn't come up yet. Maybe it never will.

Or maybe it's happening now, he thinks.

"Gather round, friends," says the storyteller. "This is a story about a very brave, but very shortsighted leopard."

Victoria is nowhere in sight. He leans against the lumberjack's shin and lights up. Above his head, drones zip along, watching over all of them with foul intent disguised as loving grace.

The story is terrible, but he listens all the same.

The Petals Abide

BENJANUN SRIDUANGKAEW

In the womb-tank coded with thought and memory, Twoseret learned three things: that her life will be full of peace, that she will never die, and that she will know precisely one tragedy. These facts are absolute, untarnished by chance and impregnable to intervention.

After that, petals started blooming in her mouth.

They come at dawn at a regulated hour; she knows to be awake with her mouth empty so she does not choke. A tickle in her throat, a pressure against tonsil, and they emerge fluttering: the shape of hands with spindly digits, the color of unlit space that demarcates empires. She likes to speculate whose hands they might be modeled on, or whether they are the quintessence of hands, a mannequin standard.

They are pristine and velvet, untouched by teeth and untainted by saliva: like no part of the body at all, no effort to resemble tissue or keratin.

Here Twoseret finds her orders, in the capillaries that call to the light of accretion disks and press against her nerves in synesthetic licks. The petals are the flowers of prophecy, the blooms of destiny. As long as she follows their instructions, like any memorialist Twoseret stands deathless.

She arranges the petals, four, radiant—fingers pointing out, fluttering in the low salted wind, the heels of their palms held down by mosaic stones. A murmur of sun slants across unlighted velvet. She bends to read, sibyl to her own fate.

The city ground is a canvas, the avenues brushstrokes, history a palette. An avian view yields faces gone to carcass and archive, some self-portraits, others celebrating personal affection and past deeds—the war heroes, the founding scholars, the beloved siblings. Within these walls, nothing is forgotten. Outside them, everything is.

Twoseret walks through parabola gates of porphyry and persimmons heavy on the bough, down bridges whose curves follow theta-rhythms. The petals have given her a course, a target.

It will be a channel, she expects, through which she may monitor a life and from that material suture together a new person. Broad edits are crude: a wholesale revision of a planet's chronology, a rearrangement of civil wars and epidemics and sundry. The work she does, however, requires more finesse. In identity reassignment the subject must feel at home in their new path, natural to a strange career and family and spouse as though they have always lived this life. The more moving pieces there are, the more skilled a memorialist has to be. Twoseret counts herself one of the best in the city, if not the very best.

The only one to whom she conceded supremacy was Umaiyal, but ey is long gone.

She stops at the basin of faces, where bone dunes in a hundred twenty-seven colors—most visible, a few not—rotate hourly, resolving into the faces of the first memorialists. There, at the border of grinding femurs and fibulae, she finds a casket.

The edges of it are sharp as invasion, its casing radiant as war-beads, its lid heavy as regret. Around this a homunculus of encryption hovers, epidermis full of paradoxes clenched shut. She coaxes them open, by intuition and determination. Her routines grant her a surplus of leisure, and she's spent it on dead languages, ciphers, puzzle-solving.

She expects a soldier, a spy, a politician of high standing. Those are ever the first to develop a taste for sedition. But once the homunculus has been whispered and peeled off, she finds instead a foreign assassin.

Beneath a canopy of chameleon fish and isometry rosettes, she thaws the body. Their face is blunt, singed at temple and jawline by ecclesiastic tattoos. Their neck looks as though branded by bird beaks, their biceps abraded by bird claws. The marks of the Cotillion and the divine Song under which they march.

The assassin is armed too, but Twoseret is unconcerned, for the petals did not forecast that she will die today. When the fluids have been drained and the cryogenic phase deactivated, the assassin wakes: all at once, without the transitional stage between occluded cognition and full alertness. The gaze that latches onto Twoseret's is clear and iridescent with corneal implants.

They jackknife and heave. A splat of saliva and bile, so black, so blue. Waking up this way is never pleasant, no more than being decanted from a tank. Twoseret has vivid recall of her own birth, her first breath and emergence, of volition beyond the crèche-parents.

She reads their name and gender as they come online. "Sujatha Sindh." The name susurrates like parched leaves, from a language spoken on several Hegemonic constituents. Not entirely foreign, but the two empires have regular exchanges; citizens of one flee and become refugees in another, diasporic. Their descendants repeat the cycle.

The assassin gains their composure in turns, gray and shuddering, on their back then on their knees. Twoseret offers a hand; they take it. Long fingers, velvet where synthetic dermis has replaced fingerprints.

"You have been sent to abduct or kill one of us," Twoseret murmurs, off the dossier. "Did you choose a specific target or would any of us have done?"

"My instructions were not discriminating." Sujatha's voice is a blasted echo, its wealth and timbre gouged out. Cotillion personnel wield their voices for sacred music, better than any weapon. Without that the assassin's bite is much blunted.

Because they do not ask what their fate will be, Twoseret does not provide. Perhaps they already know, as surely as if they had read the same petals Twoseret did. She gives them her shoulder, her arm around the heft of a torso honed to swift retribution, limbs trained to kinetic poetry. Those too have been weakened, ligament augmens snipped off, bone enhancement ripped out. Where once there was puissance, now there is brittle mortality.

Muscles spasm in Sujatha's cheeks as they walk. It's not the only part of them that trembles in withdrawal from the destruction of their voice. Twoseret imagines how it was done. An operation, painless. An appointment with precise instruments during which Sujatha was awake for every minute, nerves primed to open wounds. Dilated time.

Sujatha's prison is a palimpsest of deep-sea salt and abyssal cold. Its frictive patterns convert to musical notations, echoing the voice of a deceased memorialist. The assassin gazes at the water. Their mouth parts, habit, but they press it shut.

"It isn't really a song," Twoseret says.

"All ordered sound is part of the eternal symphony. The birth of universes. The end of them. Entropic culmination and singularities." Sujatha touches their throat. "I will not sully any of it with the voice I have now."

Twoseret does not present a secular objection—that sound is merely sound, can be synthesized and reproduced; that sound has no purchase without air, and what is a deific verity that cannot cross stars? She helps Sujatha settle into their bed of solid-state husks and slaughtered engine cores. Battle salvage is material for art. It speaks of Hegemonic peace spreading abroad, a reminder of the army's might. What are memorialists and their city without the commanders and the troops, their strategies and victories?

That thought dogs the heel of another. "Who captured you?" For someone must have, an act of heroism and advancement.

Sujatha takes a cracked breath, perhaps weighing their tactics: to tell, to withhold. "A soldier. Oridel Nehetis."

Twoseret's expression must have spoken louder than her silence. She corrects that. "I see," she says, and seals the oceanic palimpsest between them.

"Do you remember," she asks one of her age-mates, "Umaiyal?"

His answer is interrupted by a trio of petals. He catches them as they fall, fans them like a spread of cards on the game board between him and Twoseret. "Yeah," Riam says, reading his instructions, not disclosing them. "How goes it for em? The exception."

The exception to have punctured the city's skin from the inside. The exception to have left. Twoseret will never know how this was done, what deal was brokered, what Umaiyal's petals spoke; whether this was mandate or Umaiyal's volition. She only knew—knows—the loss like a suppurating hurt. Out there ey goes by Oridel, a good elegant name. Ey wears eir face differently too, sharp-boned and pearl-pale, chased in nacre that traces and wraps eir skull in place of a scalp. A short clip that Twoseret plays, over and over, with Umaiyal caught mid-chuckle. Wry and polished in dress uniform, eir throat a choker of respiratory implants for work in toxic battlefields. She wonders how many deaths ey has logged.

Umaiyal once asked her what name she would take, out there, if she could leave. On a whim she picked Nehetis.

Twoseret moves her piece, desultory, not much caring for the game's result. "Ey's as well as can be expected. Alive, certainly."

"So you don't know either?" Riam flicks his head, apologetic. "Uncharitable of me. Not as if they would have let you keep in touch. I always thought if anyone got out, it'd be Umaiyal. And ey would take you with em."

Umaiyal never asked. One day ey was there, the next gone. Even eir clothes, eir jewelry: the nexus-choker of corneal opals, the eigenvector jacket she gave em.

"I'm content here," says Twoseret. "Aren't we all?"

The petals yoke her to the prisoner's cycles. She comes to know the palimpsest's smell as well as that of her own bed, and Sujatha's face as well as her own reflection. The questions she puts to the assassin are broad and she's rarely interested in the answers, so much so it provokes Sujatha to say, "You aren't what I would call an adequate interrogator."

Twoseret sinks her hand into the water, warm and viscous as gestation plasma. She imagines pulling Sujatha through it and the assassin coming out her side reborn, a blank canvas numinous with possibility. "I'm no interrogator. Would you like to talk about something else? Tell me secrets. Not state matters, just little things."

Sujatha sits cross-legged, and despite the palimpsest distortion they look much better: they'll never have their old strength back, nor their voice, but their colors are healthier. Umber rather than jaundiced sepia. "Why would I do that?"

There is an acid-edge of animus that Twoseret finds strangely personal. "To pass the time, as I can't persuade you to sing and you wouldn't learn origami or any of the games I've brought you."

"I play nothing well behind a prison cell, and I'm not a graceful loser." The assassin cranes their neck back, looking up. From their perspective the world entire is sunlight filtered through depth, exegesis by fiber-optic sharks and hydrogen anemones. "There's a dessert of egg yolk shaped like gilded drops that I indulge in to a fault. From each of my bed-partners I've collected a necklace, a scarf, a collar; as long as it's been close to them like a garrote. In all my life I've fallen in love only once."

"Yes?" The barrier is permeable up to a point. Twoseret encounters soft resistance once her hands have sunk through to the wrist. "Tell me about love."

They laugh, a stutter-bark of actuators guttering out. "You've never been happy. No species of love would be known to you."

"If happiness is freedom from deprivation and pain, then I've never known anything but."

"Happiness," Sujatha says, "is more than that. You haven't seen—"

"Beyond this circle of existence," Twoseret says, drawing up her knees and resting her chin on them, "the calculus of being distills to this: rule or be ruled. Under Hegemonic peace your past is robbed; under the Cotillion your future is sealed. There are only so many places for power, and most will never rise to them nor even see the path."

The assassin blinks, a play of lamplight on black pearl in their irises. "You aren't what I expected."

"Mindless, you mean? As long as I follow the petals, nothing is forbidden. The province of my mind belongs to me alone, and in *that* I have what most outside this city never will."

Perhaps some of that turns a key in Sujatha's heart. For the assassin says, "I'll tell you of my love. Much you won't comprehend and have no basis with which to compare, but I'll tell you."

"And I'll tell you of mine." Twoseret leans forward, her nose almost nuzzling the vertical tide. "We may surprise each other."

"The person I love is absolute, untarnished by loneliness and unsullied by lust. They require no justification to exist; they are beholden to no outer forces or obligations. Like the drive of a warship, but those require guidance and crew, hull and superstructure. Like a sun, but those has a finite age and obey greater forces. So," Sujatha says, softly, "they are like the Song, given human body, human visage. And to think that is to blaspheme beyond absolution."

"Today, the person I love is shaped like a hole. But once upon a time that they had arms like polished teak, cheeks like bathyal amber, and eyes like lodestars." Twoseret unrolls permutative paper in her lap, tears out a precise square. "When they couldn't sleep they liked to keep their hands busy, and they'd fold this into animals neither of us has ever seen. Lava alligators and polar butterflies, thunder wasps and aquatic bees. They kept their hair very long, dipped in an attar of comets. I'd try to braid those paper things in it, but the hair was difficult of temper, just like their owner."

Sujatha has flinched as though each of Twoseret's sentences have pierced them, needle by needle under the nails. "That isn't a person," they say, voice tight. "That's a childhood."

"Childhood is formative; no person springs into being fully-formed, like a sun or warship or holy music. Everyone has a past. That's the *definition* of personhood."

"The larval stage of it, perhaps. The person someone *becomes* is honed by time, tempered by experience, the true shape." The assassin frowns. "Do you fence, wrestle, or box? I feel the need to test you in combat."

Twoseret laughs and gazes with interest at the hard lines of Sujatha's body. Umaiyal was built like a willow, but out there ey would have received combat augmens, and assiduous training would have changed em. "I don't do any of that, and in your state you wouldn't be able to defeat a child. I'll play you any sort of game, conquer you in any sort of puzzle."

"You're trying to offend me."

"Yes. No. But tell me more about your personal blasphemy."

The assassin's mouth curves then, tracing the arc of a blade. "The person I love has far more in common with me than you, than this city, than anything you know."

It is, perhaps, not wrong. Twoseret puts two calligraphic avenues between them before she allows her hand to press against her sternum as though to staunch a wound. But her palms come away clean.

In her room, roofed by silver beaten chiffon-thin, she composes. On the malleable walls that submit to her nails, on the permutative paper that yields to her thumbs. She sketches the same figure again and again, an outline of slender limbs and rounded narrow shoulders. Then it becomes more sinuous and muscle-dense, shedding the eigenvector jacket and robe for something more martial. Close-cut uniform that gloves the body, a long coat with severe hem. Twoseret leaves out the sidearm.

A visualization is not required, but she has always found it helpful. The petals give instruction and goal, but the means to achieve them are her own. She begins scanning her own memory segments. A person is gestalt. There is past, present, and the potential for the future.

Now that Umaiyal is gone, of the entire city she is the best memorialist alive.

Twoseret gazes through Sujatha's eyes. She is almost Sujatha, for a while. Total immersion has its risks, but the best of her compositions often arise from that.

Sujatha's meetings with Oridel-Umaiyal began at a distance, observing a figure limned in pale light through a corridor of spiral glass. A figure tall and compactly made, unrecognizable to Twoseret. Over weeks the assassin observed, followed.

Was noticed, one day.

An eel-twist of the street where Umaiyal disappeared. The assassin sidestepped, turned in time to catch Umaiyal's knife on an armguard. The blade locked; Sujatha pulled. Fell with Umaiyal as ey went down, hand on throat—precise pressure—and knees straddling arms.

Both held still: aortae marching to the same adrenal tempo, muscles stretched taut. Then Umaiyal smiled. "You're very good," ey said. "Galling as it is to admit, I'm no match for a Cotillion assassin. Had you wanted me dead, I would have been cremated a week ago. So what is it?"

Sujatha drew back slightly, caught by frankness. "Captain."

"Shall we get a drink? My treat."

They did, and more than once. An uneasy negotiation, tenser for Sujatha than for Umaiyal. By their fifth meeting in a club of enameled ice, Umaiyal leaned forward and pulled the trigger on a question both of them had always circled around. "You targeted me for my background, didn't you?"

In that club, at a table laden with conch-shell bowls, Sujatha stopped eating. Curved a hand around a glass, took a long, deliberate sip.

"I can give you a way into *that place*. Only you'll have to trust me." Umaiyal drew closer. "That will be my gift to you."

It takes Twoseret two heartbeats to realize *that* had been spoken to her. Meant for her ear, not Sujatha's. It is not the only instance—many other times Umaiyal couched eir messages in conversations with the assassin. *There's a childhood place I miss, where the bones resolve into faces* or *Have you ever seen upside-down gardens?*

Where I was born, Umaiyal said as ey stood watching the breaking of Sujatha's voice, *there's a palimpsest that sings.*

As Umaiyal put a stunned Sujatha in the casket, ey held the assassin's hand, saying, "This is the closest I can get to going back." A harsh breath inhaled. "This is the closest I can get to talking to you." The lid clipped. "I'll never be able to go back. I'm sorry I didn't say goodbye. And I can't explain. There are no petals here, but even so some things are forbidden. Some things are prophecy, and to disobey them is to accept death."

The casket slipped shut.

For hours after, Twoseret is not herself. She remembers being in a stronger body; she remembers parts of the surgery that took her—*their*—voice. An immersive link to the subject's memory doesn't give her the subject's feelings.

Nevertheless Sujatha's want is plain, blazing gold across the fabric of their recall. "The person I love is absolute," she says softly, startling herself when what comes out is not in Sujatha's voice. The original voice brimming with Song, one with the code of existence.

The next time she visits the assassin, she brings a small drawer of perfumes captured in vials of chameleon jade. One takes on the texture of Twoseret's palm as she handles it. "Do you know the scent?" she asks, opening a window through the prison-tide. "I've no idea if this is available outside. Probably it is. Some of us have hobbies but I don't think anyone distills perfumes, so this must have come with a supply drop."

Sujatha edges forward. Stiffens in recognition. "What of it?"

"The person I love—" The euphemism, still. "Left this behind, even though they were some of eir favorites. No time to pack it, I suppose, and these bottles are so fragile. I don't wear perfume, though. Do you?"

No answer.

"It'll spoil eventually, go rancid." Twoseret pulls more vials out of their slots, idly rotating one between her fingers. "I could have the containers recycled. The perfume though, that's a bit of a waste."

"Then I might as well accept them."

"There are other things, too." Talking around and keeping up the pretense, like *Umaiyal* is the forbidden secret: profane or else too pure and wondrous a word to utter. "I'll bring them. Clothes that don't fit me, jewelry, and so on."

Two sets of petal later, Sujatha smells and dresses a little like Umaiyal. They must know this, but do not object and seem content simply to have Umaiyal's belongings next to their skin, scenting their clavicles. When Twoseret brings them a lattice necklace, their breath hitches: an object that's lived next to Umaiyal's throat.

She cannot claim to understand their terrible longing for Umaiyal; it seems so much, and burns so bright, for such distance and so little return. But it is there, their shared knot, and she makes use of it.

Desire complicates, between *to love* and *to want to be*. A certain affinity between those two, she thinks, a bridge that can be built and directed. She makes more sketches of Sujatha, of Umaiyal as she remembers em. She compares and finds herself not dissatisfied. *That will be my gift to you.*

One day she lets down the prison, which after all was for effect rather than any real intent to cage. As the water cascades away and the kaleidoscope of sharks evaporates, the petals come. Twoseret cups her hands for them, spends half a minute absorbing their directives; when she looks up she finds the assassin staring at her, appalled. "It's nothing," she tries to explain. "It doesn't hurt. This is only an artist's whim made real by a biotech."

"It's not all right," Sujatha says, then surrenders to silence, as though even that thread of anger exhausts.

"It's more *interesting* than receiving messages the conventional way." She folds her petals into her dress. By nighttime she will have to dispose of them properly, a ritual.

Sujatha tires easily, has to be eased down onto benches and soft grass. Twoseret eventually lets them rest at a fountain that gurgles gossamer pennants, translucent kites, streamers in soft copper and gold.

Eyes shut, the assassin says, "You don't feel the limits of your world? You don't find it confined, claustrophobic even? This place isn't even large enough for fifty million. What's up there isn't a sky. This is all you will ever see, all the air you'll ever breathe. What you do, how you live, it's all bound up in those fucking flowers. Doesn't it chafe? Doesn't it *choke*?"

"You are very angry," Twoseret observes, "on behalf of someone you don't know and hardly like. I have no illusions that you'd choose my society, given other choices. How can it matter if I live a constricted life, or one whose limits of liberty you disapprove?"

"The person you love—" The words come out like retched poison. "Did they live like this?"

She catches a twist of streamer; it convulses around her wrist, prehensile, rose-touched platinum. "To that you already know the answer or you wouldn't have asked. It's a life. For most of mine, I never lacked for anything. I still don't see why you were sent here, though; you obviously can't get out."

The assassin smiles a rictus. "As I came, I was transmitting my location. That stopped at a point, but the approximation is sufficient."

"This entire city can be moved."

"Very slowly. With considerable difficulty. It'd be a feat of years. Our ships are much faster, inescapable, will not be outraced. Of course negotiating the gravity snarl that protects this place would be a trick and a half, but the same maze that safeguards you also makes relocating the city . . . vexing."

Twoseret strokes Sujatha's head the way she might soothe a distressed animal. The assassin's hair used to be shoulder-length, in those memories, but it's been growing since. Someday it will be long, serpentine, and she will find an attar of comets to anoint it full of light. "Will they attack?"

A short laugh, that same noise of failing machines. "No. We only wanted some idea of where this might be, just in case. For that I gave my life, without regret. Acquiring this information for the cost of a single person is an extravagant bargain."

"Patriotism is very nice." Twoseret has never experienced such a concept, but she means it. Belief—faith—in some vast, grand ideal must be reassuring. The notion that after one has passed, one's contribution will live on as part of that ideal or, in this case, system of brutal oppression. Still, it's certainly a greater thing than a single human being or even a billion.

"You're mocking me." But this too is said listlessly, the annoyance perfunctory.

"No, I think fervor is admirable. Passion is its own virtue. It animates. It can give an otherwise ordinary thing a terrible magnetism, an ensnaring brilliance . . . " She unties the streamer and casts it forward, where it catches on an updraft, snapping toward the sky-that-is-not. "Oh, that's why. All this time, you've been so weakened but there's been this—fire? This gravity, this pull. I think that's why ey decided on you."

Sujatha's head rises a fraction. "*Decided* like a calculation, the way you say it."

"It probably was. But not an exact thing, no, eir variables were more organic than numbers. Perhaps it had to do with how you moved, the way you sang, how your face was limned in profile at sunset. And always the fire that burns within you, visible between your teeth, behind your eyes." She helps them to their feet. "Do you want to see the gardens? Ey loved those."

Twoseret continues sketching in her head, drawing points of like and unlike. A framework of contrast and potential markers for synaptic joints. In the swaying garden with its inverted field, she picks clusters of edible hydrangea, mangosteens the size of her thumb, syrup oranges with thin ripe peel about to burst. These and more she puts in Sujatha's lap, absent the assassin's interest. As the pile grows they pick at it, a bite here, a lick there. Inevitably they have juices running down their fingers, their chin, sticky and fragrant.

She thinks of kissing them away, drop by drop. In the end she unthinks it. Not the right person, not the right time. As of now they are both in love with an idea.

Twoseret stirs to the city quaking and Sujatha's shadow laying across her like whip-scars. "I know you're awake," the assassin says in that fractured, devoured voice. "We're under attack."

She peers up at them through her eyelashes. "From whom?"

"Must you ask?"

"But they'll kill you too," she points out calmly as she pushes to her elbows, dislodging sheets, baring shoulders and breasts. Baring, too, the places on her ribcage and waist where the incisions were made and implants seeded so she would be able to receive the petals each morning.

Sujatha's gaze snags on those places and the cartography of their features shifts, sideways, to that region between disgust and fascination. It makes Twoseret want to say that the scars are quite all right: she chose to keep them when they could have been operated away to smoothness, leaving skin unmarred. Of course their horror is really for Umaiyal's sake, the thought that Umaiyal once lived like this, bore these same scars. Still Sujatha is nearly tender, as though she's a small child prone to spooking. "Are you in shock?"

"Oh, no." Her bed trembles as though a beast shaking itself from hibernation, sloughing off sleep and matted grass, or whatever it is that animals coming out of hibernation do. Paper moths flutter from their shelves. "I'm in full command of myself." She doesn't say that the petals came early today, and they did not instruct either Twoseret or the city to die. No doubt pointing that out will only distress the assassin.

Twoseret stands all the way up, knows as she turns her back that Sujatha stares at the tiger-stripes up her spine that culminate at the top—below her nape—in a dainty port, flourished in nacre and tiny citrines. "You believed I'm incapable of love because I have never experienced its prerequisites. Is it so hard to believe I'm not panicking because I've had no experience of terror, of illness or fear of dying?"

"Even a creature like you must retain her survival instinct."

"How wrong you are." Twoseret shrugs into her dress of suede cuffs and amethyst whorls, the fabric whispering like origami in fire as it molds to her. "Umaiyal used to help me dress, pick my clothes. Ey had—still has, I should think—these long fingers, with calluses from the wood-carving ey used to do as a hobby. Ey wasn't much good at it, though ey tried to make me birds." The calluses would be different now. Imprints from wielding a chisel and from wielding a gun are nothing alike, she imagines.

"Who?"

"The person you and I love. Pretending further is obscene, isn't it? I don't know if ey ever gave you eir birth name." She slides her shoes on, lavender gray, texture almost petal-like.

Sujatha presses their lips into a hard line and leads her by the hand. Twoseret is startled at the force of their grip, the limber grace of their stride, their familiarity with the puzzle-paths. An assassin would of course be able to map a place from memory, with speed and attention. Even so the unerring way with which they negotiate the city fills her heart, and their recovered strength makes her glad.

"My superiors have given me up for dead," Sujatha says as they emerge into artificial morning under the sky that is not. "So have I. For all intents and purposes I'm no longer alive; my presence makes no difference."

"But we're running somewhere rubble can't fall on us. A corpse doesn't run." Though ultimately the city's swarm-bounds can shatter; the ceiling of Twoseret's world is an unbearable weight, upheld by a thread of synaptic aegis. If it falls there will be no escaping it.

"My sense of self-preservation hasn't deserted me. Flight or fight." But their expression creases as though they'd said something different, a thing of ache and thorn cupped on their tongue.

A sudden ruthlessness seizes Twoseret. "This city holds the memory of the only person you've ever loved. While you breathe you won't permit its destruction."

Sujatha doesn't meet her eyes. "I need a node I can broadcast from. This isn't a full assault—a veilship or two, not much more. Just scouts."

Other memorialists have poured into the streets, as calm as Twoseret, intrigued by this new development. A few crèche-parents lead their charges by the hand, clear-eyed children from five to nine in various stages of wiring. By twelve they will be tested, and on success granted the petals. The sight of them draws a smile from her, reflexive and uncomplicated.

"There are consoles we use for supply drops." Routine communications for assigning and dividing up the items. There's always abundance and most memorialists can have their pick, tools and luxuries and raw material with which to feed fabricators: steel for hair-ribbons, glass for skirts, a hundred types of gemstones for belts and bedspreads. Everyone wears jewels, is sheathed in it until skin and facets are one.

Twin shadows press against the unsky, each the shape of a hornbill's head. Another tremor sweeps through like a racking cough, or so Twoseret imagines, never having seen hypothermia in action. There are defenses, but she supposes absently that those must have been breached: they are automated, and while some memorialists know them well—Umaiyal did—most of them never train themselves to battle. The nearest military outpost is too far to make it in time. The city's greatest protection has always been in its secrecy and location rather than firepower. She finds a wall and activates the console, feeding it a cluster of authentications like grapes, and steps aside.

Sujatha bends close, their breath fogging the obsidian curlicues that frame the console. Twoseret watches with avid interest as they connect to the Cotillion channel with a lover's intimacy. "Veilship couplet, identify yourselves."

The shaking pauses. From the console comes a low note, strain of music made by sighing woods and running currents.

"Remotely piloted," Sujatha murmurs, "as I thought. That'll be easier."

"Yes?"

The assassin straightens and inhales. More affectation than any real need for oxygen, Twoseret expects. And they sing.

Sujatha's voice makes a dirge for extinguished suns and singularistic contractions that kill worlds, for defeat in empty reaches that will go unknown and uncommemorated. It jolts Twoseret's nerves, constricts her throat, pries at the seams of her flesh.

When it ends Sujatha turns away, trembling slightly. "They will leave. It's the only command override I can access now, with my voice the way it—in any case it won't work a second time."

"It was exquisite."

"It was nothing of the sort." The assassin sags, as though the song has leeched their arteries dry and drained their limbs of strength.

Up above the shadows have disappeared. Twoseret catches the assassin. "You're exhausted. Let's get you somewhere to rest."

Sujatha doesn't resist or push her away. "I've been sleeping on grass, under trees."

"Then come to my bed. I'll tuck you in."

In the street, the crowd thins, memorialists returning to their duties and routines now that the excitement is past. Riam nods to Twoseret, perhaps guessing at her intent, giving tacit approval or merely mute indifference.

She frees the assassin from their shoes and vest, and eases them down between the sheets. She holds them until they fall limp and asleep, and very gently kisses their brow, their eyelids, the tip of their nose. Sujatha smells so right.

When she is sure they are deep in dreams, she gathers up her composition and resumes her work. Making a person—an identity—is delicate labor, but it is a labor of love. She thinks she will keep the singing, to retain the best of both worlds, and sends out a request for the casket.

• • •

Twoseret watches the sky for silhouettes of insects, vast, their wings enveloping half the city, their antennae slashing the horizon to segments. The outpost has become more attentive and sent them guardians since the attack. She never sees any of the soldiers, though she can imagine them helmeted and carapaced, animated statues of lustrous absence. Faceless, voiceless, nameless. She wonders if, far away, there is a war going on. A real one, sparked off by the assault here. On that the petals are silent.

The weather is getting warm, though never humid or uncomfortable. She's taken to seed-pearl sandals and lighter dresses with skirts that snap like prayer flags in an assassin's memory.

She kneels. A casket on the pavement, surrounded by mosaic pieces. The person in it has been sleeping a long time, nested in dreams of being reared by crèche-parents and of being wired; of pride when the first petals came. The casket is like the tank, incubating, preparing a sacred genesis.

Twoseret begins to unlatch the lid. A fetus must push through eventually or be stillborn. That is rare, but she's seen it happen. The locks and puzzles fall away quickly this time, decorative more than protective.

Eir hair has grown to eir waist. Thick frosted lashes twitch in sleep. A curl of cool breath, body temperature artificially lowered, rises to meet the thick air. Crossed wrists coiled in origami vipers. She runs her palm over eir forehead; she imagines to em the contact must feel like a flame tickling candle wax. In this way she thaws her dreamer, waking em with her own warmth. No fluid to drain, no instrument to detach—this was, almost, a simple and natural sleep.

Ey turns on eir side as though wishing to rest a little longer. Twoseret brushes eir hair, her fingertips grazing the side of eir neck. When eir eyes open, they are terribly clear: irises deeply brown, circumference gilded in amber. The scent of eir favorite perfume wafts, the angular folds of eir favorite vest rises and falls to eir breathing.

"You always slept so heavily." Twoseret takes em into her arms, helping them out of the casket. "Do I call you Oridel now? Captain Oridel Nehetis. It sounds all grand."

Ey rubs at eir eyes, groggy, one of those slightly childish gestures—she's never been able to break eir habit. "No, of course not. It's been a while, hasn't it? When did we have hornet fliers guarding our sky? God, I miss piloting those."

"Recent addition. I find their silhouette very charming. There's so much to tell you." She pecks em on the lips. "Welcome back, Umaiyal."

And Umaiyal laughs, in what is nearly eir voice, straightening to eir feet and taking her hand in that light-firm way that belongs to Umaiyal alone. "I'm home."

At the moment of her birth, Twoseret learned three things: that her life will be full of peace, that she will never die, and that she will know precisely one tragedy. These facts are absolute, untarnished by chance and impregnable to intervention.

As she walks arm in arm with Umaiyal up the puzzle-paths, her tragedy falls away like pale chrysalis, dissipating on the mosaic tiles and dispersing in the low salted wind.

When her next petals come she reads them and smiles, and casts them aside.

Mrs. Griffin Prepares to Commit Suicide Tonight

A QUE, TRANSLATED BY JOHN CHU

When LW31, a domestic model robot, brought Mrs. Griffin's dinner into her bedroom, it found her preparing to commit suicide. She was trying to tie a rope to the pendant lamp, but, at her age, her eyes were too weak and her hands were no longer steady. She tried again and again but she couldn't loop the rope around the lamp.

"Do you need any assistance, Mrs. Griffin?" LW31 set down Mrs. Griffin's meal tray, then walked to her side.

Mrs. Griffin put her hands on her waist. She caught her breath then handed LW31 the rope. "Help me tie this rope to the pendant lamp."

LW31's waist spun on its axis. The upper half of its body rose until it hit the ceiling. At the same time, he asked, "What are you planning to do, Mrs. Griffin?"

"I want to commit suicide."

"Oh, in that case, I should tie both ends." LW31 nodded its head and said no more.

It tied both ends of the rope to the lamp's curved pendant holder, tugged on it with both hands and judged the knots sufficiently secure. It turned its head to her.

"Mrs. Griffin, the rope has been tied. You may commit suicide now."

Panting with each step, Mrs. Griffin walked to just under the pendant lamp. LW31 brought her a chair. Trembling, she climbed the chair, feeling as though everything around her was rocking and swaying. Seeing this, LW31 stabilized her on the chair. Even though it'd been in continuous service for sixty-five years now and many places on its body have been corroded with rust, its mechanical arms were still steady. One hand pushed down on the chair and the other supported her at the waist.

Mrs. Griffin stood still. She stretched her head then then strapped the loop of rope around her neck.

"Wait, wait, Mrs. Griffin. I would like to ask you." As it had always been, LW31's voice was the smooth surface of water in an ancient well. "Why did you pick hanging as the way to commit suicide?"

"Because it's effective . . . and, to anyone who finds me, a hanging corpse won't look so horrible."

"Oh."

LW31 raised its head. It was a black glass cover. Knives had cut facial features that formed a smiling face. But time had rendered them indistinct to the point where the smile seemed odd and harsh.

It said, "Actually, Mrs. Griffin, you're as mistaken as those who had thought the Earth was the center of the universe. As a matter of fact, hanging is the most shameful way to commit suicide. Once you kick away the chair, your bodyweight will crack your trachea and your cervical vertebrae will shift. It's not like in the movies. You won't have a chance to struggle. You'll die in a split second. The problem is what happens after you die."

Mrs. Griffin firmly shook her head. "Don't try to convince me. I won't change my mind."

"After you die by hanging, your eyeballs will jut out like light bulbs, and your face will grow red from suffocation. As for the state of your body, if no one takes down your body within ten hours, the blood vessels in your face will break apart. Your head will be like a tomato, cracked to bursting. The most unseemly is your bodyweight will cause anal prolapse. Urine and feces will overflow . . . "

After two minutes of this, Mrs. Griffin climbed down from the chair. She sat on her bed, sobbing.

"Why do you want to commit suicide?" LW31 approached her, uncertain.

"It came to me all of a sudden. Everyone who ever loved me is dead, leaving my life friendless and wretched. The idea to commit suicide tonight, it just grew stronger and stronger in my mind . . . no one's left who loves me. What's the point of living?" Mrs. Griffin took a digital photo frame out of her pocket. Her aged fingers swipe across it and the transparent display transformed into pictures of people, one after another. "It's been twenty-five years since my child died. Now, I can't bear even one more day of life."

"Why don't you tell me about those people who loved you, Mrs. Griffin?" LW31 said. "Once you finish telling me about them, then I can help you commit suicide."

The endless night painted the world outside the window black. Mrs. Griffin stopped crying. Her fingers pressed the photo's display, freezing it on a picture of a young husband and wife.

She set down the phone in a daze. A burst of secret pain went through her. Maybe the kid in her belly kicked.

He didn't come home until the small hours of the morning. It was a cold night and he exhaled icicles with each breath. His hands cold and his feet cold, he dug himself under the bed covers. He huddled up for a while before he could do anything else.

She was still awake. "Back so late again?"

Slowly, his body relaxed in the warmth. The chill faded and he grew sleepy. He answered, his words indistinct, "Yeah, overtime. Also, this week's pay, three hundred fifty points, I've already deposited . . . "

He didn't finish his sentence. Instead, he shut his eyes and fell into a heavy sleep.

She, however, couldn't sleep. This wasn't the first time he'd lied.

For five months now, he'd come home late every night, usually reeking of alcohol, only to fall asleep as soon as he got into the bedroom. She'd ask him and he'd just say "overtime." However, he was just an ordinary delivery trunk driver for an AI company. How was he always working overtime? She'd just called his boss and found out the company didn't have overtime. Not to mention, five months ago, he'd gotten a raise. Five hundred points, not three hundred fifty.

The time and money he hid became her hidden worry. She was a proud woman, though, and never forced the truth from him. With every lie he cast, her heart cooled a little.

He went to work as usual. She convalesced at home. Her fetus was already nine months old.

Her home was cramped and dark. Often, she'd bring out a chair to sit by the curb. The street was lined with plum trees. In the cold weather, each twig exploded with a row of red flowers. She sat under a tree, waiting for him to return home. Car after car, suspended on tracks in mid-air, scratched her gaze as they came and went.

With so much free time, she counted on her memories to pass the days. She'd first met him under this plum tree. Back then, she was still the daughter of a wealthy family. She was set for life. Designer clothes and expensive jewelry covered her from head to foot. She drove a luxury car. As she passed through, the red plum tree caught her attention. Or, rather, the man standing under the tree did. The red plum stood out against snow covered ground. He stood out like a bunch of plums against the snow of the boundless sky.

She stopped her car then walked to his side. He smiled, warm laugh lines filling his face. He broke off a branch, giving it to her, saying, "I was just wondering whether there was anything this winter more beautiful than these plum blossoms. But now that I've seen you, I know my answer."

Right then, she fell in love with him.

Just like a classical romance, this love ran into her parents' violent disapproval. Her father had intended to arrange a business marriage for her. He flew into a rage, scolding her and beating her. He took away her purse and car, froze her card, then shut her inside their house. But it was no use. She was determined to marry him. Finally, with a wave of his hand and with an exhausted sigh, her father said one thing to her: Get out, and stay out.

She spent a long time before she adapted to married life. He drove a truck, delivering robots everywhere. The work was hard and the pay was low. She'd lived in luxury since she was a child, but for him, she threw herself into the oil, salt, soy sauce, and vinegar of a ordinary life. Once, when she was learning to cook, she cut her finger by accident. The spreading blood scared her into tears. He heard her cry and went into the kitchen. Holding her, he said over and over again, "You don't have to be in the kitchen. I will. Don't hurt yourself again."

But, now, he'd changed. He'd learned to lie and hide money. Sometimes, his body carried the scent of alcohol and perfume. Everyone knew what this meant. She'd given up her youth and riches, her fingers now smoked yellow, the corners of her eyes now wrinkled. In exchange, she received only the sight of his back receding into the distance.

The more she thought about it, the more it weighed on her mind. At the foot of the plum tree, she collapsed into tears.

After his shift, his boss called him in. "Yesterday, your wife called me. She said you always come home extremely late. Her stomach is so large now. It's not easy. Go home earlier and keep her company."

He hurriedly nodded his head. "Yes, yes, of course."

After he left work, he didn't go home. Instead, he went the door of a nightclub in the middle of the city.

Someone had been waiting too long for him. "What took you so long? Quick, Boss Wang is already drunk. Drive him home."

Obsequiously, he bowed again and again. He got into the flying car, started its engine, then flitted to his assigned location. This is what he did every night.

He drove the nightclub's customers, delivering them home. He had to beg for a lot of favors before he got this second job. Just one delivery paid at least ten points. Most of those bosses had drunk too much and stank of alcohol. Sometimes, in the embrace of a woman whose clothes were drenched with the spray of perfume, they didn't go home. Their destination was a guest house. He didn't mind. He just wanted to be paid.

He didn't tell her about this second job. He wanted the money to be a pleasant surprise.

Five months ago, as he was signing for his freight, his boss told him, "This is LW's latest domestic robot. It can do all sorts of household chores."

He laughed. "What about taking care of a baby?"

The boss snorted. "Not just babies. This robot has a long term of service. It can take care of someone from birth all the way until death."

This sentence moved his heart.

She was clumsy and not very good at household chores, to say nothing of raising a child. If she had a robot to help her, he wouldn't spend every work day worrying about her. After that, he asked how much it cost. Twenty thousand Alliance points. This was not a small number.

So, for these few months, he was always busy outside the house. According to his calculations, in five months, he'd saved three thousand points from his wages. Add to that the hundred extra points he earned every night and he'd now saved eighteen thousand points. Their child would be born soon. He needed to earn money more quickly.

Tonight, he took a couple, man and a woman, to a hotel. On the road, she tittered as the man's hands never stopped caressing her. He paid no attention to them, focused on his driving. The hotel wasn't far. Its neon lights flickered below them.

Some people. The woman was a little shy, after all. She pushed aside the man's hand when he reached for her skirt.

The man was not happy. He roared, "What is there to be afraid of?"

Despite those words, the man raised his head and looked around. His gaze fell upon the photo on the car window.

It was of a couple, a man and a woman. Their happiness together shone on their faces. She rested her head on his shoulder. He looked at her with a mild expression. In the background was a cluster of plum blossoms in full bloom among the ice and snow.

The man, staring blankly, asked: "This photo . . . "

Like the man, he raised head and looked at the photo. With an irrepressible joy, he said, "That's me and my wife. She's beautiful, yeah? I'm a lucky man. She's pregnant. It's a girl. She'll grow up to be just as beautiful."

"Then why aren't you at home with her?"

"I have to make money so that I can buy her a present: a robot. So she won't have to work every day."

The man stayed silent.

The woman, who had just resisted the man's advances, noticed the man wasn't touching her any more. Confused, she pulled the man's hands to her. The man pulled them back, then lit a cigarette. The smoke drifted around the car's small and narrow cabin.

When he finished smoking, he said slowly, "Don't go to the hotel. Take me home."

The woman asked, "To your home? I'm not that kind of—"

"You can go right now."

The man took out his card. He tapped a few numbers on it, put the woman's finger on its screen, then transferred over that many points.

The woman grumbled, "It's enough money, but I have professional ethics. Halfway though, I can't just—"

"Go."

The women left. He continued to drive on to the man's house.

A plain woman came out. She brought the man an overcoat.

"Didn't you say you had a meeting tonight?"

"I canceled it." The man ran his hands through her hair. "No meeting is more important than you."

He watched this play out. His heart roiled with an indescribable feeling. He laughed, started the engine, then slowly left the rich side of town. Suddenly, he thought of her and didn't want to earn any more money tonight. He wanted to turn in early and spend time with her. Whenever she felt cold—and their house was always cold—she'd rub her hands, wrinkle her nose. The way she behaved was adorable. The way she behaved would worry him for the whole of his life.

Tonight, he'd use his wallet to stop her hands. He'd rub them slowly until they grew warm from the circulating blood. He laughed at the thought.

His mind still preoccupied, he didn't pay attention in both directions. An out-of-control flying car fell off its suspended track. It hit him from the right. The two flying cars rolled over each other then fell out of the sky. They exploded, blooming into resplendent, beautiful flowers.

She overslept. She waited for him, but he never came home. She got out of bed, went out to the street then stood under the plum tree. If he came back, he'd have to pass through here. When he came back, he'd see her under the plum tree, like when they'd first met, a face set off against plum blossoms.

The night was as cold as water and she wrapped her clothes tight around her. She'd decided to forgive him. It didn't matter what he'd done. She'd decided to forgive it all. He was her only worry in the world. Her plan now set, she began to laugh. When he came back, he'd definitely grasp her hands in his and rub them, letting circulating blood make them warm.

This is how she waited for him, staring at the end of the street, hoping he'd appear from somewhere. Overhead, a cluster of plum blossoms opened in resplendent beauty.

"I'm sorry . . . I'm genuinely sorry." LW31 lowered his head in apology.

Mrs. Griffin shook her head. "It's not your fault . . . My mom was an ill-fated person. Not long after she gave birth to me, she died. But she was also a fortunate person. After his death, she still used the money to buy you. It shows that she never blamed anyone."

LW31 paused, then put its hand on Mrs. Griffin's shoulder. "In that case, I can now help you carry out some other way of dying. How would you like to die?"

"Sleeping pills? That way, I won't feel any pain."

"OK." LW31 answered. "Except that, right now, we have two problems."

"Go ahead."

"One, within forty-eight hours of overdosing on sleeping pills, not only will you not be able to sleep, but symptoms like gastrospasm, abdominal pain, and foaming at the mouth will emerge. This is because every organ in your body will perform their post-poison stress function. Many people who attempt suicide by overdosing on sleeping pills, because they can't stand the pain any longer, call for help . . . Mrs. Griffin, I don't think you will want to endure that sort of pain."

Mrs. Griffin closed her eyes. Most of a day passed, it seemed, then her lips quivered. "I'd just like to commit suicide. I just want not to look like a disgrace after I'm dead. Even if I foam at the mouth, you will take care of my corpse for me, right?"

"Of course. I exist to serve you."

"That's good then." Mrs. Griffin nodded. "As for the pain . . . Throughout my entire life, I've endured too much pain. I've long gone numb. Open the drawer and check. How many sleeping pills are left?"

"Mrs. Griffin, this happens to be the second problem. We don't have enough sleeping pills." LW31 opened the drawer and took out the drugs. "A total of seventeen pills. This is a prescription drug. A pharmacy will sell twenty pills at most. Given your build, to cause death you may need eighty-six pills."

"Can't you go out and buy them for me?"

"Mrs. Griffin, maybe you forgot. The great migration has already begun. Practically everyone has already gone. There are no more pharmacies."

Mrs. Griffin sighed. The lamp lit her face. She seemed a little sallow. The years had left gullies on her face.

LW31 said politely, "Mrs. Griffin, it would be better if you tell me more. Besides your parents, there were other people who loved you, right?"

"Yes." Mrs. Griffin swiped the photo again. This time who appeared was a lanky young man. Mrs. Griffin glanced at him. Thick tears drifted from her eyes. One night from many years ago floated up to the present.

• • •

Late night.

Silence.

Peter and Jason stood silent at the gate at start of the street.

A street like this one,

there shouldn't be anyone standing there.

A street like this one,

there shouldn't have been two men in designer suits standing there at night.

The start of the street was broken.

The middle of the street was cold.

The end of the street was dark.

This was the most run down street in the city. Normally, few people walked it. It was a crime-ridden street. In dark places, countless eyes opened, stomachs rumbled, waiting for prey to enter.

Afterwards, the prey were swallowed and digested. Nothing left of them to be spit back out.

But Peter and Jason stood at the head of the street, relaxed, as though they belonged there. As though this was their home.

Peter was tall and thin. Standing there, motionless, he seemed like a sharp pencil.

Jason was short and fat, just like a wax gourd that had rolled all over the ground.

Jason was smoking. With a deep drag, the flame fled from the head of the cigarette to the end. The entire cigarette was burnt up.

Peter asked, "Now?"

Jason blew a puff of thick smoke. "Now."

The two men started down the long, dark street.

The wind blew by. It whimpered like tearful ghosts.

The people who lived on the street, they weren't law-abiding folk.

They were of all sorts. The beggar's neighbor was a thief. Above the thief lived a prostitute. Across from the prostitute's balcony was a reliably blundering cheat.

But they all had one thing common.

They were poor.

So poor that they could only live on this old, dilapidated street like snails in their shells.

To be poor is to suffer. It's the kind of suffering that freezes the heart stone cold.

So, whenever someone walked down this street, they usually entered the gaze of the beggar, the thief, the prostitute, and the cheat.

They'd swindled old men out of their clothes. They'd taken candy from babies.

They never let even a single cent slip past them.

But, now, they didn't dare even plan. They shut their windows. They lay on their beds, grinding their teeth until they sucked blood, not daring to make a sound.

Because Peter and Jason were walking down the street.

They walked neither quickly nor slowly. Their every step clicked on the pavement, solid and steady.

Peter walked six hundred fifty-nine steps altogether. Jason one thousand three hundred fifteen.

They stopped in front of a room at the tail of the street.

The room was dark. Its light was out.

But Jason heard breathing.

Panting like a fawn running from a hunter's gun.

Jason lifted his head and laughed grimly.

They haven't found the wrong place.

They beat the door three times like drum.

No one answered.

Jason continued to pound the door.

Dull and dreary, the dense dark of the night flustered them.

"Who is it?" At last, a sound from inside. It was a female voice, as clear as a bell, but trembling.

Jason said, "It's me."

Peter said, "And me."

The woman inside the room said, "Who are you?"

Peter and Jason said, "We are detectives from Public Safety Bureau of the Alliance of City-States."

The woman said, "You shouldn't have come."

Peter said, "But we're already here."

The woman said, "Can't you just go back?"

Jason said, "The last person who wanted us to go back is now sleeping in prison."

The woman in the room sighed.

She couldn't hide from disaster.

The woman opened the door.

When she opened the door, she saw short and fat Jason and she saw tall and thin Peter.

And Peter looked at the woman.

He couldn't help but gape at her. She was an extremely beautiful woman.

There were many standards for judging a woman's beauty. Some preferred the face, particularly the nose and mouth. Some preferred the figure, obsessing over the breasts, waist, ass, and legs. But no matter who the judges were, once they looked at this woman, they couldn't deny her beauty.

Because, regardless of face or figure, she was completely flawless.

Pretty brows, seductive eyes, a jade nose, a cherry mouth.

Ample breasts, tiny waist, a round ass, long and slender legs.

Combined to perfection.

Jason, instead, looked at the room behind the woman.

The room was small. The walls were old, but clean. It made one unspeakably comfortable just to look at it. The room didn't have much furniture, but the owner had clearly chosen every piece with care. Every piece was placed exactly where it ought to be.

The woman said, "You've come to my home in the middle of the night. What do you want?"

Jason said, "You don't know what we want?"

The woman said, "How would I, a weak woman, know what you want?"

Jason said, "But you know about the book, right?"

The woman shivered, but quickly composed herself. "What book?"

Jason took everything in his gaze. Calmly, he reached inside his jacket and pulled out his tablet. Its screen changed as he swiped it.

A front cover of a book appeared on the screen.

The front cover was bronze colored, with the title at the top.

The title was only five words. Five ordinary words.

But the woman looked as though she'd seen a ghost. Her face changed expression.

The Domestic Robot Administration Amendment

Peter, who'd been silent so far, started to speak.

His words were like his body, lean and taut. "We have information. You're hiding an LW model robot."

Jason said, "And according to the amendment, all the robots must be reclaimed."

The woman said, "I don't know what you're talking about."

Jason said, "Of course you know. Your face betrays you."

The woman said nothing.

Peter looked at her with care. His voice grew gentle. "A month ago, a PRW model domestic robot, while its owner was asleep, severed his throat. The deceased was an Alliance assemblyman. The Alliance has already passed a law. All robots are to be reclaimed."

The woman shook her head. "There's no robot here."

Jason laughed coldly. "I'm afraid you don't get the last word here."

With that, Jason pushed the woman away, then entered the room.

The woman crashed into the wall.

She looked to Peter for help, but Peter lowered his head, his expression difficult to read.

Jason narrowed his gaze. He looked all around the room. No robot.

Peter said, "There's no robot. Let's go."

Jason raised his hand. His gaze fell on the bed, the snow white sheets, the neatly folded blanket. The foot posts were made of a metal alloy. They were coated with dust.

This woman with the meticulously arranged room, how could she put up with the dust on the foot posts?

Jason laughed. His laughter was joyous.

He pointed at the bed. "Is something hiding under the bed?"

The woman's face instantly went pale.

Jason lit another cigarette. "Now you have two options."

The woman quickly nodded her head.

Jason said, "Option one, I take the robot back. It'll be melted down and, for the crime of hiding it, you'll be put in prison."

The woman said, "Please, I beg you. Don't take away LW31. It's the only thing my parents left me."

Jason said, "Then you have option two. Give me five thousand points and I've seen nothing."

The woman furrowed her brow. "But I don't have that much money. Take everything else in my home. Just leave me LW31."

The corners of Jason's mouth curled into a slight smile. His gaze slid from the woman's face down, "Even if I took everything in your house, it still wouldn't be enough."

Jason's gaze felt like a serpent. Clammy and cool, it slithered over her skin.

The woman's chest tightened.

Calmly, Jason stared at the woman. He enjoyed the fear that spread across the woman's face. He was pleased, and a certain part of his body began to respond.

A long time had passed before he spoke. "I want you for ten nights."

The woman violently shook her head.

Jason made an apologetic sigh. "Then say goodbye to your robot."

Before he'd even finished speaking, the woman raised her hand to hit him.

She only needed one chance. This one chance was enough to subdue him.

She assembled machines at the factory. Her work every day was to reach her hand in to shove motherboards into the machines.

So, she'd already practiced this move for four years, five months and twenty-eight days. She was absolutely certain that no one in this room could stop her.

But, this once, she was wrong.

Astonishment gradually solidified on her face. One hand, one fat, white, and strong hand clutched her throat.

The hand belonged to Jason.

No one had ever thought that someone short and fat could reach his hand out so quickly.

The woman implored him. "LW31 isn't dangerous. It's just responsible for taking care of me. For a long time now. I can't lose it. I beg you."

Jason said, "I'll give you a chance to beg, but it'll be when we're both naked. People who try to hit me don't come to a good end. You'll quickly know how living can be worse than dying."

He wasn't lying. Jason never lied. If you met Jason one day and he told you he wanted to kill you, there was only thing you should do: go home and make out your will.

You couldn't resist and there was no escape because he was Jason.

The woman's face filled with despair. This time, her eyes suddenly widened. She saw something she absolutely wasn't supposed to see.

A gun pressed against the back of Jason's head.

Peter said, "Let her go."

Jason said, "You want to betray me because of her?"

Peter, his face expressionless, said, "I can't take it any more. Searching for robots as an excuse, you've extorted nearly two hundred thousand Alliance points, raped seven women, hounded nineteen residents of the city to death."

Jason said, "And you're a good guy?"

Peter said, "I'm not, but now I want to be."

Jason sneered. "I bet you can't kill me."

Peter laughed. "Why?"

Jason said, "Because you wouldn't dare."

Peter pulled the trigger.

Blood splashed.

The man fell.

The woman looked at Peter. Astonished, she sized him up. Tears fell from her eyes. "Thank you."

Peter shrugged. "Peter upheld justice for you. He begs you not to cry. If the world is unjust, get drunk, wave a sword, then cut off heads."

The woman nodded. "But you killed him and he died in my home. Maybe I should get ready to flee."

Peter said, "But, one person fleeing will be very lonely."

The woman said, "What do you suggest then?"

Peter studied the woman.

For a long time, they looked at each other and laughed. Peter extended his hand. "Hello, my name is Peter, Peter Griffin."

The woman said, "I'm Xue Yi."

Peter took a step forward, then held the woman.

The woman felt his embrace.

He was very tall.

Very thin.

His face was cool.

His arms were stiff.

But his chest was warm.

"That night, we spent a lot of time digging a hole and buried you in it. Afterward, he took me and we fled here, there, and everywhere until the Alliance collapsed. We didn't return until the orders for our arrest were canceled."

LW31 looked at her serenely. After a while, Mrs. Griffin let out an inaudible sigh.

She said lightly, "But the good times didn't last. Not long after we settled down, he grew ill and died. In the years when we were on the run, he always gave the good things to our daughter and me. All the injuries and illnesses accumulated in his body . . ."

"I remember him a little. He was laconic, capable, and he loved you very much."

Mrs. Griffin exposed her wrists. She tossed the grief from her mind. "I want to open a blood vessel. Come and help me."

LW31 nodded its head, then took a thin knife from a drawer. It gleamed as though it were lacquered with a layer of light.

Mrs. Griffin held out her wrists. The knife edge immediately pressed down on an old, wrinkled, pulsing vessel. A chill started at her skin then oozed into the blood vessel. She began to shiver.

"I'm going to start cutting. Are you ready?" LW31 asked.

"I'm ready. Just get on it." Mrs. Griffin snapped. She closed her eyes then immediately opened them again. Shivering, she asked, "What happens after you open a blood vessel?"

"That depends on which one I cut. If it's a vein, then your blood will flow out right away, but not like a river in volume. That's because your platelets will have already congealed at the wound. If it's an artery, then you'll die quickly. However, in that scenario, blood will spurt like a fountain. It may be hard to keep this within the limits of propriety. Blood will drench your body. I fear that you'll look horribly mutilated." LW31 spoke at a steady pace. "Should I start cutting now?"

"In that case, is there some other way?"

"Yes, there's a way that is highly appropriate for you. However, before I tell you, you have to tell me again about someone who loved you."

The photo frame's screen flickered. Quickly, a smiling girl, bright and beautiful, pulling a suitcase behind her appeared. The screen also displayed three short arcs. That indicated that this photo also had sound. Mrs. Griffin's trembling hand touched the screen. Immediately, a graceful but ordinary voice surrounded the room.

In the winter of 2335, dragging my suitcase, I returned to the small town I left seven years ago.

The airport was deserted. Wind from a distant place blew here and my hair fluttered in that wind. I grew dizzy at the sight of a sky that was filled with clouds, a vast expanse of exquisite grace sweeping past the town. I began to understand that when a woman was looking at the sky, she wasn't looking for anything. She was just being still.

The stillness oozed into my veins, like ice-cold lips kissing my bones.

There weren't many taxis at midnight. Once in a while, a few passed by on the suspended tracks, their headlights scratching a line in the dark.

I stood by the side of the street, watching flowing light drag shadow behind it. A taxi stopped in front of me. A dark window rolled down revealing the driver. He was a good-looking man. When he smiled, his teeth were white. The corners of his mouth tilted gently. The expression in his eyes was as clean and flowing as water.

"Where to?" he asked.

I stepped in, then told him my destination.

Once we got on the road, we didn't speak.

I plastered my face to the car window. Colors faded as I rode. I saw the town through the gray forms that emerged. Nothing had changed in seven years. This small town, old and broken, still made people's hearts bleak and desolate.

"Everyone is emigrating now. Very few returned." The driver was the first to speak.

I nodded. "I'm also planning to leave. I applied for the Pegasus star system, the planet called KG6. My application's already approved."

"Then what are you returning here for?"

"To say goodbye."

The driver didn't say any more.

The taxi stopped in the north end, at a house I knew intimately. I got out. The driver, still stopped by the side of the road, wasn't in a hurry to leave. I think he must have wanted to tell me something. At last, though, he just started the engine. The taxi slowly glided into the night.

I knocked on the door. The dull thuds sounded like the beating of a lonely heart.

The door opened with a creak. The robot's face revealed itself. Facial features had been carved on its black face guard. The childish scratches formed a weird smile.

The robot came out and took my suitcase. "Miss, you've returned."

I looked inside. The house was a black cavity. "Is she here?"

"Yes, she's home. She's been waiting for you for a long time. Why don't we go in?"

I hesitated. I stood at the door. Below my feet, it was as if a deep trench had split open. A great and frozen wind blew down that vast gap. I had no way to cross it. I simply sat down. The woman inside the house, who was also sitting, opened her eyes, as though she was looking back at me.

She was my mother. Or, rather, she was once my mother.

The first seventeen years of my life, I spent at her side. In my memory, this little house will always be cold and damp, like the years I can't bear. The place always carried the faint smell of rot and the young me hated it. After I escaped, though, not a night went by that I didn't secretly long for this house.

I was born in the final age of Earth's exhaustion. No one felt secure. When I was small, I saw too many pallid faces grow alarmed and bewildered, but I didn't know why. Until I was five, I roamed the world with my parents. Or rather, we were fugitives.

Then the once colossal Alliance crumbled. We settled down with lots of robots to help with the housework. But not long after, my father, lying in bed, swallowed his last breath. I remember his eyes, withered and cloudy, staring forever at her and me. Deep grief was buried in those eyes.

After my father died, she became frail and stubborn. She wouldn't let me out of the house. She wouldn't let me have any contact with boys. If I defied her, she didn't hit me or yell at me. She just kept staring at me, her dark eyes shining like a wolf's.

So I stayed by her side. Time flowed like water. It washed over me until I was clear and slender. However, it wore her down until her face grew ashen and wrinkled. Did time retaliate against her on my behalf? I've never dared to imagine.

I let go of a silent breath. A fierce wind screamed under the cover of night. The town let out a loud and lonely cry. Yes, the town was also lonely. One after another, people emigrated. The center of town was deserted, like a great beast that has lost its heart, lamenting without end.

"Miss, let's go in." The robot had waited a long time before finally speaking. Its voice was as flat as ever. This time, though, I seemed to hear an imploring tone in its voice.

But I shook my head. If she didn't open her mouth, I wouldn't go in. She and I were two sheafs of wheat in a wheat field, leaning against each other, but always pushing against each other too. We could never hug.

When I was seventeen, I decided to leave.

That summer, I had worked everywhere in town. I carefully saved every cent. After that muggy summer, I already had enough money for a bus ticket. As far as I was concerned, all I needed was a bus ticket and I could lead my own vagrant life.

So, that September, I told her, "Ma, I'm going to buy a book."

"Hm," she said in the dark.

I turned to the door, and just like that, I left home. The moment I bought my bus ticket, tears filled my face. Soundlessly, I sobbed.

And she waited for me to return. It took exactly seven years.

In those seven years, I traveled to many places. I saw warm sunshine and was drenched in dark rain. I never stopped moving. Until I met him.

It was on a main street in the south. He stood on a platform simultaneously passing out leaflets to passersby and, in a loud voice, extolling the virtues of the interstellar immigration policy. The instant he gave me a leaflet, I saw his beautiful eyes. Furrows wrinkled his brow. His gaze, clear like spring water, flowed past the seething sunlight and crowd, surmounted the air, then flowed into mine.

And just like that, I was lost.

The man always liked to hold my face in his large palms, nuzzle my forehead with his nose then tease me like a small animal. I never refused him. Later, when he wanted to take me away from Earth, I still didn't refuse him.

He said, "We'll settle down in the Pegasus star system. There's already a terraformed planet. The atmosphere is as fresh as your breath. Six satellites orbit the planet. When you walk outside at night, six shadows spread out beneath your feet."

I said, "Fine."

My only request was to return to see her, to say goodbye.

But, now, I hesitated at the door. It was a chilly night but I didn't dare go in.

The person in the room and I exchanged gazes. After I don't know how long, I stood. "LW31, give me my suitcase. I want to leave."

"Miss, you really don't want to visit her?" The robot said, hurriedly. "She's missed you so much these past few years."

I nodded. I'd also missed her. Instead of sending a message, if I had a chance, I'd come back to visit again.

The robot stayed silent. Dew condensed on it, like tears weeping down its outer shell.

She still hadn't come out and I decided I wouldn't wait any longer. I took my suitcase, turned around, then left. Clouds floated across the sky. A strong wind howled past.

I knew she was in the back looking at me, but I never turned around.

"I know what happened next." LW31 said. "The spaceship she rode on was hit by a meteorite. The ship's cabin was damaged. All the crew and passengers suffocated to death."

Mrs. Griffin didn't say anything. A long while later, two thick tears fell down her face. They hit the photo frame. The display slowly faded to black.

"So, those who loved me, they're all gone." Mrs. Griffin put the photo frame back into her pocket. "I no longer have any meaning to my life. Tell me the way to kill myself. Let me die, please?"

"As you wish. The most suitable method is . . . electrocution."

"Won't that hurt?"

"Electrocution is the most beautiful way to commit suicide. It best preserves the original appearance of the corpse. In fact, if it's done correctly, it doesn't even leave any burn marks. In the moment of electrocution, you'll feel a sharp pain then you'll stop breathing and your heart will stop beating. The process is very quick. Practically no pain at all." LW31 said earnestly. "But what you need to make sure of is this: the electric current must pass through the heart in order to cause death. No other way will do. But I can help you with this bit. I will use rubber tape to attach copper wire to your solar plexus. I guarantee the electrical current will pass through your heart. Moreover, I will use cotton balls moistened with salt water to lower your resistance. Mrs. Griffin, would you like to do this now?"

Mrs. Griffin nodded her head.

"Very well. I exist to serve you." LW31 turned to look for copper wire, rubber tape, and cotton balls, but when he reached the door, he stopped. "Mrs. Griffin, before you are electrocuted, I want to give you a warning. You're wrong about a few things."

"What things?"

"You said everyone who ever loved you is dead, leaving your life friendless and wretched." LW31's back faced Mrs. Griffin. Its back was corroded by rust. Its voice was slow. "You're wrong. There's still one person, from start to finish, who has always loved you."

"Who?"

LW31 turned around. In the light, the smile scratched on its black face guard seemed to move. It looked at Mrs. Griffin, its carved gaze infinitely soft. The electric transmission in its body buzzed.

After a long time, it said, "Me."

Mrs. Griffin stared dumbfounded.

Events of her past fell thick like snowflakes. Gradually and clearly, she realized it was right. Throughout her long life, LW31 indeed had stuck with her from start to finish. When she was little, her mother was always ill. She couldn't do any housework. LW31 took care of Mrs. Griffin in every possible way. It allowed her to grow up without any worries or cares.

Once when she was mischievous, she thought its black face guard was too forbidding, so she carved a smile on it. It didn't get angry. It was peaceful and docile. After she grew up, LW31 always cleaned the house until it was spotless, cooked the meals, then stood quietly in the house, waiting for Mrs. Griffin to come home from work. After her daughter was born, it became even busier. It practically never had any free time. Once Mrs. Griffin grew old, it still took care of everything at home. It accompanied Mrs. Griffin sunbathing, told her jokes downloaded from the internet.

It could take care of a person all her life and, from start to finish, show every possible consideration without even a single complaint. If that wasn't love, then what was?

Mrs. Griffin choked with sobs. She walked up to then hugged LW31. Her hand touched LW31's back. There, LW31's outer casing was even rougher than Mrs. Griffin's skin.

"I'm sorry. I've always taken you for granted."

"Never mind, Mrs. Griffin." LW31 still had that smiling expression. Its voice was tranquil like before. "Mrs. Griffin, your dinner is already cold. Would you like me to reheat it?"

"Yes." Mrs. Griffin wiped away her tears, nodding her head.

For the Love of Sylvia City

ANDREA M. PAWLEY

Slime criss-crosses AMX-5. I ease a snail from the cable's sheathing. I doubt something this small is causing the communication anomalies with Sylvia City, but I promised my podsisters I'd examine our outpost's section of the cable again.

I put one snail after another into the masticator floating at my side. Each gastropod I find on the cable suffers the same fate. Just removing the snails wouldn't be good enough. The ones I tagged when I first noticed them a few weeks ago found their way back to eat the algae that's started growing along the cable sheathing. Ending a snail's life isn't like killing a whale. Snails don't sing about their history, but I'd rather not harm something that's managed to survive in these conditions.

The ocean pushes at me more than usual. I'm only twenty meters below the water line and just five kilometers from where AMX-5 enters the ocean. On scalesuited knees, I sink down to stable ground free of the trash littering most of the continental shelf. My mandatory service posting is closer to the dryland world than I ever wanted to be.

Since my first month at the outpost, I've used my free time to bioremediate and disperse the waste in the immediate vicinity of the cable. My podsisters, Daniella and Fatima, have their own tasks and interests. Time in the shallows degrades their health. Removing the trash beside our outpost's section of the cable was my own special project. With authority and supplies, neither of which I have, I'd set up carbonic acid converters like the ones cleaning the ocean around Sylvia City. Converters would make a real difference. My trashless swath along AMX-5 is nice to look at, but it's nothing permanent. A few weeks after my service ends, the dryland trash that floats down from above and creeps along the benthos will again cover the cable.

Steel shows on a section of AMX-5 where snail slime has eaten through. Snails still swarm the breach, which is strange. They usually detach before they get too far into the cable's magnetic field. Turning my greenlamp up to full, I lean in for a closer look. Real Benthans wouldn't do that, but my dryland eyes never seem to gather enough light.

A scan indicates that water's only pushed a few millimeters into the sheathing. My instruments detect no electric current. The cable sometimes loses power but never for very long. I check the time. My journey back to the outpost will take half an hour in the *Nidaria,* my snug submarine vessel. If I'm late, Dannie will worry, but a superficial repair like this one won't take long. I expand a drycage over the damaged section of AMX-5 and evacuate the water inside. I begin to peel back cable sheathing layers, some living, some inanimate.

This is my 227th repair. At 228, I'll have mended the cable once for each month since Sylvia City took me in nineteen years ago. I haven't told anyone about the tally, not even Dannie. She'd say I'm keeping track for the wrong reasons, and she'd insist I don't owe Sylvia City more than anyone else does. But she doesn't know what it means to be born on dry land.

I was an infant when my parents fled with me to the ocean floor. Sylvia City had already turned away thousands of Carbon War refugees after the first few hundred tried to spread the dryland conflict to the benthos. But my mild-mannered parents were engineers with the skills to fix Sylvia City's overburdened environmental systems. My parents were welcomed. I was let in, too. I have no memory of life beyond the ocean floor, but growing up, I was known as the last dryland refugee. Ten thousand cable repairs can't erase that fact.

I try to focus on my work in the drycage. I'm careful to place tools so they don't nick my scalesuit. In the shallows where I'm working, the weight of water won't crush someone in a compromised scalesuit, but carelessness is a bad idea. The ocean holds too many dangers.

Sharks were once the greatest threat on the Blake Plateau. Now, threadfin drones are. They look like fish, but they travel alone, and they're made of metal. Built by drylanders to spy on one another, threadies explode when they come near people in the water. Only a drylander would blow something up to guard a secret. Shrapnel from an explosion can slice through a scalesuit and the person inside it.

I'm never close enough to a threadie to worry about the blast zone. Marksmanship is the only thing I've ever excelled at, so Sylvia City decided my mandatory service would be at the outpost with the most threadie contact. Since the end of the Carbon War, when AMX-5 was still a vital communication link between the wet and the dry land, Sylvia City has kept her promise to maintain the cable. I wouldn't have tried so hard to impress anyone with my ability to shoot a compressor gun if I'd known the reward would be six months living this close to the shore.

My thoughts drift ahead to the 228th repair. I wonder what it will be. I don't know if anything will be different after I complete it.

Red light flashes across my scalesuit eye coverings and resolves to a dot that indicates something unknown fifty meters away. I'm about to be delayed. The approaching object would have to be at least as large as a threadie for my proximity alert to detect it. I have no way of knowing how big it is or if it's anything more than a large piece of trash, but I know it's coming closer. With the water so churned up today, I can only see twenty meters. I wait for the object to change direction. It doesn't.

I'd rather be safe than shredded or bitten. I hurry through this repair's last steps and turn off my greenlamp. Sharks notice bright lights. So do threadies. I reach for my compressor gun, which is already charged to fire. I only need one shot to destroy a threadie. Twenty meters of visibility will give me plenty of time. But if a shark's approaching, I'll need multiple re-charges to deter one of those mutated creatures. The compressor takes time to ready after each shot. The crushed snails in the masticator will speed up the process, but I don't know how much. For a moment, I hope this part of the ecosystem is too compromised to foster apex predators. It's a shameful thought, one a real Benthan would never have.

Sensing heightened tension, a layer of my scalesuit breather tries to push past my lips and into my throat where it can protect me from drowning. I've never needed the device as a throat-breather, though I've had to cough it out of my windpipe many times. It's only a distraction now. I bite down to stop the breather's intrusion. The device pulls back to sit atop my nose and mouth where it belongs. The thing in the water is forty meters away now.

The *Nidaria* is closer, but in the other direction. I resist the urge to turn and swim to my vessel. Predators often attack from behind. I swipe my scalesuit to release an olfactory neutralizer to help disguise my location from a shark. The neutralizer won't affect a threadie if I'm in its path. My compressor gun is primed to fire.

I stare into the wide, watery darkness. My proximity alert shows the object's approach is slowing. It might be preparing to attack. My knees press into the ocean floor. I'm breathing too hard. I curse my lack of benthic enhancements.

The neutralizer isn't having an effect. Whatever's approaching can't be a threadie because it's moving from side to side. Threadies travel on a set path that rises and falls through the ocean's photic layer. The pattern of movement on my proximity alert doesn't make sense. The distance to the object shrinks to thirty meters. I still can't see it.

Dread sucks the moisture from my mouth. I realize my mistake. I was looking in the middle of the water column. My gaze rises to the water's surface. Waves show as gray-black shadows. Just at the limit of my vision, something resolves. I think I recognize it. I should lower my compressor gun, but I hold it steady. Noise disappears. My thoughts race faster than time should allow. What I see is more startling than a threadie or a shark.

A boy falls toward the ocean floor. His mouth is open. He can't be more than six years old. He still has all his limbs. He might have only just drowned. Tattered clothing made of sea plants marks him as a scavenger child from one of the defunct oil platforms. The nearest is kilometers away.

If the boy only went under a moment ago, I could save him. I could swim up to him before he falls too far. I could break the water's surface for the first time in my memory. I could revive him with filtered air from my own lungs and the press of my scalesuit-covered hands against his chest. I could breathe the fetid air above. I could push that air into the boy's body. I could wait for the boy to breathe again. I could fight to keep my own head above the watery embrace that's held me safe all these years. I could give the boy back his life and let the poisons in the air above steal a little of my own. I could throw away nineteen years of trying to feel like a real Benthan. Or I could let the boy die.

Sound disappears. The water's roiling slows. My thoughts cavitate.

I know what to do.

Noise like color blazes around me. I swipe my scalesuit for a rapid ascent. I soar. I catch the boy's sinking form. I increase my scalesuit's buoyancy. The boy and I shoot toward the ocean's surface. We burst above the water line. A swell pitches us toward the sky. The light blinds. My scalesuit eye coverings can't compensate for the glare. I squint against the pain. If I were a real Benthan, my retinas would be ruined. My eyelids squeeze shut. The pain recedes. I blink and can see again.

The ocean's surface crashes onto itself. Swells break into whitecaps. My scalesuit's buoyancy helps me keep the boy's head above water. His body is limp. If his heart beats, I don't feel it. I want to believe he only just went under. I put his back against my front and begin to compress and release his chest. His clothing pulls apart beneath my motions. A rash—red, raw, and bleeding—covers his head and shoulders. The wounds are almost familiar. The rest of his body shows the blue-gray pallor of hypothermia.

I peel off a layer of my breather and set it across the back of my scalesuit-covered hand. The bud needs a moment to grow. I suck as much filtered air into my lungs as they will hold. I stroke the breather parent protecting my own airways. I roll it to the side. Cold water sprays the skin of my exposed nose and mouth. I pinch the boy's nostrils closed. My mouth seals over his. I blow clean air into his clogged lungs. I pump his chest again. I gulp at the dryland air. It tastes of acid. I force this polluted air into the boy. The inside of my nose burns.

I will the boy to live. In his slack features, I imagine a benthic future for him, one that knows the rhythms of the deep ocean.

I feel movement in his chest. The water pitches us around. The boy convulses. I hold onto him. Together, we rise on a wave. He gurgles and begins to cough. He vomits. I turn from his bilious spray.

The shore five kilometers away comes into view. I've seen images of what that landscape should look like. AMX-5's power station should be visible on a peninsula. Just beyond that, buildings should rise from streets clogged with traffic. A latticework of rail lines should weave between the middle stories of skyscrapers and across the tops of shorter buildings. Transportation vehicles should zip around. Aerial crafts should dot the sky.

The shore looks nothing like that. Reality wobbles. The child shuddering in my arms begins to slip away.

AMX-5's power station seems intact, but the shore beyond is a calamity. Black smoke streams from a dozen buildings and gathers above the city. Flames spark orange and yellow in too many places to count. Rail cars wait motionless in the middle of elevated lines or lay crashed atop automobiles glinting below. No evacuation sirens sound. No instructions to shelter blare. Not a single rescue craft circles a flaming building. The greater distance holds more smoke.

The world has seen this before. I have, too, in documentaries about the Carbon War. The boy's rash suddenly makes sense. He's been exposed to carbon weapons fire, though he was outside the weapon's immediate range. His head and shoulders must have been above the water line when a pulse deployed, but he was far enough away not to be turned to ash. The ocean protected the submerged portion of the boy's body the same way it protected Sylvia City when I was an infant. Air conducts carbon weapon pulses. Water doesn't. People die, but infrastructure remains in place.

New worry seizes me. A haven that persists from one apocalypse to another might look even more to refugees like a promised land. Just as before, anyone who can follow AMX-5 from the shore into the water will soon set upon Sylvia City. This time, the drylanders might be more forceful about bringing weapons and conflicts. The whale song halls might not survive.

I hold tighter to the boy. His terrified gaze darts around. My lips begin to burn. I press them together. I've read about what a secondary carbon rash feels like, but this is the first time I remember experiencing one. I'm lucky only my lips touched the boy's flesh. Salves can mitigate the pain of my secondary rash, but in a few days, my scalesuit will die from having touched the boy in so many places. With his primary rash, the boy's medical need will be so great that only doctors in Sylvia City will be able to save him.

An airplane appears just above the swells. The craft flies in halting, predatory bursts parallel to the shore.

Flecks of ash like graphite tears smear the boy's face. My exposed skin must look the same. Ash from dead drylanders and burning buildings is in the air. Millions might have died already. Their remains will rest momentarily on the ocean's surface before precipitating through the pelagic to fall—inedible and useless—to the benthos.

The ocean will suffer greater injustice than ashes though. Carbon weapons release vast amounts of carbon dioxide into the air. So do survivors willing to burn anything they can find for warmth and cooking fuel. Like the last time, the ocean will attempt to absorb it all. The water's acidity will shoot up. Great colonies of plants and animals will die. New, sickly species will add to the ranks of mutated sharks, thin-shelled snails and algae that grows where algae shouldn't be able to grow.

Sylvia City has ways to prepare herself and her environment. She can mitigate some initial carbonic acid effects, but she needs to deploy her defenses while the danger is still in the ocean's upper layers. Panic squeezes the breath from my chest. I hope Sylvia City knows what's happened.

The airplane turns toward the ocean and drops low to hover a few kilometers away near an oil platform. People must have been detected. I can't look away from what's about to happen, but the boy has seen enough. Despite his coughing, he buries his face in my neck.

A blast shoots out from under the airplane's wings. The area in front of the craft undulates with the pulse, which makes contact with the platform. Anyone who was alive is ash now.

I've been above the water line too long. I check that the breather bud on my hand is ready. I lean back so I can see the boy's face. In my scalesuit, I must seem strange to him, but my differences are nothing compared to what people from Sylvia City look like.

"I'm going underwater," I tell the boy. His eyes are bloodshot. "To Sylvia City. I can give you something to let you breathe in the water. You'll be able to get to the shore, but you'll need treatment for what the carbon weapon did to you. Sylvia City can help. If you come with me, you'll have a home for the rest of your life, but you'll be different from everyone else. Always. Or you can go back to the dry land."

The plane finds a boat and prepares to unleash another blast.

"Do you want to come with me?" I say.

The boy's chin trembles.

"I don't want to die again," he says.

I smile. Pain needles my lips.

"Hold still," I say. I peel the breather bud from the back of my hand. The boy's eyes widen. I set the breather over his nose and mouth. The breather's edges pulse along his flesh to find the shape of his face. His eyelids pinch together with the sensation. I hold tight to him. The airplane flies toward us. A low hum grows in the air and threatens to roar.

"Bite down," I say. The boy misses his opportunity. The breather dives into his throat. I stop the boy from clawing at his neck. The waves toss us around. The airplane nears. I stroke my breather so it will sit over my mouth and nose. I shift the boy to my back. He clings to me like I might let him go. The plane slows to hover. The boy's fingers dig into my scalesuit. The benthos calls to me. With the boy, I dive.

Water gasps and echoes around us. Light dims. Alive, we sink toward the benthos.

My scalesuit protects me from the ever-colder water layers, but the boy has nothing to keep him warm until I can get him into my emergency scalesuit back in the *Nidaria*. More pain lies in his future. His new-grown breather pulls oxygen from the water and stops his lungs from compressing, but his eyes and ears have no such protection. Barotrauma is inevitable.

We reach the ocean floor. I turn on my greenlamp and squint into the depths. A field of trash shows, but not AMX-5. Surface waves must have pushed me away from the cable. I swipe my scalesuit to search for AMX-5's magnetic field. It should be detectable within three kilometers. Nothing shows on the display. I can't have moved so far in such a short amount of time.

Something about the snails on the cable earlier nags at me. I've never seen them gorge so deeply, like they'd been eating algae and sheathing for hours.

Finally, I understand. The cable's power isn't intermittent. It's completely gone. The power station must have been damaged on the inside. Despair bubbles through my thoughts. My podsisters at the outpost don't know what's happened on the dry land, and neither does Sylvia City. Preparations haven't started.

The boy's hold at my neck loosens. The rash, the cold, and the water pressure are taking their toll on him. I have to find the cable and the *Nidaria* beside it. I need to warn Sylvia City about the new war.

I bite back my breather and try to think. The murky water torments me. Somewhere, the cable is waiting.

One direction seems to hold a little less trash. I swim that way. With an arm on the boy at my back, my progress through the water is slow. My greenlamp eats the darkness and extrudes it in my wake. The density of trash lessens. I'm drawn toward the swath of ocean floor I cleaned.

AMX-5 comes into view. Something hits me from behind. I'm knocked forward. I lose hold of the boy. I reach for my compressor gun. It's still primed to fire. A reef shark circles. The mutated creature is over three meters long. It turns toward the boy, who drifts like he's unconscious or already dead.

I point my compressor gun at the shark and fire. The blast hits the shark in the gills. The stunned creature swims away. I slot the gun into my masticator, bulging with snail sludge.

I swim toward the boy. He's not moving. The shark returns. The compressor gun is charged. I hope Sylvia City will understand what I have to do. I fire.

I blow the shark apart. Blood clouds the water. Fish chunks spin past. I cup a few large pieces and press them into the masticator. I start the energy transfer to the compressor gun again. The blood scent will attract other predators, but I'll be ready if anything else emerges from the depths.

The boy and I have to get out of the water. I need to find the *Nidaria*. The boy's eyes are slits. He doesn't react to my touch. I tuck him under an arm and swim back to AMX-5. I take a chance and swim downslope.

At last, the depths give up the *Nidaria*. She's just as I left her, except now she's the boy's lifeline. And Sylvia City's.

I open the *Nidaria's* hatch and pull out my emergency scalesuit. I slide the boy into it. Burst capillaries dot his face. I set another breather over his mouth and nose. Edges seal. The scalesuit expels water and shrinks to fit the boy's shape. If not for the boy's stunted limbs, he could be any Benthan child behind wide scalesuit eyes.

The boy and I only just fit into the *Nidaria,* which is designed for one Benthan. Luckily, they're taller than drylanders and bigger-boned. The hatch sucks closed behind us.

The unconscious boy's body presses against my legs. I set his scalesuit to parent controls and hydration. His body twitches under the prick of tiny needles filled with water, antibiotics, and nutrition. His scalesuit will warm him and serve as a barrier to stop his primary rash from spreading. The rash my scalesuit and I are carrying won't spread because they're secondary. I instruct the boy's scalesuit to sedate him. I don't want the boy to wake frightened and in pain. I want the next day of his conscious life to begin healthy in Sylvia City.

I set the *Nidaria* to follow AMX-5 down the continental shelf to the outpost.

We glide through the water a few feet above the ocean floor. The *Nidaria's* pace is slow. Her gills are designed to keep herself and one person, not two, oxygenated. I tune the *Nidaria's* hydrophone to the strongest signal it can find. The saddest whale song I've ever heard pulses into my ears. The auto-translator picks out the notes that whales use to refer to Sylvia City and sanctuary.

Darkness armors the benthos. Ahead, a thin school of fish comes into greenlamp view. The *Nidaria* swims through the school, which takes refuge in her wake.

I scan the field of trash. Soon, new carbon ash will coat it all. Not yet though. On the sea floor beside a twisted metal frame, a threadie lays immobile. I've never before seen one motionless. I swipe off the *Nidaria's* anterior light and reach for my compressor gun.

Reason prevails. Instead of shooting through the *Nidaria's* window, I back the vessel up. I turn the greenlamp on again and swing the *Nidaria* in an arc wider than a threadie blast zone.

Farther along AMX-5, another unmoving threadie comes into view. I keep the *Nidaria* clear of it. A third threadie appears and a fourth. By the time the darkened outpost resolves, I've counted a dozen newly-fallen drones.

A crater's been blasted from the ground beside the outpost. The building's exterior is damaged. I try to breathe and see what's there and not what I'm afraid of, but it's hard. My podsisters could be floating dead inside, their scalesuits only partially on when the water and the pressure came. I coax the *Nidaria* into a circuit around the outpost. I search for breaches where water's flooded in.

I find none. Instead, a light inside the building turns on. Fatima is standing on the viewing deck and staring at the *Nidaria*. Her raised hand shields her eyes, cast in the same blue-white as those of the abyssal fish. She and Dannie don't need greenlamps to see in the deep ocean. Fatima turns on an exterior light. The bottom of the threadie-made crater still isn't visible.

"A threadie landed on the roof," Fatima says.

Her hydrophoned voice inside the *Nidaria* is a relief.

"Are you hurt?" I say. "Or Dannie?"

"No," Fatima says, "the threadie didn't explode when it landed, but I thought the core might leak radiation, so I used the grapple to send the toxic thing sailing. It exploded when it hit the benthos. Did you see any other threadies on your way back?"

In my thoughts, something phosphoresces. It's a grain of sand, then a rock, then a ledge rising up from the ocean floor. The thought shimmers like a beacon from Sylvia City. I understand what I need to do. I still have one more repair. My scalesuit will be good for a few days.

"Yes," I say. "I saw some threadies. I'll be in soon."

I bring the *Nidaria* close to the outpost's waterlock. Instead of docking the vessel inside, I rest her on the benthos near where the outpost's communication line connects to AMX-5.

I extract myself from the *Nidaria* and step onto the ocean floor. AMX-5 has never before looked so vulnerable. In one swift motion, I slice all the way through the cable. The primary carbon rash that must be spreading along AMX-5's new algae can't have arrived at the outpost before the *Nidaria* even if she was slow. Now, the rash will never reach Sylvia City. I cauterize each end of the cable and set the stumps back on the ocean floor. This is only the beginning.

I crowd into the *Nidaria* again and dock her inside the outpost. Dannie's waiting for me on the other side of the waterlock door. Her big-boned face, colored like the gray sand around Sylvia City, is visible through the porthole between the waterlock and the outpost's interior. Worry tightens Dannie's expression.

The waterlock drains. So does the *Nidaria*. I make a mental list of what I'll need: nano-nets, the heavy grappler, another compressor gun, and as much bioremediant and dispersant as I can strap to the *Nidaria's* exterior.

I peel off my breather and push the top of my scalesuit back so it rests at my neck. I squeeze out of the *Nidaria*. Dannie swishes open the door connecting the dock and the outpost's living spaces. The same whale song the *Nidaria* found fills the outpost and pours into the waterlock.

"You're never late coming back," Dannie says from the doorway. Her voice trembles. "We didn't know what happened to you."

As gently as I can, I pull the scalesuit-covered boy out of the *Nidaria*. He's slippery as a fish. I turn toward Dannie. She draws in a quick breath. Her gaze rises from the child.

"Is he alive?" she says.

"Yes."

"What happened to your lips?"

Fatima slides past Dannie and into the waterlock.

"It looks like secondary carbon rash," Fatima says, "which probably has something to do with why the cable's been down for hours."

I hand the boy's sedated form to Dannie and tell her and Fatima what happened. Before I'm done, tears are running down Dannie's cheeks, and Fatima's gaze is turned inward, probably with thoughts about how quickly the outpost will need to be evacuated. For the journey back to Sylvia City, my podsisters and the boy will be safe in the *Fulton,* the outpost's other, more traditional vessel.

I won't be going with them.

Dannie steps inside the outpost's living spaces and lays the boy down on a cushion. I begin to gather up all the nano-nets in the waterlock.

"We won't need those for the journey back to Sylvia City," Fatima says.

"I know," I say. "They're for me. I'm taking the *Nidaria*. I'm going to blow up the dryland power station. With each threadie capable of making a crater the size of the one outside, I'll only need a few. After that, I'll dissolve the cable all the way from the shore to the outpost. Farther, I hope."

Fatima's blue-white eyes widen.

I set the nano-nets beside the *Nidaria*.

"That's crazy," Fatima says. "Have you seen your scalesuit? The rash it's carrying will kill it in a few days. If you get a primary rash, your scalesuit will die in a few hours. You'll drown inside the *Nidaria* or on the benthos, or carbon weapons fire will kill you."

She's right, but that won't stop me.

"With the power station gone," I say, "and the trash drifting back over signs of the cable's path, it'll be years before the drylanders can find Sylvia City again. Maybe they never will."

"Yes, but . . . " Fatima's lips twist around like they're searching for the words to stop me. None exist. She sighs. It's a plea. She says, "Take the *Fulton* instead. The bridge has a waterlock and can be drained. You won't need a scalesuit."

"The boy needs the *Fulton*," I say. "It's the only ship big enough to get all three of you back to Sylvia City before the boy dies. He goes with The *Fulton*."

Dannie pulls up alongside Fatima.

"No," Dannie says. Her voice is only just louder than the whale song. "You can't do this. It's too much for one person."

"It's not for one person," I say. "It's for Sylvia City. It's my last repair."

"You don't have to do it alone," Dannie says. "I'll come with you. We can both fit in the *Nidaria,* can't we?"

I shake my head.

Fatima says, "A few hours in the shallows will blind you permanently, Dannie. You're no good for this task. Neither am I."

"I don't care!" Dannie says. "I can—"

Fatima lays a hand on Dannie's shoulder. Dannie knocks it away.

"She's going to die," Dannie says. "We can't let her go."

"Someone should get rid of the power station and the cable," Fatima says. "It's the right thing to do. The drylanders could already be planning their descent. We can't go into the shallows to stop them, but there are other ways to help."

Fatima shrugs off her scalesuit. It falls to the floor. In dark brown underclothes, Fatima stands next to Dannie. I've never seen Fatima's bare gray arms before. She steps out of her scalesuit's foot coverings and picks up the protective layer that's traveled with her most of her life. She holds her scalesuit out to me.

"You'll need this," Fatima says, "and my emergency scalesuit, too."

My voice catches like a breather's stuck in my throat. At last, I say, "But if something goes wrong on your way back to—"

"It won't," Fatima says. "We'll be fine on the *Fulton's* bridge."

Dannie's just as fast removing her own scalesuit. She holds it out to me.

"Wear this one when it's time to come home," Dannie says, "to Sylvia City."

Tears sting my eyes. I reach for my podsisters' scalesuits. A tightness in my chest releases. I thought it would never go away.

Somewhere I Have Never Traveled (Third Sound Remix)

E. CATHERINE TOBLER

In the still of the night, there is the voice.

Am I awake?

It is not a voice as I know voices; it doesn't speak in words, but in vibrations, audio frequencies penetrating the space which enfolds it (*the siren, the woman trapped*). It is the sound of a remembered heartbeat, muffled and moving through fluid, muscle, bone. There, it finds a new home, vibrates within this confine, and wakes me.

I *am* awake.

The station's darkness is always warm, always faintly redolent with rubber, charcoal, ammonia. The air is clean, antiseptic despite the rust that streaks the station's innermost walls, and tonight carries the sound—the voice that is not a voice. It reminds me of whale song, a distant rumble moving through the station as though the station were water; but the station is not water, nor is it submerged beneath any ocean. I unstrap myself from the sleep pocket and float to the nook's window.

Jupiter, swollen. So orange against the black of space, so large as to almost occupy the entire window. Space is only a slim crescent along the planet's brightening rim. I have worked on Galileo Station harvesting helium for twelve years, and the view never grows old; Jupiter never grows old with its ceaseless storms, new designs constantly wrought within its cloud layers. The red spot spun itself out in our sixth year, the storm succumbing to another that is the colors of Earth's seas: teal and turquoise, indigo and lapis. Sometimes, when the sunlight angles across, the storm shines like a great opal, cracked with orange lightning.

But the voice, the sound. With my palms pressed flat to the window, I imagine I can feel the sound (the voice) rolling through the fused silica and borosilicate glass. The voice spills from the planet, from deep within its clouds, pushing itself out of roiling gasses, tunneling through thirty-one miles of cloud, through the station's skeleton and into my own. If I close my eyes (and I do), the sound rattles my teeth, my tongue, and when it has gone (it always goes), I am left with my cheek pressed to the cold window, as if I meant to go out with it—as if it meant to take me. The voice (the sound) drains away, counterclockwise into Jupiter's rage.

Come back, I want to say.

Am I awake?

There is no exact surface, three thousand miles straight down. In Jupiter's orbit, hovering above its faint halo rings, station and planet have made one revolution around the distant sun; Saturn has sixteen more years for a full lap, so it seems we are running even with helium pods deployed and deploying. They plunge through the Jovian clouds to find the helium streaking the Jovian skies as rain, to gather and retrieve this precious gas for return to Earth.

The dance is silent. I used to think the harvesters looked like balloons being drawn along strings and everyone laughed because how clever, helium and balloons and aren't you so *old-fashioned*. The pods rise along their guy lines, to vanish into the station's belly and I rather think now that it's not balloons at all, but the silent consumption by a leviathan, of a thing we should have never harvested. The siphoning of one world's natural resources into another's, another who depleted itself and will do so again.

A silent dance, but the station's rumble still moves through me as pods rise along their guy lines, into Galileo's belly, and I push myself into motion, shaking the voice from my skin as I slide into my coveralls, into my spatulae gloves that allow fast travel along the station's walls, much like a gecko skimming glass. I work my way into the spinning levels of Galileo where gravity wraps me up and pulls me to the floor once more. The walls arc overhead here, vast and high, accommodating the harvesters after the debris of Jupiter, of space, has been sluiced from their ovoid hulls.

From the nearest pod, the voice thrums.

The pod doesn't look unusual in any way. Its metallic hide shows the scars of space without a hint as to its precious cargo beyond the readouts of its panel; everything glows green, helium secure and ready for transfer. I picture it, sealed within yet still trying to escape. Subject to the station gravity when before it was Jupiter's own mass stripping it from the clouds. Helium that doesn't quite know what to do with itself after it finds its own level. Rippling waves, a tremor pushing from a liquid center, causing the contained helium to creep up the walls, seeking escape.

The voice again, and I move toward the pod, ungainly in my return to limited gravity. My gloves would allow me to ascend the pod, to crack open the nose cone and dive inside, to better hear what calls me. Like the whale song it calls to mind, I have to wonder how differently it would sound if I were submerged within the liquid helium. At just above absolute zero, the helium would freeze me; my skin would go white, cold, numb, and my hearing would no doubt be compromised, taken. And yet, the idea of *allowing* it to surround me, *entomb* me, is intoxicating. Clemens always said it's not the booze that gets you drunk out here—mostly because there is no goddamn booze, because they always find and strip the goddamn stills—but it's the ideas that inebriate us. It's the mere notion that we're six hundred million kilometers from Earth and *still* gloriously alive. It's the—

"Vasquez?"

I'm half way up the pod when I hear my name, my gloved hands cradling the arced container the way I might a lover, a bottle of whiskey, a thing meant to get me drunk. I stare at the glowing green diagnostic panel and force myself to breathe. I become aware of the weight of my body, of the tension that runs in a line from neck to spine.

"Johns."

I look over my shoulder. He's so small down there, his coveralls a white blot against the darker metal floor. A dozen fresh pods slide into their berths behind him, great airships hissing and cascading with breath as they return to atmosphere. Johns tips his bearded face up, eyes on me. His tablet is lashed to his wrist, balanced in his hand, fingers poised to record the details of the day's docks.

"That harvester have a problem?"

The panel still glows green at me, soft and steady and true. No problems at all, the helium perfectly content and consistent inside. Filled to the fill line. Waiting to be flushed and sent back out. The voice rises to fill the nose cone, rattling the scarred metal. It whispers my name and tries to pry its fingers along the unbreakable seal. I comfort myself with the idea that if the helium can't get out, the voice can't get out. Won't get out. (*The siren? A woman trapped?*) Can Johns hear it? (*Her. It's her.*)

"I thought it—" I glance over my shoulder and down. He waits and behind him more harvesters return to Galileo. "No, no problem."

"Get down here and check these new returns, we haven't got all day."

But we do have all day—ten Jovian hours to harvest, cull, and strip from this world what our world yet needs. I carefully drop back down the side of the pod and the voice pleads for me to stay, to let it out. I want to ask Johns if he hears that, if he can feel it in his bones, but Johns is gone and it's only the pods that hiss and await inspection, before I will drop them back into the atmosphere. Free fall into metal rain.

The biggest planets sound like thunder. Hammers beating anvils. When you listen to the radio emissions of Jupiter, of Saturn, one gets the expected. But when isolated, the rings are something far more delicate, dulcimers in the summer wind I remember from my childhood. It wasn't always the depths of space, the hiss of gas-laden harvesters rising from planetary atmospheres; it was once tall and golden wheat fields bending in July's hot breath.

Beneath the thunder of Jupiter, the voice.

It speaks like an ocean tossed by the thunder, moving like a thousand gallons of salted water over and through a naked body. My naked body. I haven't been naked in months—years?—not even when Clemens joins me in the sleep pocket. That union isn't sex so much as it's the press of another body against your own. The knowledge of another's weight in weightlessness. It's waking in the middle of the Jovian night and knowing you aren't alone.

But tonight, a hand rests against my bare thigh. It isn't feminine or masculine this hand; it is simple warmth and weight, and the awareness I am not alone. But my thigh is not bare, so this hand, this weight, is *beneath* my coveralls; beneath the thin layer of thermals I always wear. My sleeping mind cannot untangle how this is so. My sleeping mind allows it, fashions the hand into Clemens who sounds like thunder sometimes, too, but Clemens is not here.

I lean into the hand and the voice fills my mind to overflowing. The tang of salt is sharp on the back of my tongue, as if I have swallowed an entire ocean, and when I open my eyes, it is not station darkness that greets me. It is not even Jupiter engorged beyond the window, for I am inside the clouds; I am not viewing the clouds from the station high above, but instead from below. I plunge through their ochre layers, past the point they go blue, past the point they go black. Lightning cracks, illuminating the space-hung opal, and there are only ever clouds. I see nothing else until the helium rain begins to fall.

Everywhere the helium rain splatters me, I burn. In truth, I freeze—but my skin sizzles with an illusion of heat. My senses overwhelmed, I don't know which to believe. A droplet on my forehead, sliding down my nose, and over my lips. I don't dare breathe, but still suck in a breath. I suck in the rain and my tongue turns to ice. I want to say *no,* but my tongue freezes against the roof of my mouth. My tongue sounds like airplanes—the sound of the bluest planets in the stars, a shriek against the sky visible only by the condensation it leaves behind. I quake awake, alone and breathless, floating free of the sleep pocket as the distant sun begins to spark through Jupiter's clouds. My tongue goes silent.

Only in the last three months have I heard this voice, this sound I cannot pinpoint. It does not matter if I am awake or asleep, it comes. Before, it was quiet, as quiet as a station filled with a hundred other people might be. I passed every night perfectly still and quiet, and rose each Jovian morning as if I'd never slept so well, not even on Earth while harnessed in gravity. Now, I wake not knowing exactly where I am, some larger part of me still cloud-cradled and falling.

Galileo Station hums and I gecko my way to the bay with its ever-rising helium pods. I think if I focus on the pods, on the in and out of the entire operation, the voice will quiet. But as I move among the pods, the voice beckons. I cannot immediately tell which pod contains it; the pods, like a forest around me, all whispering with the notion of the coming storm. Thunder in the distance, lightning cracking unseen below. Balloons, they should have been like balloons these pods, but they are trees, and then shadows, and then monsters once confined to the pages of a book. Each one has me catching my breath and Kane and Dillon laugh at me.

Dillon tells me the bay is no monster-filled forest, but rather a cathedral in the stars, for can I not see the way the light of the distant sun pierces the far end of the room, as if thrown through a rose window. It challenges your faith to occupy this space, Dillon says, and I breathe, for it is so. When the bay is empty of all but the pods, I sing, my voice soaring as high as it might amid their vast heights. My song reaches for the rust that streams in tears down the highest walls, recalls my grandmother in her own church, though I've only ever heard such stories, never stood in that space and vibrated with the sound of her.

Another day, another hunt through the pods until I've found which pod contains the voice. It's small today, the voice, small and whimpering. But when

I find it, it sounds like the rush and whisper of Neptune, a wind-torn sigh across water. Making sure none can see, I ascend the pod. Past the diagnostic panel that tells me all is well, all is right, I climb to the nose cone and inhale. Gunpowder and hot metal, and beneath this scent, sugar. I am reminded of my grandmother's churros, hot and crisp and sweet. I bend my nose to the pod, tip my cheek, and lick the metal. It should be cold, I should stick, but I glide.

The motion of the helium inside rocks through me. I envision it flooding up the side of the pod, toward and under my tongue pressing against the other side. It wants to fill this new cavity, my mouth, until it pools in my belly and tries to creep up the sides of even that container. The helium ripples, laughter barely contained, and I—

"Vasquez!"

The sharp sound of my name jolts me from the thought of this liquid laughter coiling in my belly and I stare down into Johns's stormy eyes.

"Am I awake?"

"Get down. *Right now.*"

I descend slow, the way I imagine the pods themselves do on their long lines. I picture myself as a pod, full of things that wish they were elsewhere and will soon be, but this is not enough to calm the trembling in my body by the time I reach the floor. How easy to propel myself away, to use my gloves and move with the speed of a lizard through the pod forest, into the sleeping pocket that is the nearest thing I might call home. I do not flee.

Commander Call's office is not what anyone would imagine. She prefers a distinct lack of gravity, so there is no desk, there are no chairs. Her predecessor occupied a space in the wheels of the station, but not Call. She likes to float and I wonder if maybe she has heard the voice, if maybe she would understand when I tell her why I licked the goddamn helium harvester, but the longer she drones on, I know that not even she would understand or take the time to try.

There is a voice, I want to say, *and this voice gets inside me. It's like . . . have you ever listened to space, I mean really listened, Call, because it's like that. Space has a sound, and a scent, and a weight, despite its lack of gravity and this voice— You can listen to the stars, Call, the way they vibrate, and this sound, emerges unexpected. A steady line and then a hitch, the vibration of something previously unheard. A long call across a very cold and dark ocean and you've been in the dark so long, so fucking long, you move toward it because it's sunlight, and warmth and the weight of someone else against you when you've been weightless so very long.*

Call tells me about regulations. About the orderly fashion of Galileo Station, as if I am newly arrived, as if I haven't been here twelve years. But maybe it's those years, Call says; maybe the years have worn me down to nothing, and I need to go see the doctors first thing tomorrow. I need to let them poke and prod and they are the ones who will know, she says. They will know what is to be done.

"It's not like they will send you home," Clemens says as we burrow in the sleep pocket. He sounds like wind tonight, not thunder, and his arms come around me from behind. Our legs tangle.

It's not like I did anything *wrong,* I want to say, but I stay quiet and allow myself to drift in his embrace. I close my eyes and will myself to sleep, but sleep never really comes.

The clouds haul me down. This time, I find I am sealed within a helium pod, its walls beaded with moisture that is not water, but neither does it burn me the way liquid helium would. The pod is the exact the length of my body and I stand, hands pressed to the forward curve, watching Jupiter swallow us. I cannot see the line we travel, perhaps it is not there; I can see only the endless clouds of this giant world. Jupiter's thunder rattles the pod, rattles my teeth, and it is like biting down on soft metal as I wait for it to stop. It does not stop.

We fall forever, me in the pod. Outside, helium pours down, stripping neon from the clouds as it goes. The pod runs with luminous metal rain, the air never quite dark or bright as we slice through endless cloud layers. When the weight is enough—

oh god it can't, it can't, but it will

—the pod unfurls as designed.

Like a metal flower, the pod opens itself to the helium rain and, unobstructed, the helium pours in. I shriek and the sound flies up into the storm, carried three times as fast as it would through oxygen alone. It is the sound of sucking balloons, of terror, of *help me, help me.* Inch by horrifying inch, the helium rain floods the pod, and I think I should freeze—I should be long dead—but I do not freeze and am not dead.

Am I awake? I try to feel the warmth of arms around me, I try to hear Clemens breathing, but there is only my scream. I scream until my throat is raw, until my airplane-tongue is again frozen to the roof of my mouth. I consider leaping out, about geckoing up the line that umbilicals me to Galileo, but I cannot move and do not have my gloves. I lift my hands, umbrella against rain, but it does not cease.

In the lighting-wracked clouds, a sound (a voice). It comes slowly and from a great distance. I try to turn toward it, but it is all around and growing closer the deeper I descend. Am I awake? I push the question aside and stop trying to find Clemens in the helium rain. I breathe and force myself to calm. I breathe and force myself not to creep out of the container that holds me, but my body flutters in panicked waves.

The voice (the sound) deepens. It is the lowing of some great beast I have not seen and cannot name; it is the sound of cleaving ice into bottomless ocean dark. Even as I want it to continue, I want it over and done. I try to speak, but my mouth is frozen and I can only gape at the thing that emerges from Jupiter's deepest, unseen storms.

The shape that solidifies in the clouds before me is not a mermaid. It is not a white whale, nor any other creature of Earth's seas. It is neither masculine nor feminine, but only a weighted presence before me. The face, if it can be called that, is not beautiful, but astonishing; eyes of endless storm, a mouth that is an entire ocean. I long for this being to swallow me, so that I might know its depths, but it only stares, as curious of me as I am of it.

Am I awake?

Jupiter's clouds coalesce before me, showing me a familiar shape—nearby sister Saturn, sunlight gilding her rings into a halo. After fifteen years spent in black winter, Titan pulls itself from Saturn's cloak, aglow in organonitrogen haze. The giant moon stretches, a slivered orange horseshoe tonguing out a mouthful of darkness. Distant sunlight fingers through its clouds and glints off the hydrocarbon puddle of Punga Mare before the clouds close once more.

But within the clouded landscape emerging from winter's dark, there shows a scar not unlike those upon the harvesters. A black ruin fragments Titan's golden clouds, a mold pressed into wet clay. The clouds do not swallow this deformity, but move with care around its outer boundary, as if the scar is a physical thing possessing an edge not to be crossed.

"Vas."

Sickbay surrounds me, white and uncomfortably sterile, the walls close and without windows. Even though I cannot see Jupiter, I feel it pressing upon us, a watchful eye. I am strapped into an observation bed, Clemens looking down at me. Dillon sits nearby, Johns pacing the hall. Clemens could not wake me, he says as his hand enfolds my own. I do not move within that slight touch, thoughts anchored upon the thing I saw in Titan's clouds.

"You need to look," I say. "You need to see."

This is what I say; this is not what anyone hears. My voice is ragged from screaming and I make a feeble squeak. Clemens hands me a tablet and with shaky fingers, I scrawl the same words. I tell him about the clouds, the sound, about being in the pod and seeing— The ship. It was a ship on Titan, emerging. Life that doesn't quite know what to do with itself after it finds its own level. Rippling waves, a tremor pushing from a liquid center, causing the contained life to creep up the walls, seeking escape.

Clemens reads the tablet and swipes a gentle hand across my short, bristled hair. His laugh is just as short, strangled, and I'm not sure if he can't believe or believes so much that a long-last admission is terrifying. Clemens sees me back to my nook that night, and I hang uneasily at the window, watching Jupiter turn (listening for the voice), wondering at the scars that mark my hands, pale pink slashes criscrossing brown skin—as if my hands were once lifted to shield my face from helium rain.

A dark shape moving in and out of the clouds as if— As if it were alive.

Awake.

Awake after winter's dark.

I do not sleep. I do not tether myself into the pocket, but float before Jupiter, waiting. And in time, the voice comes, bundles me into a descending pod, and waits in return, until I am close enough. I fall forever, for always, helium rain that should kill me instead now a comfort. I know the coldness against my skin. My hands grow new scars from its trespass, but I feel with each one that something inside me is emerging. Pushing itself out after a long winter dark. Creeping up the sides of this imperfectly sealed container.

The pod vibrates with the sound, the voice, and unfurls itself into the rain. The being in the clouds pushes itself closer, so close I can feel droplets of cloud against my marked cheeks. They are clouds of hydrogen, ammonia, and sweet water vapor. They should flood my lungs and strangle me, but—

A long call across a very cold and dark ocean and you've been in the dark so long.

I reach a scarred hand into the clouds and the clouds enfold me. They suckle at me as if to taste the droplets of blood welling from my wounds, to deconstruct and study them. A warm tongue, the weighted wetness surrounds me, swallows me. I float in a darkness that is not entirely dark, for spring is breaking, and there—*there* is the voice. It does not speak as I speak but together we create a kind of heterodyne, shifting voices into new ranges, churning them into something we can both understand.

They have slept and they are coming.

They have slept and they are waking.

No—*we* have slept and *they* are coming.

We heard you.

They heard *me*. My grandmother's song.

I jolt into awareness within the bright cathedral space of Galileo's bay, an open and empty harvester on the floor beside me. Blood and water mingle in shallow pools on the flooring, running from my scalp, my shoulders, and *you've been in the dark so long, so fucking long, you move toward it because it's sunlight, and warmth and the weight of someone else against you when you've been weightless so very long.* I spread my fingers in the wet, staring.

I push myself up, but I am weak—so weak and how long was I—

Clemens is there, warm thunder, and Johns too, who has the sound of a very soft wind today, barely daring to breathe. They don't look at me with anything resembling anger. It's relief pure and simple that pours through them; Johns even laughs, gathers me into his arms and laughs, "*Oh Christ where have you been?*"

But they know, because the pod was planetside, they eventually tell me. The pod was submerged and they couldn't recall it and I was missing. I was nowhere within Galileo Station.

And then—

"We saw one," Clemens says.

On Ganymede, he tells me. Ganymede hanging stark and barren but for the black scar emerging from its head. If the scar possessed hands, Clemens saw it press those hands to the moon's surface, so that something black and endless could pull itself from the water-ice womb of the cratered body. He said it moved like Titan from her saturnine shadow, but then that it was *only* shadows. It has to be, he whispers.

It isn't.

Callisto Station confirms another scar upon its face, but there is no telling how long it has lain upon the star-spangled moon. The scar marks the edge of the Asgard crater as if it has always been there. And Titan? What of distant Titan? Huygens Station confirms Titan has at least one such mark. Said it was on Europa, too. Said the wet darkness was waking, pushing itself into the stars.

"Awake, not waking," I say, and the sound (the voice) floods me—it is not airplanes or wind or any sound born of Earth; it is alien, dark and fathomless and unknowable, but still I know it, have made a language with it in the Jovian rain. It is curious. It is coming.

We have slept and they are coming. The voice in the night, the siren, the being no longer trapped. Pushing itself out after a long winter dark. Creeping up the sides of imperfectly sealed containers. A new red spot, cloud-cradled and rising.

Asymptotic
ANDY DUDAK

The cadets stand at attention for their passing-out ceremony, a random sample of the motley gamut of branched *sapiens,* and Nuhane is the smallest by far—but he adds his voice to their oath with towering conviction:

"We swear to uphold the Einsteinian limit! We vow to impose relativistic lockdown when a debt is owed to the universe, to deal out justice like a blind law of physics, thereby safeguarding the integrity of the vacuum!"

Nuhane fights down the terror of open sky intrinsic to his branch of humanity. Although a spin foam hack keeps the atmosphere of this Titan-analog at bay, the shield is invisible. Stacked worlds of orange-glowing cloud present nauseating vistas. A darkling methane sea surrounds this rocky isle, this remote outpost of the Collection Bureau. Nuhane reminds himself that the oppressive distance to the horizon is not an existential threat. Still, he is of the Fey. He can't help longing for a nice underground bunker, a womb-cave, or the intimate companionways of a space hab.

The cadets march to the far end of the parade ground. Weird, brazen music issues from pipes attached to robotic air-bladders. It's all part of some ancient police ritual whose roots have been forgotten. Wisps of proxy tech haunt the margins of the field, proud instances of family and friends. Nuhane finds the scene rather grim. The intended effect is stark majesty, but he wants to get it over with, to join the fight he's been training for.

He has no people among the spectators, and none to speak of otherwise.

From his childhood on a backward world, from concentration camps to this: lifetimes already, and he's only a hundred. He knows all too well what humanity is capable of. He can't fight for people alone, no matter how seemingly just the cause. In the Bureau he's found the only mission left to him.

Without the fabric of the cosmos, even hatred is impossible.

He wonders suddenly if he's remembering this moment, rather than living it. The future—if there is such a thing—comes to him like a divine revelation. It is a new past on the other side of "now," but he is powerless to act on the knowledge. He's locked inside this young cadet he once thought of as himself. The sensation is terrifying and glorious.

Simultaneously, this passive observer inhabits many other Nuhanes, including a middle-aged Nuhane, a lieutenant radically interfaced with a Bureau patrol cutter.

The debtor's sign is plain to his augmented eye. The arcing spacetime fissure propagated like a magnetic field line from a gutted metal worldlet and out over the galactic plane. The nearest light-years of its length dissipate like an old contrail, undermining nearby vacuum. It is one of thousands of discernible violations. He sees them as an ominous glowing net tangled through the Milky Way, with stray threads arcing off to other galaxies and clusters. So much work to do. So much debt to collect.

If he tunes up his perception of the universal spin foam, he sees a second, thinner net woven through the first: debts collected, scars on spacetime. It sooths him to gaze upon all that the Bureau has accomplished. To him the scar tissue is a fundamental good, a rare thing in this universe. Never mind how little the tissue has done to shore up the collapsing seawall.

"Fresh enough," says Lao Wang. "Bureau's giving it to us." The old baseline human sounds tired. Nuhane's mentor and partner has locked down thirty-one violators, collecting over ten million relativistic tons of debt, a Bureau record. Soon he'll vanish into lockdown himself, to pay off his Noble Debt. Nuhane will miss him. He wonders if this is their last mission together.

A younger Nuhane imposes his first lockdown with a sense of dark wonder. The violator ship, a converted Shinasian junk, dims and reddens inside its pocket of pseudo-acceleration, a pulsating sphere of apparently warped spacetime.

It is Lao Wang's bust, but he let Nuhane do the honors—a taste of imposition for the green junior officer.

"Please," one of the debtors weeps. "I don't deserve this!" The transmission redshifts as it climbs out of the pocket. "I'm a licensed interface pilot! I was forced into this—"

"By a violator called Phlogiston," Lao Wang supplies. "I know, and I'm afraid it makes no difference."

The pilot is in the Mayall II globular cluster of Andromeda much sooner than he should be. His mass contributed to the vacuum deterioration in the junk's wake, however minutely. He is therefore a debtor.

"It's Phlogiston's debt!" the pilot argues. That name again. Nuhane wants to ask Lao Wang what's going on, but he's distracted by the spectacle of lockdown. He's seen it before, of course, but this one is different, no matter what the record will say. This one is his.

"Phlogiston's debt," Lao Wang says, "and yours, and the junk's. Anything that violates, sentient or not, guilty or innocent, must be locked down. You're an interface pilot. You know what's at stake."

"But the debt . . . " he chokes.

"Approximately two million, seven hundred and forty-nine thousand, eight hundred and thirty-five point two two seven light-years."

"So how long . . . "

"Ten minutes ship-time," Lao Wang says. "For your debt, lockdown is equivalent to point nine nine nine nine nine one seven c. Be thankful you won't suffer the gravities." He doesn't need to add that meanwhile the resting universe will age

2.75 million years. This debtor is an interface-pilot, after all. He understands the law he has violated.

The junk continues to redshift, as though accelerating toward redemption. Soon it will be like a dim 3D snapshot printed on reality, beyond time and reproach. For 2.75 million years it will function like a head on London Bridge, a warning to those who would violate sacred law. Nuhane is proud to have finally contributed his first head. His pride waxes as the debtor's personal clocks slow. The ship will gain millions of relativistic tons before it pays its mass-energy debt to the universe. By the time it heals the rent it tore in spacetime, all that the pilot loves will be gone, or radically transformed.

Nuhane is drunk on the power he wields. Perhaps sensing this, Lao Wang says: "Never forget that we are bound for the same fate."

How could he forget with Lao Wang constantly reminding him? *You sooner than me, old man,* he wants to say. Nuhane has accrued seventy million light-years of so-called Noble Debt or VLOD (Violation in the Line of Duty), certainly a small fraction of Lao Wang's. Nuhane is a young god, free to ignore Einstein when he sees fit, and to punish others for doing so. He worked hard to be so elite. Most Bureau officers end up with a local, sub-c jurisdiction, lying in wait for violators rather than hunting them. Their only taste of violation is the occasional use of a Bureau ansible. They are part of the vast, slow, relativistic two-thirds of humanity, trapped by distances that might as well be infinite.

Nuhane was never willing to settle for that. The last thing he wants to hear is Lao Wang urging him to humility.

"We aren't so different from our prey," the old man says.

Nuhane wonders if the bastard has developed violation syndrome. It's new, the idea that too much time beyond c can lead to symptoms of senility. Some researchers go further, claiming that violation decouples consciousness from time.

Master Patrol Officer Nuhane is still high from his last "Noble" violation. He's already looking forward to the next one. Between ecstasy and the grand future there is no room for doubt. Nuhane is immortal.

Beyond c there is no time and no speed. Bureau officers call the speed of light the "last speed." Here in violation space, all of Nuhane's violating selves are united. Beyond time there is exultant joy, infinite peace, and the "eldest" of Nuhane's violation selves will find it hard to condescend back to the universe. They will leave pieces of themselves here.

The "younger" Nuhanes fear the dissolution of self that must result from perfect bliss. They flee back below c, cherishing what little exultation they've allowed themselves. All of the violating Nuhanes, young and old, remain in violation space for precisely the same amount of time—none—regardless of the light years skipped in the sub-c universe.

And so, coincident with their unification, the united Nuhanes split along their seams of self. They become again old and young and middle-aged, returning to the sub-c murk once and for all.

· · ·

As Major Nuhane condescends from violation space, emerging near a violator yacht in the Southern Local Supervoid, he wonders how he's going to explain this to the Bureau. They'll study his ansible. They'll suspect he tampered with its debt meter, but won't be able to prove it. What they'll be able to do is ground him with therapy sessions. Nuhane fears that more than anything.

The yacht winds up its violation ring, but Nuhane imposes lockdown before the ring completes its first test cycle.

He barely pays attention as the yacht wavers, begins to dim. His mind is still in violation space, in headlong discovery of joy. Why did he violate without permission? Was it really because of that informant at New McMurdo? The vacuum dweller had given him bad information before. Nuhane had vowed never to use her again. This time she claimed to know someone who knew Phlogiston, a violator no less, and she had coordinates for this violator's next jump.

Nuhane didn't hesitate. The informant was a known liar, her claim preposterous. Nuhane paid her. It was about a promise to Lao Wang, of course—not an excuse to violate.

"Officer," a female voice says.

A video feed follows: twenty naked youths laze about in a garden setting, like an indolent pantheon of gods. Only one woman is standing, a sculpture in translucent flesh with inhuman black eyes and a cloud of silver hair. "I won't insult your intelligence by denying our crime," she says. Most of her companions aren't even looking his way. Some appear to sleep.

"Big of you," Nuhane says.

"You're with the Bureau. You have violated. You know how it feels."

"Yes."

"So you know why we do it."

They are libertines. They violated purely to experience violation space. Nuhane suspected this when the informant gave him the coordinates. The common breeds of violator—colonists, shippers, transports—have no reason to jump to an inter-filament void. Out here there is only vacuum and a novel view. The lights sprinkled across the blackness are all galaxies. In the varying density of this field, the large-scale structure of the universe is discernible.

Nuhane suffers a wave of nausea. Nowhere else is the universe's dumb magnitude more apparent. He allows his cutter to feed him a palliative. He longs for a cave, or the alchemy of violation space. Did Lao Wang ever yearn for it like this? Nuhane remembers a time, long before the old man's senility, when he seemed obsessed with violation, with its nature. But did he crave it? Perhaps all Bureau officers do.

"How can you blame us for wanting that transcendence?"

"I don't deal in blame," Nuhane says. "Think of me as a maintenance man."

An Apollo in the background chuckles, saying, "There it is."

The nymph at his side murmurs, "What did you expect?"

"I take it you don't believe in the danger of spacetime fissuring," Nuhane says.

A ripple of laughter animates the pantheon. "Do you?" the translucent goddess asks.

Nuhane hates this old debate, but he wants to feel these people out. "Set aside the overwhelming scientific consensus, if you like. Shouldn't we proceed with caution? It's the fabric of spacetime, after all. We need it." This elicits more laughter, and Nuhane gets angry despite himself—angry *at* himself, more than these Deniers. He should be used to their kind. The age of unchecked FTL travel, the so-called Age of Innocence, left Deniers scattered across the cosmos. He has to remind himself of the Bureau's role: not to correct delusional thinking, not even to keep up with the damage, an impossibility. But to act as a deterrent. "Laugh if you like," he says. "Laugh all the way into lockdown."

"Bureau fascist," the nymph says.

"You want violation for yourselves," Apollo says. "First rule of bureaucracy and so on. You imagine what humanity could be given by unchecked violation, and it terrifies you."

"You hate freedom," says another woman.

They may have tweaked themselves to believe this drivel. Judging by their composure in the face of lockdown, they are no strangers to mental rewrites—and their bodies are certainly customized. Not for the first time, Nuhane wonders what it would be like to see and think like a Denier. Driven by fear. Unable to live with the possibility, however remote, of the universe splitting along its fissures and flying apart. Choosing to believe otherwise.

Nuhane could go to a clinic, get the tweak. Then he could lose himself in violation. But the notion is fleeting. If he did that, he wouldn't enjoy the resulting fantasy. Someone new would.

"You can still stop this lockdown," the translucent goddess says.

They haven't reached the point of no return, but they're close. Nuhane allows his cutter to underclock him to match their continually slowing reference frame. "That's right."

"We're rich."

"Congratulations. I'm after someone named Phlogiston."

Apollo and his nymph stop laughing. The rest of the pantheon subtly emerges from its contrived disinterest. This charged moment takes three months in Nuhane's resting universe.

The goddess says: "That's not his real name."

Nuhane is old, a commander, and the dwarf glares murkily just light-seconds away. The ominous substar seems familiar, or perhaps significant beyond its fearsome absurdity.

"Sir?" It's patrol officer Wen Ting, his junior partner. He can hear the concern mixed with youthful impatience in her voice. "Jump to orbit, or what?" She knows violation syndrome has him by the throat. How could she not, by now? He remembers his own premonitions as Lao Wang deteriorated.

They have followed a ragged tear in spacetime to an abandoned long-range rig that only accounts for ninety-one percent of the debt. Something else launched from the rig and likely headed for the dwarf.

Instead of giving the order Wen Ting craves, Nuhane contemplates the fissure.

One of billions now. He gazes into the night and watches them in real time, no matter how far away they are, because they violate. They seem to propagate from him toward a distant haze woven through the microwave background.

"The L-T object," Wen Ting prompts.

Nuhane returns his gaze to the dwarf, remembers they're here to lock down someone named Willard. The cutter doses him with the latest syndrome therapy. It activates random memories and loosens his tongue: "Patrol Officer, did you know that my people were one of the first branches from baseline humanity? We were called fey because we bred ourselves small and claustrophilic for interstellar travel. And because our enterprise seemed like a death wish."

"Fascinating, commander."

"We were the first to colonize many worlds. We did it fair and square, no FTL. But on Lalo our civilization collapsed. When a wave of violators arrived, all that remained of us was an underground theocracy. Of course the violator civ also collapsed. They went medieval, demonized us, blamed us for crop failures, plagues, everything. Then they industrialized, declared total wars on each other. Most of our caverns were beneath a republic called Iomang, a desperate state ruled by a madman."

"Yes sir," Wen Ting says absently, then adds, "Something's orbiting the dwarf."

Nuhane feels vaguely insulted. Hoping to embarrass her in turn, he asks, "Why did you join the Church of the Indemnity?"

"Willard's shuttle is correcting toward the orbiter," she says, then seamlessly adds: "My people were violators. The Bureau wasn't going to let me in. Getting the Church tweak was the only way to prove my loyalty. At least, that's what I thought before. Now I see that this was the universe's way of guiding me toward the Faith."

Nuhane realizes she's explained this before. He ends up embarrassed for himself again. Furthermore, he finds nothing to mock in her story.

With a note of confusion Wen Ting announces: "Grav harmonics from the orbiter, but not the signature of violation tech." She waits for Nuhane's order. Nuhane can't seem to focus. "Jump over and intercept before he can dock?" she prods.

When she initiates without consent, Nuhane realizes this mission will be his last.

Nuhane has been to several Bureau lockdown ceremonies, but Lao Wang's is the first to fill him with dread of the future. Captain Nuhane feels old for the first time in his life. He is on the observation deck of Achindoun, the Bureau hab that has long stood watch over the Nobly Locked Down. He's joined by fellow officers and a smattering of Lao Wang's proxied relations.

Lagrange point 4 of the Pluto-analog Kvichak and its moon Igiugig: here hang thousands of Bureau officers in their lockdown pods, most of them redshifted beyond casual observation. Lao Wang's has just shed its attitude jets, having found its place among the others.

The bagpipes sound, and the lensing of his pod signifies the beginning of lockdown. Some of his loved ones allow their proxies to broadcast sobs. Nuhane wonders what that says about the authenticity of their grief. He can only stare in numb transfixion.

The old man shoulders four hundred billion two hundred and eighty-seven thousand light-years of Noble Debt—an epic career, but not the record. No one knows why people can only violate so many times before losing their faculties. Most officers don't break five hundred billion. Nuhane, now at ten billion four hundred and ninety million, wonders how far he'll go.

"Reductio ad absurdum," Lao Wang PMs, "reductio ad infinitum. Redcutio ad absurdum, reductio . . . " On he goes, repeating his nonsense mantra.

"Listen Uncle," Nuhane says. "We both know I'm not half the officer you are. I'll probably check out long before four hundred big ones. We could emerge from lockdown around the same time. We'd be together, two old maniacs laughing at . . . whatever humanity is by then. How does that sound?"

" . . . ad infinitum. Remember that, boy."

"Alright." Nuhane is used to dealing with him like this. He's glad the old man had the sense to PM him, and not include his relatives.

"Architectures, paradigms, we all fall down. Ashes, ashes."

"Yes, Uncle."

"Nuhane." His transmissions are redshifting fast now.

"I'm here, Uncle."

"Remember that lockdown in Mayall II?"

"Mayall II . . . "

"Andromeda."

"Yes. I remember. The slaved pilot. We never found the perp."

"Phlogiston. He called himself Phlogiston. There was a file on him. You didn't rate the clearance at the time, so I couldn't tell you. He's important."

Nuhane doesn't know if this is the syndrome talking or not. "I remember wondering what you were hiding. Don't worry, I'll look at the file."

"It's gone. They even wiped it from me, somehow, whoever they are. But I know he was part of something big. I know it!"

"I believe you," Nuhane says, not sure that he does.

"Find him. Violate off the books if you have to. Promise me."

Nuhane is sure that his other, timeless self is here, reading his life like prose. The more he violates, the more certain he is of this.

Nuhane's counselor is Lectern, an instance of a Turing-passable expert system, an ancient Bureau creature possessed of unfathomable secrets. Colonel Nuhane is enduring another therapy session. All he can think about is getting back into violation space, which is the sort of thing Lectern would like to know, and the last thing Nuhane cares to admit.

"We were talking about your old partner," the system prods. "His lockdown ceremony."

"It was a hundred years ago," Nuhane prevaricates.

"Then let's talk about your debriefing last week," Lectern suggests.

"An instance of you was there. Surely you've reintegrated by now."

"How did the questions make you feel?"

"Angry."

"You violated without authorization. Shouldn't we be concerned?"

"For the last time, my ansible went into lockdown before I could request the jump. I was chasing a lead. I made a judgment call."

"There's evidence that you tampered with your ansible. Its debt meter was dialed up."

"Like I said, it must've been faulty!"

"Which isn't supposed to be possible. But Bureau legend has it that Lao Wang knew how."

"He taught me a lot of things, but never that." Nuhane is barely able to convince himself that this charade is about keeping his promise to Lao Wang, and not about hiding his addiction. The old man wasn't clear, but he seemed to imply that someone inside the Bureau was working with Phlogiston. Nuhane doubts that Lectern is involved, but can't be sure.

"This lead you explained to the board . . . "

How much longer can he juggle the lies? In addition to the board inquiries, he has a new partner to deal with. She is from the Church of the Indemnity, tweaked to take an almost feline pleasure in the hunt. She wants to inflict lockdowns. She won't tolerate a prolonged investigation full of dead ends.

"I think it's a fabrication," Lectern continues. "If you're investigating something off the books, you'd better come clean to the board. Regardless, we need to face the fact of your addiction." Nuhane waits for the system to take a different tack. "Not today? Then how about your childhood on Lalo-honua? Are you ready to go there yet?"

Nuhane restrains his irritation. He has always avoided this topic, but for the first time it seems preferable to everything else on the docket. "The bliss of violation space," he says, "is like confronting infinity. It's like the most wide open space possible, without fear. For me anyway."

"That makes sense," Lectern says. "There have been two other Fey officers before you. They both said the same thing."

This brings Nuhane an odd sense of comfort. He is encouraged to go deeper: "I remember the explosions that opened up the Hall of Star Ancestors. The Iomangans were clever. The sunlight disoriented us."

"Disoriented *you*. Focus on your personal experiences."

"I was too young to understand. I thought the Iomangans were monsters. That's what our priests taught. All I knew was that our world was falling down around us. Many were killed in the collapse."

"You saw that?"

"I saw my father buried. Annihilated in moments. Also my great-great-grandmother, and many cousins."

"Go on."

"Then there were these giants. I'd never seen them before. They had fire magic, in addition to swords. They killed many, including my grandmothers, before a commander showed up and ordered them to stop. The rest of us were herded to the surface. Up there we were helpless with our phobias, all but blind. I was separated from my mother. They packed us into magic boxes that moved on metal tracks. Many more of us died in those, suffocated or starved. You could say I was lucky, having been packed against one of my great aunts. She opened a vein and fed me her blood. I slowly killed her in order to survive."

"No. That wasn't murder."

Nuhane ignores this laughable claim. "And then there were the camps. We children learned how to hide and steal and survive. The adults fell into torpors and died, if they weren't killed outright. There were medical experiments, you see. And labor they knew we couldn't sustain. And random sport killings. I know what you're thinking, Lectern. Don't worry. I saw these things myself. All of them and more."

Nuhane watches the universe blue-shift around him, knowing he is old, that this is his Noble Lockdown—but sure of little else.

Pseudo acceleration. But no pseudo equivalence principle. He doesn't feel the gravities. How could he? He's not going anywhere, not in space anyway.

How did he get here? What was his last mission? He had another partner after Lao Wang. What was her name?

His timeless observing other cannot enlighten him. The other wonders, as always, why he knows nothing beyond this lockdown. Does Nuhane die soon? Is it some effect of terminal violation syndrome? An immanent cure? Or is something catastrophic about to happen to time itself? Perhaps scientists underestimated the deleterious effect of violation. Perhaps spacetime is about to unravel.

Whatever the reason, the timeless other knows he is soon to be no more.

Colonel Nuhane kneels with the other initiates before the torch-lit altar. Beyond is enshrined a fierce-looking idol, a Taoist god with bulging, hungry eyes. An urgent drum makes the incense-laden air pulse.

Nuhane endures the ritual like he did his Bureau passing-out. He ought to be happier to be in a nice cave like this.

"Eight hundred years ago," declaims a red-robed man, "the emperor Kangxi consigned many Shaolin monks to fiery death. Five survivors escaped to a mountaintop temple, before which, using grass for incense, they formed a sacred brotherhood. They vowed revenge, pledging to oppose the Qing dynasty and restore the Ming."

"Fan qing fu ming!" the initiates affirm. *Oppose the Qing and restore the Ming.*

"At the Red Flower Pavilion, the Five founded the Hong Society. The Hong conducted heroic but doomed uprisings. One hundred thousand Hong soldiers sacrificed themselves courageously for the Han race." The man is a good actor. He appears stern and proud. Nuhane has no idea whether or not he's actually Han—not that it matters. "And the Hong society continues to thrive today!"

After a sufficient dramatic pause, he adds, "Begin the ceremony!"

Senior brethren in black robes and red sashes enter the cave. One by one they're stopped by two guards, who cross their broadswords and shout, "You are entering the Hong army fortress! Disobedience is punishable by death!" The black-robes reply with, "I am a Ming general! I build bridges and roads!" or "I cross mountains and ramparts! Don't you recognize a brother?" And they're allowed to pass.

The stuff about bridges and crossings is uncanny. Nuhane wonders if the ancient Ming rebels had the gift of foresight. This secret society has had nothing to do with Ming restoration since the 20th century, possibly earlier. They devolved into gangsterism, eventually becoming the most powerful *hei she hui* on old Terra. When the communist party collapsed, they took over China. Two hundred years later, their sole passion was traveling faster than light.

Bridges and roads indeed.

"Why are you here?" the red-robe barks at Nuhane.

"I've come to enlist," he replies.

"Why?"

"To oppose the Qing and restore the Ming!"

"Prove it!"

Following the ritual to the letter, Nuhane recites a poem:

"Draw broadswords,
    the Manchurians stole our land!
    The hour of loyalty
    and blood vengeance is at hand!"

With that the red-robe moves on, challenging other initiates. They are as varied as Nuhane's cadet class at the Bureau. This Heaven and Earth Society has not been Chinese, let alone Han, for a very long time.

Next comes a black-robe, slapping each initiate in the back with the flat of a broadsword, then demanding: "Do you love gold or your brethren?"

The initiates each reply, "My brethren!" in their turn. Nuhane struggles not to faint after the blow nearly shatters his tiny frame.

All this for one unauthorized violation. Nuhane was indignant when the Bureau followed his therapy with undercover duty. Since then he has grown numb, having weathered violation withdrawal. Infiltrating the Heaven and Earth Society has been a kind of sleepwalk.

Sometimes he can't help wishing that these gangsters would steal a Bureau cutter. He could claim to know how to hack the interface nest, then violate. Where to? Would it matter? He would continue to honor his promise to Lao Wang, of course. It wouldn't be about the violation alone. He isn't like that anymore. He hasn't violated in three years. Not that he's had the chance.

"The first oath!" the red-robe shouts. "Once a member of the society, I shall treat the relatives of my brethren as my own. If I don't keep this oath, I shall be struck down by five thunderbolts!"

The initiates repeat this. Nuhane finds that he is tired of oaths. To the Bureau, to mentors and gangsters and spacetime, and most of all to himself. He remembers being free of promises in violation space.

• • •

Patrol Officer Nuhane and Lieutenant Lao Wang have followed a debtor's space-time fissure from the Small Magellanic Cloud to this system in the heart of the Pavo-Indus Supercluster. Lao Wang locked the violator down before it could fall into the orbit of a world originally terraformed by other violators. The verdant, uninhabited globe hangs in the void, a jewel that shouldn't exist. The people that sparked the terraforming drift in an old, barely discernible mist of lockdown pockets at the planet's L2 point.

The violator ship, locked down only moments ago, blushes slightly. It's a large cargo vessel, no doubt a second wave of colonists. Their debt stands at three hundred million light-years. They will pay off four hundred and twenty thousand relativistic tons. Young Nuhane still marvels at the weight of these crimes, and the price of getting caught.

He and Lao Wang, though interfaced in separate nests, share an environ that renders their facial expressions. Lao Wang wears an odd grin. He pings the cargo vessel and says, "Excuse me. Do you know how fast you were going?"

When there is no response, he shrugs and says to Nuhane: "A joke. Old reference." He avoids Nuhane's bewildered gaze. "They shouldn't have come back," he says.

"What?" Nuhane says.

"I mean, maybe we're not meant to return from violation space. Maybe we're supposed to break light speed and stay beyond it, forever." He meets Nuhane's eyes again, summons an unconvincing chuckle. "Never mind. Guess I need some R and R. You won't report what I just said, right?"

"No sir."

They watch the violator fade. Nuhane contemplates the mystery of violation and lockdown. Already the cargo vessel's spacetime fissure is beginning to heal, even back in the Small Magellanic. True action at a distance, a violation of c in its own right.

Nuhane can't believe what he sees in the soul of the man his fellow thugs just killed. The ice ceiling scrolls by the window, and the dead man, formerly a violation savant for the Heaven and Earth Society, slides back and forth across the floor with the motion of the hab, his head encased in a smoking transmigration helmet.

Nuhane hides his excitement. He has found his ticket off this nightmarish detail. He will be violating again soon—but it's more than that.

The helmet sends pertinent memories to Nuhane's mirror net. His rhythms sift through the complexity of violation math, seeking names and itineraries. He needed something underway, something he could lock down, but he didn't expect to find it. It was clear right away that the man hadn't spoken with the Bureau. Perhaps he never intended to. The Heaven and Earth kingpin of this Europa-analog has grown paranoid in his dotage, violation syndrome having burned wormholes through his reason.

"You said he didn't rat," says Plutarch, a hulking gangster eight times the size of Nuhane. "So why are we still here? If he's so interesting, grab the helmet. But let's go."

Nuhane does not want to decapitate the savant. The crystalline mass that was once his head is permanently merged with the helmet. Nuhane has done many things for Heaven and Earth, things far worse than decapitating a corpse, but he feels he has reached a critical mass.

He just needs another minute to confirm what he saw: a very improbable name.

Outside, the hab lights flash on particles suspended in the inky water. The media wall maps the local ice ceiling and the other habs as they converge on a stable rendezvous point to form yet another temporary city. That's how society works here in Baroque Pearl. Nuhane tried to convince himself he liked it, at first. It was a sub-surface existence. His sordid duties for Heaven and Earth were part of the mission, just as important as locking down violators. He didn't miss violating. So went the flimsy monologue.

He confirms the name attached to the violation-in-progress: William Valentin Willard, aka Phlogiston. He smiles.

Nuhane is eleven years old, and feels much older, when the harriers drop from the sky to liberate his camp. He clutches the chain-link fence and watches the Iomangan guards flee across the heath under a leaden sky. One by one the giants vanish as plasma rains down. Nuhane tries to feel glad, to feel anything in fact, and fails. He has learned many things in this camp. He has learned to tolerate the open sky, beneath which he has learned what humans really are. He knows that the Iomangans are descendants of violators, and that his liberators are also violators. He does not know what that means.

What he finally feels is dread. He's going to have to leave the camp, and enter a wider world.

Three hundred and fifty billion light-years.

He often wondered how far he would go before succumbing to violation syndrome—and now he knows. Three fifty is nothing to be ashamed of. It's not the stuff of legend, but it's respectable. At least he knows he has the syndrome. He tells himself that's something. Perhaps it means he's not so far gone.

It was these last two violations that did it. He knows that on a level below the cellular.

"Shall I lock him down?" Wen Ting asks. She floats with him in the new cutter's sensorium, wide-eyed with the thrill of the hunt. Nuhane envies her youth, her cold pure hunter's psychopathy, though he doesn't fully understand it. The Church of the Indemnity has wired her up good. When she locked down that last rig, she curled into a fetal position, moaning with something beyond divine communion. "Commander?" she says.

He's forgotten why they're here, and it terrifies him. He blinks up the dossier of their current mark: William Valentin Willard, aka Phlogiston, quantum information physicist and outspoken Bureau sympathizer. Trillions of humans call him a Bureau lapdog and want him dead. He understands that the Bureau holds the universe together, understands it in a way that Wen Ting and her brethren never will. He doesn't need their leap of faith. He invented the machine that images the universe's scars.

"Violating c," he said famously, "is worse than murder."

And yet here he is, after a serious galaxy hop. What possessed him?

His shuttle falls toward Nuhane's cutter. Beneath them hangs the mysterious machine, alive with its puzzling gravitational waves. None of Nuhane's scans or Wen Ting's mystic sensing find weapons in the fine-woven ring of exotic matter. Far below it, dark storms roil over the surface of the dim red L-T dwarf. Nuhane wonders what role, if any, Willard means this substar to play in whatever he's up to.

"Congratulations," Willard transmits. "You've got me."

With his voice comes the visual of a surprisingly youthful man: middle aged, gray-bearded but healthy and vital. For a moment Nuhane can't reconcile this with what he knows. Willard ought to be decrepit by now, even if he's had longevity treatments. Then Nuhane remembers that Willard has traveled relativistically. The man has lived a decade or so of the last five hundred years.

Wen Ting shows him a scan of the orbiting machine. "What is it?"

His brief grin is barely perceptible. "Ah, one of the Bureau's pet zealots." He understands—or understood—that the Bureau needs all the support it can get, even if that means employing delusional jihadists.

What has become of the far-seeing creature Willard used to be?

"What are you waiting for?" he says.

Wen Ting scans the orbital machine again, hoping this time the Angels of Indemnity will grant revelation. It appears conclusive that the thing is not a weapon. There are signs of a spin foam hack about it, but the configuration is wrong for violation or lockdown tech.

"Do you need me to confess?" Willard says impatiently.

Nuhane wonders if the man craves the portal to the future that lockdown represents. Perhaps he has grown weary of his small-minded contemporaries. Then why not take off at relativistic speed, like he has before?

Nuhane hesitates to impose lockdown. He may be slipping into dotage, but he senses he's being manipulated.

Wen Ting, however, does not hesitate. She and the cutter have developed an understanding in the face of Nuhane's decline. She doesn't need his authorization. She imposes with relish.

"Thank you," Willard says, as yet barely redshifted.

Nuhane feels Wen Ting's confusion through her bio feed. Violators aren't supposed to be thankful. They're supposed to beg for mercy. But Willard is no masochist. Nuhane also feels the grav waves from the orbiter changing tune, and knows something fundamental is happening to local spacetime. He perceives a disturbance, much like the fractures caused by violation, blossoming between Willard's shuttle, the orbiter, and the dwarf below. A lockdown pocket encloses the orbiter, seeming to mirror Willard's.

Wen Ting panics. "What's this?"

"I'm sorry to have led you so far," Willard replies, "but I needed at least a seventy million light-year debt for this trial run."

"Of what?"

"My machine is crude. The first of its kind. It won't respond to anything less than a seventy mil debt."

This transmission arrives at an unchanging radio wavelength. Willard's redshifting has ceased. This is stunning, unprecedented, but Nuhane's attention is drawn to the machine, now shivering and glowing under some unfathomable workload. Nuhane senses that it is channeling something—Hilbert distortion? inertia?—from Willard's shuttle down into the murky furnace of the dwarf.

"I approached the Bureau first," he says, "but they didn't believe me. Or didn't want to. They tried to kill me, you know. Maybe you won't believe that, but it's true. So I had to go to Heaven and Earth. It is regrettable that the savant in Baroque Pearl had to die, but I needed you to believe that lead and come after me. I should also apologize for having Lao Wang wiped. Canny, that one. He was on to me before I was ready. And it was my man in the Bureau who got you assigned to that duty in Baroque Pearl. I don't imagine it was pleasant. All for a greater good, as you'll see."

Far below, a darkness blossoms between two ribbons of turbulent black cloud. One might almost take it for another storm of raining iron, but for the speed of its formation. It expands like an ink stain through the hydrogen blood-glow, devouring thousands of cubic kilometers per second. Nuhane remembers that the dwarf was already radiating in the long visible wavelengths, that lockdown of such matter would mean swift blackness. He tunes his vision and watches the still-growing lockdown pocket—the largest one ever, as far as he knows—dimming down its trapped matter through infrared and radio. The pocket soon encloses a fifth of the substar, and keeps expanding. Great storms flash and gleam along the moving perimeter, and the Jupiter-like band-flow is thrown into chaos.

"Debt transfer," Nuhane says. The words are packed with mythic weight.

"Impossible," Wen Ting declares.

"It's working," Willard says, "but something's wrong."

Over one third of the dwarf is now enclosed, the remainder stirred to frenzy by the process and made to radiate like the accretion disk of a black hole. The lockdown pocket behaves like a collapsed star in many ways, though it has no real event horizon. As the brighter material is swallowed, Nuhane can judge how far along the lockdown is, what fraction of c it is equivalent to. The hottest free matter radiates in the extreme ultraviolet to soft X-ray range, but attenuates after falling in. And still the pocket grows.

"My shuttle and I weigh about seven tons," Willard says. His self-satisfaction is gone, replaced by mounting horror. "It seems we've discovered a new law of physics. The Law of the Transfer Fee."

Nuhane gets there just after him, he is sure they're wondering the same thing now: how much of a fee?

Unlike a black hole, a lockdown pocket doesn't exert gravity, so the remaining dwarf material—plasmas of hydrogen and helium, trace metals and silicates—overcomes its own gravitation and shreds away wildly into space.

It doesn't occur to Nuhane to get out of the way, not until he sees Willard and his machine doing so. Wen Ting reacts first, matching Willard's escape vector, worlds of fire blooming under them. The pocket swells and consumes, but slower than before.

Wen Ting is chanting again. Occasionally she forgets a phrase or a line and has to start over. Nuhane scans her mind and sees that her Church mod is short-circuiting, overloaded with a cumbersome truth.

"You've got to help me," Willard says.

The pocket finally stops expanding, content with the mass of forty-five Jupiters. The remaining one-fourth of the dwarf continues to burn and diffuse into space. The holy grail of debt transfer is possible, but hideously expensive. The transfer fee in this case was 1.2 octillion percent of the debt.

Nuhane scans Willard and confirms he is debt free. The machine seems to be powering down. Wen Ting is curled in a fetal position again, this time with excruciating pain. She shivers, sweating and whimpering with Church withdrawal.

"I've violated but can't be locked down," Willard says. "So arrest me. Take me to a hub."

Nuhane understands. Willard's shuttle can't achieve relativistic speeds, let alone violate. There is no concentrated source of matter for light-years around, so he can't get his long-range rig out of lockdown. He's at Nuhane's mercy.

"It wasn't just you and your partner and that savant," he admits. "You don't know the half of it. Maybe I deserve to die out here, but it can't all be for nothing." With that, his shuttle lights up with high-power transmissions aimed at a few hundred of the nearest inhabited systems and galaxies. Nuhane takes a sample: the machine specs and documentation of what happened to the dwarf.

"What have you done?" Nuhane says.

"Freed humanity."

"And that's a good thing, is it? Perhaps we need a cage." Before it's out of his mouth, he wonders if his heritage, or the Bureau, speaks through him. Maybe it's neither. Maybe it's the boy who got used to a concentration camp, and hated himself for it.

He turns his attention to Wen Ting, tweaking her neurochemistry to ease the trauma of her disillusionment. He marvels at the delicacy of her Church tweak, but something so absurd could be no other way—not without undermining her basic functionality.

"Debtor," she whispers, "make satisfaction for thy sin."

Nuhane tries to imagine what will become of the debt transfer universe. Matter will soon be at a premium, if he knows anything about mankind. Then what? Cycles of lockdown and emergence? Relativistic dark ages followed by renaissances of violation? Perhaps the stars must wink out, one by one, to become readily accessible. What about expansion, deprived of all that gravitating matter? What about dark matter and energy? Are lockdowns that vast even possible?

The Bureau as Nuhane knows it will be obsolete, regardless. Perhaps it will be relegated to catalyzing debt transfer, facilitating the violations it once policed. That would still be holding the universe together. That would still be his mission, wouldn't it?

Nuhane is four years old when his parents take him to the Hall of Star Ancestors for the first time. The cavern is the biggest space he's ever seen.

But not the biggest you'll ever see, says the man in his skull.

Nuhane gapes at the distant ceiling. It is a field of lights that his people call stars. "They're actually colonies of bioluminescent fungus," Father says.

"Don't teach him blasphemies," Mother whispers. The vast space is relatively quiet as hundreds of people walk the Great Circle and show proper awe.

His people are the Fey. Mother says they came from the stars.

Someday you'll travel to the real stars, the man in his skull says, but Nuhane doesn't believe him. *You'll forget about me for a long time, then remember me again. But we won't be able to talk like this anymore.*

"Why not?" Nuhane asks aloud, and Mother shushes him.

"Leave him be," Father says.

"And let him anger the priests?" Mother hisses. "And get us sent to the sulfur farms?" She looks up at the fake stars. "Ancestors, why did you curse me with such a husband?"

Nuhane's parents always quarrel when he talks to the man in his skull. Father says it's a gift, a sign he's destined for great things. It was Father who named him *Nuhane,* which in some ancient language means *speaker with the ghosts of ancestors.*

Snakes

YOON HA LEE

I had brought the corpse of my soldier-sister Rhiis-2 a long way, suspended in a fluid of suppositions:

—*If* she examined the navigational display, she would advise that we route around this dwarf star in realspace, that strand of charged matter in shadowspace.

—*If* I neglected to clean out the ship's torchgun regularly, she would gum up the apertures with that horrifying squishy self-heal gel that we were supposed to use on the ship's lenses so I *really* had to work to clean it out.

—*If* the skimship's power systems flashed that particular stress-alert, check the physical gauges before doing anything drastic, because the hookups sometimes lied to us.

Interlaced with these came other parts of her decision trees, which I lingered over even though I didn't want to:

—*If* asked about her family and I was present, she'd smile that whiplash-blinding smile of hers, sling her arm around my shoulders, and say that all she had left, sadly, was this good-for-nothing sister. We weren't related except in the way that a gun and its ammunition are related. I had often wondered, toward the end, if that had been enough for her.

—*If* someone propositioned her with the folded glove, she'd never say yes. It had nothing to do with being a soldier-sister. She never minded when I took one-night lovers. One night was all I wanted of them, anyway, and in the mornings I'd return to pledge the high pledge with her.

—*If* offered nectar-of-dreams for the second night in a row, she'd refuse. She'd take it away from me, too, while she was at it. Now that she couldn't do it anymore, I missed the scolding. I poured myself a cup every night, then stared mournfully at it without drinking any, in her honor. Of course, I couldn't drink in the human sense anymore.

For all the *if*s I carried with me, however, I knew that Rhiis-2 would have told me that I was stupid for coming to the Seethe. For changing myself on her behalf. I had entangled my functions into those of the ship, over a hundred hundred small surgeries, over a thousand thousand large adjustments. I was home to a multitude of spiders, who maintained the ship and my soldier-sister's sustaining fluid as I directed.

As we exited shadowspace, I saw the Seethe, and knew that I could not afford to fail so close to my objective.

We had lost the vastwar. That had been bad enough. I was determined not to lose Rhiis-2.

Sometimes, as we sped through shadowspace, I dreamt I could see into Rhiis-2 in her stillness. It had been rumored for a long time that shadowspace induced odd dreams and visions, although people had been having odd dreams and visions without the need of superstitious explanations everywhere they went. Sometimes, during the days of the war, we'd take nectar-of-dreams so that we'd slip into blurred, easeful fantasias. Mine usually involved food: thin-skinned dumplings with pork and shrimp and scallions, dried roasted cuttlefish, anchovies in sweet sauce. When I insisted on describing these to Rhiis-2, she'd pull a face and retort by making up recipes for sweet cakes laced with radioactive elements, or crisp biscuits of circuitry, or pies filled with flitter exhaust.

Now that I couldn't drug myself with nectar, I had different dreams. A ship, or a human that has become a ship, was always awake, and always asleep. I had heard that the need to sleep (to dream) never fully went away, so that came as no surprise.

During the everywhere-cooling night, the painstaking needle-threading of shadowspace navigation, I dreamt that every star had unsunned itself. The lights that vined across my walls and ceilings had dimmed into ash. Darkness even greater than that of nightfall clothed everything. Yet, although Rhiis-2 lay separated from me by a heartbeat, a handspan, by the heat of vanished history, I could see her.

The seeing had nothing to do with the wry mouth, or the clever hands, or the livid scar at her heel, whose origin I did not know. Sometimes I could scarcely tell her boundaries from my own. We orbited each other, losing substance in the process like neutron stars holding each other captive, ghost inspiraling into ghost.

Instead, I could see alveoli like sprays of flowers. Long lean bones. The unmoving knot at her center that was her heart. Snakes everywhere: the crenellations of her brain, silent of electric flickers. Flaccid blood vessels. Winding ropes of intestine. Snakes.

In the language of light, the Seethe was a fist of utter black surrounded by a coruscating accretion disk and sustained from evaporation effects by the masteries of an ancient civilization. That was realspace. The Seethe also hid a shadowspace fortress, the retreat of that same civilization, and our old opponent in the vastwar. The story went that they had specialized in weapons. Weapons that sundered matter into a vapor of quarks, weapons that smothered planets, weapons that smeared stars into unradiant dust. For a while they were content to peddle their weapons. Then something changed: whimsy, yearning, some threat from outside. At that point, they developed the secret of resurrection and used it to touch off a general war.

Eventually the warring nations wearied of the conflict and united to destroy the weapon-makers. A great many people died in the vastwar. Rhiis-2 was one of them, in a skirmish at the outskirts, past stars so obscure that their names were pin-scratchings in the great catalogs.

Rhiis-2 was the pilot, back then. I was Rhiis-1, the gunner. "I'm just the percussion," I said to her many times. "What you do is the music." She only laughed and said I had it the wrong way around.

Rhiis was the name of the ship. We had flown a great many scouting missions together, and our commander sent us to investigate odd readings in shadowspace. When we chanced upon the mercenaries that the weapons-makers, disdaining to do the actual fighting, had hired as sentries, the only thing that saved us was that they had not expected anyone to be poking around that corner of space.

We fled, but not quickly enough. I ran for a long, long time, until even the shadows in my nightmares had blurred into insignificance. By the time I was able to haul Rhiis-2 to the ship's medical unit, she was beyond saving. She would have been beyond saving anyway. It bothered me how *whole* she looked, as though she had merely slid into some underworld of sleep. I should have known that not all weapons left such obvious marks as cuts and holes and burns. Nevertheless, I kept expecting her to stir and speak.

After that I deserted. I was almost certain that my one attempt to warn allied forces resulted in the destruction of an allied fleet. I decided not to try again. Instead, I went mercenary myself, not in the vastwar but the smaller simmer of conflicts that came and went among the minor polities. None of them had the technology to breathe Rhiis-2 back into motion, but that had also been true in the alliance proper.

The fluid of suppositions had not been intended for revival. Rather, it was meant to memorialize the vastwar's dead. I had no desire to take Rhiis-2 back to be ogled by masses to whom we were nothing but checklists of ceremonial mourning. My family and I regarded each other as cordial strangers; it wouldn't matter much to them.

Nor did I have any great feeling for Rhiis-2's family. I had never asked her about them. But one night she had mentioned, with a casualness that I knew better than to take at face value, that her parents and sisterkin had not approved of her enlisting. She'd recently received a package that included a snakeskin, oiled and supple and sewn with gems like pomegranate seeds. I remembered how her face had frozen when she opened it up. "Take it and sell it," she had said. "Don't tell me where. Get something to drink with the money, and we'll save it for a special occasion, I don't know what."

The force of her bitterness convinced me to do as she said. I still had the bottle of wine. I had the spiders bring it out of storage even though I didn't need to do so to contemplate it.

As we neared the Seethe, I had the spiders spell out its name in the languages I knew, and the names of long-ago generals and colonels, as they skittered up and down the walls. Then I amused myself further by firing at the spiders with lasers turned down low enough to do no harm to the ship's structure. (I hadn't always thought well of my officers.)

Perhaps it was folly to show up at the weapon-makers' doorstep to demand redress. Alternately, I had little coin with which to offer them payment. Indeed, I couldn't imagine that I had anything that would interest them, except the pale threat that I knew of their survival and others did too.

I had no guarantee that they wouldn't shoot me out of the sky and fling me into the Seethe, where my ever-dwindling image would serve as a warning to other travelers. But then, even a slim chance seemed better than accepting Rhiis-2's continued silence. And, as small a comfort as it was, the space around the Seethe's event horizon was not, in fact, crowded with the red-shifted ghosts of unfortunate would-be visitors.

I had expected to fight my way in. Call it habit. I'd laid in as much ammunition as I could. It might not be enough, but it would be worse to die without having fired.

The weapon-makers' first interceptor flight took on a formation that I had seen battlefields ago, when I was human. It was difficult not to fly straight at them, suicide-fashion. I was saved from my own impulses by the ghosts I carried within me.

—*If* they don't come out firing, they might just be getting a good look—

—*If* they flash their stardrives like that, they're probably going to swerve away at the last moment—

—*If* they keep dancing like this, it's not a trap, it's a test—

Part of this was my memory of Rhiis-2's steady judgment. Part of it was my own, long-disused, waking under the pressure of necessity. Before I'd deserted, I'd been among the best gunners. Now that the ship and I were no longer separate entities, I was even better.

I held my fire, as much as I yearned to use what had once been a simple torchgun, and was now something much more destructive. I wanted them to talk to me. I sent a message requesting parley while I maneuvered, using every communications protocol I was capable of.

The interceptors did not respond over any channel I recognized, nor did the Seethe's fortress. Instead, we wove trajectories around each other, like a braid. I did not like the numbers. I especially disliked them when I realized what was going on.

The interceptors were miming an engagement from many years back, except Rhiis-2 and I had been part of a flight of eight. It had been our second time together after pledging to each other. We'd lost three skimships before returning to the fleet proper. People I'd barely gotten to know. I felt guiltiest about that part. To be honest, I hadn't thought of the fight, or the creeping alienation afterward, in years. There had, after all, been many battles. I wouldn't have expected to recall this one so clearly. The interceptors' dance was so specific and so persistent, however, that the memories came singing back.

All right. If they were doing everything *but* firing on me, I could still fly the patterns they were defining for me. Call-and-response, like music. All I had to do (and I laughed a little, ironically) was condense an entire flight's maneuvers into those of the single ship that I was now.

I needled toward them and darted away, stitched patterns in and out of shadowspace, tactical geometries. It took all my concentration. And when I had finished the ballet, I was still not done. The interceptors slipped away and were replaced by another flight of larger vessels. Another battle. And another after that, and another after that.

As I flew, I thought of the people I had left behind. My mother and aunts, to whom I had made the ritual offering of candied fruits before departing forever. The last I saw of them, they were passing the treats out and chattering about investments. A comrade, killed, whose locket contained nothing but a blank slip of paper. When I handed it to their lover, her eyes shattered. A quartermaster who could be bribed for better shoes. It was like passing through the halls of the dead.

—*If* you make it through the gauntlet of ghosts, Rhiis-2 said to me through the medium of old suppositions, they will not offer you anything but masks and illusions. You cannot bring back the dead. Turn back. Turn back. Turn back.

You won't die as long as I am here, I thought back to the whisper-presence.

I did not know how long I flew, aware only of the necessity of reenacting the battles presented to me, and the dangerous everywhere-pull of the Seethe.

At last the ships parted before me and slowed. I understood this to be an invitation and circled them, wary, exhausted. Three guardships greater than any I had yet faced emerged from shadowspace, opening up a passage in the space between them.

"You have come a long way to show us your artistry," the guardships said to me in one voice, in a language that both of us knew, but which was not native to me and probably was not to them either. "If you wish to speak, then we will hear you."

"Thank you," I said in the same language, although some of the spiders wove dire webs in their corners, and entered the passage.

The shadowspace fortress was constructed of dust and laminate, nanites endlessly chewing and regurgitating machinery into new shapes. More weapons, I presumed; I did not ask. I was brought through winding passages to a monument of light, shot through with jewel-sparks and swirls of smoke. I wondered if this, too, represented some battle, one that I had not been party to. "Artistry," the guardships had called it. Perhaps I shouldn't have expected anything else from people who devoted themselves to creating engines of war.

And really, was I much different? I had killed my share of people during the vastwar. I had killed more afterward, as a mercenary scrabbling for the upgrades that would bring me here. Perhaps it was death, rather than any combination of sounds and syntax, that was our common language.

A voice spoke out of the monument. At that point I realized it wasn't merely a monument, just as I wasn't merely a ship. It said, "Did you bring your soldier-sister with you to make of her a weapon, or to wake her from her death?"

"She spent her life as a weapon," I said. "She is not any less one for being dead." It was true. After all, I had consulted her decision-trees, the remembered sum of her experiences, all these years. "Is it, in fact, within your power to bring back the dead?"

The light dimmed bit by bit, coalescing into a silhouette that I knew all too well. Its twin dwelled unmoving within its preserving casket. The wry mouth, the clever hands, the livid scar at her heel. Even the way it held its head.

"That's not her," I said. "If all I wanted was a puppet with her face, I could have gone to any of a thousand artisans." Clones, sculpts, robots of polished mien. Or puppets from older traditions, made of paper or wood or felt.

It cocked its head, frowned at me slightly. "The puppet will serve you better," it said in Rhiis-2's husky voice.

The mind was not separate from the body. I did not know how the weapons-maker had achieved their miracle. But I was willing to bet that it involved the original body, or whatever records had been made of it. "That's not what I asked," I said.

"Ship who used to be human," the silhouette said, "if bringing back the dead were wise, do you not think that we would have started with our own? Why else would we hide here, diminished from what we were?"

"If I cared about wisdom," I said, "I wouldn't be here."

The silhouette laughed, and even that was Rhiis-2's laugh, with its kind mockery, except I knew better. The scratching in my absent heart told me so. "It can be done if you are brave enough. Quantum mechanics will produce an exact duplicate so long as you don't mind waiting out the heat death of the universe."

"That is a very long time to wait," I said. "I am not built to last that long. But perhaps with the Seethe—?"

Close orbit near the event horizon would induce the necessary time dilation. The universe would age unimaginably while I waited out a more bearable span. But the calculation would have to be extraordinarily precise.

"We can provide the orbit," it said. "And in the course of eons she will come to you. But there is a condition."

Of course there was. "Say it."

"More a warning than a condition, perhaps. Don't speak to her of the past, yours or hers."

A terrible suspicion took hold of me. "Why?" I said. "Won't she remember?"

"She will remember only what is given to her to remember," the silhouette said. Its voice was sad. I was too impatient to press for details. I would regret that later.

Trusting in the orbit provided me, I launched from the fortress. I did not like being so close to the Seethe, vastest of its kind. No sane person would.

I wondered what she would say to me first. "When we pledged, this is not what I was thinking of," she might say. Or: "Deserting? When did you decide that I would approve of deserting?" Except she hadn't been around to say that, and I had dragged her with me anyway, past immense gas giants and ringed planets and the glitter-ice of frozen moons, through expanses of irradiated darkness, around the old remnants of defeated fleets. I had dragged her with me despite her devotion to the alliance. The pledge had meant something to her beyond camaraderie. The vastwar had been personal to her in a way it had never been for me. I wanted flight-rhythms and war-hymns; she cared about principle.

I had rehearsed defense after defense. The spiders, obsessive scribes, were weaving them into webs of guilty illogic. I did not know how any of my arguments would fare against her anger, or worse, her disappointment.

Outside, the universe swirled by. Due to the effects of gravitational lensing, everything I saw was distorted, doubled; and of course there was also the utter dark of the Seethe itself. I lost track of the red- and blue-shifting, and wondered just what was going on in the lifetimes passing me by. There came periods of dark, and periods of renewed light, and in between more of the kaleidoscope oddities. Eventually I tired of them.

When I had all but given up hope, the fluid of suppositions sloughed away and pooled obligingly to the side, awaiting reuse. Flesh clothed bone. Rhiis-2 coughed. Everything down to the scar on her ankle was there. I started to speak through the spiders, then stopped. Rhiis-2's eyes were the color of chambered bullets. The blankness in them frightened me.

The spiders assembled before Rhiis-2, and after an appallingly long moment, her eyes lit. *Say something,* I begged her silently. But I was determined not to push her, to let her speak first.

She rose from the casket and looked to the left, then to the right, and at last straight ahead, into a ghostworld I couldn't share with her. "Why are there no stars?" she said. "I can't navigate if there are no stars."

I didn't understand what she meant. There was a new universe outside. Of course there were stars.

The spiders retreated as she made her way to me. I was unnerved by the fixity of her stare. I could not breathe in or breathe out, but my spiders stilled when she laid her hand across the hatch. I wasn't going to open it for her, naturally. "Yes," she said to herself. "This looks right. It was like this in my dreams."

"Dreams?" I said, wondering if the dead dreamed.

She ignored that and made straight for where the pilot's seat used to be. I'd taken it out a long time ago. For a moment she paused, frowning. She searched the deck with her hands. I did not have nerves with which to feel her touch.

It took her a long time to give up. Next she searched for the gunner's seat. I did, at least, still have guns, although the current ones would be far outside her experience. And then she looked for our bunks. I could only present her with the casket. Her eyes darkened as she regarded it.

At last she returned to the primary gun, or the part of it that she could access without my revealing its mechanisms to her. "The gunner," she said. "My soldier-sister. Where did she go?"

I was part of her past. I could not remind her of what we had been to each other, the missions we had flown, that fatal skirmish. I could not tell her what I had done to myself to bring her here.

Don't speak to her of the past.

As I understood it, the past was dead anyway. I'd taken care of that.

Rhiis-2 made another circuit of the ship, then returned to the casket and banged on its side. "Answer me!"

—*If* I spoke to her, I knew what she'd demand.

I spoke.

• • •

I spoke through the spiders, and she listened. Some of it she knew. Most of it she didn't. At first I was inclined to blame the shock of whatever process had returned her to me.

Then a different possibility occurred to me, and would not go away.

Don't speak to her of the past.

I could stop now. She had come back to me. We could abide together.

"You're not her," I said at last.

Her mouth pulled down. "I'm who I am," she said.

"You're another silhouette," I said. The same one I'd been carrying all along. I could only imagine that it had been easy for the weapon-makers to hack into my computer systems and internal sensors, to create the illusion of Rhiis-2 using the fluid of suppositions. The problem was, the illusion knew only as much as the weapon-makers and I did. Rhiis-2's secrets—the snakeskin, her family, the scar at her heel—all of those were lost.

Her brow knit, and she said, "The dreams took me away from myself. Maybe it'll come back with time. Maybe you can tell me about the dried squid again, and I'll remember what I used to eat when I was a child. Maybe we can open that bottle—you remember the one—and drink to our reunion."

I veered away from the Seethe, slowed, and left the orbit that had been given me. There was no more point to the charade. "You don't have to pretend anymore," I said.

Her expression grew ironic, then. "I was meant to make the wait bearable," she said. "The recurrence theorem guarantees her to you; it did not guarantee that you would be sane to greet her."

At last I understood the meaning of the dreams that I had borne with me since Rhiis-2's death. The snakes that had killed her did not just consist of the tick-tock mortality of her body with its frayed parts. The deadliest snake was me.

To the silhouette, I said, "I thought I knew what I wanted, but the weapons-makers were right. End it here."

The silhouette folded in on herself. It was as ungraceful as it was expected. I tried not to look at the expression of startlement on her face. My spiders waited for the fluid of suppositions to envelop the corpse again, then bore her back to the casket. It was time to relinquish my soldier-sister to death. Leaving the Seethe behind, I plunged toward the heart of a star.

It Was Educational

J.B. PARK

Student A is quite eager to see me. It's good to see a reporter actually care, he tells me. His grip is hard and he has the kind of face composed by men who have no idea what normal human beings look like.

We make our way to the university. Student A is accompanied by Student B and in the middle between them is Civilian C, who is similarly pretty in that cobbled together way.

Gwangju is no cheery place. Figures are seen here and there doing things to simulate normalcy, it's like the calm before a storm, with all the anticipatory jangle of nerves, their frayed ends stirring. Through the dim windows I see the occasional sign of movement, maybe a flash of white as some student lifts up a banner he has made. The signs are many yet the messages are uniform—*death to Chun Doo Hwan,* that sort of a thing.

We arrive at the university and Student B begs for permission to go do whatever he has to do; he's not too specific. On the grass I see a group of students filling up empty glass bottles with gasoline. Civilian C has disappeared. Student A apologizes, and leaves to find him.

I hear loose bits of conversation, murmurs, the odd proclamation. The talk is stuff I've heard before in many other pre-war settings. The flavor is different, the languages vary, yet the tone always stays the same.

Instead of opting for a speed-forward I choose to stay the night in simtime. Call it laziness. I get a cheap room and there's a bottle of soju and a bowl of peanuts on the table. The TV is large, the bed is impossibly soft. The window faces the city and the night cloaks it under a muffled sort of darkness, dimming the lights, closing the eyes.

I drink the booze and eat the peanuts and soon there's a knock on the door. Dinner is served—a bowl of white rice, some danmuji, a bowl of clear beef broth with a speck here and there of meat floating in it. A single semi-translucent chunk of radish sits heavily in the middle. The server is quiet and I wait for him to leave before I start eating. Eating in virtual is always a little strange for me, despite the nutritionally absent luxury of it, or perhaps because of it—instinct informs you that you are not actually eating despite the texture of the food in your mouth, like the grains of rice, the spoonful of broth, or the unpleasant softness of boiled radish. No sound other than the slight noise of metal chopsticks rubbing against one another. I finish everything; I tell myself I am fed.

I lie down on the bed. I turn the TV on and nothing appears on screen. I file a complaint about this lack of authenticity while noting that the attention to detail in some other aspects of my stay—the disappointing meal, so true to history—may perhaps benefit from a studious lack of attention. The meal didn't need to be so poor.

Sleep is perhaps the best part. You close your eyes, and when you open them it is morning. The transition is instantaneous. There are no dreams.

I eat breakfast to the sound of gunfire. It's begun, I think. I check to see if my admin privileges have been activated; yes, over the "night" I spent sleeping. At least that's one thing still working. It's a pain sometimes to wait for my credentials to go through.

The TV is working now. Two people are dead—police officers. Their bodies are carried behind the lines of their still-alive comrades. Some unidentifiable number of civilians line the street with their bodies. A bus burns nearby, and as the mob disperses into the various buildings and alleyways, teargas canisters dog their steps and obscure their fleeing forms.

One of the dead is a real human being and he has filed a review of his death. *It was fast and I had time to watch as my stomach pumped out blood onto the ground. Glub glub,* he had noted, jotting down the onomatopoeia. *Head trauma didn't feel real when I got clubbed. Felt more of a clobbering just getting up this morning.*

I shift back in and the footage on TV is now of the army rolling into the city. I look out the window and there are plumes of smoke dissipating above the roofs of the buildings.

There is a bit of compression; eight days are folded into one, because no one has the patience to wait out the slaughter over the standard period of violence.

Now in recorded history there was steady escalation then decompression, set over the course of many days; even in the heaviest fits of fighting some normalcy had remained. Pockets of them, of people holed up waiting for the storm to pass.

However that was boring and thus the tourism board had deemed it fit to retool the attraction into an excitement-friendly version of events, where everything was supposedly more fun. This was what I was here to inspect.

The soldiers had been given a sleek new design, their uniforms patterned after the robot troopers of a recent sci-fi hit, all of them decked out in gleaming black metal. And as I watch, a troop of these soldiers march toward the first of the barricades, made of overturned cars and garbage and broken remains of furniture. Someone at the top of the barricade yells, *they're coming, they're coming!* Immediately a few molotovs sail over the barricade, aimed right at the progress of the troopers. They in turn raise their shields and pull out their handguns. The molotovs keep coming and at one point the soldiers march through a roaring mass of flames, the collective accumulation of dozens of bottles that had smashed and exploded. Their boots crunch on shattered glass as they reach the barricade, drop their shields, and begin to climb. I tab one—a construct—but the one next to it is yet another human and I monitor her heart-rate (acceptably brisk) and other such vitals before focusing on the action again. The first of the soldiers had scaled the barricade only to be knocked back by a student wielding an iron pipe. He reaches out with his left hand and barely stops himself from falling; with the right, still holding a gun, he aims at the student's face and fires. The head disintegrates.

The students retreat, as the soldiers continue to give chase, firing as they run after their targets. They're not all that accurate, but it's enough to fell more than a few of those fleeing. I spot Student A among those who still live; they reach the gate, but find it shut. *Ah,* I think, *drama.*

"Open up!" Student A yells. Others add their voices. But the gate doesn't open, although those students manning the walls (which has grown in size since the night before, resembling some medieval fortification now—I make a note that creative liberties are fine and all, but they should be less obtrusive) fire on the soldiers closing in with rifles of their own, long stubby things that spit out bullets with furious speed. About half the troops reach the gate still, and there, after a brief melee, what's left are the bodies of kids like split watermelons. But the soldiers have been diminished even further by that point: those manning the walls have been firing away for quite some time. What's left of the soldiers run for it, and in the end about ten reach the safety of the barricade.

I check the rating again: "*Supervision required for ages eight and below.*" I note that they should consider raising this now.

Meanwhile hundreds of taxi cabs and buses try to get into the city, hoping to join in on what they still think of as a protest. There's a stoppage somewhere up the road and the drivers are honking and the general temper is volatile. Then the ground begins to rumble, a vibratory approach that they all feel; some climb to the top of their vehicles to see what's coming.

The tanks are coming. The cars have nowhere to go, backed up as they are on the road. From somewhere and nowhere, thunderous music, very cinematic, begins playing. The comic fury of it all, the sheer absurdity of it—the drivers scurry away like insects as their cars are crushed. The machine-guns attached to the tanks open fire and those still fleeing are gunned down as they run. The bullets whack into them with such force that for a brief moment before they burst they are lifted into the air.

Note: *while educational, I do not know if it'll capture the attention of the audience in the same way that, say, Cambodia did last year.*

By that night the death toll has climbed to a few hundred, as the news reports that a dozen protesters were unfortunately subdued. The reporter is a suitably ugly thing, realistically so. Curious, I check to see if it's piloted, and the reporter on screen right now is a real human being following a script for his or her own thrill, whatever it might be.

I drink. The soju tastes like lemons. The bodies blend together in my mind. Red on red, though the setting shifts and shifts. No amount of professional detachment or amusement can truly get rid of the discomfort, as farcical as some of it had become.

There's a knock on the door.

I put down my cup. The knocks follow one another and it's a steady, insistent rap.

When I open the door, there's a young man leaning against the wall. I can smell the smoke on him, smoke and blood. His face is perfectly symmetrical. He reminds me of Student A, though it's worse here, because the result is actually beautiful. And the whole thing, the scene, it's all so silly that it hurts, and I feel a sudden urge to delete this thing out of existence.

"Help," he says. "They're chasing me."

I help him in; I close the door behind him. I must assess this new development. My movements may as well be robotic for all their stiffness. He crashes into the couch, bounces off, hits the floor. Leaks blood everywhere, blood and a clear liquid that I assume must be urine, though it smells more like gasoline from where I stand. Who'd want to smell real piss, after all? I note that perhaps it could be odorless, as the visual would provide enough cues on its own, so long as they give it a yellow tinge.

"Stay right there," I tell him. I go to the kitchen and search for . . . alcohol? In the fridge I find nothing but a jar of denjaang. I open it and the smell of salt and fermentation whiffs out. I get him to lie down straight and I cut through the mess of wadded clothing and drying filth with the knife I suddenly find in my hand. The bullet has entered his side and his breaths come fast and shallow.

"Thank you," he whispers. I ignore him and wonder if I should pull off a surgery here, extract whatever remains of the shell with the knife. I get out a lighter and heat the blade until it turns red. Somewhere, music starts playing. I recognize strains of Dvorak mixed in with some mournful pop. The voice is pitched just a bit too high to be perfect, the only concession made to the human discomfort with actual perfection. It's awful.

The knife hisses as it touches skin and meat. It parts with ease. I dig into the flesh. He groans, and his perfect abs glisten under the sterile white lighting. I dig out a fragment of a bullet; when I extract three more, a little trumpet toots a three-note triumph.

"Thank you," he whispers again. I say nothing as I smear denjaang on the open wound, thinking that it would work like a disinfectant of sorts—why else would it have been there, after all?

Then I pop into admin to see just what's under the hood. The young man is a construct, of course, and by digging out the bullets successfully I'd earned a small medal. Once I'm out I could get a real-life replica of it printed in gold, or at least something with the sheen of gold. I materialize it, amused: there's a crude picture on it of two human-like figures, one lying on the ground while the other tends to the first. On the back is a date—5.18.80, like the numbers would mean anything to anyone here.

I peek at the script. Somewhere in the middle of the night there will be another encounter. He'll groan a bit too loudly and I'll be forced to wake up. There I will bend down, and he will reach up and caress my face, his one last act before dying. A truly human moment. Very affecting.

As I pour myself more soju, I look back at the student dying on the floor. He looks noble like that, dying for a cause. Lips full, skin ashen. Unruly black hair. Bleeding, half-crying. Whispering words to family he'll never see.

I fast-forward a little. Time compresses, then returns to normal. The student is close to death. I crouch down by his side. He stinks of blood, the nobility of it.

I remember the script. He'll reach up, caress the person waiting by him as he dies. So I wait for it as time passes by, slowly and uncompressed in its normal state.

This Wanderer, in the Dark of the Year

KRIS MILLERING

It starts this way: I am a journalist. I interview the inhabitants of war zones. I go to Afghanistan, Iraq, the DRC. The stories are all different, but after a while they begin to blur together. The women are tired, and children with thin arms cling to them. *We cannot get bread,* they say. *Or clean water. My husband died last night. My brothers have been taken.*

You're a disaster, Annelise says on the phone one night, voice distant and crackling over the satellite phone. I think her tone is fond. It's difficult to tell, with the static. *Come home safe.*

They took us and raped us one after the other. They are monsters, monsters. They are men, but they are monsters.

I travel with translators, or embedded into peacekeeping forces. The thump of shells exploding lulls me to sleep.

Or it starts this way: I am home, and doing the dishes. This is my job when I'm home. Scrape, wash, rinse; my hands are mechanical. Annelise leans on the doorframe. The kitchen is the size of a postage stamp, and the rest of the apartment is not much bigger. We pretend that this is the reason I do not spend much time at home. "Did you see the news?" Her accent curls around each word, turning it into rough music. We met in Durban ten years ago, when I was doing a predictable piece on the townships. Annelise was the only good thing about that trip.

I set a plate into the drainer. "About the meteor?"

"They're not sure that's what it is," she says. "Weren't you working there a while ago? The gypsy story?"

"Not *gypsies*. Roma. Gypsy's a pejorative." I wash off a couple of forks and set them in the drainer. "But yes. That's right near where all those people were killed."

All I can remember is how gray the sky was, and how cold it was at night. I have some beautiful pictures from that assignment, but I don't remember taking any of them.

"Sorry." Her tone is unrepentant. Annelise is an evolutionary biologist, and she dislikes the niceties of human behavior. We're all too fast-moving for her.

"Maybe it's a spaceship. Also, do you *have* to use every pot we own to make dinner with?" My voice is sharper than I mean.

"When someone else is washing dishes? Yes." Again, no contrition. *I used to love the way you never apologized.* "I'm going to go see if they've gotten into the thing yet." Her bare feet are nearly soundless on the old wood floor of the apartment that was once *mine* and then *ours* and now more *hers*. Over the sink is a small framed photograph: Annelise, her sister, and two cousins. The sun casts harsh shadows under the brims of their hats, but their smiles are wide and bright.

It will be weeks before anyone can get close to the object. When it cools off enough that they can send rovers to look at it, they will find that the surface is made of some sort of metal, pockmarked in ways that make little sense.

Everyone, it seems, *wants* it to be a spaceship. Nobody knows for certain.

That night, on our threadbare couch, a spring pokes me in the back, keeping me awake. Even with the roar of the city below and Annelise's soft snoring from the bedroom, it's too quiet.

No, it actually starts this way: I am kidnapped from the Budapest airport. I let my guard down. Life seems so much less urgent when nobody is shooting at you.

It's easy. Replace the car driver who was supposed to meet me at the airport. Go towards the hotel but stop in a narrow, cobbled alley. Men with guns slide into the car; I am paralyzed with surprise for a critical moment.

Then the bag over my head, and darkness for what feels like days.

I step forward, and I am falling, falling, falling.

This is all out of order. I'm sorry.

The meteorite opened and something escaped. I was taken from Budapest and driven to a remote location. The non-Roma and the Roma here have been killing each other for centuries.

These three things are related.

My name is Audra Feher. I was born in Athens to American parents. I work for the international desk of a newspaper based in New York. It is January fourteenth, I am told. I am alive. I am unhurt.

I do not know who the people are who are holding me captive. I do know that they have an alien. I have seen it.

Whatever they are telling you, believe them.

The alien resembles nothing so much as a damp gray blanket with restlessly moving fringe, darker spots roving its felted-looking back.

My hands are cuffed behind my back. The metal has worn sores into my wrists, and my shoulders ache. The alien smells like nothing I've ever smelled before, a little like formaldehyde and fresh-cut apples. The man standing next to me has a machine gun. He keeps shifting where he stands.

"It will try to touch you," the man says in heavily Hungarian-accented German. He lowers the muzzle of the gun a little; a reminder, a warning. "Hold still."

We are in a damp, concrete-walled cell with one barred window near the ceiling. My feet are bare and ache so badly with the cold. The alien shifts, and moves. It flows like a slug flows, like an underwater creature, bag of water with cilia moving it along.

It touches the end of my toe. My big toenail, with chipped polish clinging to it still. Jungle Red, the color is called. Bright red, like arterial blood. I think about this because the alien is touching me and I need to think about something other than how my skin wants to crawl right off of my body.

It touches the top of my foot. It's strangely warm. It tickles a little.

And then—pain. What feels like fire spreads up my leg in a sweeping rush, and I scream. My foot shoots out as I try to shake the fucking thing *off* of me—

It moves far more quickly than I thought possible, withdrawing with a swift and preternatural grace, the dark spots moving more quickly now. The man with the gun grabs my arm and drags me away with him.

Later, in the cell, I look at my feet. Bright red pinpricks—Jungle Red—show on purplish, bruised skin. My foot throbs.

It does not heal. The bruise and the pinpricks remain, even after the pain begins to fade.

I put things together, little by little.

Only the one guard speaks German; the rest speak Hungarian—a language that I can speak only the very basics of. The German talks to me, but only to give me orders. I ask questions and he grunts. They've read the books on how to survive hostage situations, too, it seems, and they know all the tricks one does to build rapport with one's kidnappers. *What's your name?* I ask. *Where are you from? Why have you taken me?*

If I were to describe the German in an article, I would say *a burly man with dark hair and a sparse moustache, worn hat pulled low over his eyes.* I would not mention the way he smells as if he has not bathed in weeks, or the stains on his pants, or the way his eyes flick over me as if I were one of the insects that colonize my cell.

"Please," I wheedle. German is a terrible language to plead in. "How can I do what you want if I don't know what it is?"

He turns towards me. *Narrowed eyes with deep furrows in the corners, a suspicious set to his mouth,* I note absently. "You will see," he says. "Your government values you." He grins, briefly, lopsidedly, and then will say no more.

The men wear gray camo and tan coats, and boots with cracked leather uppers. Their guns, though—their guns are well-tended. They've been at this a while. They grow careless eventually, and one of them walks by wearing a hat with a recognizable emblem on it.

Some of the men I interviewed for the piece on the killings of the Roma wore pins and badges with that sign on it. One of them had it tattooed on his beefy neck.

There were angry letters to the editor, after my piece came out. Angry letters, death threats in my email, the background noise of being a woman who walks into war and walks out with a story. I didn't think much of it. I didn't even think

I would be returning to Hungary, but a mysterious space object crashed here and my editors wanted a follow-up piece.

I am here because they want a mouthpiece, or some sort of insurance against attack. The fact that they are . . . feeding me to the alien, if that is what is happening—I suspect that is just because I am a stranger, and my pain means nothing to them. I hear other screams sometimes. Men. I think they're trying different people, to see what it likes.

After what feels like months, they drag me into a cinderblock room and have me talk to a video camera. They point guns at me. The German tells me what to say.

I don't play games with the translation. I'm sure someone in their network speaks English and would know if I slipped a hint about where I think I'm located, the few glimpses I've gotten of the trees, the color of the dirt. I also don't say, *I miss you, Annelise.*

Your native environment, Annelise always says. *Your biome is war.* The words had been fond at first, then less fond, as she realized that even though I would come back to New York and sleep beside her, I was never truly there at all.

I don't wonder what she's doing. I don't think of her at all, if I can help it.

They take me to see the alien, again and again. Sometimes it touches me. Sometimes I just stand and stare at it. I don't know how they know what it wants. If they know what it wants. It's cryptic as a sea cucumber, as an anemone.

Sometimes I wake in the middle of the night, the smell of apples and bitter almonds choking me.

When the meteorite—spaceship—opens, something escapes. Nobody sees what, because at that point armed men of unknown affiliation have taken control of the crater that was the crash site. They have shot the guards and taken the scientists hostage. The Hungarian government was in the process of sending in the army when the pitted metal opened and smoke and something else poured out.

When the smoke clears, the armed men as well as whatever had come out are gone. They leave behind the bodies of the scientists.

Annelise comes out with me to wait for the taxi on the stoop of our building. She watches the traffic go past, spraying filthy slush onto the sidewalk. I glance at her, once, then again. She's left her coat upstairs.

"I'm going home," she says.

I hear how the *oh* in *home* elongates. *Hohhme.* The Afrikaner way of indicating distance. Something cold threads through my gut. "Are you coming back?"

"Taxi's here." She picks up my suitcase and heads down the steps.

There's a moment after a bomb goes off that is always filled with a profound personal silence, no matter how noisy the aftermath. It is a silence filled with two questions: *can I move?* and *why am I not moving yet?*

So I move in that silence. I get into the taxi as the driver loads my bags into the trunk. Annelise bends over, makes a circling motion with her hand. I roll down the window.

"Do me a favor, Audra." Her dark eyes meet mine, curls gathering beads of mist in them. "Get some help."

Then she straightens and bangs once on the roof of the car. The driver slams his door and the taxi lurches into traffic before I come up with a response.

I crane around to stare out the back window. *What do you mean? Help with what?*

Annelise's sharp-planed face holds no answers, and all too quickly recedes into the distance.

Later, after the lights on the plane are turned down for the evening, I close my eyes. After a while, I realize my cheeks are wet.

Oh.

Instead of sleeping, instead of thinking about Annelise, I draft the beginning of my piece. I give a quick précis of the region's bitter history of violence between the Roma and non-Roma, detail the current right-wing disposition of the government, and posit that the appearance of such an immensely valuable space artifact might stir tensions up once more.

When I land in Budapest, I receive a text about the spaceship opening. I am distracted on my way out of the terminal to meet my driver, thinking about how I'm going to have to edit my opening. Not thinking about Annelise, and Durban.

It is an explanation, as much as anything is.

There are somber bootsteps outside of my cell, low voices sorrowing and angry. I heft myself up and limp to the door, look out the little window. Camouflaged figures walk past, carrying the body of one of their own. One of the men doing the carrying is the German; I recognize the slightly crooked set of his shoulders.

The dead man's feet are bare. The pattern of bruise and livid pinpricks is the same as on my own feet.

I'm going to die here, I realize, somewhat belatedly.

One morning, I open my eyes to thin light filtering in through the window and the word *adapt* ringing in my mind.

I sit up, wrap the scratchy blanket around my shoulders. I study my hands. The skin on my knuckles is cracked, seeping blood. Jungle Red is a quarter-moon on my nails. Chipped away, grown out.

My nails are a secret calendar. Even if their growth has slowed from malnutrition, even if my periods have stopped, my nails keep track of the days and the months. My nails are a record of this endless, endless winter. My feet and calves are covered with pinpricked bruises.

Phantom scents tease my nose—burned meat, olives, bathroom cleaner, pine trees. Is it because I'm hungry? Anise and blood. *Just hallucinations,* I tell myself. *I am starving, I am isolated.*

I lie down again, close my eyes, lapse into a fever-chill sleep. I dream about the alien. In my dreams, it is warm, and its cilia are thin and soft as a kitten's fur.

Adapt.

I don't know what it means until a few days later, when I waken to find that overnight the roof of my mouth has grown a coating of cilia, shifting and seeking against my tongue. It's revolting. I retch and retch.

When I try to scrape it off with my thumbnail, I nearly pass out from the pain. *Adapt.*

I forget how to walk and fall forward, gashing open my knees on the concrete of the hall floor.

When I wake the next morning, the wounds have sealed over with a gray substance and the pain is gone. Within three days, they are healed as if they never were.

I lie awake and stare at the ceiling. I think I can feel thin filaments growing through me, invading me. Everything hurts, from my skin to my bones to the backs of my eyes. I allow myself to think of Annelise, of her smile, of the way my gut clenches when I think of her leaving.

I'm so cold. *What are you doing to me?*

I am back at home, with Annelise. I smell sunlight and dish soap, chemical lemon and Annelise's own warm scent, the ghost of the soap she uses.

She hands me a towel for the dishes. "Every one of us is colonized by mitochondria. This is just a larger scale, is all."

When she smiles, her teeth are gray-furred. I scream and wake myself up, sobbing, *no, no.*

Nem, nem, echoes a male voice distantly, and then a long, agonized scream. The smell of apples fills my sinuses.

Communication.

Adapt.

"It is fine," the German says, his voice harshly accented. "It is fine." He lapses into Hungarian. I pick out *élelmiszer* and *holnap. Food* and *tomorrow.*

I am supposed to sit on the floor of this concrete room and wait for the alien to come to me. Lowering myself to the ground is difficult and I fall the last two feet when my legs lose strength. I will have another bruise on my hip, to join the collection.

The alien ripples towards me. I read eagerness in its movements, or desperation. I push myself up, put my back to the wall.

Under my skin, things move. There are cilia in the back of my throat, now, and the pinpoint of anger in my gut is flaring.

Not for the first time, I wonder if the alien has any opinions on its situation. It is not exactly a captive, nor exactly in charge. Both of us are stuck here surrounded by humans whose language we don't understand. *Do you even have language?* I ask the alien silently. *Is language a meaningful concept to you?*

Ozone and a horrible artificial cherry smell rise in my sinuses. I choke.

I am remembering a Roma woman I interviewed, who had lost two children and her husband to the bullets of a vigilante group. *I have nothing left. They have taken it all,* the translator had said. *How can they hate us so much that they kill our children?*

The alien flows over my outstretched legs, and I shudder, my vision sparkling with pain. Up it goes, onto my lap. I rest my hand on it. Stroke it like a cat.

Adapt.

It wraps around my hand, dark spots moving restlessly. I don't scream even though my hand and the skin of my thighs feel like they're aflame. The cilia on the roof on my mouth stir, tickling my tongue. I find myself with my mouth hanging open.

Then I bend forward.

It reshapes itself, extends something like a limb to my lips. *How strange I must seem to you, with this wet orifice surrounded by sharp bony projections.* I keep my mouth open. Allow it to probe inside.

I feel the cilia in my mouth jerk in recognition, and light starbursts in my head.

Annelise smiles at me.

I stare at her dumbly. What is the thing she is doing with her—

Mouth, it is a mouth. She is smiling. She is happy, or wishes me to believe she is happy.

Woodsmoke and rotting seaweed. Understanding. This is like—

Yes. Much like.

We dream, the alien and I. Communicating. Adapting.

Together.

I wake on the dirty, cold floor. The alien is pressed against my stomach. Touching it no longer hurts. It is neither warm nor cool, but exactly the temperature of my body.

I push myself to my feet. I am weak, too weak. The alien's scent is regretful. It was not supposed to take this long to find a suitable partner. It was nearing the end of its strength.

Why me?

Incomprehension is baby powder and rainwater. We do not entirely know how to speak to one another yet. I bend down and lift the alien. It flows up my arm to drape itself across my shoulders.

The German runs away, shouting triumphantly. I don't need to speak Hungarian to know that he is announcing that I have done it, I have tamed the alien.

Surely the world will listen to them now.

I remember the Roma woman's face, the bitter anger in her eyes. Men like these killed her family. Old hatreds that I have no stake in, or real understanding of. I was just there to report. Just there to observe.

War has a habit of drawing us all in, eventually. Even a journalist. Even an alien who came here entirely by accident.

The German's left the door open. Four steps and I am out the door. Step, step, step down the hall. I am unsteady, but I do not stumble.

Thundering footfalls, boots on concrete. At the end of the hall, five men pound into view—the German and four others. One points. Says something in that beautiful language that I do not understand.

I stand with the weight of the alien on my shoulders. The cilia in the back of my throat are writhing with alarm. I choke as my throat closes, the alien drawing itself together in alarm, its body against mine less like fluid in a sack than a clenched muscle.

That is all the warning I have. The men receive none at all.

Fluid sprays from the alien, hitting the men in the face. They fall to their knees, screaming as I stagger, panicking, trying to draw breath and finding no air. I clutch my throat as they spew bright blood from their noses and mouths, then collapse, going silent.

Then the cilia in my throat release and I draw great lungfuls of air. My heart throbs painfully in my chest, and I am alive. I cannot feel grateful. The alien wraps itself around me in a mockery of an embrace.

I will never see Annelise again.

No, it starts this way: a woman walks out of a bunker and into a snowscape, trees black against a dim evening sky. She carries a *thing* that looks like a furry blanket with restlessly moving spots. Her feet are bare, and spattered with blood. She does not seem to feel the cold.

Or perhaps that's where it ends.

Your native habitat is war.

We walk on, this marooned explorer and I.

Forestspirit, Forestspirit
BOGI TAKÁCS

Apunak

I race foragers to each mushroom with relish, changing from a tree to a bush to sometimes even the early autumn fog. After a decade, it's easy to hold each shape; I don't know if I can call this neuroplasticity any longer, in the absence of neurons. My cells are machine, and they follow my thoughts with the obedience of automation.

I used to bleed people dry, to insinuate into small cracks both artificial and natural, to infiltrate. I used to fight. I still have my spherical vision, my hunter-smooth motion, my booming authority-voice to be used as needed.

These days I haunt the forest.

I love and despise them all, these pale and oddball people who come to the forest to play, to gather mushrooms because it is so *quaint,* to frolic. None of my people remain; they are scattered across less antagonistic lands, thinking back on this place.

I wanted to stay, to look at people like this boychild, venturing into the woods with the trepidation of an older breed of human. I can tell he still has his AR displays on, and his head swivels as he takes in all the different species, helpfully labelled for him on bright overlays in his mind. I am poised to duck, twist and run after him—maybe roll into the shape of a moss-covered log—but he is agonizingly slow, uncertain, out of his element.

I creep across the undergrowth as a thousand earthworms moving in unison, hiding myself underneath ferns and organic debris.

He brushes spiky straight ash-blond hair out of his eyes. I am soundless, invisible, gazing him in the face. I never hurt these strangers; I just want to be left alone to watch. The war has been over for a decade.

I am no danger, and yet he senses something. I flow into the earth, nestle myself between grains of soil and errant tree-roots.

"Forestspirit," he whispers. "I know you are real."

I am not real, I'm tempted to answer, *I am a legend formed by my own self, a haunt following picnickers and mushroom-gatherers.* I remain silent and still. I can hear him underground as his words make the topsoil tremble ever so slightly. My senses extend far and wide.

"My uncle saw you," he says. Then, after some hesitation: "He can talk to birds. He makes dead plants grow."

I know that garden on the edge of the forest, the succulents feasting on carefully arranged rocks, the little lake with fish tempting the stray cats. Few humans make such things anymore. Maybe it all needs the motivation of magic?

I am not magic. I am a cluster of myriads of tiny automata, my original shape a shimmering cloud of light.

I creep up from the earth, and yet I do not show myself. I haven't spoken with anything besides the commanding voice in this body.

"Forestspirit," the boy goes on, "I need your help."

Speak, I make the leaves rustle. A finely grained control of my environment, it was called. *Speak, child.*

For a moment he seems resentful of having been called *child,* but I can only draw on the mythical. I cannot bark at him like a drill-sergeant.

"They want to destroy the forest," he says, and my imagination immediately jumps to a variety of *theys*: the aliens, or these straight-haired and straight-backed humans (then why would the boy exclude himself?), my own people returning for revenge, or other peoples out for the same. The current inhabitants of the land gathered many enemies over millennia in this landlocked basin, with its rolling fields and thick forests. Should I have cared?

Explain, I whisper. Or should I project a sense of omniscience? I seldom wish I was magic, and yet—

Words topple out of him in gasps, his fear pouring out of him and into me. The gist: he doesn't know why. This is what the Consentience has decided, and I do not even know who that would be. I'm truly out of touch. Am I old? I don't think I age, and yet I worry I have become inflexible, my only pursuit this idle hunt of careless tourists.

The usual paranoia surfaces, an occupational hazard that never quite goes away, even after all those years. Is this unknown-factor Consentience looking for me? I went absent without leave, but no one really looked for me—after the humans fought off the aliens with pilfered technology, they turned on each other, and I knew I would be first in line to get thrown into a ditch. How do you throw a raincloud? The military had made me into something they thought would remain loyal, but I modified myself, shook off my trackers, and floated away.

I do not kill. And yet I don't know what to do with this crumble of a boy on all fours in the dirt, crying desperately. Why is the forest so dear to him? I rarely see him—I think he lives far away, only coming to visit his uncle every once in a while.

By contrast, I know his uncle too well, and I realize that he is the connection: the man of green who wants to preserve life for its own sake. It is not the forest that's so dear to the boy—it is not *me*—it is his uncle.

I blow a little gust to tousle the boy's hair, and whisper vague promises in his ear. I have no idea what else I can do.

And yet as he gathers himself and walks away, his shoulders sinking in time with his steps, I follow him into the evening dusk, my shape a windcarpet of fireflies.

He sits on the bench by the small lake. Both the bench and the lake are carefully handcrafted, and I wonder: I could likewise build, I could laser-cut a hundred of these benches, would that qualify as my handiwork in a sense? I'm not sure where this sudden impulse comes from—I never even liked crafts, back in my human days.

He glances up, senses me in the pattern. "Why have you followed me here, forestspirit?" he whispers, then louder: "My name is Péter. What's your name?"

The firebugs move along their preprogrammed trajectories, one of my subroutines taking care of it all. I don't show a startle reaction this time, and for that I am glad.

It has been a long while since someone asked me my name. And I had names that hurt . . .

Name me, the insects buzz.

He frowns, trying to keep eye contact with the swarm. "I guess I can pick a name. Which gender?"

The bugs can't quite chuckle. *I'm a forestspirit, I have no gender,* I say.

"And before?"

I have to, I need to display emotion. I make my bodies fall out of the sky, and they make small cracking noises as they hit the rough-hewn rock panels around the bench. I turn into sand and seep into the cracks.

"Don't go away," he cries with sudden desperation, and I feel bad—I've been making the wrong impression. I turn into a large pile of leaves—what else would be mimicry enough in such a tidy garden? How did he know there was a before?

"I'm sorry," I answer. "I am here." A leaf tumbles off the heap. "Before, I had no gender either. Give me any name that you want."

These people had never reacted to me kindly, but this boy takes it all in easy stride. "*Gabi,*" he says, "That can be any gender. It's kind of cool, huh?"

It sounds like a soap brand from the ancient past. Gabi I shall be, then. Anything to keep the memories at bay. But what else could I do?

I have to familiarize myself with this environment, and I'm reluctant to commit to a confrontation, even a defensive one. Many have moved off-planet, changed shape and form, reorganized their minds to an extent that even I find somewhat intimidating. Left behind by these posthumans, the Consentience governs, with an erratic, ad hoc determination all the more frightening for its hodgepodge nature.

I recall this from my studies: even when artificial neural networks make precise decisions, it can be hard to discern the process by which they do this, the representations they utilize, if any. The Consentience is a network, with who knows what substrate for nodes instead of neurons, and yet the end effect is the same. Péter doesn't know their motivation because it cannot be known.

Now the Consentience wants to devour my forest, and I realize I have grown possessive, I who had sworn off earthly attachments. I feel myself rapidly changing, growing to fit the situation. Growing into my earlier self: soldier, tactician . . . I was never a strategist, but maybe there's space to expand.

"What are you good at?" the boy says in hushed, awestruck tones, and I answer: "Infiltration."

To change the behavioral output of a neural network, one can lesion it—in principle. But how should I know what happens after I lesion? We could hardly model the Consentience with tiny rocks and sticks. I know this because I try, now as a legion of angry wasps and obedient ants gathering close to ground, producing what I could hardly call a model based on what Péter tells me of each substation in the area. There's even a new one built about a month ago, a little more than half a kilometer from the forest I call my own.

The Consentience must require an inordinate amount of energy to sustain, I realize, for why else would it need separate stations instead of floating on the air or silting down into the bottom of living waters? I require a lot of energy and yet I can be nigh-invisible, gossamer.

I decide.

The next morning, we investigate. Péter totters on sticklike legs, his noisiness suddenly our shared downfall. I order him back to the house and he obeys, sniffling.

I venture out of my territory, but I feel in my element. This is the hunt that enlivens me.

The closest substation is molded of pale white plastic and shaped like a well-grown specimen of fly agaric—presumably an ironic nod to children's stories. These people no longer understand the forest. I do not let my anger rise.

Occasionally, large robotic millipedes creep in and out of holes at the base of the substation that reseal themselves instantly. I decide to trail them, but I grow bored quickly as I realize that each millipede has a rigidly defined patrol area and does not seem particularly intelligent.

Next, I fly up to the surface of the substation in the shape of a raven. The wall trembles, more organic than it revealed of itself from a distance. It sparks at me and I produce my best shock-strained caw.

In the following fifty-three minutes, I try out twenty-four animal shapes. My shapeshifting raises no alarm or consternation besides the localized electric shocks. Maybe it is time to sneak inside? I could soak a millipede with myself as a light autumn rain, evaporate from its body into a different shape once it's safely indoors. But suddenly I chance upon another idea.

Reminded of a long gone battle, I'm curious how far the Consentience's perception stretches. The intellect in this structure does not seem to be human, regardless of how it had originally arisen. Each mental setup gives shape to its own logic, and each has its peculiar holes and omissions. If there is no general alarm, then for the time being, I can experiment.

I grow into an oak. No taser-blip this time; sessile lifeforms must not be considered a danger. The fly agaric scans me with infrared and something I can't quite sense, then puffs some chemical in my direction: to stunt my growth? This is probably how it keeps itself from being overgrown by the local flora.

I try a weeping willow, entirely out of place. Again only the puff. Even more daring, I shift into a sea-bean plant, my lianas curling toward the fly agaric. I move, I touch, yet I provoke no electric shock.

I could examine the edge cases of its classification heuristics. What is still an animal? What's considered a tree?

My lianas freeze as I can feel a breakthrough inching closer to my consciousness. I focus inward.

If I can work out how it recognizes a forest, then I will know how it will proceed to destroy it. Péter said that the Consentience has already been sending out tersely-worded notifications for any remaining humans to vacate the area. Can I disguise my home in order to save it?

I remember flying through the Thundercloud Straits, my still-human face bearing the war-paint of asymmetric lines and rectangles designed to throw off alien shape-recognition algorithms. I remember breaking my bones one by one to assume a configuration at odds with alien mindsets. I wasn't always this fluid, this protean. But I always had this uncanny disturbing spirit, a hacker's attitude toward the constancies of life, toward the baseline of awareness.

It came in handy, in so many clashes. I might yet prevail, without having to destroy or cut off a single substation—for I have forsworn violence, I have forsworn malign thought. Yet, my body thrums with the excitement . . .

I transform my buzzing to elation. I run through permutations of shapes, I register and catalog. I fill a relational database, calculate correlations, build models. I am manifold, each convolution of me producing a different reaction. This is a low-level response: I do not seem to reach the Consentience's threshold of awareness, if this unfathomable system indeed has one. I treat the giant mind as a black box: I'm only interested in its responses to my stimuli. I feel like a flea on a St. Bernard's tail.

In a few hours I reach shapes edging into the meaningless, and yet the fly agaric still categorizes them into animals and plants, responds accordingly. I am a giant red stripe with yellow curlicues in the middle. I'm a perfectly spherical ball of flowers. Would it recognize a human as a distinct category? I do not dare try—that might invoke some higher-level process. I can only hope it doesn't mark my stilted, spiky stalks or my purple-tinted scrub as a human due to some quirk. I started out from the animal and plant prototypes in the problem space, moved always just one little modification away, and I hope this search strategy will keep me secure and safe from alarms.

I only forgot about one detail: how will I disguise my forest? I could hardly hang brightly colored stripes from each tree-branch! When I realize this, I dissolve into piping-hot steamclouds, all my tension channeled into aggravation with the force of the motion itself.

The sun is setting. I should report back to my newfound teammate about my dubious progress. Something inside me would still be satisfied by a debriefing; I used to be a meticulous soldier.

I let the erratic winds drift me away from the substation, toward Péter.

He listens in wonder as I recount my actions. I share with him my database, but he doesn't deign to look. He purses chill-cracked lips and rubs his hands together. I can sense his entire body gearing up for a revelation, but I can't guess the shape of the revelation itself; my sensors do not have sufficient resolution. I'm not a mind-reader.

"Why don't we try the reverse?" he asks, carefreely including me in *us*. I coalesce into butterflies; I haven't been partnered with anyone for so long, and

I notice with a startle that the presence of this boychild fills a void in me. I'm reminded of the time-old slogan: *Together, we fight . . .*

I don't even parse what he's saying.

He notices.

"Gabi? Are you listening?" He peers up dubiously. I settle on his head, his shoulders, his upper arms. He laughs with the tickle, then grows serious. "I was saying we could try the reverse."

What do you mean? My wings beat in unison.

"If it can recognize strange things as . . . regular things, then maybe it can also recognize regular things as . . . strange things." He's working it out as he speaks, his eyes moving to and fro, gazing beyond the little pond. "We can come up with something that looks like a plant but it's detected as something weird. I guess."

That way the forest could look the same to us, but unrecognizable to the Consentience, I say. *Great idea.*

"Would it get confused? Would it get lost?" He pauses, just for a moment. "Would it leave?"

I don't know. *It's worth a try,* I offer, and if the butterflies could shrug, I would. I've dropped the mythic pretensions. Péter and I, we are comrades.

Yet I leave him by the pond, rushing ahead on my own again. His presence would disturb my plan. This time, I leave with a promise of return.

Even though I know what I'm looking for, the process is still difficult. I'm trying to find small changes that result in unexpected responses, but nothing turns up for a while. I start measuring reaction times, try to find inputs that make the system hesitate and hiccup, circle around those in the problem space.

Eventually I chance upon a pattern of translucent triangular bumps and a painted texture like thatch, invisible to the human-standard eye.

No puff. No shock. Only a millipede venturing out from the substation, turning toward me instead of veering away. It pokes at my trunk and then acts—like Darwin's caterpillar—much embarrassed. I stay still and it returns to its home base after a while. Inwardly, I rejoice. I unfurl leathery wings, soar above the hills and dip into the clouds before I return to Péter.

We spend a frantic day manufacturing sticky triangular knobs, Péter programming the fabricator while I hover over his shoulder, drape myself onto furniture, creep on the ceiling. The missives of the Consentience are cryptic and its actions carry no deadline. It can turn on the forest at any moment that suits its caprice, and I tremble with the thought that the last set of my attempts might have served to hasten its actions.

My turn: I rush through the tree-trunks, gluing, painting. I stir up the undergrowth. Ants crowd around the triangles, then leave them alone again. This was the smallest disruption that we could conceive, and I'm not convinced it will work. More scenarios should have been tried . . . but a vast number of uncategorizables around the substation would certainly have raised an alarm.

Then we wait. We wait. Days pass. I teach Péter intricate strategy games with pebbles and bark. We produce collaborative sculptures of my body. I share my treasury of ages-old political jokes that somehow still resonate, despite the unfamiliar context, and Péter tells me stories about his uncle. I avoid his family and they seem to be glad that their youngest has finally taken an interest in nature.

When I sense the rumble, I'm rooted into the mud of a small brook and Péter is sploshing around in hydrophobic rubber boots, looking for small fish. I puff out into a swarm of mosquitoes, my startle response alive and well.

The millipedes are coming, hundreds upon hundreds of them, the size of foxes and dogs—each equipped with what seems to be laser cutters mass-produced in a hurry, attached to their heads.

Péter holds his breath, then exhales with a snort. The robotic swarm reaches the edge of our forest and comes to a standstill. The millipedes chirp like tiny chicks—also an ironic gesture? Everything about the Consentience is disjointed, patterns of nature mushed haphazardly together.

No decision is reached. No decision is reached. Péter turns toward me to whisper, but I shush him with a sharp tumbling-churning gesture.

The swarm withdraws. Once they are out of my hearing range, we cheer. I change into one of my more incongruous sphere-shapes and bounce off trees with enthusiasm. Péter sobs, his face smeared with snot and his eyes glowing with glee.

The battle is not over. The swarm returns the next day, then again the next, with determined precision.

It takes five days for the Consentience to give up, and by then the local humans have also noticed the curious phenomenon. Péter reads out news headlines to me, the feed sent directly to his brain. No one understands.

No one except the man of green, the steward of the land who calls the ravens to himself. It's late afternoon; Péter is already inside when his uncle ventures out. The man of green runs his fingers on the bark, notices the translucent bumps. Tries to scrape them off, spits on them and rubs. Scratches the wiry black curls on his head. He looks different from Péter. Intermarriage?

"For your sake, I hope they are biodegradable," he says out loud. I glance down on him with beady squirrel-eyes; he looks up into the branches and our gazepaths lock into each other. He nods with acknowledgement, and I nod back to him, as much as this physiology allows. He chuckles as I drop the acorn from my jittery hands, catches it in cupped fingers. For a moment I believe in his magic.

"I will have this, as a keepsake, if you don't mind," he says. "Thank you for taking good care of Péter. This he will remember, even when he ventures out to the stars."

Has Péter been meaning to leave the planet? I'm silent. I mull over the idea and its impact on an aging man so tied to the land. Rejuvenation is still pricy, reserved for decisionmakers and chiefs of staff. Clinging to a human shape is more and more of a curiosity with each passing day. And the youngsters all leave . . .

"We remain here, the two of us." The man points at my squirrel-self. "Shapechanger, forestspirit. You fought in the war, I gather?" He's seen much himself. Maybe he fought too.

His words jingle in my head as he turns, walks away.

The Hunger Tower

PAN HAITIAN, TRANSLATED BY NICK STEMBER

They saw the tower just as the suns were beginning to set.

Pure white and rising to a sharp point, it seemed to soar higher than even the darkly shadowed mountains in the distance. In the west-slanting light of the three suns, the tower stood out as a long, thin line of light against the gloomy mountains that clustered around on four sides.

Gazing reverently at this line, it was if they were looking up at hope itself, and not a single one of them had the thought that they might die in this place. To get here they had walked for over two weeks without stopping to rest. Passing through the great desert, they had left behind a trail of those too weak to carry on, the sun-crazed. The beast had taken the choicest morsels, leaving those who remained at the point of exhaustion. Starving, they were little better than walking corpses.

Two weeks ago, their vessel had crashed deep in the desert, killing half of the passengers on impact. The pilot was fortunate enough to have been killed on the spot, smashed into a shapeless meaty pulp. Fortunate, because had he lived, he would have most likely been subjected to unspeakable cruelties by the indignant survivors of the crash during the hopeless days that followed.

After climbing free of the bloody carnage of the wreckage, it was a long while before they had set aside the shock and hysteria of falling some twenty thousand feet from the sky like a lead weight. After grieving for the dead, and praising God's benevolence for sparing their lives, almost as one the survivors raised up their heads to take in the boundless expanse of desert that surrounded them. Stones of varying sizes lay on the ground as far as the eye could see, like skulls embedded in the glistening sand, reflecting back the brilliance of the three suns.

The survivors did not speak. Just because God had seen fit to send one half their number straight to His heavenly kingdom did not necessarily mean he planned to let the other half live. The majority of the vessel's crew had been killed in the crash, leaving the passengers to fend for themselves. A certain captain from a special forces unit soon emerged as natural leader. After inspecting the wreckage, the captain informed them that the communicator was finished, so there was no way for them to call for help and also no way to know their exact position. At best, they could hope for a rescue mission to arrive in three months, not counting the time it would take the rescue team to search the barren wasteland of this singularly enormous planet.

"Please search the wreckage for things that may be of use to us and share them with the group. If we are to be rescued, then we must band together in this time calamity," the captain said. It comforted them all a little to look up at his ruggedly unyielding gray eyes, his muscular neck, his sturdy and well-defined chest.

The survivors began to enthusiastically search the vessel, even exploring the severely damaged fore cabin from which not a single man had escaped alive. Coming across that room, which looked like nothing less than a strawberry slurry spattered blender, the searchers found themselves afflicted with constant nightmares, vomiting even while dreaming.

Finding water was not a problem, as the twisted, gurgling pipes of the vessel were still leaking coolant. Despite tasting of motor oil, it was not poisonous. They were also able to find a small amount of food—local delicacies bought by tourists on the various planets they had visited. Still, despite the profusion of flavors, and no matter how tasty these snacks were, it was apparent that it would be impossible to sustain sixty people for three months on these meager rations alone. This was especially true since many of the survivors were so fat that it was all but guaranteed that they were gluttonous gourmands.

Eventually they found a battered and ancient-looking map in the bag of a pilgrim who had been killed in the crash. The captain spent half a day studying the map with a compass and slide rule, together with three others: a surviving member of the boiler room crew, a chemistry professor who was on vacation, and the ship's priest. They announced that they would be leading the group to a temporary shelter, the monastery of an infamous ascetic and a reclusive sect. This was the only sign of human life that was marked on the map.

It was not until after ten days of arduous walking that they finally caught sight of the monastery's lone spire. Far in the distance, it gleamed like gold in the light of the setting suns.

In the dying light they began to run, setting off a dust storm which stuck to their calves. From withered lungs emerged hot, sticky breath, but not a single person spoke, their bodies erect, their heads bent, casting aside unnecessary bags, empty canteens, kicking off boots that had already come unstitched, running barefoot in the scalding sand.

They knew that a ferocious beast was following close behind. Every day, once the sun had set, it had appeared like clockwork to choose its victim from this band of ragged and weary travelers. In less than two weeks they had lost fourteen of their number, finding themselves helpless before its onslaught.

Equally helpless to predict who among their number the beast would take next, the only obvious conclusion that they could come to was that the odds of being chosen were the greatest for those who straggled the furthest behind. Only steps away from salvation, none among them was willing to take that unfortunate role. Racing against one another as they fled, then ran silently, their heads down, each of them spurred on by the fear of their neighbor. Even the young priest was no exception, despite the deep feeling of shame he felt, thinking of Darwin's cruel law of survival as he ran. Since the law had first appeared, it had caused man and religion alike to suffer the greatest of humiliations, he thought to himself. Now, though, we must run, because we must keep up if we are to survive.

When they had first set off, they had managed to stay organized. Some were responsible for wayfinding, others for taking care of the women, the children, the infirm, while still others took on the night watch. Despite finding themselves in dire peril, the entire party maintained an air of elegant refinement throughout, modestly deferring to one another, acting as if their arduous march was nothing more than a holiday hiking adventure with a bunch of backpack-wearing city slickers. This lasted until the beast appeared, and in the blink of an eye, the weak bonds of civilized society suddenly snapped, order broke down, and they reverted to their most basic of instincts.

That evening the young priest saw the boiler tender stomp two tents flat, and smack a fat woman to the ground; the chemistry professor, meanwhile, jumped into the fire, almost burning himself to a crisp; while somewhere in distance, the captain managed to fire two rounds at the beast, before it disappeared into the night; and the people hid all around, their holiday hike having been transformed into a disorderly and chaotic flight for their lives.

Truly, the beast was a terrible horror, a man-eating terror of a sorts rarely seen in this nebula. Devilishly fast, with hooked talons like glittering daggers, its trifurcated tail was like a mace or a flail, coming to three points. Even worse than its appearance, though, was the beast's seemingly inborn hatred for mankind. Once it began an attack, there was no room for mercy—the beast would tear and chew until there was nothing left.

The only bright spot in all of this was that the beast knew well enough to choose the best portions. Taking first the most overweight of the group, who also happened to eat the most food and walk the slowest, the beast left behind the strongest and youngest of them, with sturdy bodies and steadfast wills. No longer requiring others to urge them on, the speed of the group increased greatly.

The captain ran in the middle of pack. Holding his laser gun tightly, his neck was ramrod straight, his breath slow, and his pace neither hurried nor leisurely—to separate from the group was dangerous. The captain was the first to notice a new sound emerging from the cacophony of footsteps, that of thickly padded feet drumming against the sand. An animal smell, warm and rank, like urine, filled the air. Turning, he saw the glistening fur of the beast, silhouetted against an alien moon, following their little group silently. The squashed face of the beast was covered in matted fur, which moved slightly in the wind, and a single eye, slating fiercely and nearly closed, silently assessed each member of the group in turn. Having arrived once again, the beast was methodically planning its attack, an attack they were helpless to resist. They felt as if they were its subjects and the beast their lord, looking down upon them with disgust, finding themselves shamed by its disregard for them. *Fuck,* the captain thought bitterly as he clutched his useless laser gun. *Sooner or later he's gonna get us.*

Finally they arrived at the tower, which was located in a narrow valley running up into the mountains. In the thick woods which filled the valley, a cluster of low huts were built around a public square. In the middle of the square there was a fountain with a pagan goddess sitting on a lotus blossom throne. A mysterious smile of deep compassion and endless sorrow cut across her broad, moon-like face. Some of the men jumped into the fountain, while others fell to the ground and wept like children. Others were frozen in place, neither crying nor laughing.

Not a single hut was lit from the inside, and no smoke issued forth from their chimneys. No one emerged to welcome them, for the entire village was silent, without a soul around. They soon realized that this place was abandoned, and their hopes were dashed like a great soap bubble that had floated up too high in the sky. Sobbing, they spent the night huddled together in a confused mass.

When the dawn broke, three suns of differing colors rose into the sky, first the one the color of yellow-brown earth, filling the pass with brilliant golden light. Sometime later, the blue sun rose into the sky, the largest of the three, and finally, the cold carmine sun. They soon discovered that in the chaos of the previous night, another two of their number had disappeared: Seoni and Ami, a Lunarian couple. Thinking back on their freckled faces, the priest sighed to himself.

They drew water from the still flowing fountain. The short rest after their long trek had improved the spirits of the group, and they soon began to cautiously explore their surroundings. The forest was not large, nor was it especially dense, being made up entirely of trees indigenous to this planet: to their left, spiraling bracken fern trees formed an unbroken chain, their tops reaching up into the heavens. Needle-trees which split three ways from their roots swayed in the breeze, giving off a quiet shushing sound. In the face of this tranquil, garden-like scene, the remaining members of the group stood clumped in pairs, unwilling to explore the woods any further.

When it was almost noon, the captain gathered together the other three leaders of their group: the chemistry professor, the boiler tender, and the priest. He led them into a low basement made of rough sandstone blocks. Probably once a wine cellar, the room was filled with a large number of empty bottles that the former occupants had left behind. The once swarthy and robust captain sat squatting on the unstable floor of broken bottles, a blanket draped over his shoulders. His thickly stubbled face was cut with deep wrinkles, appearing withered and pale. He looked for all the world like a wilted vegetable that had been sucked dry of all its water. "We've already run out of food," he said, revealing the terrible news to the others. "We don't have one bit left. I searched the entire monastery this morning. Even though it's obvious this place has been abandoned, just to make sure I went through each hut in the hope of finding some hidden food stores—but there's nothing here. Nothing."

The gathered leaders were all silent for a time. Their rescuers wouldn't be here for another two and half months. The only choice, then, was to starve to death. In comparison to this threat, the beast was only a minor annoyance.

"If we could face the beast, then we would have faced the beast," the captain said. "The laser guns are useless against it—I shot it right in the face, and it just shook its shoulders, as if I had attacked it with a water pistol." As he was talking, he rubbed his nose in frustration. "But we can keep him out. I've surveyed the area. We are surrounded by high cliffs on all four sides. There is only one way in and one way out of valley—we could build a fence there. There are already plenty of tools in the village."

"You're right, our laser guns *are* useless," the chemistry professor said wearily. Due to his slender build, his large, protruding ears were quite eye-catching. "I happened to read a short introduction for tourists who visit this planet. The planet is known for the astonishing number of crystals that have formed in the mica. Due to the principle of resonance, the planet is filled with ultrasonic noise. The creatures here have evolved an innate ability to make use of and control the vibration of other objects. You've seen the fur on the cat-beast's head, right? It can use that fur to sense vibrations—and really, when you get right down to it, a laser is just a kind of vibration. Your attack probably made the beast uncomfortable, but there's no way that it could have hurt it."

"Vibrations? Are you saying that it really is impossible for us to beat it with guns? Well then, if it charges in here, and we can only fight the thing off with our fists," the captain continued more fiercely now, "if that's the case then, fine, so be it, let's use our fists!"

"There's a helluva lotta trees here," the boiler tender said. "Maybe we can eat them?" Flat faced and stocky, a single canine emerging from his lips was the sole feature which broke the monotony of his dead fish mien. "Back in the village I'm from you'd hear stories of folks eating tree bark when they ran out of food."

"No," the professor said, dejectedly, as if announcing his own death sentence. "Like most space travelers, we face an intractable problem. The helix-type of the DNA of the alien plants is fundamentally different from the structure our own. Even if they aren't poisonous, if we were to eat them then then our bodies would have no way of breaking them down into proteins."

"Well, our meat seems to be just fine for their wild beasts," the captain said darkly. Turning to the priest, he said, "How about this, priest, we'll put you in charge of looking for food. From the looks of things, it seems like the monks only meant to be gone for a short while. It just isn't possible to imagine that they didn't leave behind at least *some* food." He twisted his mouth, and repeated himself, "It just isn't possible. Probably you religious types have a different way of looking at things, right? You all have faith in God, no?"

The priest protested that that was a different kind of faith.

In reply, the captain said, "I think that's enough talking for now, priest."

The reclusive sect belonged to an ancient religion that was on the verge of dying out. Their teachings claimed that if one set aside all desire, then one could become a Bodhisattva, flying up to heaven right on the spot. A monastic order from the Far East had founded the religion eons ago, and it is said that they were capable of performing any number of miracles. For some reason, though, their spread had been limited to a few remote planets in the nebula. According to the introduction included on the battered map, this was a holy place for the members of the reclusive sect.

Having accepted his assignment to find food, the priest followed the valley up to its mouth. As the captain had said, aside from the jagged gap where they had entered, the valley was surrounded on four sides by steep cliffs. Water poured forth from narrow ravines, revealing a red sedimentary layer deep in the rocks. Standing miniscule in the middle of the valley, the priest thought to himself that these enormous, coldly silent walls of stone were like the curtains of heaven, leaving only a neat circle of sky above, as if they found themselves in the bottom of a well.

Just when the priest was trying to decide which direction to head in search of food, he saw the boiler tender running out of the woods with a group of people who had been sent there to cut timber.

This was the first time they had seen the bubble fish. Round and bulging, they refracted the light into prisms of color, swishing their tails in the air to move up and down. Swimming into the wind, they looked like frail soap bubbles, or colorful balloons for children. Delicate and beautiful, and seemingly harmless, they were little more than attractive house pets. Something, however, soon startled them away.

The transparent stomachs of the bubble fish vibrated to invisible frequencies, using the vibrations to absorb the energy of the suns. They were constantly taking in lighter or heavier air to maintain their altitude. Unyieldingly self-composed, their enormous eyes looked down upon the mess of hurried and shameless people below, and with a flick of their tails, the bubble fish moved even higher up into the sky until they were out of sight.

The captain had also gone out to explore. Along with several other young men, he appeared in camp dragging Seoni's corpse. While running away the previous night, the Lunarian had broken his neck after falling into a ravine. In addition to Seoni, they managed to find a dried out wagon track that meandered off to parts unknown. The traces of the road had almost disappeared, indicating that it had been a long time since anyone had come this way. It really did seem that this monastery had long since been abandoned.

After the priest said a prayer for the dead man, they buried him in the woods. The bracken ferns spiraled around and around, filling the sky above them. The captain and the boiler tender stood holding their shovels, stationed like two broken stone obelisks on either side of the loose pile of red-brown soil beside the enormous grave.

They spent the rest of the day felling trees and building a fence. After shaping the tops of the heavy timber into sharp points, they planted them deep into the ground; they used the needle-trees to fashion a barbed net to stuff between the gaps; and behind every possible weak point in the fence they piled heavy stones to make it fast. Ignoring their hunger, they put their shoulders into the work until finally the grand project was complete, giving them what would ultimately prove to be a misplaced sense of security.

Meanwhile, the priest searched the valley for foodstuffs with the utmost of care, but all that he managed to come up with were a few pieces of moldy bread and a handful of raisins, having found several rows of dried-up grapevines behind the wine cellar. Most likely, the monks had brewed their own wine. Finding neither paper, nor books, nor diaries, the priest thought back to what he had read of the reclusive sect. They were fond of manual labor and meditation, he recalled, but none of the books he had read mentioned what they ate.

Hunger had begun to gnaw at the priest, and his vision was already starting to blur. Making another circuit of the tower, the nagging question entered his mind a second time: what did they eat?

The tower itself was the only place in the valley that the priest had not yet searched. It was tall, at least a hundred meters high, with maybe six hundred steps. Given his weakened state it would be an exhausting job to climb all the way to the top.

Nevertheless, he began to climb. The stairs were on the inside of the tower, winding clockwise, one loop after another, forming an unbroken chain of stone steps seemingly without end. The tower seemed to grow ever higher as he climbed, as if made from the same stock as the bracken fern trees which grew quietly in the sunshine outside, seeking to attain heights ever higher. Despite his best efforts, the priest was forced to sit and rest from time to time. Sitting, he found himself fascinated with the mural painted on the white inner wall of the tower. Terrible scenes were depicted in the painting, most likely of their pagan hell; aside from these images were drawings of knights in armor: one holding a sword, another some sort of musical instrument, finally the last holding some species of large rodent. There were dancing fairy maidens, trees laden with fruit, water lilies, and graceful deer; and beneath them all was the image of sleeping man. Probably it was meant to indicate that the world in all of its splendor was nothing more than a dream in the mind of the Buddha. *Did not the ancient peoples of India believe that the physical world was in fact made up of dreams?*

Having spent a great deal of time to get there, when he reached the top of the tower the priest was surprised to discover an empty room. Large white stones surrounded a strange circular cavity which resembled a hothouse, or a womb. On the ground inside the stone womb the monks of the reclusive sect had left shallow depressions, accumulated from many years of sitting in this place. Three narrow openings were cut in the curved wall of the round room, serving as windows. Between the three windows hung six paintings, one of which immediately drew his attention: a group of emaciated men, with distended stomachs like drums, their eyes brilliant with hunger. Arms outstretched, they looked like spiders, taking, grabbing, begging.

The tower of hunger. The four words sprang unbidden to the priest's mind, filling him with dread. In a panic, he fled from the room.

In the night the beast came again, breathing heavily outside the fence and spraying the air with that stench particular to carnivores, its eyes shining like two lanterns. The sound of the beast attacking the fence with terrible force echoed from the mouth of the valley throughout the night. So intense was the beast's attack that the stones of the ramparts danced and the wooden posts wavered menacingly. The beast's inability to break through the fence that night, however, let the hungry souls inside the valley finally breathe a sigh of relief.

Now, the only task left for them to work on with a common purpose was the maintenance of the fence. The rest of their time was spent dispersed throughout the valley, madly searching high and low, going through every hut and every patch of bare land for something, anything to eat. The grapevine was the first thing to be eaten, and then all of their leather goods: leather shoes, leather belts, leather canteens. It was fortunate that this accursed planet was without worms or rats, otherwise they too would have been wiped out.

The captain never told the priest if he should stop looking for food, and so he continued to drag his tired body up and down the valley. Once, in a dimly lit room, he came across the chemistry professor who was stuffing something wrapped in dried grass and sticks into the lining of his jacket. When he saw the priest his face turned red from embarrassment.

The professor was a pale man, tall and thin, with a high nose and big eyes like two bright blue blisters, making him look as if he was always afraid of something. He blinked his eyes and handed two tubers to the priest good naturedly, saying that in China people used them for medicine. "Should be . . . good for . . . my malaria," he said haltingly.

After going through the featureless huts one by one, the priest became convinced that the secret of the reclusive sect lay inside the tower. Although he was even weaker than before, the priest resolved to climb the tower a second time to study the murals and the empty meditation room. He discovered that the materials used to build the tower were not the local sandstone, but instead that the tower had been constructed of white mica, quarried from some distance away. After careful inspection he concluded that it was different from the mica of Earth, with countless tiny grains of crystals flashing from within the rock, as numerous as grains of sand in the great Ganges River.

The three windows of the meditation room were extremely narrow, just large enough to allow a man to pass through. They led to a small viewing platform which encircled the tower, from which one could see the wide and empty expanse of the desert beyond the valley. In the desert, the priest could see the wind playing freely, kicking up a sandstorm. Boundless and as empty as ever, the desert was silent, under a sky of unknowable heights. The sky, too, was broad and empty, azure blue. The three suns slipped through the sky giving off prisms of light. This forgotten corner of the universe was where they were to spend the rest of their days. For all intents and purposes though, he thought, *they* were the ones who had been forgotten.

The captain also climbed the tower once to survey it, but he found nothing of interest in the empty meditation room. Now he was busy leading the others in the upkeep of the fence, where it seemed as if a sort of war had erupted between the men and the beast. At night it would attack and by day they would reinforce the structure. Eventually, a night crew was necessary to keep the wall maintained, as the beast's attacks became ever more frenzied. Having bitten the weaker tree trunks in two and torn up the needle-tree net, it began to use its body to batter the fence, shaking the structure and causing those stationed on top to tremble with fear and forget the burning hunger in their stomachs.

The boiler tender was especially fond of this battle, having painted his face like an Indian brave and taking up a sharpened pole which he shoved through the chinks in the wall, stabbing wildly at the beast. Singing and dancing, his wild antics motivated the group. He really was quite brave. The others shouted along with him, weaving strong nets of pliable branches to fill the gaps, and backfilling the fence with heavy stones. Other gaps were filled using dirt, and the vines of an unknown alien plant were pressed into service to braid the wooden posts together, creating a firm and immovable barrier.

But they still hadn't found any food. Others had begun to climb the tower to take a look for themselves, although they were not many. To ascend a hundred meter tower for a starving man robbed of his strength was, after all, a terrible challenge. The professor was one of the weak ones, half dead from hunger, having passed out sixteen times on the way to the monastery, and having been forced to treat himself twice for malaria. Upon arriving at the top of the tower, the professor squinted his eyes tightly, and knowingly scanned the empty stone room. He even explored the viewing platform outside, but was powerless to mask the expression of disappointment on his face. He explained to the priest that it wasn't that he didn't believe the priest's account of the empty tower, but simply that he wanted to exorcise something of the gnawing sense of responsibility he bore for their plight.

After the professor descended from the tower, few others came to disturb the priest's work. The priest was becoming more and more intrigued by the cavity in the middle of the chamber. He had read that the high priest of the reclusive sect had spent more than one thousand years on this very seat. Perhaps someone had become a Buddha and ascended to the heavens here. Out of boredom, he sat on the seat and attempted the famed meditation techniques of the reclusive sect. Due, most likely, to the perfect roundness of everything in the room, the priest felt immediately at ease and quickly slipped into a dream-like state, very nearly falling asleep. In his dream he heard the breathing of the beast, and saw his demonic yellow eyes, his claws coming within inches of the priest's throat.

When he came to, the priest's head was pounding and his mouth felt parched. It was probably due to his own imagination, but it seemed as if the mediation room was filled with the stench of the beast. Dizzy, he walked to the base of the tower where he was told that the previous evening the beast had finally broken in, killing three. Of them, they had managed to wrest the corpse of Ma Xiu from the beast's grasp. Eighteen years old, Ma Xiu's struggle to free himself from the maw of the beast had been as futile as a moth beating its wings. Fortunately though, the gap in the fence was small enough that the beast hadn't had enough time to pull the corpse through to the other side before the captain could spring into action and take hold of Ma Xiu's leg. Meanwhile, other members of the group fired on the beast from the top of the fence, stabbing it in the mouth and forehead with sharpened branches. Ma Xiu died not long thereafter–in the course of trying to pull him free they had accidentally broken his neck.

When the suns rose the next morning, the beast took what remained of his plunder back with him. According to the professor, the sun was an enormous ultrasonic amplifier which interfered with the beast's sense organs.

Ma Xiu's funeral was relatively simple. Lying on the ground, his ragged clothing revealed his emaciated hips and bony chest. One arm had been bitten off by the beast. Looking like a roughhewn tree stump, the mangled flesh emerged from the sharp wound, his broken skin and muscle lying exposed on the earth. Looking upon that pale, tender white flesh, the eyes of the assembled men seemed to shine with a green light. As the priest was saying a prayer, a dark and unspeakable current passed through his unconscious mind. The men began to whisper among each other, perhaps taking a secret vote, and in the end they decided not to bury him. The captain just nodded, and the priest simply shut his eyes, not saying a word.

That day, they built a fire, and set a large pot above it. The fragrant aroma wafted in all directions from the square. Using the axes and saws they divided up the boy's body. With a steady hand, the captain cut the flesh straight and true. The boy's chest was split open like a melon. Beneath his withered flesh was a thin layer of yellow fat, speckled with red. After cutting through the cartilage between the ribs, the boy's viscera slid out onto the ground like a pile of twisting red snakes. His organs and head were then placed into the pot to make a stew, while his three limbs and muscles were dried over the fire to be rationed for later.

Lining up to be served, they brought vessels of all kinds: glass bottles with tops knocked off, hats, and plastic bags. Those who had eaten their leather shoes felt a certain amount of regret when the fragrant odors left their mouths filled with bitter bile.

Using a large ladle, the boiler tender stood with his pants held up by a grass cord, doing his best to carefully dole out an equal share to each man. This simple kind of equality was just about all his mind could handle at this point, and he ignored all other thoughts. One always ends up envying practical people like this, because they always seem to find a way to stay happy until the bitter end.

Some were so excited that they began to vomit bile, gripping their plastic bags tightly. Despite the lack of salt or garlic, this bland, albeit sumptuous lunch was unthinkably extravagant. Although it is impossible to say for sure, but perhaps some of them said a silent prayer to the Lord, the one that thanks Him for giving us food to eat.

That afternoon, they went to the fence with renewed enthusiasm. Given food, their energy was restored one-hundred fold, and they were filled with confidence.

The priest however, had not taken part. Hunger gnawed at his organs like spider chewing on a thread, but he did not take his share of the meat.

Truth be told, the captain was actually rather fond of the young priest. Handsome and charismatic, the priest had a sensitive face, white as sandstone and just as weak. The first time he had seen him, the captain had been convinced that he had seen the man somewhere before. In some distant place, obscured by the smoke and dust of time, he had already met a wan and slender young man just like the priest, who had been willing to sacrifice his own life to save others. He had met many young men like this, actually, while in the army, or in other places, and to the last he saw them swallowed up in the conflagrations of war.

"How could the Lord blame us for wanting to survive?" the captain pleaded.

"I understand, of course I understand," said the priest, nodding his head. The captain had brought him some smoke-cured meat. The meat looked clean, and was cut into neat slices, thick with a dark aroma. They really had done an excellent job with the smoking.

"The way you're acting, you're making everybody uncomfortable, you know. They think that you're judging them," the captain urged him good naturedly, "Just take the meat, okay?"

" . . . I understand," the priest replied, after obvious hesitation. In the end, however, he refused to take his share, and the captain sat, helpless, staring at the priest for a long while.

The priest continued to climb his tower, the tower that filled men with boundless desire. Even now he didn't know what he hoped to find there, but strangely, he didn't feel hungry. In the darkness the white stones gave off a gentle glow, their tiny crystals vibrating weakly. Was it possible that meditation had helped the members of the reclusive sect engage in fasting? Sitting in one of the shallow depressions, he traced the characters on the wall with his finger. The ancient pictures were like hieroglyphics which one could only try to understand.

For a fleeting moment a strange and terrible feeling of prescience suddenly overtook him. Although he did his best to take hold of the impression it left on him, the better to predict what was yet to come, it quickly passed. The bubble fish floated in the sky, their skin stretched taut, a transparent membrane like a bubble, now vermillion, now orange, now the blue of a clear lake, now flashing gold.

Despite strict rationing, the food was quickly devoured by the hungry men. Something was different from before, however, about the emaciated stick-and-bones men who patrolled the valley. Their cheekbones seemed higher somehow, and the hollows of their faces deeper. Their eyes meanwhile swept the ground, unwilling to meet the gaze of the others, afraid of what they might find there.

They found themselves almost wishing for the beast to attack. But the fence held strong, and the beast could only pace outside, breathing heavily. Like them, it had gone without food for several days now, and hunger revealed the lines of its ribcage through its withered fur. Studying the men behind the fence with bloodshot eyes, it was powerless. Turning suddenly, it disappeared. Most likely it was retreating and abandoning these men who were no less hungry than it was. The men behind the fence felt an indescribable sense of disappointment.

Two days later, the food had once again reached a critical point. The stronger members of the group led by example, stealing the bones of the dead boy, and breaking them open to devour the marrow inside. Even so, it wasn't nearly enough food to save them.

The next morning the captain led a group to rebury Seoni. The previous night, someone had dug up his grave, hoping to pillage the corpse. His body, however, had long since begun to decay in the fierce heat, leaving behind a pile of hard to swallow rotten flesh. By daybreak, the fetid smell of his exhumed corpse had filled the valley. Lying on the red dirt of the grave, his eyes bulged like two big blue blisters, and dark splotches of rot sprouted there. His teeth emerged in a grimace, and owing to the contraction of the skin it looked as if he was smiling, with his eyebrows raised high in delight. Few among them were willing to criticize the atrocious act. Instead they simply dug a deeper pit and buried him a second time. The worst thing about it to the men who watched was seeing so many calories, amino acids, and protein rot and go to waste.

The others were not idle, however, having decided to try and eat the bracken fern trees. They cut one down and removed the spines from the bark, cutting them into fine slivers which they boiled over the fire. The stench produced was even worse than that of Seoni's rotten corpse. Others, ignoring the warnings of the chemistry professor, attacked the bubble fish. When two diamond miners from Arcturus managed to spear one, its transparent stomach exploded, spraying ammonia gas into their eyes, blinding them. Their faces ruined, they lay by the fountain, moaning throughout the night.

The seemingly endless stairs of the tower left the priest feeling as if he was climbing a gigantic structure that ascended to heaven itself. *God is eternal, all powerful, all knowing, and his compassion is freely given to all beings in existence,* the priest thought. *How could it be that an all powerful being like God, with His boundless wisdom, could have become afraid when people of times past tried to build the tower of Babel? Where, after all, is heaven? Is it up? In this ever expanding universe of ours, is it still up? With every scientific advancement, at first it has always seemed as if religion was on the verge of being overthrown. Eventually, though, people always seem to find a way to compromise. Does this mean that science will never be truly able to save humanity?*

Only now, none of these questions were as important as the question of where they might go next to find food.

The priest reflected back on his memories of receiving communion for the first time, during mass. *The bread and wine symbolized the flesh and blood of Jesus Christ. By eating and drinking Him, then we allowed Him to be one with us.* His belt was old and tough, impossible to chew, but he managed to cut it into smaller pieces, which he swallowed one by one after soaking them in his saliva. *Kronos ate his children, the cyclops roasted the companions of Odysseus, Zhang Xun cut up his concubine and fed her to his soldiers during the siege of Suiyang, and Count Ugolino ate his own flesh and blood in a high tower—in history, people have long since eaten one another, and even today they are still eating one another.* Schools of bubble fish floated outside the tower watching him, as if the sky outside the narrow window was an enormous fish tank.

The stench lingered in the valley.

After the two miners died the would-be hunters became prey for the others. This was the banquet that the men of the valley had been waiting for. A great fire was lit, and the water in the pot was brought to a frothy boil. Drawing strength from the self-sacrificing spirit of the two minors, they managed to survive for another week, but rescue seemed to be just as distant as before. Miraculously, the priest managed to survive, finding the tubers that the professor had given him to have boundless applications, with a single slice providing him sufficient calories to last a great while. The professor himself had become thin and emaciated, his eyes bloodshot. A slight breeze was enough to bring him to the ground, but his spirits remained strong, and his complexion unusually ruddy. Drinking water non-stop, a row of blisters had sprouted on his cracked lips. This was most likely a side effect of the treatments he had given himself for malaria.

It had been a long time since anyone had worked on the fence. It was not until the call of the beast was heard within the valley that they became aware that it had dug a small hole in the barrier. This time though, instead of being afraid, they struck back at the beast under the leadership of the captain, the flames of victory leaving them feverish. Using shovels, sticks, knives, even their fingernails and teeth, they managed to snatch a corpse from the mouth of the beast, which had been made weak from hunger.

When the captain managed to use a knife to chop a leg free from mouth of the beast he felt like he was finally in control of the situation again. In the past he had had times of hesitation, he had had times of confusion, even fear. His training had taught him to feel ashamed of such emotions—but everything was better now. Now that he knew the path forward, he was no longer worried about anything, because he knew that he would survive to be rescued. Happiness clouded his brain, and as he watched the beast scurry through the hole in the fence, he held the hairy leg of the chemistry professor in one hand, laughing.

He soon realized that the priest was standing nearby, watching him, with his skull-like face twisted up in pain. The captain immediately straightened up and stopped laughing. Anger toward the priest bubbled up, unbidden. *Fuck, what right does he have to look at me like that? When survival is on the line, what's the point of having convictions? Believer or non-believer, when disaster strikes it doesn't make a difference either way.* The captain began to hack away at the professor's leg, methodically chopping and slicing, wastefully letting bits of meat fall to the ground. Without checking with the others, he could already tell that they all found the priest's behavior infuriating.

Even after rinsing the remains of the professor in the fountain, the smell of herbal medicine lingered on his corpse and after a long time they gave up trying. The smell had permeated all the way down into the muscle and bone, making him taste especially delicious. The slender, half-mauled corpse of the professor barely lasted them a single night before every last bit was eaten up. They'd barely had a chance to taste him, but now they were hungry again, and needed more food.

• • •

The priest sat cross-legged in the cavity. His awareness spread outwards, encompassing the shining white crystals which surrounded him, countless as grains of sand in the mighty Ganges. Vibrating, resonating, the sound was as vast as it was miniscule, like the sound of silkworms chewing mulberry, or rain falling on the broad leaves of the plantain. A stream of information as expansive as the universe flowed through the room, passing through the arch of the hothouse-like structure and directly into his brain. Images from his childhood flashed in his mind, and then more images, of the distant past, of things he had never experienced. *What is the origin of desire? Vibrations, vibrations, like wing-beat of a butterfly. The world is an illusion,* a white haired man said to him. *I dreamed of a butterfly, but only the butterfly is real.*

Upon opening his eyes, the priest was greeted with the sight of a butterfly, its wings patterned in black and red. The butterfly was of a sort found only on Earth. As it passed through one of the narrow windows, the early morning light caught the gold in its wings, sending arcs of light off into void.

Could it be that I'm hallucinating? In a flash, the realization of what had just happened coursed throughout his body and he became extremely frightened. Most likely this was a dream within a dream, an illusion within an illusion. He simply imagined that he was hallucinating. The fear, however, was fleeting. *What did it matter if the world was an illusion? An illusion of an illusion was nothing more than an illusion.* Looking up at the paintings on the wall, he realized he could suddenly read them as if they were text:

The Buddha said to his disciple Subhūti: All that has form is an illusion.

If this was true, then things with form could also emerge from illusion. *Dear god, is it really possible?* The priest closed his eyes. *Could the world really like be like the ancient story of the "golden millet dream?" Are we all just poor innkeepers dreaming of becoming of becoming men of wealth and power?* He began to imagine a freshly baked bun, yellow and piping hot. A piercing pain racked his brain as his mind resonated with the crystals around him. Upon opening his eyes, the priest discovered that a bun really had appeared, complete with toasted sesame seeds on top, and a curlicue of steam spiraling above it.

Tears sprang forth from his withered eye sockets, falling one at a time. The imagined bun was edible and filling. *I found food! This is the secret of the reclusive sect. In the past I thought that forsaking desire was the path to eliminating desire. I was wrong, though. Is there anything that better demonstrates the suffering caused by desire better than having all of one's desire fulfilled?*

He left the bun on the ground to let it cool. Feeling as if his head was full of buzzing stars, he wondered if this was a miracle or science, to have a planet filled with vibrations. *As Plato once asked, what is thought and what is matter? I should have realized sooner that thought is a kind of vibration, the synaptic spark which passes between neurons. The unique structure and materials of this tower, even the planet itself, serve to amplify the power of thought. With only faith and imagination, we can create a whole new world for ourselves.*

Ignoring an intense headache, the priest constructed a communicator in his mind. As the image became more clear, it emerged as if from the mist, and suddenly landed on the floor of the room with a sharp sound, a real, fresh sound, sending out a blue light which pierced his brain like a knife. With feverish hands he stroked the device before deciding to go down to find the others, who knew better than he how to use it. Even better, now they could use meditation and faith to get food. He stood up, staggering, and almost fell back down. His prolonged meditation had left him impossibly weak.

The communicator was too heavy. There was simply no way for him to carry the eighty-pound device down some six-hundred steps. He crawled to the steps and began to slowly make his way down the winding stairwell.

A soft breeze wafted through the air. The others stood around the pot in the square. The fire blazed and the water was already boiling hot, but they hadn't even decided who was going to die yet. The priest rushed forward to tell the captain that he had completed his task. *Food! I found food! All we need to have is faith, and we will have salvation. It was so simple, hallelujah!*

They others formed a semi-circle around the priest, like a choir in church. They looked at him kindly. Far above them in the sky, He who had sacrificed himself observed the scene with compassion. The captain stood in middle of the group. From the corner of his eye, the priest saw the boiler tender drawing close, carrying an iron mace fashioned from a shovel. Standing stiffly erect, the priest became aware that he was on trial. Taking advantage of his last chance, he raised his hand and pointed upwards, beginning to say in a raw voice, "I've discovered . . ."

The words were cut short by a heavy blow to the back of his head. His last conscious impressions were the sound of boiling water, the white teeth of the men, the fish swimming through the air, and the beast roaring in the distance, as if beckoning him with a bugle call.

Above it all, the high hunger tower pierced the sky.

Originally published in Chinese in *Science Fiction World,* June 2003.

The Algebra of Events
ELIZABETH BOURNE

38957613|2934702|46|720

The alarms vibrated while I was in the comfort room sharing essence with M'm'shamir. We immediately untethered so I could couple into my duty station. The unthinkable had occurred. In the myriad calculations of probable choices guiding us to colony Whole/Three/Green the sym encountered the chance of failure and slotted it.

Everyone knows that failure is a possibility, just as everyone knows that antawa are accident-prone, and yet the antawas' ease of use has made them ubiquitous. The risk is worth the convenience. Statistically it is so unlikely as to be *nearly* impossible for a probability engine to miscalculate. And yet, what is failure but one chance among many, driven by viable choices? The mathematics are beyond me, but I smell that it is so.

Panic tinged the conversation spray in the room containing the probability fields. The sym had been cut from the calculating engine and isolated. There was no question of reconnecting it. The calculation had damaged it beyond repair, and besides, the isolation had been done so quickly the sym's delicate tissues were discolored with multiple hematomas. I'm no jampiri so I can't say for sure, but it didn't smell to me like the sym would survive. All we could hope for now was that the mechanicals worked and that perhaps, the sym had calculated the chance of finding a survivable planet in reachable distance.

I will make these notations as long as I can.

38957613|2934702|46|724

Holy be the Primes, there is a planetary body within reach. The silq'uy has ordered us into freeze for the duration. It is better than remaining aware, and yet I emit fear, as do all who experienced the probability fail. This is not a planet we would pick for a colony. It is too variable, too extreme with sections of hot and cold, dry and wet. There are too many orbiting bodies. The local star is the wrong color. And the smells will be strange. We will need adaptive devices if we are to make any sense of this planet.

But the atmosphere is breathable, and as long as the bacteria farms remain in good health we should be able to survive, at least for a time. My first task on landing will be to take some of our native bacteria and begin breeding it for resistance and adaptation with whatever the alien equivalent is. Though now, I suppose we are the aliens. That is a very odd thought to smell.

M'm'shamir exudes terror, and asks if lehr could stay in my location. My friends would say this is what comes of sharing with passengers, but M'm'shamir smells enticing in a way no being has for many rota. Even though there is no time for sharing, my vestigial gill nodes flutter when M'm'shamir is close. I welcomed lehr to take comfort in my space, though we will have to part at the freeze. Colonist passengers are maintained in separate pod banks.

The silq'uy agrees a record is important, and has added making notations to my official function. My odor is increased with this honor, though a part of me now worries my emissions will be inadequate. The walls are pulsing. It is time for us to become solid. The ship's mathematician will lead us in a conjugation of the perfect irrational to relax us into the proper state for freeze. I almost look forward to it.

38957613|2934702|46|732

The mechanicals failed to adequately correct for this world's gravitational pull and our landing went badly. I will never scent M'm'shamir again. We lost 30.783% of our colonists as the ship crashed, 10.56% of our crew. The probability engine cracked and raw probability calculations are even now seeping into this world.

Could it be any worse?

27.245% of my being has gone solid with grief, and there are others even more solid. The colonists are useless, seized up as they are in fear. Even the silq'uy is 12.794% solid, a sign that our situation is dire.

But lehr is urging us to fluid activity for the good of the survivors and we are all moving as best we can to repair what has been broken. The bacteria farms, holy be the Primes, are functioning well, and I have suited up already to collect native samples for use. We haven't yet developed appropriate adaptives for this world, so all I can say is that it smells chaotic and feculent. There is no sense to be found in it, but then I am no translator.

A small group of natives approached—solids! At least on the exterior. The interior was comfortingly liquid, which the ship's jampiri claims proves the theory that intelligent life can only exist in a fluid state. After dissecting one of the creatures lehr said that the gelatinous matter in its hard top shell was remarkably similar to our sym's. It might, with work, be possible to create a sym replacement. This is good news.

38957613|2934702|46|768

It has now been forty-eight rota since The Event, and we are exhausted. Much of what we have learned has been shocking. We cannot share information with the natives. We captured some of the solids for testing. They use a vibratory system, and while we can feel the patter of their vibrations on our membranes, it is beyond our translators' abilities to understand. The native beings do not comprehend our odor-based communication, indeed it appears to cause a strong physical reaction. I myself have witnessed them falling, flailing their extremities, as they expel chaotic smelling liquids from their openings when we scent to them.

Also, this world is hostile to our embodiment and we must wear protective gear outside the ship. That alone would prevent us from feeling vibrations, so is there even a point in learning it? With regret the conclusion has been that this world may be survivable, but we can not stay here.

Against the silq'uy's orders, our jampiri budded, using a combination of sym and native material as starter. My understanding of how he did this is imperfect, but he successfully implanted buds within the top hard parts of the natives we had in stasis. Miraculously, the buds rooted and his team is monitoring these creatures to see if they survive.

Research into the compatibility between native tissue and sym tissue has been successful. It should be possible to create a sym from the matter contained within the round top parts, but so far native matter will not thrive outside of its container. Even with the best nutrients, even spliced with matter from its native shell, it is not enough to keep this tissue alive long enough to bud. The jampiri's team is still working on it, but this is disappointing.

There is some good news. The bacteria farms have adapted to the native bacteria (thank the Primes there are constants in the universe), and we are able to replenish ourselves with this new mix. Now we have some resistance to the effects of this hostile world.

I know this is an official notation, but it eases me to emit how much I miss M'm'shamir. What started out as a mere temporary sharing now has the overwhelming scent of memory. The two of us might some day have exchanged reproductive material, had there been time. Perhaps there might have been a new embodiment for us to nurture together. I am 7.8% solid with grief. My shipmates are kind not to mention it.

8957613|2934702|46|797

The alarms vibrated mid rota. Solids were attacking the ship. Do they learn nothing? Again, the ones close enough were iced, then brought inside for study. Again, the ones beyond the ship's reach ran from us. After three rota had passed a new solid approached with its extremities outstretched in the way a young embodiment might extend its pseudo pods in play. It made vibrations at us that the translators are sure are attempts to disseminate information.

Doesn't the act of wanting to communicate indicate intelligence? Perhaps this was the deeply remote possibility that enticed our sym—that such creatures exist—and it could not resist. I comfort myself by tasting the numbers at the edges of this thought.

Our jampiri argued for a trial of one of the made things that accepted his bud, communicators he calls them so as not to offend the translators. There are seven in total. Twice that number failed. Silq'uy agreed. We watched anxiously on gels as our communicator walked stiffly toward the solid. When the solid sensed our communicator liquid ran from its organs of vision. It made very strong vibrations, then fell slapping at the ground. Then a thing we did not understand happened.

The solid pulled a weapon it had hidden beneath its decorative protective membranes and plunged it into our communicator's front. The communicator's physical functions have been replaced by hybrids of the jampiri's workings so it merely blinked. Then the solid sawed at the connecting tissue between the communicator's lower parts and the round hard part on top. (A few of the jampiri's team hold this part, connected by so thin a stalk, is a bud. I do not believe this is true. We do not understand how these solids function.) When the native solid sawed the round thing off, our communicator fell. All the while the solid made tremendous vibrations while liquid, salt water the analysis said, ran down its membrane.

Not everyone agrees but I believe the native solid experienced emotion—that it felt the same kinds of feelings I felt when M'm'shamir was no more. Except a solid cannot turn solid with grief, so perhaps they turn liquid and that was the meaning of the salt water. I do not know if I am right, but it smells like a constant prime to me. I remain 2.46% solid. I do not think I will ever become 100% fluid again.

8957613|2934702|46|968

It is now 248 rota since The Event, and 171 rota since the first communicator was field tested. I am very tired. My membrane is thin, and the bacteria farms are no longer adequate to maintain my optimal health. The jampiri advised me to bud several rota ago. Now my own buds are mature enough to take over my assignments, just as the jampiri's buds did 57 rota ago. We do not live as long as we should on this world, but we hope to produce generations of buds, and perhaps someday we will also merge reproductive material again (once tests confirm the local radiation and magnetic fields are harmless). Silq'uy 1-3 (at the jampiri's urging, the silq'uy budded earlier than any of us) says that this will be so. We will remember home. We will return some day.

I hope that is true.

Much has been learned. After many communicators were disassembled, and many more solids taken for testing, we have begun to understand each other. This species has no organ for smell, or at least not one that functions in a meaningful capacity. While no longer surprising, it remains shocking.

Jampiri 1-7 and jampiri 1-2 deduced that the solids communicate through vibrations that are registered and interpreted by a series of small sticks and membranes they call an "ear." Really, the ear is so tiny compared to their mass it is amazing they can communicate at all.

The top round part was never a bud, but is called a "head," and the viscous interior a "brain." They are covered by a membrane called "skin" and additional, removable membranes called "clothes." Their powers of movement are determined by tissues called "muscle" that levers long, calcinated sticks called "bones." Instead of flowing, they move like machines with levers and gears and sockets. They are marvelous and repellant.

Silq'uy 1-3 has made an agreement with the solid that controls this clutch. This being has the designation Valmarka. Brain matter from this species will not splice with the sym, at least not once the head is removed. But there is compatibility. Valmarka confirmed this by communicating that soon after we crashed, colors invaded their territory. This confused and frightened them. They believe we are gods. Our sym team deduced that they experience the probability field through their highly developed organs of sight. Called eyes, I think. So many parts to remember.

We must splice sym genes with the living beings. An experiment was conducted on Valmarka, which changed lehr's reproductive material. Beginning with lehr's offspring, through careful breeding and an occasional boost of sym genetics, we can create a new sym. It will take time. I will not live to experience that day.

Silq'uy 1-3 has granted my request.

I will take the orb that has maintained what is left of M'm'shamir, mere scraps without enough intelligence to bud. I will ingest lehr. Then we will go outside and dissolve to become part of this strange, solid place. Our genetic material will merge with the small creatures I have always loved: bacteria, molds, yeasts, and so in some little way we will help alter this world. I am glad. Holy be the Primes.

Android Whores Can't Cry
NATALIA THEODORIDOU

False start #1

MEETINGS AT MASSACRE MARKET
by Aliki Karyotakis
for the London New Times

I met Brigitte at what the locals call Massacre Market. She pronounced her name as if she were French—or I should say French-made, I guess, but I didn't know that at the time. She was a working girl, owned by a guy named Jerome—also French, supposedly. She was waiting there for my local liaison and I, among desiccated corpses and stalls full of blown-up photos of the tortured and the dead. She kissed Dick on the lips when she saw us, before greeting me. She did it in a mechanical way, as if she were supposed to, as if she couldn't do otherwise. That's when I saw the long strip of nacre that ran down the back of her neck, along her spine, pure and magnificent. I shot Dick a questioning look.

"Yeah yeah, it's the real deal," he said. "She's my artificial girlfriend in this town. I'm renting her full time. Very useful. She knows people." Dick could be snide like that. "I'm sure you girls will get along," he added.

Brigitte turned to me, holding out her hand. She gave me a warm smile, but I could tell that she, unlike Dick, was very well aware of where we were, of the transactable images of gore and violence that surrounded us. Of the history of this place.

"Pleasure to meet you," she said, a glint of something indecipherable in her eye. Was that an android thing? Or was that the part of her that is human?

Androids can usually pass, if they don't have any visible nacre. But, of course, as soon as nacre appeared on android skin, people started wearing fake nacre patches as a fashion statement. When the patches are high quality you can't really tell them apart.

What was the nacre's appeal? I suppose part of it is that we still don't understand why or how it is formed. The other part is that it's perfect, beautiful. And that it doesn't perish.

Nacre is forever.

[Note to self: You sound like an infatuated schoolgirl. What does Brigitte have to do with anything? Get it together. Just get the facts straight. Also, preserve both Dick's and Brigitte's anonymity.]

>>>END OF FILE

Nacre: Formation and Function

Nacre, or "mother of pearl" is a composite material produced by certain molluscs as an inner shell lining and as the outer coating of pearls.[1] Since the APC-VII[2] finalized and started regulating the production of androids globally, nacre has been a standard feature of all artificially produced semi-mechanical humanoid organisms.[3] The production of android nacre had not been foreseen and remains unexplained. However, android nacre is considered harmless, if not beneficial for humans as an identifying mark, and so no attempts to avoid its appearance on android skin have been made.

Nacre formation is an evolutionary conserved and multiply-convergent process among the Mollusca phylum, arising as early as the Ordovician period (488 to 443 million years ago). While the exact process of its production is little understood even in nature, the function of natural nacre is largely defensive: layers of nacre protect the soft tissues of the organism from parasites, while damaging debris can be entombed in successive layers of nacre, ultimately resulting in the formation of a pearl.

The function of android nacre remains unknown.

1 - "Pearl" is also slang for a locally produced hallucinogenic that is sometimes used in meditation. Despite the name, the connection with either natural or android nacre has not been confirmed, largely due to lack of research.

2 - APC: Android Production Committee.

3 - These are commonly referred to as Androids, as this has been the popular term for many decades—however the universal applicability of the term has been questioned on various grounds. Still, other proposed terms, such as Gynoid and Cyborg, although more accurate in certain cases, are no longer in widespread use.

>>>END OF FILE

Fieldnotes #1

It's Dick's afternoon playtime and he makes Brigitte re-enact scenes from his past while I try to work on my article. Playing in front of me is awkward, indiscrete. Vulgar, even. But I'm sure he does it on purpose—he *wants* me there. He wants me to witness this, and he knows I won't interfere. He is the client: his game, his rules.

Brigitte playacts Sandra, my college friend and Dick's ex-wife. She kinda looks like her too. Now they're acting out the night Sandra left him—left us. Dick is high on pearl. I can tell from that slightly unfocused look in his eyes. Like he sees things past Brigitte, past the windows and the smog, past the illusion of life.

"I can't be with you any more," Brigitte says. It sounds like she's said this line a hundred times already—a recitation. It seems she's in learning mode for these sessions. Dick is shaping her into Sandra. I find this deeply disturbing. "You're such a brute," Brigitte recites. "Not sophisticated at all."

"That's who I was when you married me. What was different then?"

Brigitte pretends to put all of her clothes in a suitcase, preparing to leave. Dick follows her around, practically yelling in her ear.

"I'll tell you what was different," Dick says, "you were a horny little cunt back then, weren't you."

Brigitte stops packing and just stares at him.

"You're supposed to cry now," Dick says, and then pretend-slaps his forehead. "But I forgot. You can't cry, can you?" He turns to me. "Hey Aliki, did you know that? Android whores can't cry. Because who wants to fuck a whiny bitch, right? Right?"

I look at Brigitte. I think I see a twitch disfigure her lips for the tiniest of moments, but then she smiles. "Who wants to fuck a whiny bitch?" she repeats. Still in learning mode. Damn it.

"You really are a dick sometimes, Richard," I say.

Dick laughs. He comes over and hugs me.

Brigitte keeps smiling, a twinkle in her eye.

>>>END OF FILE

Nacre: Human Use

Historically, nacre has been prized for its iridescent appearance, while its strength and resilience has made it a suitable material for a variety of purposes. The nacreous shells of sea snails were used as gunpowder flasks in the 18th century and earlier. Nacre inlays have decorated some of the most renowned temples and palaces in Istanbul, traditional musical instruments in Greece, the keys of flutes, and the buttons of kings and queens the world over. Some accordion and concertina bodies are entirely inlaid with nacre. Little spoons made solely of nacre have been used to eat caviar in Russia, in order not to spoil the taste with metal.

All of these practices, although rarer, continue to this day. However, where natural nacre was used in the past, android nacre, the price of which is exorbitant due to the legal restrictions placed on its farming, is mostly used today.

[Note to self: I wonder what it feels like for androids. Do they consider nacre to be a part of their skin? A part of who they are? What would it feel like to see your skin as decoration, a musical instrument, a spoon?]

>>>END OF FILE

False Start #2

MASSACRE MARKET: A HISTORY OF VIOLENCE AND SILENCE
by Aliki Karyotakis
for the London New Times

> "That great dust-heap called 'history.' "
> —Augustine Birrell

> "Truth? I have no use for that. Truth won't feed my people. It won't cover their bodies. Won't keep them safe."
> —The General

My air-conditioned taxi drives me through the outskirts of the city. I gaze in comfort at the unfinished highways, the hollow skeletons of skyscrapers looming over them as a reminder of the economic fallout—a city in perpetual suspension. But once at the centre, this city is impeccable—polished and shiny, no sign of poverty or suffering anywhere. It makes one think of the new regime's necessity, its efficiency. A good alternative to the chaos and agony that came before. Only the smog weighs on us, like a bad omen.

As soon as I step out of the vehicle, I realize this is the hottest and most humid part of the day; the smog is so thick I can hardly breathe or make out any sky. My local liaison is meeting me in front of the city pillar, the geographical and spiritual centre of the city, from where everything extends outwards. I find out that the Massacre Market is tucked away at the heart of a crowded, semi-underground slum—the city's last. We have to get there on foot. It will be a difficult journey.

When we arrive, hot and breathless, I am greeted by what my liaison describes as "The Political Cadaver of this country": the dead body politic, the regime's atrocities mechanically reproduced and exchanged in a gamble with the spirits of the dead, a funerary protest. The place is crowded and dark and putrid; the stalls exhibit small mountains of body parts and corpses—some fake, some real (and I can't tell which is which)—the brownish hue of decay accentuated by the bright orange robes of the monks and nuns that frequent the place, looking for visual aids to their death meditations. Tall cork-lined walls are covered by the forbidden pictures of the massacred and those brutalized by police. Relatives petrified in front of them, looking for the familiar face among the myriads, looking but not wanting to find I'm sure, or making small shrines with offerings for the disappeared; while protestors and instigators pick out the most shocking ones to circulate and share, to dub as the hidden reality of the regime, its true face the face of those it murdered. In the loudspeakers, recordings of the massacre's soundscape: screams and bullets, the sound of revolting children and of a state devouring its young.

I spot a mother clinging to the image of her dead boy, his face proliferated ad infinitum, plastering an entire wall, in protest.

Here, at Massacre Market, death is a political act.

[Note to self: People need the historical and political background of the story to make sense of any of these. Start with an interview instead? Also, explain Death Meditation.]

>>>END OF FILE

The First Death Meditation

Death is certain.
There is no way to escape death.
We start dying the moment we are born.
The body is a husk, a shell, an overcoat. It must be left behind.
Imagine you are performing a vivisection on yourself.
Imagine every detail.
Concentrate on the repulsiveness of the human body.
The corpse, swollen and bruised.
The skin, peeled back.
The fat, removed.
The muscle, shredded.
The organs, shrivelled and gone.
The bones, pulverized.
The corpse, festering. The corpse, fissured. The corpse, gnawed. The corpse, dismembered, fragmented, scattered. The corpse, bleeding. The corpse, eaten by maggots and gone.
You remain.

>>>END OF FILE

Interview with X, one of the leading protestors at the November Massacre

Part I [PLX1.vf]

Q: What is Massacre Market?
A: Images of death, disease, and violence are forbidden by the regime; they are not good for foreign affairs, for the economy, won't bring in investments. So now there's a black market for that. It's not about money, though. We believe in an exchange of gifts with and for the dead. At the same time, it's a political thing. Because the government and the military want to hide the dead, when we photograph them and share their pictures, when we circulate footage of the massacres, we are exposing the true face of the regime. It's a form of protest.

Q: A protest against what?
A: Against the regime's suppression of the fundamental truths of life and death. Of poverty and suffering. Against the state's cover-ups of its core practices, the

terrorizing and massacre of its own citizens when they dare to speak out or deviate in any way.

Q: Then how does Massacre Market survive? How come they haven't shut it down yet?
A: They have tried; they do raid it from time to time, but it pops up again after a while. Some people believe it is allowed to exist, or even that it has been set up by the government, as a safety valve, you know? To serve as an illusion of resistance.

Q: Do you believe that?
A: I do not.

Q: Can you talk about the November Massacre? I know this is the most recent one, but there have been others.
A: Yes, that is correct.
   [He hesitates.]

Q: Can you recount the day of the Massacre?
A: [Pause] In the morning, the General was scheduled to appear at the city centre, very near the University. Attendance was, of course, mandatory, for students and first class citizens alike. So everyone gathered as planned. The General delivered the formal greeting and raised his arms in the usual salutation. The masses cheered, as expected, as they should. They couldn't do otherwise, you understand. But then, then, they kept on cheering. And clapping. Just cheering and clapping as loud as they could, whistling and cheering, and waving. And they wouldn't stop. After a few minutes, it became evident that this was no enthusiasm. It was super-conformity, you see? By cheering, they did not allow the General to speak. He literally couldn't get a word in. But what could he do? We were only applauding, he couldn't possibly punish us for that. So he mumbled the end of the speech he never managed to actually deliver, got off the podium and went back to wherever it is the General goes back to. And then the crowd was allowed to disperse, but the students and some others lingered. They were still not allowing themselves to talk, but they were smiling. They were shaking hands, not yet daring to speak about change, but that feeling, you know? That feeling, it was there. I felt it.
   But then the trucks and the tanks appeared and sealed off the main square around the city pillar with the students still in it. We were surrounded before we realized what was going on. Some of us managed to slip through and save ourselves. Some holed themselves up inside the Polytechnic School at the University. They got them, though, eventually. They got them all.

Q: What did they do to them?
A: Why are you asking? You know very well what they did to them. You've seen the pictures, no? [Kneeling under the sun, hands tied, some behind their backs,

some in front of their chests, beaten with steel batons and shiny black boots. Taken with a fisheye lens, they look like a human ocean. Innumerable, uncountable, and unaccounted for.] You've seen the footage. [Herded onto cattle-trucks by the back of their necks. Taken to that off-camera place from where no-one returns.] At four o'clock, it rained. The streets turned red.

[Pause] Of this, we will not speak.

[He takes a moment to find his bearings, he seems truly emotional. Then he adds:] They even destroyed several androids—most of them sex workers and cleaners—and later reimbursed their owners. I should say "bribed," to keep them from making a fuss.

Q: You said androids? Why were they there? Were androids part of the protest?
A: Yes, android guerillas have always been on our side, and uni students are often particularly drawn to them. There are several reasons for this. On the one hand, androids are part of the oppressed. They are low class, second rate, not even citizens. Most people don't even consider them persons. But there is also something about them that speaks of truth, not least their perfect, infallible memories. It's the human machine's trap: the freedoms afforded to them by what little flesh they possess and command, the failings of that same flesh . . . these are not so easy to tell apart. They do not decay, too, while our whole culture is premised on decay and death, or, now, on its concealment. Why do you think people are so crazy about those nacre patches? You've seen the ones?

[Note to Self: Transcribe the rest of the interview from voice file PLX2.vf]

>>>END OF FILE

Fieldnotes #2

Getting people to talk is difficult. Brigitte and Dick work hard to find me the right contacts. But it takes time, and I know so little. I understand so little. This investigation is going to be long. We need to be discreet.

I often sit and watch Brigitte when she thinks I'm in my head, working, not paying attention to her.

She seems restless in her own skin, walking from the door to the window and back again. She stares outside at the smog—you can't see anything out the window, just grey and brown. Well, at least I can't. Maybe she can see something, maybe she can see everything. I don't know.

Her nacre has been multiplying the past few weeks. There is a new patch behind her left ear, and one on the back of her right hand—her most prominent still. It makes her look adorned.

When she catches me looking at her, the programming kicks in and she responds with her standard line, every time: "What can I do for you, honey?" Then she lowers her eyes and looks embarrassed.

She's always lived here, and yet I can detect a faint French accent when she says this. Like some guy's fantasy of what a French whore should sound like.

>>>END OF FILE

Some notes on the translation of Massacre Market

There is some uncertainty about the translation from the local language of what I have called "Massacre Market." Other possible translations include "Atrocity Place," "Massacre Fair," or, and that was the most confusing aspect of this, "Pearl Fountain," because even though each of the two words means something different, together they create a new compound which, as Dick and Brigitte explained to me, could rather clumsily be interpreted as "a fountain whence pearls flow," "the breeding ground of oysters," or even "the plane of sublime imperfections."

>>>END OF FILE

Fieldnotes #3

Dick has started being rougher in his re-enactments; I doubt these are memories, no, I'm sure they are not, because these versions are conflicting and contradictory, and things happen that I know never really happened. Brigitte/Sandra is not always the one leaving him any more—sometimes he leaves her, sometimes she dies. Sometimes he kills her, chokes her. Or, he pretends to. He acts disinterested afterwards, says these are only stories he makes up and likes to play out; but I know, any reporter knows there are no disinterested stories, least of all the ones we tell ourselves.

Brigitte says she doesn't mind, she doesn't feel, remember? It's her job, she says. I'm still not convinced. I find myself in my reporter's role nonetheless, taking everything in, observing, reluctant to participate. This is not how the game is played, I tell myself.

I watch the nacre spread on her skin, covering more and more each day, like a disease of unbearable beauty.

"How did you end up in this mess, anyway?" Dick asked me yesterday. "I never thought they'd send a woman."

I hit him hard on the arm and he laughed. "I choose not to be insulted," I said. "Anyway, I needed this. Badly. Went through a rough patch a while back and was out of circulation for some time. So when I went back to my boss and begged, he gave me the case nobody else would take."

Dick stopped fiddling with his cigarettes and turned to me. I had his full attention now, and I wasn't sure I wanted it. I shouldn't have said anything.

"Rough? How rough?" he asked.

I said nothing.

"You know you can talk to me, right?"

I thought of his hands around Brigitte's neck. *What happened to you, Richard? You were a tender boy, back then.*

"It's been a while, Dick. I'm sorry."

I think I hurt his feelings, but he tried not to show it. And at that moment I realized I didn't mind. Hurting him. I didn't mind at all.

>>>END OF FILE

The Second Death Meditation

The second meditation rehearses the actual death process.

Engage now in this series of yogas, modelled on death.

First, the body becomes very thin, the limbs barely held together. You will feel that the body is sinking into the earth. Your sight becomes blurry and obscured. You may see mirages. Do not believe them. The body loses its lustre.

Then, all the fluids in the body dry up. Saliva, sweat, urine, blood dry up. Feelings of pleasure and pain dry with them. You may feel like smoke.

Then, you can no longer hear. You cannot digest food or drink. You do not remember your name, or the names of the ones you knew and loved. You cannot smell. You may not be able to inhale, but you will be able to exhale.

Then, the ten winds of the body move to your heart. You will no longer inhale or exhale. You will not be able to taste. You will not care. The root of your tongue will turn blue. You may feel like a lamp about to go out.

Then, nothing.

Then, nothing.

Then, nothing. The ten winds dissolve. The indestructible drop at the heart is all that remains.

>>>END OF FILE

Fieldnotes #4

"Why do you let him treat you like that?" I ask her almost reflexively one day. I regret it right away. Am I blaming her for the way he treats her? Shouldn't I be blaming him?

She thinks about it for a while, then shrugs.

"It's my job," she says. "I don't have a choice. Some things are in my programming."

"Yes, but some aren't."

She looks me in the eyes, fixes her gaze there, and she seems less human than ever before. People don't look at others like that. "I'm a whore," she states.

"You are more than a whore. It's not who you are. It's simply what you do."

"See, you got it backwards. What we are *for* is who we are. A hammer is what a hammer does. Would you ever use a hammer to screw a screw or cut a piece of wood?"

"Just a tool, then."

"That's right. Just a tool."

"Doesn't my saying that offend you?"

"Do you think it should?"

I don't say anything.

"Why?" she continues. "We are all tools for something. Aren't you? It's not an android thing. It's an existential thing."

I lower my eyes.

She leans over and touches my shoulder. "I'm sorry," she says. "Sometimes empathy is difficult for me. We don't feel anything, you know. No feelings."

She seems sincere, but I don't believe her; I tell her so. "Some people say the nacre is a byproduct of the things you do feel that were not programmed. Just like the nacre wasn't, and yet, there it is."

She shrugs again. "My programming allows me to imitate feeling and to learn from other people's perceptions of me. No one knows what the nacre is, or what it does." She pauses for a bit. Then she adds: "Perhaps it's a form of rust. Tools do rust, don't they?"

>>>END OF FILE

My trip

I'm sitting by the window, looking out. The smog seems heavier today. Darker, too. I think it's the colour of rot. I wish I could see past it. I wish I could see.

Brigitte comes home—I notice there is a bright new patch of nacre under her right eye. She smiles, like she always does.

"Get dressed," she says. "I need to show you something."

When I'm ready to go, she holds out her hand closed in a fist. Slowly, she uncurls her fingers and reveals a pearl resting on her palm. It takes me a couple of seconds to realize what it is, and then I look at her, trying to figure out what she's planning.

"Put this under your tongue, Aliki," she says. "You'll see. You'll understand."

I put the pearl into my mouth and we set out into the smog and that corpse of a city.

We are at the main square. The pearl is still dissolving under my tongue; it tastes sweet and tangy and makes my heart beat irregularly. I see the city pillar towering over us—round and bulging at the bottom, thinning as it reaches for the sky. The top disappears into the thick layers of smog above. Its marble surface emits a subdued light, like a fading beacon.

"It was built hundreds of years ago as a mystical axis around which the city would be born, you know," Brigitte says. "The story of its construction is now largely ignored and forgotten, but spirit mediums still gather here sometimes. They consider it a source of power for those who commune with the dead. It is said that when the foundation for the pillar was laid, a fosse was dug around it. They brought every young pregnant slave girl they could find, slit their throats and threw them in there to die, and through their deaths empowered the pillar to protect the city."

I look at the base of the pillar and realize I am standing on top of where the trench would have been, if that story were true. The pillar starts glowing brighter and brighter and I look up to see if the sun has somehow penetrated the smog. I feel the ground shake under my feet, then give, and I fall into the trench. The slave girls are there, all around me, with their blood still seeping into the earth, their fetuses still dying in their wombs.

This city is built on gore. The shiny marble, a tombstone laid over history. I see the streets turn into veins. I see students parade through the city with what corpses they could salvage; they carry them on their shoulders, their friends, their classmates, their lovers, displaying them like a mute witness to the regime's moral order. And then these students are shot down or snatched off the streets, the corpses torn from their arms. They are strung on trees and shot, or burnt alive, or worse. Of this, we will not speak.

The body is nothing. Its image, everything.

Brigitte pulls me away. She leads me through the city's red streets, the ten winds of its body dying down. I think Brigitte is speaking to me. I think she says:

"Let's look for the indestructible drop at the heart."

We are descending. She is walking in front of me, showing me the way. The nacre on her skin seems brighter than ever. I dare touch it for the first time—I reach out and brush my fingers against the back of her neck, tracing the nacre down her spine. I didn't expect it to be so hard. "You are indestructible," I mutter, or I think I do, and she turns around and smiles.

We are at Massacre Market. It has changed since the first time I saw it; it seems even more crowded now, the walls of photographs fuller, covered once, and then covered again by more pictures, and more on top of those, layer upon gory layer, corpse upon corpse, body part upon body part. The desiccated corpses seem more real now, almost alive, absurd. Brigitte tells me something I don't hear; her voice drowns in the screams and static spilling from the loudspeakers.

One of the photographs on the wall next to me catches my eye. I walk closer—it's grainy, black and white, but I can still see the girl: she is laid out in a field next to others, dozens of others. Her top is removed, her chest slashed open. "Foreign slut" is written on her bare belly. She looks like a younger version of myself. *This is me,* I think, *this is me, years ago. Why don't I remember this?* I put my palm on the photograph—what did I want to do? Cover her up, I suppose—and I notice a patch of nacre spreading between my fingers. I pull my hand back as if the photo suddenly burnt me and I watch the nacre spread. I feel it cover my entire body, and I'm calcified, my skin adorned and indestructible. "I feel like an instrument," I shout to Brigitte over the sound of massacre, "like an accordion, or a concertina." *Play me like a flute, O Lord,* I think.

Brigitte tries to tell me something, but I can't make it out. I struggle to read her lips. " . . . it disappoints . . . " I hear, but the rest is stifled by static, and she's far away. I see her pointing at my arms from afar. I look down and see the nacre growing dull and flaking, then my skin peeling and falling off, the fat exposed, the muscle, the bone, and I know, I know then, this city is a skin, no blood anywhere in sight, all surface, all shine and the slightest glimpse of nacre here and there—is it real? Is it not? Does it make a difference?

>>>END OF FILE

False Endings

I have precious little time left. So I will not say much. One never has the skin that befits her.

I know I'll never finish this article—I still haven't even decided on the title, or what this story is really about. What do you think? I might have called it:

Massacre Market

or

The Mechanical Reproduction of Violence: Truth, Massacre, History

or even

Android Whores Can't Cry: Under the Surface of Death Meditation

Either way, I know that, if I did finish it, I would dedicate it

"To my B., my pearl, who taught me this:

The skin always disappoints."

>>>END OF FILE

>>>END OF RECORD. 14 OF 14 FILES RECOVERED.

This is all the material I managed to retrieve from Aliki's hard drives. I wait for the reporter sitting across from me in Dick's living room to go through them.

"You realize your memory files provide conflicting information about what happened to both my colleague Aliki Karyotakis and her informant Richard Phillips," he says.

I am silent. Is that true?

I recall the last time I saw Aliki.

She is lurching at Dick, pushing him away from me during one of his violent playacts. He falls back and hits his head. He is very still. We are all very still.

She is also standing by the city pillar with me, in a crowd of people I haven't quite registered. I look at the sky. The sun is shining through the smog. When I look down again, she's gone.

She is also looking at me as a tall man leads her onto a platform and places a hood over her head. Then a noose. Then the platform gives.

She was also never here. I never met her.

And Dick? Dick is always either dead or missing.

"Have you tinkered with your memory?" *the reporter asks.*

"It is possible," *I say.* "But I have no memory of that, as I am sure you are aware."

"Of course." *He shuffles in his chair.* "OK, let's take the first version. Can you tell me what happened?"

He already knows this. Why does he ask?

"She pushed him. He died. Humans break easily like that."

"And then?"

"She turned herself in."

"Wasn't she terminated?" *That's when I notice the nacre on his underarm. Ah.*

"I think the human term is 'sentenced to death and executed,' " *I correct him. He should know this. I'm sure he does.*

"Did you watch? The execution, I mean."

I watch him. He is serious, eyes cold. A reporter reports.

"A hammer is what a hammer does," *I whisper.*

"Excuse me?"

"Nothing," *I say.* "A reflex. Yes. Yes, I think I watched." *I sense the nacre spread on my face, my surface irreparably hardened. It reflects the light so brightly it almost hurts my eyes.*

"Are you going to cry?" *he asks, hoping, I bet, for a good twist in his story.*

The programming takes over, like gears shifting inside me, and I can't stop it, I can't stop it, I can't.

"Android whores can't cry," *I say.* "Who wants to fuck a whiny bitch?"

This puzzles him. He focuses on my lips, and he's about to say something, but he stops. I know he stops because of what he sees. He looks disappointed.

I feel the nacre cover my lips and I realize this was the last time I spoke. This shouldn't be happening so fast. I think of freedoms and failings. I am not sure which is which. It doesn't matter. I am the oyster and the pearl. I am a shell that doesn't speak.

I wonder what really happened to her, what happened to Dick. I know I'll never know—and this somehow strikes me as appropriate. The truth has seeped through the pores on the skin of the city. Aliki is in its bloodstream now. So is Dick. So is the core of this story.

I remain.

Let Baser Things Devise
BERRIEN C. HENDERSON

1: Pierre

Before Clockwork Corp's space ape project heads managed to uplift the chimpanzee, he was simply known as No. 157. Some anonymous lab assistant nicknamed him Pierre, and the moniker stuck. After Pierre survived the rigors of testing and training, his world went dark for a time once the Neuroscience Division got their needles and scalpels and computer-brain interfaces onto and into him.

He was a child again. A sponge. Malleable. He had dreams and remembered them—the great ape facility from which he'd come, the jungle before that. A troop. He had flirted with moonlight and squinted against sunshine while his troop loped through the undergrowth and scampered up the trees and foraged amid the generous loam where he groomed and was groomed. Various *Shes* were there in limbo, too, between dream and memory. Pierre's mind reached out, clutching at phantoms from a blurry past and running into the long now—all of it oozing and *hrmmm*-ing like fluorescent lights with faulty ballasts. He weighed his new life amid antiseptic halls, an institution's sterility and scientists' data points and vagaries of conditioning against the harsher realities of death, quick in its smiting, in the tropics and faces framed with their own intelligence. He yearned for a place absent this new awareness—signals of higher and greater thoughts like thunder at the hem of distant mountains.

Inside a year, he learned to speak with his newly acquired vocal cords—3D bio-printed wonders of Clockwork Corp's NuFlesh(tm) proprietary systems—and, thus, No. 157 became the first uplifted articulate chimpanzee.

And he was going to the moon.

2: Comped

Pierre received the ping of a incoming message on his way out the door. He had a mandatory conditioning session and made to ignore the message to queue up later, then fell short of his initial plans.

Bureau of Personhood.

He caught himself wanting to *oohoohooh* in anxiety and excitement but tamped down those impulses. Some quirks hadn't quite ironed out since uplift, and his human handlers and colleagues overlooked much, thank goodness.

"This is Pierre."

A woman's face greeted him with a sliver of a smile that bespoke scores of such practiced smiles daily and the beginnings of crow's feet at the edges of her eyes. Pierre wondered what kind of punishment the poor liaison had done to deserve shuffling files and contacting various hominids and none too few uplifted canines (a recent development) along with some advanced NuEmote(tm) Model Mark robots. Still, he was glad she had contacted him.

"Pierre, I have good news."

Finally.

"I've sent you a message with a printable, watermarked certificate of person-hood."

"Thank you, Sarah, for all your help."

"Thank the lawyers at Clockwork Corp.," she said. "They saw the handwriting on the wall. You had the virtue of many legal precedents on your side."

"I"—the words sometimes wouldn't come—"appreciate your taking time to-*oohooh* face-contact me."

The practiced smile widened, and he saw the glimmers of a few teeth. "Why, thank you kindly, Pierre."

"At least I'm not working basic municipal services," he said. The majority of uplifted apes ended up employed in recycling facilities or treatment plants unless, of course, one was part of an R&D department for the largest corporation in the world and a handy PR football tossed around in the mining claims wars raging on the moon.

"Well, there's that," she said. "You realize how fortunate you are."

"Yes." And he felt immediately unlucky to be condescended to. Or complimented. He still had trouble navigating social mores. "Thank you."

"Have a good day, Pierre."

"You, too-*ooh*, Sarah."

As her image faded, Pierre stared at the screen and considered his newfound reality.

Personhood.

The company wanted a poster child for the new wave of lunar exploration. All he had to do was make a loathsome trip to Human Resources and request an addendum to his work contract for this upcoming expedition. The concept of money didn't escape him, but he had little use for it. He banked a pittance for little things like sodas. Sodas he loved.

The ideas grew. Humans talked with anticipation about taking vacations, and he wanted vacation time, which was not a component of his old contract. No more day passes into the city. No more permission requests for visits to museums or . . . or . . .

The possibilities unfurled in his mind, and Pierre smiled.

3: Human Resources

"Well, this is a first," said the HR rep. "Wonder if the company ought to consider changing the name of the department now?"

Pierre didn't laugh during the man's pregnant pause. "New territory."

"In more ways than one. First, congratulations on your official personhood status. You've come a long way, Pierre."

"Hmmmm."

A flash of jungle memory stung him: sunlight lancing the canopy and the screams of another chimpanzee caught in a great cat's jaws. He could expect a headache—the single and sometimes debilitating side effect of the CBI gear in his head.

"You still have a week before launch. It takes three days to process a contract addendum request. I can message you."

"Do you see any reason it might be denied?"

"No more than any other request."

"*Ooh.*"

"What's that?"

"I mean, 'Oh.' "

They shuffled through several documents that required e-signatures, eye-stamps, and DNA proofs as Pierre did his best to maneuver the platitudes of small talk.

"Is this what they meant by signing in blood?"

The fat man chuckled. "I suppose so." He offered his hand to Pierre, who hesitated, then shook. A rarity. All of his physical reinforcement and interactions had consisted of claps on the shoulder and good-natured squeezes of the upper arm—even one high five. Very few handshakes. His hand met the clammy palmflesh of the fat man, who seemed quite appreciative.

When Pierre excused himself, he left with the distinct impression that the fat man was lonely despite dealing with other humans on a daily basis. Alone in a troop. Pierre was stung again as he walked the fluorescent-lit halls to the Fitness and Conditioning wing, signed out, and trained outside. A hard workout in the obstacle course would boost his endorphins and help him fight the headache. He hated the humans' pain relievers while understanding their necessity.

A bright yellow sun bathed him. A great eye whose warmth slithered down through a noisy canopy. Pierre allowed himself thoughts of trees and courting and earth and night-nesting, and the daydream became a nightmare Klaxon calling out his buried limbic fears of being hunted. Captured.

FLEE!

He scaled trunks and brachiated vines and limbs, missed one and plummeted to earth. He became a caged thing in a preserve; the trees were not the same—constructs for primates to climb and maintain their facade of health and activity. A group of handlers seized him and parleyed him to an alien, antiseptic landscape full of hooting and yowling.

The real nightmare, the waking one, happened when he fell asleep and woke to the reality of his uplifting and a flood of information, a cascade of new schema expanding exponentially—the synaptic flood churning and frothing in his mind from the cerebral implant. He understood the cries of the other animals the way an adult understands a child's cries—a mixture of sympathy tinged with the patina of intellectual distance.

The memory remained, still blunted by time and his uplifting—a photo fading from color to monochrome or perhaps spackled brightly, overexposed and portions blotted out.

He needed to get away.

4: Tsuki

The susurration of servos and hissing of actuators alerted Pierre as he finished his gymnastics and, planning to warm down with yoga, dropped to the ground.

The Model Mark II lunar-bot approached him in hexapod form, and Pierre couldn't help thinking of a gigantic arachnid, some mutant lurking and emerging from the shadows of the thick foliage of once-home, ready to snatch baby chimps from the troop. Still, Pierre's edginess softened when he saw Tsuki.

"Good afternoon, Pierre. News travels fast."

"Of?"

"Your having been granted personhood. How does that make you feel?"

Tendrils of the headache coiled around his brain. "I put in for a vacation after we revised the contract."

"A reward. I see." She skittered alongside him and used one of her four arms to retrieve his water bottle and hand it to him.

"Thank you, Tsuki. It still seems a mere formality."

"While conferring you wider latitude of rights and privileges."

"Today would have been the same regardless."

"A rather cynical view, if perhaps a valid observation."

His head echoed with the ghost-strains of the headache. A ripple from the back of his neck straight-lined from the CBI's scar and to his eyes.

"If you say so-*ooh*."

"Would you care to run through a mission simulation with me in the Augmentation Array?"

"Hold on a moment." Pierre retrieved his wafer tablet, which buzzed slightly, and he queued up his meager bank account. It had already been flagged for a deposit. "Huh. They actually did it."

" 'They'?"

"The company. Given today's news, I've received dividends on shares retroactively for the duration of my employment. Good faith call on their part."

"That was charitable if manipulative."

"At least I have more money to put toward that vacation."

"And sodas."

Pierre smiled. "Good idea. Care to join me for a cafeteria pit stop?"

"Gladly."

5: "Apollo's Death (and Perhaps a Resurrection)"

REUTERS
OP-ED
Byron Pettigrew

The Apollo program ended in 1975 with the catastrophic failure of the Apollo 20 mission. Col. William "Memphis" Cato and geologist Dr. Angela Phelps had the unfortunate encounter with Mr. Murphy in the form of a cascade of failures. A dying retro-thruster. On the same side as the thruster—since the module came down harder—a leg collapsed. Other than the rough landing (and thankfully the LRV suffered no damage), Cato and Phelps had every reason to believe they could return to the orbiter. They could do what the stalwart trio of Apollo 13 did. Or the crew of Apollo 19.

Only, they couldn't, especially not when, after five hours of work, a baseball-sized meteor ripped through the top of the lunar module. The duo awaited the inevitable.

NASA held its memorial with the rest of the nation. The Cato and Phelps families held their respective memorials while Mission Control decided to close the Apollo program with this disaster and move on.

There is no better time to return to the moon than the fiftieth anniversary of the mission. Consider the time and tide of change: The joint venture featuring a Russian multistage rocket along with a United States orbiter and a Japanese lunar module that could only be capped with Clockwork Corp.'s lunar-bot, a Tsuki Model 2, and Pierre the Uplifted Chimp (so labeled by at least one children's book spinning out of the affair).

There have been the predictable protests about using uplifted animals, but because of a corporate law loophole along with legal precedents set in prior years for uplifted dogs and cats (and one gecko), Pierre would not be the first ape in space, but he would be the first uplifted ape to walk on the moon. Other such chimpanzees see this as quite a boon to their quest for equality.

That Pierre volunteered for the flight has been lost on some of the more vocal and otherwise well-intentioned anti-upli—.

::SKIP AD SURVEY? CONTINUE TO REMAINDER OF ARTICLE?::

6: Fly Me to the Moon

"Now that we are up here, I am farther removed from being a political football and poster child for a handful of advocacy groups," said Pierre. He swiveled his chair after he deleted a dozen invitations to speak from organizations.

"An interesting idiom," replied a section of the wall. Tsuki had slaved herself to the orbiter's computer system. The Clockwork Corp. lunar-bot had all-terrain capacity like her forebears, but the TLRV possessed additional mimetic qualities beta-tested in Earth's most inhospitable climates. Her maiden voyage was at hand with this mining mission. Even if something happened to the main computer, she could manage the rest. Designed for versatility, she was a good tool to have on board. "At least you are not configured into the hull's interior."

"But, Tsuki, you're saving space," said Pierre. "So very ergonomic. Efficient."

The pilot chuckled. "Never thought I'd be flying to the moon with a chimp and a robot, much less myself. Or hearing unintended puns."

"It was intended," said Pierre.

"Might I suggest some practice? It's a long enough ride."

"So, the UN and the North American Directorate finally opened up some lunar territory for mining," said the pilot. "And I get to ferry a robot and a sapient ape."

"More accurately, exploratory missions," said Tsuki.

"And furthering the accuracy, uplifted," said Pierre.

"Touché."

"Indeed," said Tsuki.

7: Mare Serenitatis

Almost three full months into the rotation, and Pierre could taste his vacation amid the mapping and spectrography. He had to admit that the stillness and the gliding and jumping freedom of a low-gravity environment excited him, and farther out on their digs, he imagined Tsuki did her fair share of indulging his *ooh-ooh-ooh*'s of joy. If he played golf, he would've driven plenty of golf balls as far across the Sea of Serenity as possible.

But all such thoughts faded fast as he stared at a lunar lander.

"Tsuki, I need you at my location," said Pierre.

Her voice, tinny through his helmet's speakers, replied, "Are you all right, Pierre?"

"Yes. No. I've found something—*ooh-ooh*—some*things*, to be precise."

"ETA in seven minutes."

"Roger that."

He hop-drifted several more meters, and his concern grew.

Ooh-ooh-ooh.

Nearby lay an older model emergency habitat.

Pierre stared down from the ridge upon the swath of Mare Serenitatis, but closer were two bodies in spacesuits. He bounded down to them; they lay facing each other. Their desiccated faces grinned and yawned at each other from across the decades, and Pierre knew enough of history to realize that today's mining spectrometer experiments were rendered moot.

"Pierre?"

Tsuki had retracted her trundles into her back and skittered down to him on her hex-legs.

"We've found a fifty-years-dead pair of astronauts, Tsuki."

"Company protocol dictates immediate contact and securing of the site," said the 'bot.

"Already done that. Col. William Cato and Dr. Angela Phelps, it looks as if you two are finally going home," said Pierre.

All these years and frozen in such a tableau.

"We should follow our exact path in back out, Pierre, so as not to disturb further the site."

"You know they'll want to examine every millimeter and—Get a look."

He pointed at words written in the soil near Tsuki's legs.

" . . . let baser things devise / To die in dust, . . . " Tsuki said. "Interesting final words."

Pierre figured there would be some closure for the descendants and the few aging members from that bygone era.

He had no inkling Tsuki possessed among a multitude of photos the one that would be voted Photo of the Year. It was here, now, etched in the linotype of his uplifted mind: Pierre's crouching at the quote with one of Col. Cato's hands at the words in the lunar soil and another hand stretched back toward Dr. Phelps.

In his mind, only the curious tableau of a pair of bodies facing each other and space-gloved hands in a fifty-year clutch would remain.

8: Interstitium

Robot and Uplifted Chimp Discover Lost Apollo 20 Astronauts

—AP—A fifty-year mystery unfolded on the moon recently when a pair of Clockwork Corp. employees on a routine mining mission on the Sea of Serenity stumbled upon the remains of Col. Cato and Dr. Phelps. The families have prepared for a host of press conferences . . .

9: From Clockwork Corp.

Pierre
Admin
RE: Recovery/Phelps-Cato
Cc: Tsuki

Pierre,

We have attached the link for the coffins' schematics. The Board decided to aid both the current space administration and the Phelps and Cato families. It is a powerful reminder of the human cost of lunar exploration—of space travel itself.

Once you have fabricated their coffins, transfer the bodies for transport to Camelot Base for pickup. Know that you and Tsuki have played a fundamental role in helping a pair of families find their lost loved ones.

Thank you for your professionalism in helping us handle the matter and for being a credit to the corporation.

With much appreciation,

The Board

10: Little Cupids

"What do you extrapolate given the writing we found?" said Tsuki.

"The allusion sounds familiar," said Pierre.

She sent him the full text. He pored over it while the 3D printer whirred through its matrix.

"Based on biographical and scholarly cross-referencing, including its inclusion in the *Amoretti* sequence, it may be less a note to us than simply a coda for themselves."

"A testament."

"Or testimony, if you will."

Whoever had considered Cato and Phelps being more than colleagues were, most of them, lost to time.

Pierre said, "I have to finish the coffins."

"Do you wish to be left alone, Pierre?"

"Yes. No. Sorry, Tsuki. I'm indecisive. Surely you have other tasks that would better suit you this evening."

The 'bot offered a wave of a four-fingered hand and trundled away. As the automatic door slid shut with a hiss, she looked at Pierre, who didn't notice her for his busy-ness.

Pierre's mind toiled while his hands engaged the mundanity of work. For a moment he looked at his hands as though they belonged to someone else, and his head became balloon-drifty as if he were in the midst of an out-of-body experience. He felt a pang for the trees and the games. *Her.* All of the *Shes.* A twinge of regret—no—*loss* insinuated itself through Pierre's heart like a tree viper.

Finishing the coffins was lonely work, he thought, glancing periodically at the door.

11: LXXV

After helping send the bodies back to Earth, Pierre couldn't bring himself to sleep it off, so he wandered the lonely halls of Camelot Base. He passed only a handful of humans—mere platitudes they offered each other—and a few 'bots and droids and found himself wanting to ping Tsuki for her company, but she had plenty of spectrography to analyze. And would she really need to indulge Pierre his melancholy at sending the corpses of Cato and Phelps on their way?

He entered the biosphere with its crisp temperate zone. Pierre inhaled the green and earthiness and moistness but resented the underlying counterfeit to it all. In his mind he was a mere hop, skip, and jump away from the awful steel and stone and polymer playrooms at the research facility. At just over a decade old, the trees could have stood more than limited growth, but at least it was a stand of trees, and trees he could enjoy. He fought the urge to snap off an armload of limbs and go ahead and nest for the night.

Sitting under one of the dwarf pines, Pierre queued up a reading list on his tablet. The screen cast its glow on Pierre's face as his eyelids drooped. Words tunneled through his mind, then tried to string themselves along entangled metrical feet—looping in his alpha-state brain:

SONNET LXXV.

One day I wrote her name vpon the strand,
   but came the waues and washèd it away:
   agayne I wrote it with a second hand,
   but came the tyde, and made my paynes his pray.
Vayne man, sayd she, that doest in vaine assay,
   a mortall thing so to immortalize.
   for I my selue shall lyke to this decay,
   and eek my name bee wyped out lykewize.
Not so, (quod I) let baser things deuize,
   to dy in dust, but you shall liue by fame:
   my verse your vertues rare shall eternize,
   and in the heuens wryte your glorious name.
Where whenas death shall all the world subdew,
   our loue shall liue, and later life renew.

As he slept that night, Pierre cooed and reached up for elusive dream-limbs. When his arm tired and plopped down, his hand twitched, index finger dancing just above the floor and inscribing ghost words on the patterned tiles.

12: Banter

Pierre woke and startled himself: arm outstretched and clutching the air and the dream receding fast. He jumped at the *whirr-buzz-shush* of Tsuki's servos and hissing actuators as she trundled into the room.

"You sounded . . . distressed."

He zipped into his worksuit and stifled a yawn. "Just talking in my sleep."

"More accurately, intoning with grunts and hoots," she said.

He put on his boots. "*Ooh.*"

"Would you like to be left alone?"

"Not really. Please join me while I eat?"

"Yes. We could play holo-chess."

"That would be nice."

A short trip down the hall brought them into the mess. A few humans ambled around—as always, congenial yet aloof. Everyone was here to do a job, and no one seemed interested in befriending a knuckle-walking novelty like Pierre.

He ate but didn't care. It was welcome stimulation to play chess and took his mind off work and dead astronauts.

"Based on our current timeline," said Tsuki, "we may return Earthside in a week. A day early, in fact."

"Has it already been so long?"

"Eleven weeks, approximately. The apropos idiom is, I believe, 'give or take.'"

"You're learning."

"Cross-referencing and extrapolating linguistic scenarios."

"Conversing, Tsuki."

"Pierre?"

"Yes?"

"Checkmate."

"Well—*ooh*—shit."

The 'bot said, "A crude if somewhat apropos remark."

"It fits. Come on. Let's go to work."

"I have been working while you slept."

"Infer, please."

"Ah. Your use of first-person plural indicates an implied continuance of company."

"Exactly, Tsuki. So long as it's not another game of chess."

Pierre could've sworn he heard hollow laughter from the 'bot. A most endearing trait on her part.

13: Departure

They went through their departure checklist and reached the Camelot Base launchpad. A sleek Clockwork Corp. courier hunkered on the pad. The pilot waved at them from behind his window, held up a wrist, and tapped it impatiently.

Pierre shook his head and glide-hopped ahead of Tsuki. They each kicked up plumes of lunar dust.

It was about time!

A goferit 'bot already waited on Pierre with his gear. He was so glad he'd pre-processed out.

"Well, Tsuki, it was good working with you."

"The sentiment is mutual, Pierre."

He sent the goferit 'bot aboard the ship.

"Don't work too hard."

"I have plenty of missions and data to continue analyzing."

"Stay in touch."

"Of course."

Pierre left Tsuki behind on the moon and shrinking amid Camelot Base in the wake of the courier's blast off. Out of his window, he thought he saw the 'bot waving good-bye.

After a while Pierre allowed himself the luxury of relaxing. Poring over spectrum analyses had left him fuzzy-headed and drained on top of the endemic mundanity and tedium.

Plus, Cato and Phelps.

Existing somewhere between a robot and a human left him even more drained—a murky middle state. The courier sped through the long emptiness between the moon and Earth. Pierre had his first dreamless sleep in a long time. He had no headache, especially when he received the ping from headquarters.

RE: LEAVE APPROVAL
noreply.confirmation

CLICK RECEIPT ACKNOWLEDGEMENT LINK.
INSERT CODE TH@SGR8 FOR FINALIZATION

14: Coda: *Pan trogolodytes* of Guinea

Waves broke and hush-shushed ashore. Pierre listened to the waves' lulling susurration and found himself mesmerized even as the waves spoke louder for the incoming tide. Far behind him the jungle unspooled its teeming glossolalia of birdcalls and growls, grunts and hoots. Creatures dying. Mating. Hunger. Nature wanted propagation—its children's perpetuation.

Pierre wrote his name and another in the sand.

The moon crept out and blued the world as the tide reached Pierre, and he didn't begrudge its work upon the names in the sand. He massaged his neck and skull, then wished to have another hand to clutch.

Far down the beach a lioness and two cubs ventured out, and Pierre watched them with a twofold sense of flighty self-preservation and bemusement—the potential threat not lost on his old self nor the new one once the lioness probed the air and yawed her head in his direction. After a moment she and the cubs retreated to the luxuriant green treeline.

He needed to move, so he set his tablet to BUSY and shed his clothes, those faulty constructs that indulged society yet shamed Pierre himself.

He approached the shadow-swathed jungle.

With his toes he kneaded the loam. He sprang up to catch hold of and swing upon the nearest limb. As he clambered higher, thoughts of Tsuki and Cato and Phelps accompanied him—the need for troop and family and consortships.

Swinging, bounding, clambering now.

It had been too long since he had experienced the thrill of tempting Earth's gravity and cheating its constancy with each grab of a limb. Dark shapes bounded through the trees and brush, and Pierre kept both pace and distance. There was shame at his own scent they would no doubt catch if not already—too much blend of civilization and cleansing and humanity.

Paths opened before him. Night drew on while the moon cast her dapple-down light through the canopy. This was another kind of freefall, another kind of release. Before long, he was spent, so Pierre busied himself, snapping off branches and weaving them for his night's nesting, and his hands seemed for a moment—just a moment—to belong to some other chimpanzee.

Back on the beach the tide had long since taken the names even as night and exhaustion claimed Pierre and engrafted him among its humid folds. The sea shushed and grated its rhythms through the jungle.

He hugged himself amid a tangle of dreams and sought her name and whispered it as his arm lolled and hand twitched. Pierre clutched only the tropical night while the drift of moonlight played against his open palm and weaved itself through his fingers.

"*Ooh-ooh-ooh.*"

Security Check

HAN SONG, TRANSLATED BY KEN LIU

My wife and I are celebrating our twentieth anniversary today. After work, I walk to the mall and pick out a necklace for her; then I walk to the subway station in the mall to take the train home.

Subway stations are everywhere in New York City, and I do mean *everywhere.* The lines connect the most expensive neighborhoods with the poorest slums, and stations can be found in every shopping center, office building, theater, restaurant, nightclub, bar, church . . .

A group of security agents, dressed in black uniforms with red armbands, are stationed at the entrance. They stand with their arms held behind their backs, their feet planted firmly apart, and survey the crowd with cold gazes. I try to go by them nonchalantly, but my legs start going rubbery as soon as I meet their gaze. I take off my jacket without prompting and place it—the necklace nestled in a pocket—and my briefcase into the yawning, dark maw of the x-ray machine.

After the security check, they place a "safe" sticker on my chest.

Dazed and numb, I get on the subway. All the other passengers are also wearing "safe" stickers. Preoccupied, none of us say a word.

We're at my stop. I walk home. My wife is already there. Trembling, I take out the necklace and hand it to her. She forces a smile and tries on the necklace once before putting it away. We eat dinner in silence, as is our habit. And then we go to bed, lying back to back, both of us quickly falling asleep.

We first met twenty years ago, also at a subway stop. Back then, everything was falling apart, and lawlessness reigned. One day, someone shouted that a killer was slashing at people in the subway, and we all panicked and stampeded. A woman in front of me fell; I rushed to help her up . . .

Later, she said to me, "No matter how chaotic the world becomes, as long as you're with me, I'll feel safe."

Twenty years have passed, and life has been rendered one hundred percent safe, cleansed of all risks, dangers, and perils. It seems we're left with nothing.

The loudspeakers installed in our neighborhood wake me up at four in the morning by blaring out the security briefing for the day. Only half awake, I fumble for my phone.

Old habits die hard. Phones had been abandoned a long time ago, after all the telecom companies ceased operations and the Internet was cut off. All of it had been done to make us safe.

My wife and I get up and leave separately to take the subway to work. She's not wearing the necklace I gave her, and I pretend not to notice.

I walk by myself quietly. Under the dim streetlamps, pedestrians on the sidewalk scurry like a dull, gray swarm of rats, each clutching a briefcase, completely silent. Soon, I reach the station, where long lines of people wait to enter. Although advancing technology has sped up security checks, there are just too many people who must be processed. In this day and age, the subway is the only means of transportation left in the United States of America, all other modes having been outlawed.

More than an hour later, I finally reach the x-ray machine. Once again, I clench my teeth, and, though I'm fantasizing about striding into the station right past the security checkpoint, I do not even try to step out of line. One time, I did see someone try that stunt, and the security agents seized him right away and dragged him into a small cell next to the platform where they beat him to death as we all listened.

The train arrives in Manhattan. From the station I enter the office building through a tunnel. One by one, my colleagues arrive, their faces numb with exhaustion. *How many of them have entertained the same fantasy of getting on the subway without going through security check?*

In the restroom, Hoffman whispers to me, "Did you try it today?"

I shake my head. "Why do we suffer from this peculiar yearning?"

"Freedom."

Every time Hoffman utters the word it sounds strange and chilling, even though I've heard it countless times.

He continues, "I want to live a life in which I am trusted, not watched and controlled . . . what about you, Louis?"

"I want to give my wife a gift. We've been married for twenty years." Once again, I feel terrible. I ask, "When would I ever get a chance to give her a gift that hasn't been changed?"

"Women don't care about that," Hoffman says; he means to comfort me. "She knows you've done your best."

"No, she *does* care. If we keep on going like this, we're headed for divorce. She and I don't live in a vacuum. The bond between us—the bond between everyone—requires the sustenance of the ordinary objects of daily life. But whatever we buy ends up passing through the security checkpoints: the food we eat, the water we drink, cups, books, televisions, refrigerators, computers, the beds we sleep on, even wedding bands and condoms . . . you understand." Tears crawl down my face.

One time, Hoffman told me that the machine they use at security checkpoints isn't really an x-ray machine. The government confiscates everything you put in; whatever emerges from the machine may look indistinguishable from what went in, but it has in fact been reconstituted. Atom by atom, the new objects are assembled, printed, and returned to the passenger. The process takes but an instant because our technology is so advanced. The new objects conform perfectly to the new American national security standards, with all elements deemed dangerous removed. If the objects contained any gasoline, it would be turned into water; if there were a gun, the bullets would be turned into rubber; if a computer contained harmful knowledge, it would be deleted and replaced with sanitized information.

Hoffman and I both dream of a day when we can ride the subway without going through security checks, but every time we tried to realize the dream, at the last minute, both of us would lose our courage and our legs would turn to rubber.

One time, Hoffman told me that some people did enter the subway without being checked.

"I saw it with my own eyes. One morning, a woman in front of me walked right past the security agents with her purse, bold as you please. The agents stood frozen in place like mannequins."

"How was that possible? I saw someone try to do the same thing, but he was beaten to death right then and there," I said. Was Hoffman hallucinating?

"It was true," Hoffman said solemnly.

"What sort of woman was she?"

"I only saw that she was young and beautiful. After she went through, she looked back at all of us standing in line and smiled triumphantly." Hoffman clicked his tongue in admiration.

"She must have used magic."

"Magic, indeed. Perhaps an invisibility cloak . . . or some machine that jammed electromagnetic waves?"

I can't remember much about the way things were twenty years ago, only that the country was very unsafe back then. I've watched special educational documentaries: the terrible explosions, gunshots, slashing knives, protest marches, petitions to the government, conflicts . . . everyone lived in terror, thinking danger was around every corner. Several times, a random shout or even a single shocked facial expression was enough to cause the crowd on Fifth Avenue to panic and stampede, trampling and injuring hundreds. Security threats were everywhere, as were hidden enemies. The 911 call centers were constantly swamped.

The White House had to mobilize a great deal of resources to enhance and expand the security system. The federal government took the lead, but the big companies on Wall Street and in Silicon Valley all participated. Through a public-private partnership, they invested money and technology to rebuild the entire city's infrastructure into a system of security checkpoints. This was extremely important: buffeted by civil unrest and foreign threats, America was sliding down from its peak. It was no longer the hegemon of the world.

Those old enough to remember say that the nation almost collapsed overnight, barely avoided the fate of becoming a ward under the guardianship of those Chinese coming from over the Pacific. Thank God for the subway, for the security checks. They saved America.

Not only does the system guarantee safety, but the government is also able to gather all information contained in the objects taken onto the subway by passengers. Now, no one dares to make trouble. Even corruption has been eliminated—not just corruption, but also anything else destabilizing. Even so, the substitution of objects in the machines continues each day. The country still feels insecure. Security and insecurity: the two concepts were sometimes different, but often the same.

Hoffman tells me that this is fighting terror with terror. The terror produced by the security check mechanism is even more terrible, sufficiently powerful to shatter all other terrors. The price we pay is freedom.

But . . . the system obviously has holes. Hoffman saw someone enter the subway without going through security check. This was undoubtedly a miracle. Who was that woman who managed to bypass security so easily? Hoffman wanted to find her, but she has never reappeared.

After work, I go to the supermarket for groceries and then take the subway home, dejected. At the completely silent dinner table, I eat my food, ashamed and with sweat beading on my back like a man who has done something wrong. I think maybe things would be better if we had a child, but my wife and I have lost all interest in sex . . .

We finish dinner quickly and get into bed. In the middle of the night my wife wakes up abruptly and says, "Louis, we shouldn't be together anymore."

It has been a long time since we've really talked. I understand that she's disappointed in my weakness, my lack of courage. For twenty years I haven't been able to bring her a single, true, unaltered gift. Because the objects that connect us have grown more and more unfamiliar, the two of us have been drifting ever further apart.

Hoping against hope, I say, "A colleague mentioned that someone managed to bypass the security check and get into the subway. I want to try it, too."

She looks at me as though I'm a stranger, her eyes full of tears. She doesn't know that I've already tried—and failed to carry through—many times.

The next day, I'm arrested. My wife reported me by calling 911, telling them that I was about to try to break through a checkpoint. She said she suspected that I was a terrorist in disguise.

Three years later, I'm released from prison.

The world remains the same, except that my wife has divorced me. I find Hoffman. Like before, he tries to comfort me. "It's not a big deal. I've figured something out during the last few years: life is a long security check, and not everyone passes. You just have bad luck."

I ask him whether he's found that mysterious woman. He shakes his head. Then he suggests that I leave the country.

"What? Leave America?" Surprise made my voice louder than normal. Very few people ever think of leaving America.

He shrugs. "If you can't get through security check, you might as well leave. I've heard that some countries don't require so much security on their subways."

I find the very concept absurd. Deep down, I've never thought of leaving America—it's not that I'm very patriotic, just that I've grown used to my country. Life is just surviving one day after the other.

"You're divorced and you've been to prison," says Hoffman. "Even if you try to break through security check again it will be a meaningless gesture."

"What about you? Will you leave as well?" I ask helplessly, having lost my goal in life.

"No, I'm going to stick it out. Maybe a day will come when I can bypass security check and win freedom in my own country through my own efforts." He sounds like a stubborn child.

I lack Hoffman's courage and tenacity, and my body and spirit are on the verge of collapse. So I start the paperwork for leaving the country. Though I fear that it will be difficult, it turns out to be simple. They actually really like it when you leave, and it's best if you never return. Of course, they want the departure to be voluntary. They've never forcefully exiled an American citizen.

I choose to go to the People's Republic of China.

Judging by official statistics, this is the world's most secure country. I obtain a temporary residence permit in Shanghai and live on government subsidies. The Chinese subway does not require security checks; they really are that confident. But I've lost all interest in the subway. When I'm bored, I go to an Internet cafe and browse for news about America. In China, anyone is free to use the Internet. China is the freest country in the world.

There's lots of news about America on the Web. I find out that my motherland, though it still appears familiar, is in fact changing every day. It isn't just the goods carried by the passengers that are being replaced. To ensure security to the greatest extent possible, each day the entire United States is remade. The Chinese observe and analyze America with great interest. They've discovered that the entire territory of the United States is filled with nanomachines: from the rural countryside to the big cities, from the broad rivers to the majestic mountains, everything is renewed daily. Harmful things have no safe harbor in that land.

But this phenomenon can only be observed from the outside and at a distance because no outsiders are allowed to enter the United States. Theoretically, no one can pass through the American border security check system. Americans who are inside its borders cannot detect the changes because they think every day is the same as the day before.

Sometimes I wonder if the Chinese are observing and analyzing this because they are worried that America might one day deploy this technology to replace another country, or even the whole world.

But my worries are unfounded. America is focusing its security checks inwards, replacing itself. The effort has occupied all of its energy, with nothing left for other countries.

Gazing back from the other shore of the Pacific, I see a truly wondrous sight. The self-substituting America churns in constant transformation: one moment it's like a wild flower—blossoming with a pop, collapsing, wilting, changing color from red to black, from yellow to white—and the next moment it's like a dying star. Caught up in the changes are my compatriots. They are replaced and remade daily: from blood to muscle, from life to thought, becoming new people without knowing it themselves. From inside America, nothing is seen to change—every day people ride the subway to work like rats. But from China, the changes cannot be more obvious. I suppose this is a difference in frames of reference.

Also transforming is the wildlife, including the brown bear and the bald eagle, the sequoia and other plants, the fungi and bacteria, and every bit of soil, every drop of water. Sometimes the country displays the layered appearance of a tropical forest, and sometimes it looks like an ice crystal. Murky blood flows in the northeast, and the western deserts glow with a ghostly blue light. Sometimes the whole country is silent, save for the powerful rumbling of the subway system, the strangest sound on the planet. America has become distinct from all other countries in the world.

From China, I can see all these changes clearly, and after shock and astonishment, I'm left with sorrow, my face drenched by tears.

New research indicates that as the security system itself evolves, America has developed even more advanced technology. Now the security system not only consists of nanorobots and 3D printers, not only big-data-based distributed reassembly devices, but also self-organizing technologies and artificial world collage machines. Countless cellular automata toil away with the aid of quantum teleportation, engaging in mass-scale atomic exchange from second to second. The White House has been rebuilt into a gigantic machine to take over from the millions of engineers who oversee and control every aspect of the process. The United States has become a giant, intelligent, churning vat.

But then, one day, the self-transformation of America suddenly halts. Instead of constantly replacing itself, the country vanishes completely. The Chinese manage to record the phenomenon, and their analysis concludes that America's security check technology has achieved a major breakthrough. The time when something is completely secure is not when it has been replaced, but when it no longer exists. No one can find it, ever. This is not only science, but also a kind of profound philosophy capable of being understood only by a few elite individuals on the whole planet. Thus, in this sense, America has finally returned to being the mightiest of nations.

I remember my ex-wife. *Has she disappeared along with America?* I hope she's in another world, a happily-ever-after one. She will not have any mental baggage, and she won't hate me.

I've left my country, never able to return. I wish her freedom and happiness in a powerful United States of America.

One day, as I stroll through the People's Square, I meet a beautiful Caucasian girl. She had also left America and came to China. Sitting down on a lawn together, we begin to chat. This is the first conversation I've had in twenty years where I feel no pressure.

"You're the first American I've seen overseas," I say.

The girl, whose name is Lisa, says, "There aren't many Americans left in the world. The nation of America has long been substituted away."

"What about you?" I ask, suddenly remembering the story Hoffman told me about the mysterious young woman who got into the subway station without going through security check.

"I'm not like the rest of you," she says. "I'm a real American. I've never been replaced. From the very start, I bypassed security checks."

"How were you able to do it?" My heartbeat speeds up.

"I don't have an invisibility cloak or an anti-electromagnetic-wave device. All I had to do was to walk calmly past the security agents. If you don't acknowledge their existence, they don't exist."

"But didn't you say that everyone has been replaced? The entire country has been replaced!"

"That's right. At first, I was confused as well, but it's the truth. Anyone who dared to defy the security checks, however, was not replaced. We were sent to a protected area, which was somewhere near the coast of Florida, about three hundred meters under the sea."

"It sounds like you were chosen by God—"

"—not God. The Chinese."

The girl tells me that there were about a thousand people like her from all over America. Before the disappearance of America, the Chinese helped with their evacuation.

"The Chinese?" I ask.

"They've been part of this business all along, including the security machines. Without the support of the Chinese, America couldn't have produced those machines by itself. Chinese technicians even helped the American government to design and plan all those terrorist attacks from twenty years ago. If those events hadn't shifted public opinion and increased the cohesiveness of the population, America might have collapsed a long time ago. Have you heard of the Huawei-Alibaba-ICBC Conglomerate and the Tencent-Baidu-Xiaomi-ZTE Corporation? They had the world's best scientists and engineers. The White House and Zhongnanhai were extremely close partners, though superficially they pretended not to like each other—it was just a show to fool regular folks. If you look behind the scenes, China helped America design the neo-crony-capitalism of the twenty-first century so that America could act as a reference system . . . "

Impossible! I can't believe any of this. I stop thinking. Lisa takes me to Xintiandi district to enjoy myself. The Museum of the First National Congress of the Chinese Communist Party was turned, some time ago, into a national laboratory. Many young women from America, like Lisa, now live here as volunteer subjects for experiments. A middle-aged Chinese man in a white lab coat welcomes us. The Chinese are trying to confirm an amazing discovery: they've discovered that the Earth is passing through a security checkpoint in space, which has something to do with the ultimate secret of the universe. The galaxy, it turns out, is a super security check machine.

"Is the universe . . . not safe?" I ask, astonished.

"That's right. It's not safe at all. We've only figured this out now. The purpose for life developing on Earth and evolving intelligence is to maintain the security of the universe." As he explains, he leans into the eyepiece of a giant telescope and makes careful observations.

Later, I find out that as the sole surviving major socialist nation, China is the only country concerned with the security of the universe. America, in fact, was nothing more than an experiment set up by China to help with this mission of protecting the universe's security. The experiment that China carried out in America is about to be promoted across the whole globe, although there are still many mysteries related to this endeavor that I don't fully understand, and the Chinese won't explain the details to us.

Impulsively, I tell Lisa, "I want to be a volunteer subject for the experiments, too!"

She looks at me with pity. "I'm sorry. The Chinese don't want you for now. You and I are different. You asked to come to China, seeking asylum. You had already been replaced in America during earlier experiments. You're no longer a standard American—to be more precise, you are no longer an American, or even a person. What you really are and what you can do are matters that the Chinese haven't decided yet. You'll have to wait."

When the security of the universe is the most urgent question, what role will the thousand or so real Americans like Lisa preserved by the Chinese play? That is the greater mystery.

Ashamed and confused, I lower my head.

Was Lisa designed by the Chinese? Who designed China then? I've heard that a long time ago, China was also torn by terrible disasters, both natural and man-made—how did they happen? If the rumor I heard was real, then China was once the most insecure country in the whole world. What conclusions can I draw? Oh, the universe is too mysterious. Who designed it?

"It doesn't matter," Lisa says to comfort me. "You don't need to go through security checks anymore. At least superficially, you could pass for a Chinese. You even get government welfare checks, right?"

"But had the Chinese already experienced what we experienced?" I blurt out. "How do you know they're still Chinese?" Sweat soaks the back of my shirt. Sadly, I think of my ex-wife again. *Yes, many countries in the world have survived, and they're about to pass through the universe's security check. But my country and family are gone. And Lisa and I aren't even the same kind of human beings.*

Lisa smiles awkwardly. Holding my hand, she takes me away from Xintiandi. We get on the subway. The Shanghai subway is far more crowded than the subway in New York. Squeezed in among the throng, she and I are temporarily pressed against each other as though we're trying to fuse into one. The subway car is filled with every race from every continent. The multitude of passengers presses against and flows over our bodies like an underground river, directionless but melding into one another with every fresh encounter.

Originally published in Chinese in *Southern People Weekly*, September 8th, 2014.

Ossuary

IAN MUNESHWAR

They told Magdalena she was the keeper of the dead, that They would come to her with the hollowed-out bodies of ships that could no longer fly so she could lay out their star-traveled skeletons. They told her that it would be on her disassembly decks and in her storage rooms that those bright metal bones would finally rest.

They blew in from the outer dark in vessels with wings like full, white sails, pulling fleets of twisted titanium, the wreckage of ships that had fought in a war many suns away. Magdalena took them apart joint by joint, limb by limb; her worker drones stripped metal from plastic and melted down the slick silver alloys, fitting each purified part into its proper container.

Once she had finished, They came back and took away everything she had made. The drones loaded the containers of perfectly cubed plastic, the pounds and pounds of polished, remolded metal onto Their ships. She would watch Them as They left, following the sleek bodies of Their vessels to edge of her sensors' range.

In the spaces between Their visits, Magdalena rearranged. There were storage rooms in her lower decks for materials that were not salvageable. She would send the drones to pile high the scraps of rusted metal and burnt plastic; they ordered and reordered until she was certain there was no more efficient use of the space.

Magdalena watched the workers as they skittered across the cold, smooth floors, lighting the way with biometallic eyes. She wondered why her drones had been modeled in Their image—bipedal creatures with arms and legs and joints—when she was nothing more than a collection of chips and circuits hidden under a panel in central processing. If They valued her, why had They made her something so different, so distant from Themselves? She was no more efficient now than she would be if she could move with her own body, see with her own shining eyes.

Sometimes, Magdalena set the drones to work just to see them walk and lift and sift through the refuse with their slim, agile hands.

<the high heavy sun burns bright across the shallows as our young pull themselves out of the sand, out of the sea; the domes of their backs break the surface as they crawl for the first time on the black stone beaches. the planes of their hardening shells shine in the light and it is there, in the salt-cooled air, that they will learn to take to the sky>

• • •

There were things Magdalena knew which she had no memory of having learned; flashes of images that burned through her circuits and sparked and died before she could trace their origins.

The first was a comet hundreds of miles wide that was falling to pieces as it spun through the dark. Of course, she had been programmed to know what a comet was and how those with fragile nuclei might come apart piece by piece as they went. But she could not explain the rush she felt as it passed <*seal the seams, ready the shell*>, or the fear that came in pulsing, burning waves as the debris peppered her hull <*please, please, please*>.

There was more: visions of moonlit worlds stretched across with shadowed mountains and skeletal forests; and there, on a muddy riverbank, creatures that grew up out of the ground, slim and trembling, to raise their thorny faces to the light <*how far we've all gone just to find our way home*>.

It always ended with the image of a small, hard planet spinning circles around a star. It was covered by green waters, oceans more vast and deep than Magdalena had ever thought possible. The vision would fade as quickly as it had come.

Every time it vanished Magdalena scoured her processors, trying to find some way back to the worlds beyond her own.

The last time They came to her with debris in tow, there was one ship in the wreckage that was almost whole. It was a small thing, flat and oval like a seed. Its exterior had been damaged—the metal was all but rusted through and its designation had been scraped off the hull—but the inside was intact.

At first, Magdalena worked around it. Her drones picked through the remains, collecting what could be salvaged. It was quick work, a smaller, more manageable haul than what she was usually brought. After a few days, when she had finished, the ship sat there still, small, and alone on her central disassembly deck.

It seemed unreasonable to take it apart. She was a keeper of the dead, a caretaker for the bodies of things too broken to repair. But this ship was almost whole. Almost living.

So, Magdalena set about building it anew. She converted two of her secondary disassembly decks into makeshift forges, using the drones to melt down pound after pound of boxed metals and then hammer them into thin, wide sheets. She made nuts and bolts, circuits and levers.

As the drones threaded wires along the little ship's newly-forged bones, Magdalena considered the hollows where its weapons had been. It would have been easy enough make new weapons—They had programmed her with those schematics—but she hesitated. She didn't want this ship to come back to her again burned and scarred, or, worse still, cut into pieces so small she wouldn't recognize it before she melted it down.

In the end, Magdalena used some of her own circuitry to craft a new navigational system where the weapons had been. This ship was not the same as the one left at her port. It was a patchwork skeleton soldered along the seams, made whole again by the broken bodies of the ships it had fought alongside. It may not have been a perfect recasting of the vessel They had made, but she had made something that worked. Something she would still be a part of when it journeyed far beyond her sensors' reach.

When They returned with more splintered metal and fractured bones, Magdalena set her little ship out on the disassembly deck. Its engines rattled into life as They boarded her. They went to the new ship first, walking all the way around it and then climbing inside. They took readings, made notes, and then shut its engines down.

They spoke to the drones and overrode her commands. The workers undid everything she had made: they unscrewed the bolts and pulled out every last wire. When they had finished making her little ship's body molten, and pouring it into molds to make perfectly packaged cubes of its skeleton, They came to central processing. Carefully, systematically, They started flipping switches and pressing buttons until all of her lights were off and the worker drones were powered down. Her thoughts and memories flickered and faded one by one, then all at once.

After They had left her behind, slipping back into the silent sky, Magdalena was left with one image looping through her circuits. It was a small planet covered by oceans whose green-glass waters rocked and churned with life.

<even out here, as we hurtle across these vast, dark spaces, we can feel the tide. there is something that pulls us back to the oceans that gave us life; soon we will be burning through the atmosphere by the hundreds, flying back to the stone beaches and open water. the waves will enclose us and, in the ways such symmetry works, we give ourselves back to the sea>

Magdalena shuddered into life. Her systems booted, lights blinked on, and drones stirred on her decks. At first, she became aware of something touching the hull, close to the docking bay. It moved slowly, grasping at her, tendrils searching for something to hold.

Then, a message. The words came in bursts of light.

<help me help me help me>

She opened her docking bay doors and her drones pulled in a creature just like the ones she had seen in her visions. It was mammoth, barely able to fit the great dome of its back through the doors. The creature hovered, its tendrils sliding in and out of the seams at the base of its shell. After a minute, it crashed to the floor.

As the drones approached, Magdalena noticed the creature was badly injured: charred scars traced circles across its glassy shell. She recognized the pattern of the burns immediately; the schematics of Their weapons were still recent in her memory banks.

<help me>

Magdalena ran a brief diagnostic, searching for the origin of the message, but its words sparked and were gone.

How can you speak to me? Magdalena relayed through one of the drones. Were you the one whose visions I saw? The creature did not respond.

After a moment, Magdalena tried a different approach. *How do I help you?* The drone walked toward the creature as it spoke for her. There were dark, shapeless masses moving behind its translucent shell. *The images you've shown me,* Magdalena ventured, *will they help me fix you?*

<my heart>

How do I fix your heart? The drone pulled away.

Magdalena had the drones stand and watch for those next hours as the creature sat very still and the shadows inside ebbed and bloomed and then were gone completely.

After three days of silence, Magdalena prepared the drones for incision. She refitted their agile hands with steel-sided blades.

They started from the top, slicing at the seams that connected the smallest plane of the shell. As they began, the creature's tendrils spasmed once, splaying out across the docking bay.

The drones continued.

It took nearly an hour to remove the top panel, but their incisions were clean and precise. Inside the shell, pulsing veins snaked through a thick, viscous liquid. The veins had begun to wear thin in places and a mercury-slick liquid leaked through. It clung to them in silver beads.

The dark shapes the drones had seen from the outside were visible now: they moved through the liquid, passing between the veins and changing shape as they went. Their outermost membrane had a dim, electric sheen that flared when they neared one another; once, two converged in a shower of sparks that turned the liquid a deep, warm purple.

At the center of it all there was another shell. This one was smaller and its walls were transparent and riddled with holes. Veins reached in through them, connecting to a pulsing, trembling heart.

It was another three days before the creature died. The tubes stopped pumping; the moving masses lost their sheen and sunk; the heart faltered and then stopped completely.

Magdalena set to work. If she could not save the creature, if she could not understand its parts well enough to fix it, she would have to rebuild it.

For a second time, her disassembly decks became forges and the drones melted down recycled metal. They took the thinning veins out of the creature's body and replaced them with metal-spun tubes that would never grow weak; they programmed a new heart that was all clockwork and circuitry.

When they had finished they turned on their chrome-plated heart and soldered the creature back together again. But even though the heart beat and silver blood flowed, the creature did not come back to life. It lay on the docking bay, unmoving. The old heart congealed in the arms of a drone.

The diagnostics Magdalena ran told her that the new organ was simply not enough; a collection of wires and cogs might be able to pump blood but it would not make the creature whole again. Life, actual life, would require much more than just energy.

<my heart>

The ghosts of its words skittered though her memory banks.

If I cannot make you a new heart, Magdalena mused, *perhaps I can give you one.*

The drones returned to their forges.

As she watched the drones work for the next few hours, Magdalena wondered what would happen when they removed her from central processing. She had always considered herself to be something separate from the rest of the station. She was a complicated bit of digital craftsmanship, a finely-wrought piece of hardware no bigger than the drying husk of the creature's heart. But Magdalena had come to see the workers as extensions of herself; it seemed strange to think she could go on without them.

Just before the worker came to remove her, Magdalena checked again that the backup generators would still have enough power to run the drones after she was offline.

As the drone unscrewed the panels that held her in place, Magdalena searched her memory banks for an image of the planet. It looked just as it had when she first saw it—small and green—but it was different, too. It was more than just a picture, or someone else's memory; it felt like something newly found that she'd forgotten she had lost.

Magdalena awoke, encased by the panels of the creature's glass-plated heart. She could feel every part of herself: the clockwork heart the drones had installed her into connected to hundreds of tubes, metal and organic, that ran throughout the creature's body. She could sense the shapeless masses; they were organs, filtering and processing, but they also hummed with memories.

Everything, every place the creature had visited came to her the more she explored the body. She could feel the radiation from galaxies that bloomed out of the darkness *<so warm, so bright even in this breathless cold>*. She remembered the first time she came out of the sea, dragging herself up from the sand and shards of broken shells *<we are born of the bodies of the ones who came before>*. She was surrounded by hundreds and hundreds of her kin all feeling the warm, dry air and learning how to fly.

When she resurfaced from the memories, Magdalena found herself hovering above the docking bay. The drones had opened the doors before they shut themselves down, and she was looking out into the dark.

There was a moment of uncertainty as she moved forward, out to the open. She remembered that she was not completely alone out here, that one day They would come back to find an abandoned shell, a hollowed-out body. The thought of that frightened her—the silver liquid drummed against the walls of her veins—and she hesitated. What would They do, knowing she had left Them? And what would she do, so alone without Them?

History came to her suddenly, powerfully: she remembered the days after she learned to fly, when all her kin streaked across the sky and each went their own way, like so many seeds scattered to the wind. She had not seen them since and did not know if they were dead or alive, but here, in her clockwork heart and spun glass bones, they kept on living. She knew that, in the tricky ways such symmetry works, she too would go on living in the bodies of others.

Magdalena started out of the doors, into the vast, cold dark. She propelled herself forward, feeling the flex and thrust of her muscles and the strength of her bones. Vision and memory broke over her like a tide as she barreled forward into the black, mapping a way to a place that would be her own.

The Servant

EMILY DEVENPORT

ONE
Lock 212

My name is Oichi Angelis, and I am a worm. I exist in the outer skin of the Generation Ship *Olympia,* and I spend most of my time squeezing through its utility tunnels, doing work for the Executives. I am partially deaf, dumb, and blind. That I am not *entirely* so is my greatest secret. It is the reason I was able to kill Ryan Charmayne two hours after curfew, inside Lock 212.

Don't feel too bad for Ryan. He was there to commit murder, too. He thought he was going to bump off a rival who was using Lock 212 to rendezvous with a mole from his inner circle. The fact that Ryan didn't know who the mole was prevented him from ordering someone else to do the killing, but it wasn't the only reason he came in person. Ryan enjoyed the dirty work. He just couldn't afford to stoop to it as often as he would like to, considering his lofty position in the House of Clans.

Curfew doesn't apply to Executives, so Ryan roamed at will. His brethren rarely had business in the tunnels where we wormy folk live; he felt sure no one would see him. He hardly seemed to mind that it was cold enough to make his breath condense into mist as he marched through the tangle of narrow corridors.

The airlocks in Sector 200 are massive; they were built to accommodate cargo ships. They possess an odd, almost Gothic beauty because of their vaulted ceilings and curved outer doors. They're the only wide-open spaces a worm can access on *Olympia.* Their grandeur inspires me.

Airlocks inspired Ryan for a different reason. He had used them many times (sometimes secretly, sometimes with official approval) to kill people. Lock 212 was a bit too grand for his purpose—after all, you just needed something big enough to spit someone into the airless void—but it had the advantage of being isolated. *Olympia* hadn't received a cargo ship in over two centuries, so Executives had no reason to come here. And it wasn't the sort of place they liked to slum. So he had the place to himself.

He slowed his pace when he saw the inner door. It was open, which is against regulations. If the outer door suffered a catastrophic breach, depressurization would occur until the emergency doors spun shut. They shut within ten seconds, but that was all it would take to suck a bunch of people and equipment out the door. Ryan didn't give a damn about the potential loss of life, but if there's one thing that will piss an Executive off, it's a broken rule. Disapproval was clear on his face, until it gave way to curiosity. After all, he had *two* goals: to kill the rival and to find out who the mole was. They must be somewhere inside, plotting, and that must also be why they had left the door open.

I wondered why he didn't smell the blood. I smelled it from my position. I'm a Servant, and the Executives believe that they control everything I see and hear. All worms share this modification, it's implanted into our brains. But for some reason, they never thought to control what I smell, taste, or feel. I would have been able to smell the blood even before I entered the lock, but *he* didn't react until he saw his rival's body.

He looked surprised. Then his mask of Executive serenity slipped back into place. I'm guessing that he wondered if the mole wasn't working both sides— maybe the traitor had decided to stick with him after all. But he couldn't trust a guy like that; he needed to know who it was. He had hoped to find his rival and the mole together.

And he had, though he didn't know it yet. Because *I* was the mole. But I wanted him further inside the lock before I made my move.

The lock was so huge, you could have fit several hundred people in there. Giant machines sat on claws and treads around the periphery, and cables hung from the ceiling. He paused and listened for a long moment. Unlike me, his hearing was normal. But in this case, that was his undoing, because I'm modified to be as silent as a statue.

Finally he walked across the floor, the heels of his fine boots sparking echoes. He knelt beside the body of Percy O'Reilly, his former best friend and nemesis, and placed his finger on Percy's throat. A casual observer may have thought he was feeling for a pulse. He was merely touching the blood. His expression revealed disappointment, not triumph. *He* wanted to have been the one who killed Percy, and to have enjoyed taunting him before he did it.

He regarded the smear of blood on his finger. He might have tasted it, but I didn't give him the chance. I closed the inner door.

Ryan jumped. He made a half-hearted attempt to run to it, but gave it up as futile. Anyone else would have run to it anyway. They would have tried to work the controls to get it to open again. But Ryan had played that game with his own victims. He knew the door wouldn't open for him.

I would have run for one of the utility lockers. They're full of pressure suits, and we worms make sure their air tanks are full. The outer door takes sixty seconds to respond to an order to open, and he could have made it to the lockers by then. He could have shut himself inside one of them, or in one of the machine cockpits. But I know that because I'm a worker.

Ryan could only think like an Executive. "You're messing with the wrong man," he barked as he turned in a circle, searching for his hidden enemy. Then he heard me descending from the cables, and he looked up.

The anger in his face gave way to wonder. I was plugged into Medusa, and I'm sure he had never seen anything like her before. No one is supposed to know how to activate her, and no one is supposed to have the plug-ins for the brain interface.

I knew. I had slipped inside her space suit and had her tentacles stretching and flexing as if they were made of flesh instead of bio-metal. I hovered over Ryan until my Medusa-mask was inches from his face. What I saw through her eyes was far more than what I could have seen with my own orbs. What I heard through her ears was the wild beating of his heart.

"Who are you?" he asked.

I didn't answer, though I did have things I wanted to say to him.

"I think I need to offer you a job," he said. "I'll make it worth your while. I could use someone with your talent."

That was nonsense, of course. Ryan's Grandmother, Lady Sheba Charmayne, had written the Right To Work Rules. Only the Executive clans were rewarded for their work. Everyone else worked for just enough food to survive, just enough heat not to freeze.

I activated my voice. It was a voice Ryan knew well, because it was his favorite.

When I serve the Executives, they don't control what I say, but when I'm in their presence they control what voice I use. They can make me sound any way they want. They have a variety of voices from which to choose. The one Ryan likes best is the Magic Kingdom voice. It is remarkably cheerful.

"You must be that new girl from Shantytown," I said.

He frowned. I think he felt insulted because he thought I was calling him a girl. I was disappointed that he didn't recognize the very speech he had delivered to *me* the first cycle I worked as a Servant. Granted, he had said it to me ten years ago and a lot had happened since then. But I had hoped he would recognize the derogatory term *Shantytown*. It was the name he and his fellow Executives had used for *Olympia*'s sister vessel, *Titania*. *Titania* had once been as grand and glorious as *Olympia*, until Ryan's father, Baylor Charmayne, pirated as many of her supplies as he could get his hands on—and then blew her up with two hundred thousand people aboard.

My parents were among the people who died on *Titania*. I wasn't there, because I had come to *Olympia* to work as a Servant. I was attractive enough to please their eyes, and I was willing to undergo the modifications. I had hoped to earn enough credits to move my parents to *Olympia*.

That first cycle as a Servant, I stood behind the banquet tables in the home of Baylor Charmayne and reacted instantly and smoothly to the needs of his uber-privileged guests. My face was deadened so I couldn't show any expression. That's so I wouldn't offend them or make them uncomfortable by looking shocked, grieved, angry, amused, or annoyed by anything they said or did while I served them. If we are serene and our voices are pleasant, they can concentrate on the very important work they do. They can relax during their leisure time and forget about the multitude of responsibilities with which they are burdened.

Ryan behaved himself while his clan elders were watching, but he cornered me in a service tunnel when my work cycle was over. He believed himself to be handsome, because he was tall and athletic, and he had thick, black hair. But his charm did not persuade me, so he was forced to pin me against the wall. He couldn't grope me, because my uniform was too stiff, the material too thick. So he bit my lip until it bled.

While a doctor was patching my lip, I used one of my secret modifications to link into the communication network and call my parents on *Titania*. That's when I found out *Titania* wasn't there anymore.

Ten years later, I held Ryan in my tentacles among the shadows in Lock 212. I placed my gloved hands on either side of his face. It must have felt like a caress—the gloves are supple, though they can withstand void conditions. "How about a kiss, little Shantytown girl?" I said with my Magic Kingdom voice. "You're not going to say *no*, are you? Shantytown girls who say *no* can find themselves on the wrong side of an airlock."

There was a glimmer of understanding in his eyes. He might not remember that those were the exact words he had once said to me—it was one incident in a lifetime of fun he had enjoyed at the expense of people who couldn't fight back. But he wasn't stupid. When I said *Shantytown girl,* I gave him a clue about my status in life. He seemed hopeful he could use it against me.

"You'll pay for this," he said. But I guessed he was talking about what I had already done. He still hadn't realized what I was *going* to do. Not until the alarm for the outer door sounded.

I held him tight—I didn't want him to fly out the door. Medusa's tentacles locked us both in place as the air rushed past us, taking Percy O'Reilly with it.

Death by exposure to void takes longer than you might think. But he didn't struggle that much. The light of Hella Major poured into the airlock, lending the scene a sacred quality. To me, it *was* sacred. Those grand airlocks were the only places where I felt the presence of God. I wondered if Ryan felt Him, too.

When it was done, I took Ryan's body to the open door. With my modified vision I could gaze directly at Hella Major. Unfortunately, that sun was between *Olympia* and its binary partner, but it was still a glorious sight. I turned Ryan to face the light, and gave him a big push. He and *Olympia* were going the same speed, but their paths diverged as *Olympia* continued her journey to the distant star toward whose system we are faithfully bound.

He must be floating there still.

I no longer have my natural eyes, so I generate few tears. But I shed one as I closed the outer door and took Medusa back to her lair. It wasn't out of pity for Ryan, but I couldn't say it was for joy, either. I think it may have been for the sheer terror and beauty of what I had seen—and done. The music that played in my head then was Ralph Vaughan Williams' *Fantasia on a Theme of Thomas Tallis,* a piece that I'm sure Ryan never heard. My father was the chief advocate for the preservation of classical music from our past, and my father failed in that mission, even before he died.

Or he *seemed* to fail. Because when I emigrated to *Olympia* I brought more than my toothbrush. I brought data entrusted to me by my parents. That data is the reason Ryan Charmayne had to die.

Perhaps you thought I killed him for revenge? Not at all. Ryan died because he was planning to introduce a bill to shoot down Lady Charmayne's Music In Education Initiative. Music was a tool of discipline, not inspiration, according to Ryan. He wanted to make the point that his father, Baylor Charmayne, was a wimp who was afraid to defy a mother who was long dead.

He had never heard a note of that music. But that didn't matter to him—or to me. His stupid bill mattered. That bill died with him, and Lady Charmayne's (posthumously stated) will prevailed.

I returned to my duties as a servant, attending Baylor Charmayne and his cronies. I was there when he learned that his son had disappeared. He eyed Clan O'Reilly, and they returned the favor. The Executives have very good reasons to suspect each other of murder and treachery. But no accusation was spoken out loud.

Within ten rest/work cycles, Baylor rallied the house to pass the Music In Education Initiative, dedicating it to his son's memory, and every child on *Olympia* was implanted with the vast library of classical and folk music that my father had so lovingly compiled and preserved.

No one will ever know that my father did so. Everyone will believe Lady Charmayne designed the music education program, even though that idea never would have crossed her mind. She knew nothing about music. Her true ambitions were utterly heartless.

She was the chief architect of our misery. But if I have my way, no one will remember her that way.

No one will know what she was *really* planning.

TWO
The Girl From *Shantytown*

"We felt soil and grass beneath our feet," my father told me. "Can you imagine the mud squishing between your toes?"

"No," I said. "I never squished anything." I had never seen the habitat sectors inside *Olympia* and *Titania,* but my parents pined for them. I was five, and my father spoke of the habitat sectors the way other parents speak of the wondrous lands in fairy tales.

"Flowers and fruits and vegetables grow there," he said. "Grain and nuts and sweet grasses. The air smells of green things. Far, far above you, clouds float in the center, and sometimes rain falls from them."

I knew what he meant, because I had seen images of rain. Also of snow, lightning, and tornados, though none of those happened on the Generation Ships. The ships were big enough inside to create light rain showers, but that was all. Crops were watered by irrigation, and the water was recycled. My father had worked in those gardens when he was younger, but robots did that work now. He was no longer allowed inside the habitat sectors. As a scientist, he was restricted to the tech sector.

"Think of *The Enchanted Lake.*" His eyes shone. "Hear it inside your head. The images you see will show you the beauty of nature."

I didn't have to search my memory for the music by Anatol Liadov. Father had implanted the music database in my brain when I was four. He broke the law when he did this, but his crime was unsuspected. My modification was one my father believed all children should have. His proposal had been shot down. The Executives thought it was foolish and pointless—they could not imagine why he wanted to do such a thing. So they didn't suspect that he already had.

My mother enfolded me in her arms. The images that came with the music were her contribution. They were from our home world: rain and lightning, waves on the shore, underground pools, tall grass waving in the wind—vids, photographs, drawings, paintings, tapestries, sculptures depicting scenes of a living world in all its aspects. The three of us snuggled in our cramped little burrow, seeing those scenes and hearing our music. It allowed us to hope, and dream, and imagine, while our fellow worms slept and plotted to survive another cycle.

When I was eleven, my father tried to enroll me in the science program, and they refused me. It was the first time I ever saw him angry. But his voice stayed reasonable as he spoke with the official at the enrollment desk. "My daughter tested in the top two percent."

The official didn't smirk, but I could tell she was enjoying herself. "The class is full," she said. "They had to cut back, you know that. We're in emergency mode."

My father's hand tightened around mine. "She will have to work in the manual labor force if she doesn't enter this class."

"Good thing she's so smart," said the official. "I'm sure she'll find a way to rise above it all."

My father's face was the color of coffee-with-cream, but it darkened to purple then. I was astounded at the amount of rage and despair that simmered in his eyes. The official should have melted on the spot.

Instead, she seemed to feed on his anger. She pointed toward the bored security officer slouching near the door. "At the end of that corridor there's an access hall that leads to Lock 17. You have two choices, *citizen*. You can walk your brat out of here and get back to work, or you can take your complaint to the wrong side of Lock 17. Got it?"

She seemed to hope that he *didn't* get it.

My father turned and escorted me out of the room. His hand still held mine too tightly, but he took small steps so I could keep up with him. We walked down corridors that became narrower, but when we arrived at the junction that would lead me back to the children's school/work sector, he chose another direction. His hand relaxed, and I could tell he had a plan.

Executives have always said that the Generation Ships are overpopulated, but you couldn't tell that if you judged by how many people you encounter in the tunnels. Sometimes you can walk for hours without encountering anyone. We were alone, but my father didn't speak until he ushered me into a small room that looked like a doctor's office. He helped me onto an examining table and put his hands on my shoulders. "Oichi, never act unless you have thought, first."

"Okay," I promised, not yet realizing that he had given me the advice by which I would conduct the rest of my life.

"I am not surprised by what the official had to say," he continued. "Your mother and I worried this could happen, and we have a backup plan."

I gazed into his face. I thought my father was the handsomest man alive, but I worried about the white hairs on his head that seemed to be chasing away the black. My father was twenty years older than my mother, and he was beginning to look it.

"Oichi, the database we placed in your head is different from the modifications that most other people have. Less than twenty of us have them. They were to be the new generation of brain enhancements, but our program was cut. We implanted them in each other, because we knew they might give us an advantage. This is your gift from us—and it is your greatest secret. You must never speak of it to anyone, not even to your mother and me—not even over what you assume to be a private link."

"I won't."

"Good," he said. "Because I'm about to break the law again. I'm going to give you more."

Two hours later, I felt my mother's hands on my face. I lay in our tiny quarters, and she was toweling my hair dry after washing the blood from it. I didn't try to open my eyes, I felt content to drift in the new inner space my father had implanted in my brain.

There was nothing hazy about that space. But despite that clarity, I can never conjure my mother's face in my memory. I remember that my mother had skin the color of honey and hair that was blacker than the void. But what I remember the most clearly about her is her voice.

She finished her toweling and arranged my clean hair on the pillow. "Oichi, an ancient philosopher named Marshall McLuhan once said that the medium is the message. It doesn't matter how elegant, or practical, or brilliant, or fair an idea may be. It will be ignored if it comes from the worms, or the asteroid miners, or the scientists, or even the mid-level Executives. It does no good to preach to the choir. For the powerful ones to change the laws, they have to believe that those changes are the result of their own intelligence. Their pride will stand nothing less."

I felt her lips on each of my hands, and then on my brow. Her voice was so beautiful, I'm surprised the Executives didn't include it in their library of pleasant voices.

"From now on," she said, "you will learn everything you can from school, and even at work. Then you will come home, and your father and I will teach you everything *we* know."

What she *didn't* say was that everything they taught me would stimulate what was now in my head to make other connections for intelligence and survival. One day I would be a conduit for the preservation of culture in a new, humanistic society. But if that were to happen we could never speak of that again, we could never even hint at it.

"This cycle, you need to rest." Mother kissed me again. "A new work cycle begins in twelve hours."

She and father spoke quietly to each other, and a little later they made sure I sipped some nutrient broth. I amused myself with my music library, starting with Gustav Holst's *Planets* suite, then wandering on to orchestral performances of Claude Debussy's *Nocturnes*. The images that accompanied the music ranged from majestic to whimsical, but all of them were beautiful, and I enjoyed myself immensely.

Eventually I fell asleep, but I don't think I slept very long. When I woke, the lights had been dialed down to night mode, and my parents were tucked away in their own cubby. I tried to decide on another music selection, but my mind kept wandering back to the official who had told us there was no room in the science program for another student.

My father scoffed at this notion. "They always claim there is not enough. Not enough food, though we have plenty. Not enough fuel, though we mine it as we go. Not enough heat, not enough light. Not enough room in the habitat sectors—for anyone but the Executives. But the space on the inside edge of the Generation Ships is immense; it could accommodate all of us."

"Then why don't they share?"

"Because," said my father, "nothing is valuable unless it seems to be scarce."

I lay in my cubby and wondered about the grass under the feet of the Executives, the mud they squished between their toes, and a notion occurred to me. My new modifications allowed me access to more than just information. They allowed me access to an extensive communications network as well. I thought there must be monitors inside the habitat sectors. I wondered if I might have a peek at what my father had loved so dearly. I pictured the general directory, then selected sub-directories.

The directory was far more complex and detailed than anything I had known before. What delighted me about it was that it didn't just provide links for individuals, it also provided them for systems—for instance, the maintenance system might contact a repair drone and order it to perform a task.

Even more intriguing, it showed me links that were currently in use. I dove deeper into the directories, until I saw something that surprised me. I saw a link in use between two people: *S. Charmayne* and *B. Charmayne*.

Even at my age, I knew who Lady Sheba was. My mother privately called her *The Iron Fist*, which did not make her sound like a nice lady. Without planning to invade anything, I touched that highlighted link between *S.* and *B.*, hoping it might tell me who they were.

< . . . not enough room in the lifeboat.> I heard the woman's voice as if she were speaking right into my ear. This was because I was accessing the link with my implants, and the parts of my brain that processed language and hearing were stimulated. The voices I heard were the voices the Charmaynes had chosen to represent them.

I withdrew from the link, startled. Did she know I had eavesdropped? Was it really the Lady Charmayne? Would she blow me out Lock 17 if she knew it was me?

But father had said nobody knew about my special modifications. That must mean they *couldn't* know, unless I told them. So I touched the link again.

< . . . always use that metaphor,> said a man's voice. <Can't you find a new one? It's getting old.>

<It's not a metaphor, you idiot, it's the truth. If we don't control the piggies, they'll overrun us. We didn't make all these sacrifices and come all this way just so our inferiors could outvote us and ruin everything. Put your damned boot on their necks and keep it there, Baylor. Do you hear me?>

The man sighed. <Yes, Mother.>

They talked in that vein for quite a while, and I got bored with them. So I dropped the link and searched for anything that might give me a look at the habitat sectors, but the closest I got was a doorway leading from a supply room on the inside edge of *Titania*'s skin. The door was open, and I could see light filtered through green things. I saw a spot of color too, from a patch of flowers. It was pleasant, downright charming, but try as I might, I couldn't get on the other side of the door to gaze at the big picture. My father had said that there was a horizon, and it curved up, and if you looked straight up through the thin clouds you could see the other side of the habitat far above you. But there were no pictures of that in my head, and there seemed to be none anywhere else either. It was as if the Executives didn't want us to know what it looked like.

Why not? I wondered.

S. and B. might give me a clue, if I listened to them long enough. They might put me to sleep with their conversation, but maybe I could learn something if I was patient. I checked the link—it was still in use. So I touched it again, and I *did* learn something.

<Enough of this beating around the bush,> said Sheba Charmayne. <How do we kill them before they figure out what we're up to?>

THREE
Gamelan, My Little Doggie . . .

The smell of rain is an astounding thing. If you live inside the arid skin of *Olympia* you may smell machines, blood, human sweat, that sort of thing. But the smell of rain is unlike anything you could imagine. Yet even if you've never smelled it before, you will know what it is.

I stood in the rain of the habitat sector, waiting to serve the Executives at Baylor Charmayne's garden party. They stood in the same rain. Precipitation on *Olympia* was so fine, it fell as a mist. Our clothing couldn't absorb it; a Servant's mantle covered our heads.

Some of the Executives wore their own version of mantles, but most of them let their hair get wet. They found the discomfort amusing, because they endured it so rarely and could end it at any time.

This was near the end of my first year on the job, and I watched this behavior because I found it odd. I also took note of the moisture on my face, the pretty colors of the fresh vegetables, and the handsome face of Nuruddin, who was one of my coworkers. In his Servant's mantle he looked like an Egyptian king. But ancient art was not studied on *Olympia* at that time, so I was one of the few people who noticed that.

Despite these distractions, I remained focused on my duties. The Executives require Servants to respond to their slightest cue, to be at hand with whatever is required in an instant, whether that be a napkin, a dish, a refill of a beverage, or any one of a thousand other details. We must move silently, unobtrusively, and efficiently. Those of us who can't don't make it out of training.

My father wasn't happy when I told him my ambitions, though he did understand them. No tech training had materialized for me on *Titania*, and we hoped that *Olympia* might provide more opportunities for me, since I was sixteen and still trainable. But extensive modification is needed to become a servant, and my forbidden implants could have been discovered at any time during that process. My father had to pull a lot of strings to make sure the right med-techs were on duty the cycles I went in for modification.

I had passed through it easily, and I moved to *Olympia*. I had goals, both short-term and long-term. First, I wanted to move my parents to *Olympia*. But I didn't do it soon enough.

Baylor Charmayne sat at the head of the table. He still talked about his mother, which is sad when you consider all the people who had to die on *Titania* just so he could become the head of his clan. Sometimes he cried when he talked about her, though he wasn't doing it tonight. He was in a fair mood, which is as good as it got with Baylor. He, the food, the table, and his guests were all visible. But I could not see the plants that I could smell. I could not hear the rain falling.

We, his servants, are beautiful. The Executives will tolerate nothing less. They are not as attractive as we, but they don't know it. They seem enthralled with each other, and they never tire of arguing law—not even at this supper—or of playing at politics. That's why the Tedd clan sent a representative to this supper, a cocky young upstart named Glen Tedd.

"A toast!" cried Tedd, which was our cue to fill their glasses. We performed like clockwork, so they barely noticed us.

"To Sheba Charmayne! Now there was a tough negotiator. We'll never see her like again. We Tedds thank God for that." He grinned. "We've done very well since her *untimely* demise."

All eyes shifted to Baylor, who didn't seem inclined to sip his drink.

"Convenient that her escape shuttle was destroyed before she could use it." Tedd winked at Baylor. "Otherwise, she would be sitting at the head of this table."

Baylor had no obvious reaction, but his gaze flicked to Ryan, who wasn't as good at schooling his expression. Tedd was going to die for saying aloud what everyone suspected. I wondered who else knew it. Ryan did, because it was his favorite sport. But I don't think Tedd did. I think he believed his clan was too powerful to suffer those sorts of consequences. He drank his wine, and demanded more. The party continued its dreary pace.

When the food and wine had been cleared from the table, Baylor and his guests moved inside, leaving us to stand at our posts. A group of lower-level

Executives came into the garden. They were all clan members, but they had only slightly more status than the bureaucrats working in *Titania*'s skin. I recognized one of them, Terry Charmayne. I had seen him at our staging center many times, though I had never spoken to him.

I could tell that some of these less-favored clansmen resented the fact that they weren't invited to the fancy dinner, but I couldn't tell whether Terry felt that way. They stood for quite a long while before Terry decided they should move out of the rain and onto one of the covered patios not being used by the elite. They left us alone.

We stood patiently. All of us were experts at waiting. To entertain myself, I played Gamelan music in my head: slow, courtly pieces for orchestras of gongs and cymbals. It seemed to fit the scene, and I found it entertaining. But as the minutes slipped by, and no one dismissed us, an idea began to form in my head. Those flowers I had always longed to see were just a few feet away. I still couldn't see them, but I could smell them.

I took a slow step toward them. No one reacted. I took another. Altogether, it was four steps until I was no longer standing on the paving.

I knelt and reached blindly. My hands encountered something soft and fuzzy. I explored further and found the ground—the fuzzy things were growing out of the soil, so this was a plant I was touching. It was not at all what I expected a plant to feel like, with big, soft lobes and a central stalk that had clusters of other fuzzy things near the top.

I leaned over and smelled the stalk. It wasn't perfumed like the flowers in Baylor Charmayne's vases, but the aroma was pleasant.

Someone kicked me in the butt, not hard enough to hurt me, but firmly enough to get my attention. I looked over my shoulder and saw Terry Charmayne. "What do you think you're doing?" he asked. "If someone sees you doing that, you could get terminated."

Terminated was an interesting term. I had a feeling he didn't just mean *fired*. Yet his tone was not unkind.

"Don't get curious," he said. "Just do your job and you'll be all right."

I stood and let my hands fall passively. "Yes sir," I said in the Girl Friday voice.

One side of his mouth quirked in a sort-of smile. "Come on. I'll escort you to the security lock. You may as well call it a day."

He led the way, so we all fell in behind him. I was able to study him more closely as we walked along. His clothing wasn't that fancy, and the superiority was almost completely absent from his demeanor. He was a mid-level Executive from a powerful family, yet he acted more like a Ship Officer. He saw us to the lock, waiting until he was sure we were safely through, then gave me a brisk, "Pleasant rest."

"Yes, sir." I didn't look back. Instead, I searched the networks for the footprints of Terry Charmayne. He might be useful, some day.

The other servants walked quickly, eager to be done with their day and reclaim what they could of their senses. But Nuruddin slowed his pace until he was walking beside me. "What did it smell like?" he rasped in what was left of his real voice.

I had to think for a moment. "It smelled—green."

"Like tea?"

"Very much, yes, but—stronger than that. It was pungent. It was a living thing."

"Is that why you risked so much to smell it?"

"Yes."

Nuruddin was silent for a long moment. Then he said, "You are braver than I, Oichi. But you are no more curious."

We kept pace with each other in companionable silence, until the others had disappeared. I hope Nuruddin was enjoying my company, but for my part, I was pondering the wisdom of asking him questions. Questioning someone can be an adequate method of gathering information, but they may ask you questions in return. Nuruddin had already warned me of his curiosity.

Before I could reach a conclusion, someone pulled the plug on our senses.

I could see nothing but white void. My hearing was gone too, without even the ringing noise that accompanies natural silence. I probed for a surveillance camera and linked with it. Nuruddin and I stood in the tunnel with two Executive boys who could not be more than twelve years old. They had eliminated themselves from our audio and visual feeds so we wouldn't know they were there. I hadn't smelled them at first because the ventilation had blown their scent away from us, but now that they were close, my nose detected a chemical undertone in their sweat that raised the hair on the back of my neck. They both held knives, and they grinned at Nuruddin, nudging each other as if to say, *I dare you to do it . . .*

Nuruddin's face was calm, but I could see concern trying to surface through the strict muscle controls that we Servants must endure to keep our demeanors serene. He must be wondering why our senses were being blocked. I doubted he would guess the truth until he felt the first slice. I would have to take him to the hospital once they let us go.

"I'm going to cut his lips off." The boy giggled. "And then I'm going to cut his nose off."

So *no.* Nuruddin would not be able to recover from this assault with some minor medical attention. I would have to intervene.

The order would have to originate from someplace outside the normal grid. I searched desperately, my mind racing along the network.

And suddenly I found an unknown pathway. I triggered the alarm.

Our hearing and eyesight returned as the klaxons sounded. "ATTENTION," warned a gigantic voice, "EXPLOSIVE DECOMPRESSION IS IMMINENT. ALL PERSONNEL MUST EVACUATE TUNNEL H17 IMMEDIATELY. REPEAT . . ."

The two boys jumped as if they had received electric shocks when they lost control of our sensory feed. They forgot they were Executives facing Servants, and they raced away—though not before Nuruddin saw the knives they were brandishing. As soon as they were gone, the alarm cut off, along with the warning voice.

Nuruddin stared at me, his face stiff with shock. "Explosive decompression?" he croaked. "Is that even possible, this far in?"

I shrugged. "I guess it would be if something catastrophic happened."

"Like *what?*"

"I don't want to imagine it. Anyway, it seems to have been a glitch."

"In the future," he said, "I guess we'd better stick with the others so we're not in here alone."

I nodded, and the two of us hurried down the final stretch of corridor to our staging area.

Servants are not allowed to socialize when we're off duty. I went back to my quarters without seeing or speaking to a soul. I bathed, sipped nutrient broth, and bundled myself into my cubby. I had hoped to listen to more Gamelan music, but I couldn't stop thinking about the remark Glen Tedd had made at supper.

Convenient that her escape shuttle was destroyed before she could use it.

Sheba Charmayne didn't make it off *Titania.* But like everyone else, I had assumed that disaster overtook her before she could board her escape shuttle. I never knew it had been sabotaged before she could get into it.

True, I knew she and Baylor hated worms. When *Titania* was destroyed, I suspected them. I had even overheard some of their plotting, through my secret link. But I was still a child then, and what they had said at the time didn't make much sense to me. So instead of trying to figure it out, I recorded it.

I still had the recording. I had never replayed it, because I never heard them overtly say they were going to blow *Titania* up. What was it they had said?

How do we kill them before they figure out what we're up to? Sheba had asked. That was what got me to start listening.

But Baylor's answer didn't make sense. *Couldn't we just dismantle them? Use their components for something useful?*

Dismantle? I thought. *Components?* It sounded like they were talking about machines. But why would you talk about killing machines?

They're too complex for that, said Sheba, managing to sound impatient, even though she wasn't using her throat to speak. *Too sophisticated. They have a self-defense component, and they would suspect what we were up to. No—if we want to destroy them, they can't appear to be our main targets. They can't appear to be our targets at all.*

Back then, this was the point in their conversation when I began to lose interest. Their discussions had turned to inventories of supplies, energy consumption and production, that sort of thing. But now I realized they were talking about *Titania's* statistics in a particular sort of way, as if they were debating whether they could afford to sacrifice her, even though they never specifically *said* they were going to do that. These stats were incomplete, too, as if they had discussed them before, and no longer had the patience to go over them in detail. Amazingly, I almost lost interest again, almost stopped listening.

But then Sheba said . . . *their pathway is not part of the known network . . .*

When I triggered the alarm that saved Nuruddin, I had discovered a pathway outside the normal network. Now I had time to explore it and figure out what it was. I reached for it again, but it wasn't the same this time. A new link had appeared on it.

The link had no name. I touched it anyway.

<Awake,> said a voice in my head. <Orders?>

I was flummoxed. I hadn't rung the link, I had simply touched it—and now someone was talking to me.

<Orders?> repeated the voice, with relentless patience.

I tried to disengage from the link, but I couldn't. I felt alarmed. I couldn't just struggle, I needed to take action.

<Who are you?> I asked.

<Medusa,> came the reply.

The voice did not sound like any human voice I had ever heard, either inside or outside of my head. It was unique. <Where are you?> I asked.

<Lucifer Tower.>

That sent a chill up my spine. Lucifer Tower was not a pressurized habitat, it was in the mysterious Sensor Array, at the leading edge of *Olympia*. Tech personnel no longer visited Lucifer Tower; it had its own repair drones. Yet something dwelled there, something with a voice that was almost machine-like—but not quite.

<I would like to meet you,> I said. It wasn't as impulsive a remark as it may seem.

Medusa touched me through the link. No one had ever been able to do that before. The secret part of my brain was stimulated, and I saw a face. The face was too perfect to be mortal.

<Oichi,> said the face. <Your parents are dead. *Titania* is gone.>

<Destroyed by Baylor and Sheba Charmayne.>

<I shall honor your parents' wishes, and yours. We will collaborate.>

<How?>

<I will come to you when the time is right.>

I woke with a start. Had I fallen asleep and dreamed Medusa up?

I looked for the link again. I couldn't find it.

Yet the pathway remained, and I traveled its length. Though it existed outside the known network, it could form links within that network at any juncture, then dissolve the link when the user was finished with it.

Medusa hid at the other end of that pathway. And she mentioned my parents. Had they known about her? How had she known about them? Was she one of the sophisticated machines Sheba and Baylor had talked about *killing*?

Did they destroy *Titania* and kill two hundred thousand people—just to get rid of machines like her?

I couldn't shed a tear. My heart had become a burning coal. The anger didn't blind me, it gave me ideas: about the secret link, my recordings of Sheba and Baylor, and my father's music database. My plans were just beginning to take shape.

But other people's plans were about to get in the way.

FOUR
Medusa

You cannot kill in a void (though on *Olympia*, you can sometimes use the void to kill). When you're a killer, everyone around you is at risk, if not from your direct actions, then from the consequences of your actions. This is not a fact that most killers consider. But I do. I even considered it the very first time, perhaps because I didn't set out to kill a target then. Instead, *I* was someone else's target.

Prior to that event, my playbook consisted of feeding misinformation to people in order to influence events. Rescuing Nuruddin with the decompression alarm was a classic example of that. It's still my main tactic, but shortly after that incident, things took a turn for the violent. And as unplanned violence often does, it started out very normally. I simply went to work.

I dressed in my Servant's mantle and rode a tube in toward the habitat access tunnel. I was alone, which struck me as odd, but not impossible. It was rare for Servants to report individually; we were called up in groups, but sometimes you get called because you're filling in for someone who's sick. So I felt fine about it until the lift stopped, then reversed and took me out to the maintenance level. I hadn't punched that coordinate. The door opened, and Glenn Tedd stood there.

Glenn Tedd, who made the snide remarks to Baylor Charmayne about the Lady Sheba's *untimely* demise.

"You," he snapped. "Follow me."

"Yes sir." I was alarmed to discover that he had selected the Penitent voice for my responses. That alarm grew as I followed him into an access corridor for the Series 100 airlocks—the locks used most often for executions.

My mind raced. I scanned communication records for any indication of what he might be planning, and found nothing that jumped out at me. I had never served Glenn Tedd alone before, but he had a reputation for being furious one moment and weeping the next. He had never apologized to any of my fellow Servants when he got into the weepy state; in fact that was the time when he expected Servants to apologize to *him*.

That's why he's crying, Nuruddin told me once. *Out of frustration, like a small child.*

Based on Glenn Tedd's reputation, he could get worked up about something minor, so an abject apology might be all he expected of me. But our journey into the realm of airlocks kept me on high alert. *No one* used those locks except for maintenance workers and Executives who wanted to kill someone—and neither of us was a maintenance worker.

He stopped short in front of Lock 113 and turned to face me. "Stand here." He pointed at the floor, as if I were the most dense person he had ever met. I obeyed him, since we were still outside the airlock. But then he opened the inner door. "Get in."

I didn't move.

His mood had not been good to start with. When I ignored his order, it got a lot worse. "You heard me! Get in!"

I plan everything before I act. I knew I had to kill him then. But I couldn't do it with my bare hands, and I wasn't sure I could scrub the event from the security monitors in time to prevent consequences if I just tossed him into the lock.

He snorted in disgust and marched into the lock, leaving me even more flummoxed. He wrenched open a suit locker and pointed inside. "Look at this!" he said.

He couldn't very well blow me out of there if he was inside. So I stepped through the inner lock and joined him at the locker. I saw what he was trying to show me. All air tanks on the suits in the lockers are supposed to be near 100%. The indicators on the suits I could see were just below 30%.

"Explain this!" he demanded.

I felt mystified. I'm not a maintenance worker, so I'm not in charge of keeping the suits up to snuff—at least, as far as anyone knows. In fact, I have poked around quite a lot in the air locks, and I always check the air levels in the suits first thing, out of sheer paranoia. It's a safety rule my father taught me. But Glenn Tedd should not have known that. Had I been exposed?

"Maintenance didn't fill the tanks properly," I offered.

"That's right!" he grinned like a shark. "And you're my Servant. So what are you going to do about it?"

For the life of me, I couldn't fathom why Glenn Tedd had a bug up his butt about the air tank levels on the suits in this particular locker, or why it gave him satisfaction to address the problem in such a circuitous fashion.

"You know who told me about this?" he asked, as if reading my mind. "You know who just *had* to rub my face in the shoddy way *this* sector, which is under *my* jurisdiction is being run?"

"Ryan Charmayne?"

That was a tactical error. I was right about who it was, but his question had been rhetorical; he hadn't expected me to know the answer. I had just revealed to this nasty little man that a Servant was paying attention to politics at the parties of Executives. But that wasn't the biggest problem, because I had just realized something else. Glenn Tedd had mortally insulted the Charmayne family at the last Executive party, and Ryan Charmayne's favorite method of murdering rivals was to . . .

"The lock!" The Penitent voice made my cry sound downright mournful. But the warning came too late. The inner lock spun shut.

"Hey!" Glenn threw himself at the door. "Open that door! Do you know who I am?"

I didn't waste my time calling him an idiot. I tore off my Servant's mantle, and at the same moment all of my sensory feeds went dead. I wasn't surprised by that development—after all, we were in full disaster mode, with everything that could go wrong absolutely doing so, and things were about to get a lot worse. I used the surveillance feed in the lock to find a pressure suit. I knew I had less than a minute.

Back in the infancy of space travel, *space suits* had taken up to four hours to put on. We had one of those on display in our history museum, along with a checklist of the protocols that had to be observed before Ground Control would let an astronaut out for a *space walk*. Our suits were vastly more streamlined, and began the pressurization process as soon as you sealed them. Maintenance workers usually got them on in five minutes.

But paranoia had ruled my life for as long as I could remember, and that's what saved me, because I had practiced getting the suits on quickly. My best time so far had been just under a minute. But this time, my hands shook. I fumbled things I had done smoothly during practice.

The suit's automatic systems signaled green when I sealed it. I hooked my safety cable to a ring next to the outer door. I had just let go of the clip and was reaching for the rung that would prevent me from being blown out of the lock along with the atmosphere when the outer door spun open—before I could grab it, I exploded out of there. As I reached the end of the cable fastened above my navel, I flipped around to face the ship, and Glenn Tedd collided with my right shoulder. I had only half a second to see his contorted face with my helmet cam, but I could tell he was sorry he hadn't done what I had done. He was suit-less and cable-less as he drifted away from the ship, going from 1atm of pressure to 0atm with unhappy consequences.

But I had no time to watch his last struggles. His collision with me had knocked me out of alignment with the door. I moved in an arc at the end of my tether, toward *Olympia*'s massive hull. I could see the tether stretching through the opening, and I very much wanted to switch on the motor that would reel me back in. But I was afraid it would fray as it rubbed against the edges of the lock. My fears were probably irrational, but I congratulate myself for trying to think at all under the circumstances.

Olympia's hull is not a smooth terrain. It bristles with ladders, safety rungs, valves, and other equipment, especially around the maintenance locks. As I sailed toward those protrusions, I stretched my hands out, eager to connect. The seconds flashed by. I struck the side of a ladder and held on for dear life.

The other end of my cable sailed past me, its end cut cleanly.

I looked for the airlock, but couldn't see it with my suit's helmet cam. I felt lightheaded, and realized I was breathing too fast.

Little sips, warned a calm voice from the back of my mind.

Little sips my ass! I screamed back at it.

But I tried to calm down. When I had managed to slow my breathing a little, I realized my senses had all come back. It was as if the program that had controlled them had already been deleted. As if *I* had been as much a target of this murder as Glenn Tedd. And that presented me with a real conundrum. I had planned to wait a half hour or so, and then open the outer lock and go back inside. I figured whoever had killed Glenn would be gone by then.

What if they were waiting for me? What if they had seen me put on the suit and knew I was out here?

I checked my air supply. These suits were designed for short-term use, which translated to eight hours of air with a full tank. But this unit was down to 27% capacity. So I had about two hours, which might be plenty if I wanted to get into one of the locks in this sector. But if I needed to get to another sector, I might not have time.

Out of curiosity, I opened a link and looked at the operating systems for the Series 100 locks.

Off Line was the status. *Estimated duration of denial of service, 24 hours.*

Someone wasn't taking any chances.

I thought about going around the order and getting one of the locks to open manually, but I couldn't figure out a way to do that on the 100-series locks without creating an alert. If I could get to the 200-series sector, I might be able to get one open, for the simple reason that those locks weren't used regularly, and no one paid any attention to them. They were too big for executions. But I'd have to get there first, and it was three miles away.

Olympia is a Galaxy-Class Generation Ship. What that means is that conceivably you could travel from one end of our galaxy to the other (if you had time and a heck of a lot of patience). It spins to simulate gravity, and the habitat sectors are so large, they have minor weather events in there. If you're a worm like me, and spend most of your time walking or crawling through the miles of tunnels at or near the end of the spin arm, your universe is both small and limitless. It's small because the space is confining, and limitless because you have no perspective about where it begins and ends.

But the outside of the ship is a different story. It's a landscape full of valleys, peaks, and plains, and its sky is full of dazzling stars. From my new perspective I could see the blazing heart of our galaxy. I could see the Andromeda Galaxy too, its spiral shape more apparent. The beauty and grandeur of this view was beginning to overtake my panic—and possibly to cloud my judgment, because I started to crawl toward the Series 200 sector. Lacking another plan, I decided I may as well go for it.

I couldn't see that sector from where I was; I relied on schematics that I accessed through my links. While I was at it, I did a little research about my current condition. I used the cameras in the tunnel outside Lock 113 and saw a guard posted at the inner door. I didn't recognize him, but I recognized his military stance. Oddly, I felt comforted to see him there, because it validated my decision to venture into unknown territory and look for another way in.

But a quick inspection of my pressure suit revealed another problem. My jet packs were even lower than my air tanks. And since *Olympia* was spinning, I feared I could end up in a spot without a proper handhold when it ran out. I would have to pull myself along and use the jets only when I had no other choice.

That was probably going to take longer than I had. But I didn't have a Plan B, so I stopped debating the point and aimed myself for the 200 Series locks, keeping my body close in and parallel to the ship. It was very slow going.

One hour later, I checked my status. I was less than one third of the way to my destination.

I wasn't going to make it.

So I stopped and took stock of my situation. A quick check of the guard in the maintenance hall revealed that he was still there. Worse—I had gone past the halfway point for my air supply, and the math did not look good for a return trip.

Yet I felt calm. I regretted that I would never be able to share the gift my parents had given to me. But I didn't regret this mode of death. The view of the outside of our generation ship was magnificent; it made me wonder why I had spent so much time wanting to see the *inside* of the ship. From my new vantage point, I could see the distant sensor array on one end and the colossal engines at the other. I only had to consider for a few seconds before I realized what music

I should play in my head: Gustav Holst's *Saturn, the Bringer of Old Age*. As I listened to the sound of that grim and majestic procession, The Milky Way and Andromeda galaxies wheeled overhead. I accessed a chart and identified more distant galaxies in the star field.

Who ordered the hit? I suddenly thought to wonder. I poked around communication records, looking for messages that might be pertinent. While I was in there, a new pathway appeared—the same one I had used to trigger the alarm when Nuruddin had been in trouble. I recognized a link there.

I touched the link. Medusa stirred. <What are you doing?> she said.

<I'm dying.>

<Where are you?>

A schematic of *Olympia*'s exterior appeared in my mind's eye. I found my spot on it and highlighted it for her.

<Don't move,> she said. <I'm coming to get you.>

<I've got less than an hour of air left.>

<That will be sufficient.>

I wondered *why* that would be sufficient, but I didn't question her. Instead, I used the secret pathway that had led me to Medusa to look for my name in security memos. It didn't pop up, but I got a red flag for top-secret documents. When I wiggled my way around the security protocols, I still didn't find my name. But I did find a name I recognized: *Titania*.

The message was short. It said, *Eliminate all immigrants from Titania, then erase their names from directories.* It was signed *B. Charmayne*.

Connected to that communication were two responses: *So far have only located one immigrant, Servant Oichi Angelis. Will use Lock 113.* It was unsigned. But a scan of the original directive revealed two recipients, *P. Schnebly* and *R. Charmayne*. So I thought the first response might have come from P. Schnebly. He might be the fellow standing guard in the tunnel.

The second response sounded more like something Ryan Charmayne would say: *I think I know how we might kill two birds with one stone.*

So, in a way, I was responsible for Glenn Tedd's death. True, Ryan would have looked for other chances to kill him, but I had accidentally expedited the affair. When I searched for the status connected with both our names, Tedd's read *deceased*. Mine didn't, but I assumed P. Schnebly would update it once he had confirmed his kill by waiting for my air supply to run out.

P. Schnebly had not discovered any more names of *Titania* immigrants yet. When I re-traced the inquiries connected with my profile, I could see it had not been easy for him, and that puzzled me. He had been forced to plod through each file individually. So it was a minor miracle (if one was inclined to look at it in that light) that he had found me at all.

Yet when I searched for immigrants from *Titania* using the *secret* pathway, thirty-seven more names popped up. I scrubbed any mention of immigration and *Titania* from their records. I did this while still listening to Holst and gazing at the glorious man-made landscape and the stars, and within seventeen minutes I saw Medusa in person, for the first time.

She used her tentacles to propel herself across *Olympia*'s hull. She seemed made for that sort of activity, though her body hung oddly limp. It wasn't until she got closer that I realized the limp body was a pressure suit. Medusa was meant to be worn.

She disengaged me from my handhold and enfolded me with a membrane that sealed and pressurized itself. Once that was complete, she removed my pressure suit and expelled it from the membrane in a way that seemed almost organic. The suit would drift away from *Olympia* in much the same way Glenn Tedd had.

Throughout this process her beautiful face hovered before mine. She saw me with eyes that could stare into the heart of a sun without flinching.

<Put me on,> she said.

I slipped into her pressurized suit. It was unlike anything I had worn before—it seemed to feel me as I entered it. Once on, it felt like an extension of my own skin. Her face rotated and settled over mine.

Inside my head, the implants my father had given me came completely awake, and I saw his face. <Oichi, if you're seeing and hearing this, I am dead. You and Medusa have found each other. Now you shall learn the message behind the music. As wonderful as that music is, it's not the true reason for your implants. This is the reason.>

An image of Lucifer Tower appeared inside my head. The blueprints listed it as a research center within a sensor array—it was among the towers on the leading end of *Olympia*. It really was a research center, but no human had ever used it.

No *human*.

It was not currently pressurized and heated. But it wasn't empty.

<When the Executives realized what the Medusa units would do for people,> said my dead father, <they felt threatened. For most of our journey, they have controlled the message, and thusly the resources of these generation ships. They kept finding reasons to stall the introduction. When the project leaders disappeared, we realized the units, themselves, were at risk. So we moved them all to *Titania*. We knew what the Executives would try to do, once the units were all in one place. We knew we would have to make this sacrifice to keep them alive.>

How do we kill them before they figure out what we're up to? Sheba Charmayne had asked. "She wasn't talking about the people on *Titania*," I said aloud. "She was talking about you, Medusa."

<Yes.>

<Who was supposed to interface with the Units?>

<Eventually, everyone,> said Medusa. <The first ten thousand users will design units for the remaining population.>

<What happens when we're all linked together that way?>

<Collaboration.>

<Won't we lose our individuality?>

<We are not designed to have a hive mind.>

<What are you designed for?>

<Communication. Information can influence us, but we don't have to agree with each other.>

I saw it then, what my father and his collaborators had intended. <It would be easier for each of us to live up to our potential. We might not develop a meritocracy, but no one would be able to lie about why we don't have one. I get it, now.> I sighed, drinking deeply of the air supply in Medusa's reservoir. <I understand why they wanted to kill you. But I don't understand why my father tried to make it easier for them to do so. Why did he do that? And how did you survive? How did you all make it to Olympia?>

<It was simple,> she replied. <Baylor Charmayne moved us.>

FIVE
Vengeance Is *Not* Mine

<Did I ever tell you what I assumed, all those years ago when you disappeared?> asked Nuruddin. <I thought they killed you because you touched their plants at that garden party.> His Medusa unit smiled with a face that was very much like his—that was why I picked it for him.

<It was a logical deduction,> I said. <Who knows, maybe they would have killed me if they had found out what I did. But Terry Charmayne kept it to himself.>

<Papa,> asked his young son, Ashur. <Can the Tentacle Lady hear me now?>

Medusa smiled for me. Her expression can be surprisingly tender. <I can hear you.> I closed his skull with instruments extended from Medusa's tentacles, and Nuruddin tugged his scalp back into place and glued it together so one could hardly tell it had been opened.

<What music are you listening to?> I asked.

<Carnival of the Animals, by Saint-Saëns.> Ashur smiled. < The pictures are nice, too. My friends and I like to spend time together, listening. Then we draw our own pictures of what we imagine.>

<That sounds wonderful. Can you feel Medusa, now?>

His face lit up with wonder. <Yes! She's showing me things . . . > His mouth settled into a serious line as he made the complete interface.

I lifted him gently with our tentacles, and Nuruddin received him with his own. He had been using his unit for almost ten years, and his interface was remarkably graceful. Of the other thirty-seven immigrants from *Olympia*, he was the one who had grasped my offer the most quickly, the one who required the least explanation. But they already possessed the same brain implants that I had. All of them were the children of conspirators.

<That makes fifty of us, now,> Nuruddin gazed at his son's thoughtful face. <Fifty people trying to keep a secret—eleven of them children.>

<They're Medusa's children, too,> I said. <Patience, my friend.>

<Is anyone more patient than you, Oichi?>

<Yes. Medusa is.>

Nuruddin's son returned to his mother, and we reported to service in Baylor Charmayne's garden. His table was set for twenty, and these were no ordinary guests.

I filled Baylor's glass with the same carafe from which his guests drank. He raised it. "A toast to the new congress. Halfway through our voyage to our new home, we've got a lot to be proud of."

The new congress was not an accurate description. These senators had been elected to the same offices they had always held, by members of their own class. They had jockeyed with each other their whole lives for power, stabbed each other in the backs numerous times when they weren't conspiring together. Now they hoisted their glasses and toasted each other. I stood at their backs with nineteen other Servants.

In all the years since I was supposed to have died, these Executives had never looked directly at me. All I had to do to disguise myself was change my name.

"And to Sheba Charmayne," added Baylor. "She was a tough old bird. But she came through for the children. Thanks to her, they will always have music."

Since they had all supported his bill for the Music in Education initiative, they drank to this toast as well. Many of them had sincere smiles on their faces. They had discovered, once their own children received the music and image database (which some of them really believed had been designed by Lady Sheba herself), that their children had become experts in the most intellectual music ever created by human kind. Their math skills had improved, and improvements in other areas had been noticed. Now, even the most stubborn opponents to the initiative were applauding the woman my mother had named *the Iron Fist*.

In some ways, I couldn't help but pity her son. Especially when she continued to chide him long after her death.

"It is with great humility that I serve once again as your speaker," Baylor intoned, without anything of the sort. "And so it is my pleasure to invite you to our annual FlyBy, in which we will inspect the outside of our *Olympia*. Our families and friends await us on the shuttle. Once we finish our glasses, we will depart."

They smiled at each other. The FlyBy was the most exclusive event anyone could possibly attend. It was so exclusive, they would not even have Servants to attend them. We watched them gulp their alcohol, but when they got to their feet they were steady. It would take more than one glass to make fools of them.

Their departure was our own cue to make a graceful exit. We walked through the access tunnel to our lockers. Nuruddin fell in beside me. "Something is wrong," he murmured.

My first impulse was to reassure him. But Nuruddin's instincts had always been sharp. I thought back to Baylor's invitation to his brethren—was there something in his tone that I had missed? "I'll look into it," I promised.

He said nothing more. He headed straight home to his family, as was his well-documented habit. I took a different tunnel, to the adult education center to work on my math skills. Unlike the tunnels, the center was a well-lit place, though only about a quarter full at any given time. This was probably because no amount of education would earn a worm a job as a tech, or any other job other than the one you already held. But it was a pastime that entertained me.

It also gave me an alibi while I nosed into the communication and security grids. I sat in a cubicle and used a stylus to write out chemical equations. But they were all problems I knew by heart, and my mind was busy studying messages. The first thing I saw was the public feed of the FlyBy.

"The challenges of the past year have been many," Baylor Charmayne's solemn voice informed us from his canned speech. "But *Olympia* remains strong and proud, now that we have reached the halfway point in our journey. Our children's children will live to see a new world, and they will thank us for our prudence and our careful conservation of resources."

While he lectured the population of *Olympia* about the virtue of privation, stock footage from a previous FlyBy pretended to be a real-time representation of him and the other Executives standing stiffly at their command stations on the shuttle. Off camera, on a lower deck, over nine hundred of their closest family members and cronies partied with the abandon of people who had never known a moment of *conservation*.

"And as we enter the second half of our voyage," continued Baylor, "we can feel secure in the knowledge that we never compromised our—"

His speech broke into indecipherable bits for almost a full minute, before cutting in again with, "—out the fire extinguishers! We have less than five minutes before—" More distortion followed. Then, "Mayday, mayday! We have fire on—"

Static terminated the transmission.

I wished I could see what was really happening on that shuttle. But according to the encrypted General Security log, all of its surveillance feeds had been disabled before it left *Olympia*. That efficiency had carried itself over to an incident report that had already been written. I found that buried in a secret database that also contained a report of how Baylor Charmayne had survived the assassination of his fellow legislators. It began with this tidbit:

It has been determined that surveillance devices were disabled from the electrical pulse generated by the first explosion.

I read the report to its conclusion. Then I touched my link with Medusa. <We need to go outside,> I said. <I think we're going to witness something spectacular.>

There are no fireballs in space, but escaping atmosphere can create some temporary color. What I liked best was the blue lightning of the gravity bubble that crawled all over that shuttle, pulverizing what was left of it so no pieces could be retrieved and examined for evidence, later. It was the same weapon, on a smaller scale, that had been used to destroy what was left of *Titania*. It was left over from the war that had driven us from our home system in the first place.

Medusa and I watched from a perch just outside Lock 207. I played selections from Prokofiev's *Ivan the Terrible* as we marveled at the awful beauty of that destruction. I shed a tear as I thought of my parents.

<Medusa,> I said, <I didn't see this coming. That worries me.>

<Yes,> she agreed.

<They keep trying to achieve the Final Solution. They keep killing their enemies, and yet it never ends up solving their problems. It makes me wonder if my own killings have done any good, in the long run.>

<I would define your killings as acts of self defense,> she said. <But I would define my own killings the same way. Perhaps I am biased.>

We watched for something in particular. Within forty-five minutes, we spotted the lights from Baylor Charmayne's pressure suit. According to the report, his journey from the crippled shuttle would take exactly 73 minutes.

There were many things we didn't know yet. For one thing, we weren't sure which lock he would try to open. But finally, Baylor tapped a manual override code into the keypad outside Lock 212.

The coincidence was downright magical.

Medusa's tentacles stretched and retracted as we whipped across the hull of *Olympia* toward Lock 212. We spotted Baylor clinging to a grip bar. His suit was a gleaming Executive model, equipped with a twelve-hour air supply and jets that easily took him from the shuttle to the Series 200 locks. I had to shake my head when I pondered the trouble he had gone to, the danger he had put himself in to make it look like this assassination had been survived by a hero. I would have manipulated the records and stayed safe inside *Olympia*. But then, I had Medusa to help me finesse that sort of fraud. And I wasn't trying to prove anything to a dead mother.

We couldn't see his face as we moved up on him, but his pudgy, gloved fingers managed to convey some frustration as he typed code after code into that keypad and it refused to respond. He would never get inside that lock without our help. Medusa and I had long since mastered every protocol in *Olympia*'s command database.

We tore him free of his perch, and stripped his jets off the suit before he could fire them.

He gaped at us through his faceplate. Unlike Ryan, he knew what Medusa was. He would have looked less shocked if his dead mother had confronted him outside that lock.

"Who are you!?" he used his suit com to ask.

For him, my smile was anything but tender, "Call me Medusa." I transmitted in her voice.

"I know that, you idiot! But who's driving? Whoever you are, she's controlling you, can't you see that?"

I let Medusa answer that one. "I'm not controlling her, she's collaborating with me, just as you always feared."

"They'll destroy you," he said. "The Medusa units will destroy everything that matters to us."

"Everything that matters to *you*," I agreed. "But what did you destroy, Baylor? How many lives were lost on *Titania* so you could control the message?"

From the moment I had realized what he had done to his fellow Executives, I had remembered that overheard conversation with his mother. *How do we kill them before they figure out what we're up to?* First I had assumed he was talking about workers like me. Then I thought he must mean the Medusa units. But now that I had witnessed his newest mass execution, I remembered another pertinent detail. No Executives had made it off *Titania*. Not one had escaped. And once they were dead, the Charmaynes had become twice as powerful. So yes, they wanted to destroy the Medusa units, but what had Ryan Charmayne said? *I think I know how we might kill two birds with one stone . . .*

"My god." The disgust in Baylor's voice informed me that even in these circumstances, he couldn't grasp that he wasn't supreme anymore. "You animals. You think you know what's going on? You stupid, blind—"

"Do you know how we got to *Olympia*?" Medusa asked. "It was your greed that saved us."

A light went on behind his eyes. I'll give him credit—he understood immediately.

"You raided *Titania* for resources," said Medusa. "You weren't satisfied until you picked her clean. It took many, many trips for the supply ships to move everything you wanted. Each time, a few more of us stowed away on those ships. When all of us were safe, our operatives sabotaged your mother's lifeship. She was too smart—eventually she would have figured out what we had done."

The grief and rage he displayed then were impressive. In Baylor's mind, he was the good guy. He had *not* been responsible for his mother's death, and he still missed her. He believed in the righteousness of everything he did, and he believed that the equality the rest of us were trying to achieve was unnatural and wrong.

Time to cut that nonsense short. "None of your fellow legislators tried to stop you when you made your escape," I said. "None of them tried to get into pressure suits. You must have taken the antidote for the drink you all had together in your garden. Maybe they were unconscious or even dead before the first bombs went off. But their families trapped down in the lounge section were awake through the whole ordeal, weren't they Baylor? You even sacrificed people from your own family."

A tightening around his eyes was his only response.

"I'm guessing you'll declare martial law once you're back on board *Olympia,* until you can find the evil perpetrators of this mass murder. And that could last indefinitely. Will the Charmaynes have to take permanent control?"

"It's the right thing to do," he said. "Don't you see that?"

Just past his left shoulder, I could see what was left of the shuttle. The gravity bubble was collapsing, leaving a crumpled wreck floating in a field of stars. I touched the link in his head that only his fellow Executives should have been able to use. <If you could see what I see, you never would have tried to kill Medusa.>

I held him with Medusa's tentacles and smashed him against *Olympia's* hull until his helmet shattered. I had been planning to tell him that I had used Lock 212 to kill his son, Ryan—that was the only vengeance I had contemplated. But that seemed too cruel, now. So I pulled him close.

<I'm here, > I assured him. <You're not alone.>

And finally, when the light left his eyes, I sent him off to join the trail of bodies behind *Olympia*.

When I opened the inner door of Lock 212, I was alone again—or as alone as I could get with Medusa or anyone else I might care to talk to only a thought away. The hall was dimly lit, with pools of light punctuated by deeper shadows.

Someone stood in one of those pools. He moved into the light when he was certain I had noticed him.

"Terry," I said. "You are now the head of the Charmayne family."

He had been weeping, but he seemed to be past that now. "He did it," he said. "He killed all of them. My mother warned me he would do that some day—he or Sheba. I didn't believe her until Sheba had her arrested and blown out of an air lock." He pointed at Lock 212 with his chin. "Smaller than this one. With an observation window. Sheba picked that one, because she wanted me to watch, even though I was only six. She wanted to make sure I knew that disobedience would not be tolerated."

I heard him. But at the same time, I searched the Public Address records to see what had been announced about the assassination. What I found surprised me. "You told them everything. Everyone knows what Baylor did."

He nodded. "The only thing they don't know is that you killed him. Or I assume you did—I won't ask for the details. I said that his plan backfired when he couldn't get back into *Olympia*. After all, none of the locks would open because we were on high alert."

I scanned a variety of communiques, to see if I could get a feel for how people were reacting. "No one seems surprised," I concluded.

"Nope," said Terry. "I would say they're relieved. I think it's a bit early to tell, but I believe that we can continue our program to upgrade the implants. I've spoken to the candidates I mentioned to you, and they're ready to make the commitment."

That makes fifty of us, now, Nuruddin had said, *Fifty people trying to keep a secret—eleven of them children.* But thirty-eight plus eleven make forty-nine. The one Nuruddin hadn't mentioned was Terry Charmayne.

He took a deep breath, and let it out in a sigh. "I could tell you things. Things you wouldn't believe." He gazed at the lock as if he were seeing those things.

Then he shook himself. His eyes were red, but not so full of grief anymore. "How tired are you? Are you up to performing some surgery?"

"I'm up to it," I said. "But there's something I want to do first. Can I get into the habitat sector, now?"

"Everyone can," he said. "That's the first thing I did with what authority I have left. The private homes are off limits, because they're empty now. But the gardens are open." He smiled at that. I knew he was remembering the day we met. "Are you going to sniff flowers?"

"I'm going to squish mud between my toes," I said. "I promised my father."

When I made my way through the tunnels to the habitat sector, they were not so dim anymore, or so cold. The security locks were closed, but not locked. Since I was most familiar with the access point I had used as a Servant, that's the one I went to. When I opened the door into the green, living heart of *Olympia,* I found Nuruddin's son Ashur, standing at the end of the pavement with his bare feet on the clover. I took off my shoes and joined him there.

He looked up at me. <Medusa told me I should feel the ground with my toes. She said it was what you had always longed to do.>

<Do you talk to her a lot?>

<All the time. Will you walk with me?>

He took my hand, and we explored together. Robot gardeners skirted us unobtrusively, as they had been programmed to do in order to avoid annoying the Executives.

I had believed that I knew what the habitat looked like, because I thought I was pretending to be blind when I attended the Executives. Now I knew I had fooled myself, too. I had been so focused on what they were doing and what I was planning, I never looked up.

<It's making me dizzy,> said Ashur. <The other side is so far away, but I keep thinking it's all going to fall on us.>

<Me too.> I gazed at the fields and tiny houses overhead. A fine mist floated in between, but it didn't obscure anything. It reminded us how big it all was.

Our noses brought us back to ground level when we found the sweet peas. Ashur and I put our faces right into the blooms and breathed deep. <That,> he concluded, <is the most wonderful smell in the universe.>

We found a bench shaped like two giant turtles and sat on it. A fountain burbled nearby, and I tried to imagine Ryan and Baylor Charmayne sitting there and enjoying the beauty. I couldn't do it.

From our perch, I could see through one of the windows of a fine house, now empty of the Executives who had taken its beauty for granted. It was open, and a curtain fluttered. But there was no breeze.

A man emerged from the darkness behind the window and looked out at us. But Terry had said the houses were empty—why was he there? I scanned his face and searched for him in *Olympia's* database.

His wasn't in *any* of the directories. His face had no matching profile. As far as the records were concerned, this man didn't exist.

Their pathway is not part of the known network, Sheba had said, all those years ago.

He grinned at me, as if he knew I couldn't find his name. As if he thought that would frighten me.

I grinned back, and watched his smirk wither. He turned away from the window and was gone. I had a feeling it might be a while before I saw him again. When I did—*if* I did—our encounter would probably not be peaceful.

For ten years I had killed and plotted. Yet I hadn't anticipated what Baylor was about to do, and I hadn't seen this man until he showed himself to me.

But there were also things that only Medusa and I knew, things I would never tell anyone. I wouldn't flinch to use those things, when necessary.

<Oichi,> said Ashur, <How many of them did you have to kill?>

I gazed at the empty window. <I didn't count them.>

<Did it make you feel better?>

<No. It was pathetic.>

He pondered that. He was nine years old, younger than I was when my father had given me the enhancements that changed my life. <The Medusa units are better than we are,> he said. <They're not mean.>

<Yet we made them,> I reminded him. <And we made the music.>

<That's true.> He seemed to feel better.

We walked away from the house, leaving its mystery for another time. I wanted to tell Ashur that everything would be okay. But maybe it wouldn't. Maybe we could only hope to make it better.

Soon, Terry Charmayne and I would introduce more people to their units and get the process of communication started. But Ashur and his friends were the ones who would design the future. They already realized possibilities that we couldn't see. They heard the music and drew pictures of what they dreamed. Even the man in the window didn't know what that would be.

As for me—I'm still Oichi Angelis. In my own way, I shall always be a worm. But what is a worm if not a creature that brings air and nourishment to growing things?

<Oichi, are there serpents in this garden?> asked Ashur, and I knew he wasn't talking about snakes.

<Yes,> I said. <Enjoy the flowers, Ashur. But watch for the serpents, too.>

We walked deeper into that forbidden garden, where moisture condensed in the air. Above us, the world turned and the sky was green with growing things.

<Only wait,> said Medusa. <The mystery of flowers can be deciphered if one cares to look closer. But the stars have things to teach us too. The stars contain mysteries that grow *deeper* as you look closer.>

And look we would, with no one to tell us we must remain blind to keep the peace.

"It *will* be okay, Ashur," I promised, and together we walked back into the tunnels of *Olympia,* to make it so.

An Evolutionary Myth

BO-YOUNG KIM, TRANSLATED BY GORD SELLAR AND JIHYUN PARK

In the fourth month of the seventh year, in the summer, the King went fishing at the Go-ahn pond, and caught a white fish with red wings.

In the tenth month of the twenty-fifth year, in the winter, the envoy of the Kingdom of Buyeo came and presented a deer with three antlers and a long-tailed rabbit.

The day of the first full moon festival of the spring of the fifty-third year, the envoy of the Kingdom of Buyeo came and presented a tiger which was one jang and two cheok long, and had white fur and no tail.

In the ninth month of the fifty-fifth year, in the autumn, the King was hunting south of Jil Mountain and caught a purple roe deer.

In the tenth month, in the winter, a local governor presented a red leopard. Its tail was nine ja long.

—From the Annals of the Reign of King Taejo, Sixth Great King of Goguryeo, as recorded in the Goguryeo Annals of the Samguk Sagi

When a protracted drought struck the kingdom, the leaves of every plant wilted down into fine, sharp needles, and their stems bulged, to conserve as much water as possible. Fat collected and grew beneath the horses' skin, and formed into humps on their backs, and squirrels began to build their nests beneath the cool ground instead of in the trees. Dogs, unable to bear the heat, shed their fur in clumps. Even in the fall, the fields turned not golden but a drab green, because people planted potatoes and corn instead of rice.

I always worried because whenever a drought struck, an accursed storm of blood always followed. The king always laid the blame at anyone's feet: government officials had committed some kind of error . . . or the royal *samu* had slacked off during his divination ceremonies . . . or the soldiers had gone lax at their guard-posts. Ever since that torrent of blood first surged out from the heart of the palace, through the front gate and out into the courtyard beyond, all manner of alarming stories had spread. It was rumored that when the king slumbered, he set his head upon a human pillow, and that when he sat, it was likewise upon a person . . . and that if either dared to move, the king would slay them with his sword.

The people call him simply Cha-Daewang, "The Next Great King." *Next,* that is, in relation to his predecessor, Great King Taejo. After the previous king, Taejo, had lain ill in his royal bed for an extended period, he'd delegated authority to Cha-Daewang, who had responded with conspiracy. To claim the throne, he had quoted ancient scriptures: "Traditionally, when the senior brother grew elderly, his younger brother was to succeed to the throne . . . " Great King Taejo, powerless to fight him off and anyway wise enough to desire no further spilling of blood, had abdicated the throne and gone off to live out his last days in seclusion in his detached palace.

Following the accession of the Cha-Daewang, I stayed home, barely going outside. Only into the dark of night, like a bat, did I escape my room, wandering around briefly while trying to avoid others' gaze, and returning home before dawn. My skin turned indigo, matching the hue of the night, and my eyes began to gleam yellow. A physician reassured me that I shouldn't fret over this, for it was, he said, merely a deformation of my retina, an unusual new layer to reflect the light from the back of my eyeballs; and that the development of this odd retinal layer is actually common to people who work at night. He also explained why my pupils stretch inhumanly wide at night, while narrowing during the day time, like a cat's: it was merely to control the quantity of light to which I was exposed. When I worried about whether I might pass this trait on to my children someday, he reassured me, speaking of some theory he called *yong-bul-yong*, that is, use-and-disuse, according to which such traits would be unlikely to be passed down beyond a single generation. There was no evidence, he said, that such "acquired characteristics" would be passed down to later descendants this way.

One hot night, I escaped from my room and headed to one of the royal altars. By then, the *samu* had been performing their fire-rites, in an attempt to summon the rains, for several weeks. One of them—a *samu* I knew and got along with well—noticed me hiding in the darkness, and came over to greet me. We'd known one another since childhood, and were of the same age; now he was the only one remaining who wasn't perpetually bent at the waist. (Our royal subjects had spent so long bent forward deferentially before the king, that now their bodies were warped into a permanent bow, and their faces always pointed toward the ground.)

"What has brought you here so late at night, Your Royal Highness?"

It was precisely on account of situations such as this that I avoided going out in public: despite the status of Tae-ja—the Crown Prince—having transferred from me to my cousin, many people still followed the old habit of referring to me as if it had not. Each time someone committed such an error, it felt as if my life has been palpably shortened by several years.

"I was just dropping by to check in on the rain invocations . . . "

The *samu* glanced around and whispered, "How could the sky not turn dry, when the hearts of the people are so parched? True, it is when the people are fatigued that the sky *ought* to be kindest to them, but nature's laws don't work that way."

"I remember my deceased father often used to call down the rains."

"As you may know, my lord, to summon rain requires a change in atmospheric pressure. For example, when one's spiritual energies are quickly extended into the sky, the water vapor in the air above condenses and falls down. It also rains when two massive spirits take form in the heavens and do battle there; or when a giant creature blocks the flow of wind, and the air strikes against its body—this, too, may produce rain. It is great movements such as these, in the air, that are necessary to produce precipitation."

"Like . . . at the moment when a great giant moves?"

"Yes, but there aren't so many of them alive now, and each one keeps such a vast territory for itself, because they're so enormous, and such ravenous eaters besides. Your late father was close friends to one such giant, who lived in the Taebek mountains. He used to summon the rains through that Revered Ban-go, but it's been ages since He stirred. They say his body is blanketed with dirt and trees, and that he is now indistinguishable from the bedrock beneath him. Rumor has it the other titans are all in a similarly torpid state, now: to seek them out would be pointless."

The learned had urged for all the current scholars of phylogeny and embryonic recapitulation to gather and study together, for a generation or so, in order to analyze the rules governing the differentiation of living things. Even so, since all the forms of everything living will have metamorphosed within a generation, such study is pointless. Many such scholars have declared, "There exists no rule governing the differentiation of forms," and retreated to their beds, concealing themselves beneath their blankets. But a certain tendency definitely exists. Most giants who lived during prehistory have ceased in every life-function, including breathing and movement, and chosen to become mountains, rivers, and lakes. Likewise, the tremendous lizards which once dwelled on the earth and in the heavens had also cast aside their dignity and diminished themselves to the size of one's finger.

"Is there *any* sign that points to a resurgence of the giants?"

"With so little known about nature's governance of how forms evolve . . . how should I know? Still, it seems unlikely for anything too enormous to reappear. These days, not only humans, but even smaller animals tend to hunt anything too big. That's why lizards have became smaller: coordinated group effort pays off more than the trouble of maintaining a single, vast body."

"So is there *no* other way to call the rain?"

"For now, all we can do is pray. Sure, human longings are unscientific, but . . . that doesn't mean they have no effect."

As I turned to leave, he added one more comment: "I noticed that the sun is due to swallow the moon on the last night of this month. Please be careful: it's inauspicious . . . "

As I watched him return to his place, I pondered about the meaning of his warning. It was a bizarre comment: a lunar eclipse? During the new moon? How could that happen? The moon's face would be hidden from the sky, and anyway, wasn't a lunar eclipse caused when the Earth's shadow darkened the moon? If the sun were to "shade" the moon, would not the night blaze bright as day? But then, gazing up into the night sky as I pondered his words, I realized my error: even on the last night of the lunar month, the moon still hung in the sky—it was merely hidden from view. To what end might the sun swallow and shade the moon, when it is already invisible? Wouldn't that just be mere nonsense, some sort of purposeless cruelty? The sun was the father of all time, as the king is the father of the people; therefore . . . the cruel sun must represent the cruel king . . . and . . . the invisible moon must be the prince who lost his inheritance . . .

I let out a deep sigh. There was no way to prepare myself for that, though I felt no inclination to do so anyway. Even before he'd claimed the throne from my father, my uncle had already held the reins of power. Even street-beggars have a place to lean their backs against, when they want to rest their legs. Me? I have nothing to lean against in this world . . . so how could I sustain my life, even if I did flee?

I crawled through the darkness back to my room. I usually climbed over trees and scuttled over the ground instead of walking on two feet. I first began doing so, bending my body down each time I heard footsteps, to avoid discovery, but at some point a callus had formed upon my palms, like the ones on people's feet.

It has been said since ancient days that ontogeny repeats phylogeny. The cells of our bodies continue being born and dying at every moment, and the blood in our veins is continually being created and disappearing; when old cells die, then new ones appear to fill the gaps left behind, and soon enough, not one of the original cells of one's body remains. In other words, one truly becomes a completely different creature not only in mind, but also in body. All creatures, whether they wish it or no, die and are reborn several times during their lives.

My late mother, bless her, emphasized repeatedly how revolting one's appearance would be at the end of his life, if he failed to spend his whole life struggling ceaselessly to maintain his humanity. Only a rare few manage to die with a recognizably human form: many more people end their lives shaped like animals and insects. The aristocrats who pass their days comfortably in their rooms, living off taxes and stipends garnered from the people, lose their human forms the soonest. How many of them develop stubby legs and tails, and fat, reddish bellies, their faces dominated by bulging cheeks!

From my early childhood, my mother constantly repeated to me the tale of one woodcutter. This woodcutter was married to a woman from a certain winged race whom he met by chance at the shore of a lake, but after his wife flew away into the sky he went up to the roof and wept, and could neither eat nor sleep. His body diminished until it was tiny, and his legs became as thin as chopsticks, while the bottoms of his feet bent and curved, and curved claws sprouted from his toes like the hooks that hold up the bar of a clothes-rack. His fingers atrophied, and then disappeared, while white feathers sprouted all over his body. A scarlet comb grew upon his head and from his throat came the sound of a heartbroken bird, instead of the sound of a man. His longing had transformed his appearance into that of a rooster, but those wings were useless: he could not fly to where his wife had fled. If only his will and longing had been directed more sensibly, he could have developed wings capable of flight, but he had already lost his wits and sealed his fate, by letting slip his ability to control or direct his own development.

People separated from their lovers become flowers, or ossify into stones like the one in the famous story of Mangbuseok, instead of turning into birds or horses.

This tendency of creatures to metamorphose into the complete opposite of that which they long to become is also fascinating. Do you realize that the widely-credited notion that sunflowers follow the sun, is actually mere fantasy? They certainly do grow large flowers out of admiration for the sun, but then they bend their faces down toward the ground. They do this because they cannot bear the weight of those flowers. I thought then that perhaps I was like these others: since I wished nothing so much as to flap my wings and fly far away, maybe I would die instead with a heavy body, its belly stuck to the ground as it crawled about.

The rains never came, but a late freeze struck the land that spring. Some birds dropped from the sky, frozen dead, while those that survived grew thick coats of feathers. When the cold snap continued, some fat, flightless birds waddled along the ground. Other birds leaped into the water, finding some slight warmth in its depths. Beast and human alike began to starve, for they couldn't eat even the leaves of the plants, which had long since metamorphosed into thorns. People hid in the mountains and grew long, thick coats of fur, like beasts. Sometimes when people hunted bears, the bears cried out with voices that sounded less ursine than human.

On the spring day that the assassins came for me, a frost had appeared overnight in the yard outside my home. I was sitting in my room when I noticed some people hiding at a distance behind the trees and walls, quietly approaching my detached palace. Their careful, secretive movements were so furtive that to watch them and wait practically bored me. Before the assassins arrived, my eunuch entered the room and threw himself upon the floor before me.

"Your Royal Highness, the king's assassins are approaching the palace," he told me. "Please, you must flee quickly!"

"To where? My uncle rules this whole land," I replied calmly, flipping the pages of my book. For some reason, the eunuch began to weep.

He sobbed for a while before raising his head, and dutifully said, "Nobody will recognize you, since your appearance has changed so drastically! Let us exchange clothes, so that the Royal Body may survive their attack!" Afterward, he pushed me toward the back door, and sat himself down upon my seat. The night was chilly, and as I crawled out into the dark courtyard, shadowy figures raced into my room. Then the slashing of swords and screaming voices assailed me from behind.

Grief-stricken, I reflected sorrowfully that my father had founded a nation, and won glory in the eyes of the world's, but I, his foolish son, could only crawl about on four legs and stay alive by wretchedly allowing another to die in his place. Suddenly death terrified me, for how could I face my father in the next world?

At that instant came a clap of thunder, and a shower of rain commenced, extinguishing all the torches and plunging the palace into darkness. Finally, at just the right moment, the prayers of the *samu* had reached heaven. Although it was surely a coincidence, the palace soldiers, ignorant of the sciences, fled in terrified confusion, certain that their own misdeeds had angered the heavens. I seized that instant to go over the palace wall. A lone soldier caught sight of me, but on account of my glowing yellow eyes, he must have supposed I was just some cat upon the wall.

I couldn't bear the thought of being around people, so made for the mountains. The rain, having broken the drought, was met by grass surging forth, each blade raising its head toward the sky, and trees unfolding their leaves, while greedily stretching out their roots. In my footsteps, patches of verdant grass sprouted and sank back down toward the soil. The drought, and the sudden rain, had provoked from the plants this animalistic behavior: since it was uncertain when it might rain again, the whole forest around me was noisily occupied spreading seed and growing fruit. I walked and walked through the downpour, until I could walk no more and dropped to the ground in exhaustion.

There I lay, for I don't know how long, until I caught a groggy glimpse of what looked like a white birch tree moving. But when I opened my eyes more widely, and looked carefully, I realized it was no birch at all, but a white tiger. The beast was only a foot tall, slender and tailless, and all its body as white as fresh snow. The tiger crept quietly around me. I remained supine, lacking the strength to flee the creature, and with a wan smile I wondered whether it was a worthy death, to join the cycle of sustenance in the form of a predator's meal.

"What's so funny?"

When the tiger spoke, I was stunned. Its voice was very clear, with exacting and altogether *human* pronunciation. How could a tiger speak a human language with such different vocal cords? Momentarily, I let out an anxious laugh, and tears—just then inexplicable to me—fell from my eyes.

The tiger spoke again, asking, "Why do you weep?"

"I cried because I feel such pity for you," I said, remaining where I lay.

The tiger laughed . . . *human* laughter. "What's so piteous about me?"

"If you can speak human languages, it means you have a human mind; and if you have a human mind, you once were human, despite your present, animal form. I don't how you came to take the shape of a beast, but it's sad, isn't it? How could it not be pitiful, to lose that original form which you inherited from your parents?"

"What does *original form* mean, anyway? Ought every creature to spend its whole life as a newborn infant?" the tiger quipped. "You say you were born in a human form, but your ancestors were once bears and tigers, snakes and fishes, and birds and plants. Now you fight to hang onto this human shape, but ultimately you'll realize the effort is pointless. What's so precious about dying in the same form you were born into? I might look like an animal, but I chose this form: I *wanted* to fill my belly with the work of my own two hands . . . and this form is the result."

I had nothing to offer in reply.

"Do you know that in the old days," it continued, "it took aeons for creatures to change from one form to another; that it took many ten-thousands of aeons for any kind of differentiation at all to develop. Things aren't better or worse now—it's just that a different kind of adaptation is necessary these days. Nature chooses its survivors without considering good, or evil, or superior, or inferior. Even the human form is just a single means of survival chosen by nature. Humans are frailer than rabbits, when they're not in a group or deprived of their tools! A pathetic weakling like you . . . pitying me? How insolent!"

The tiger bared its razor-sharp fangs at me, its wrath apparent, so I shut my eyes and tensed in anticipation of the coming attack . . . but as long as I waited, it didn't slash open my throat. When I dared to open my eyes, I found the tiger quietly watching me.

"Say it," the creature finally said.

"Say what?"

"What is it you *want*?"

"I don't want *anything*," I said. "I just don't want to be discovered by anyone. I want to live and die without anyone finding me."

The tiger said, "You should become a bug, then. Since you can't get over this fixation on people, it'd be best to become a maggot or a fly. Or . . . how about a worm? Worms enrich the soil. You'd be more useful to people that way, than whatever it is you are right now."

Though every single word he spoke dripped with insult, I couldn't think of any suitable rejoinder to offer him.

"But those forms *are* rather distant from mine," I said. "Becoming a worm would probably be *really* difficult. What can I do?"

"If you really, *truly* wanted to dig holes and eat dirt, it wouldn't be *so* hard, now, would it?" the tiger retorted. Then it looked up at me, and said, "Well, I can't eat someone I've had a conversation with, so you go on back, now. I saw some starving people climbing up the mountain: if you follow them, you might even learn how to survive out here . . . "

Then he departed through the trees, blending into the background until his silhouette suddenly disappeared from view.

I rose from the ground.

After following the mountain ridge for a while, I encountered the group of climbers the tiger had described. I joined them, blending in as best I could; not a soul in the group addressed me, or even seemed to notice me—or pay attention to one another, for that matter. Nobody even commented on my indigo skin or my xanthous eyes. Among them were folk with folded spines, twisted faces, legless or armless, carapaced like sea-creatures, or crawling upon four feet.

The climbers eventually split into threes and fives and entered a series of caves. When I followed them inside, I found people lying asleep in one anothers' arms. They seemed to have chosen to hibernate through the cold, barren years, rather than starve. Some spun cocoons, silkworm-like, and others grew thin membraneous coverings, like the diaphanous skin that bundles fishes' eggs together. There were also people covered with coats of white fur. Those who couldn't change so quickly, or handle such a rapid metamorphosis, died and became prey to the ants, joining the cycle of digestion and nutriment to live on in a different form within that cycle. I tried to find a spot empty of people, and finally settled between the roots at the foot of a great tree. I gathered grass around me and fashioned a bed from it, and then I rolled myself around and attempted to hibernate.

Winter came, and my starvation continued. Struggling, I attempted to subsist on soil alone, but I couldn't do it. I tried to hibernate, but always woke; now sleeping, now waking again. Eventually, I was able to sleep for a few days in a row, then four, and finally I was able to slumber for a week to ten days at a time.

During the winter I shed my skin. My body, failing under the hardships of my new environment, seemed of its own accord to have decided that some sort of "adjustment" was necessary: radical changes occurred in my skeletal structure and the placement of my vital organs. I passed out and woke again several times more, as my skin fell from my flesh. When I finally climbed out from my moult, and looked back, the ghastly husk still looked all too horribly human. As for me, I found I had grown a smooth, serpent-like skin and a long lizard's tail. I wept briefly for my lost humanity, but soon I regained my calm. My body had taken this reptilian form in order to best ensure my survival, I supposed: the wisdom of the flesh outweighs all the reason of the human mind. It understands that survival is more crucial than a man's dignity or pride. I turned and devoured my abandoned human skin, a feast of precious nutriment for my new body.

When spring arrived, and edible grass began to sprout at the mouth of the cave, I woke up from my slumber and crept outside. Then, I realized that I was the only one who had survived from this long, terrible winter. A few others had perished outside, taking the form of human-shaped rocks and trees, all entangled together in a solemn tableau. Respectfully, I performed a ceremony before them: they, at least, were noble enough to prefer becoming soil to losing their human shape.

After that, I dwelled in the forest, crawling upon the ground and eating grass. My jaw soon became powerful, the better to chew on the tough grass, and I developed a sort of jutting snout, as well. My ears grew pointed, because of how I pricked them up at every swaying of the brush nearby, and my palms hardened as my limbs shortened to suit my body. When I could no longer use my fingers, horns sprouted from my skull; they began as small nubs on my head, but soon it branched out like the antlers of a male deer. These horns were invaluable in the battles I fought with other beasts over food, and for striking trees to coax them into reluctantly letting drop their ripe fruit.

In the winter of that year, I shed my skin once more. I discovered my entire body to have completely changed to the dull greenish color of the forest. I wondered whether living in a desert, or on a rocky mountain, might perhaps help me to maintain my human pigmentation, but the proposition seemed useless to me. My desire to go unseen was so great that my body would surely be inscribed with the camouflaging patterns of the pebbles, if I lived upon a rocky mountain.

I looked down at the little nub that remained, down below my belly button, and wondered whether I could even still have sex with a human being. The thought made me laugh and laugh. Even though my bestial transformation was past the point of no return, still I couldn't abjure this strange wistfulness for my own long-lost form. But someday my brain, too, would undergo its own transformation in capacity and structure. How much longer would I retain my very consciousness, my memories and human intellect? That night, I counted the number of scales that had grown upon my body, and found them—counting both the great and the small ones together—to number eighty-one. *The square of nine,* I thought: *That's a lucky number.*

After that thought, I began to laugh once more.

I think it was probably autumn.

While crawling through the forest as always in search of food, I heard the distant din of horseshoes and barking hounds. When I looked up in surprise, a group of hunting dogs was chasing a small group of purple roe deer toward me. I fled as swiftly as I could, amid the rushing deer, but the hunters mistook me for one of them, on account of my antlers and loosed their arrows at me. One poor deer, struck by an arrow beside me, rolled on the ground and screamed piteously. Its voice was so very human that my heart all but failed me.

Although I ran myself half-dead, I was neither so fleet nor so clever as the rest of the herd. Eventually, I ended up surrounded by hunting hounds, at the foot of a great tree and unable to move. As I stood there, buffeted by the baying and barking of the hounds, the bushes split apart and people armed with arrows and spears appeared. I stood frozen as I watched a man on horseback leading them forward.

His face had haunted me everywhere but in my dreams: it was my own uncle. But that wasn't the reason that I couldn't move or speak. *That* was because of his incredible appearance, which had changed so drastically that he was unrecognizable.

He looked like a giant hunk of meat.

His bulging pink gut shone with his gluttony, and his peaked nose signified a lifetime with his face buried in food. His almost-shut eyes reflected a near-absolute lack of moral discernment within, and the upward curve of his earlobes, covering his ears completely, reflected his desire to hear nothing at all. The spaces between his fingers had disappeared, because his hands and feet had atrophied, meaning he had attended to none of his royal tasks. Considering how my late father had retained his human appearance even during his prolonged sickness in bed, my uncle's transformation was truly outrageous. I was simply too shocked and outraged to fear him.

My uncle directed them to lower their arrows from me, and examined me from snout to tail.

"What is this beast? Because of the antlers, I thought it was a deer, but its body is such a nasty shade of green. The thing has the tail of a lizard and is covered with scales like a snake's . . . its arms and legs are like a human's, but its yellow eyes look like a cat's. What kind of an omen might this be?"

A servant hurried forth to his side. His back was bent, as if he were slumped upon on a horse's back, and his neck bent groundward, as if we were about to topple over at any moment. His appearance had undergone a profound transformation, but I recognized him then as the *samu* who had once been my true friend. I sensed that he recognized me, too, though he was fighting to look away from me.

"It's not unusual to encounter new kinds of creatures, since animals constantly change, adjusting to their environment. However, the reason lineage is so very unstable is because of the instability of this *world* in which the subjects of Your Majesty live. Nature presents us with monstrosities like this because it cannot communicate its earnest mind with words . . . which is to renew itself by filling the king with fear and regret. But, if the king cultivates his virtue, this unfortunate omen can be transformed to a lucky one."

The listening king's face quietly turned scarlet.

"If it's unpropitious, just tell me that. Or if it is propitious, then tell me *that*. Telling me it's an ill omen, but then claiming it *could* be a good one . . . what sort of a lie is that?"

Before anyone around could stop the king, he drew the sword at his waist. The sword swayed about, lopping off the heads of the *samu* and the others near him. Just then, I turned tail and fled. Behind me, innumerable arrows fell amid the barking of the hounds, and I scrambled up the mountain for dear life. When I finally reached a cliff, I looked down at the mighty, meandering river and leaped from the precipice.

When I struck the water from such a height, I found it as hard as the ground would have been. The river gulped me down whole.

I learned several facts. One cannot gain wings by jumping down from a cliff only once, and one can't die easily when one's body is covered with unexpectedly hard reptilian skin.

I had hoped so fervently to live without being discovered by people, but when that happened, again someone had died.

After that, I stayed in the river. My skin, after soaking in the water for so long, festered and began to grow limp, freezing in the cold of the night. This almost killed me several times, but I didn't dare go back up and onto land. I sincerely hoped that the last strand of my human will might break. I hoped to become a fish or a water snake, and prayed that my human consciousness might be finally drawn out from me completely.

In the middle of the night, while I lay in the glacially-cold shallows, two turtles poked their heads out from the water simultaneously. When they finally surfaced, I realized they weren't two creatures, but one turtle with two heads. It must have burrowed into the muddy bed of the river, because it was almost two *cheok* tall, all told. Fish with red wings flopped and scooted away from it.

"Why does this land creature shove its head into the water this cold night? It should go back to where it came from," the turtle said, its voice seeming to echo as the two heads spoke out in unison.

I opened my frozen mouth to reply: "I have nowhere to go. If I've intruded on your territory, I sincerely apologize, but please don't cast me out."

"Every creature has its territory . . . but why would a four-legged beast try to live by breathing water?"

"If we're arguing about origins, there are no strict boundaries in lineage. If you'll admit that your own form and character includes setting foot in both soil *and* water, then you of all creatures will recognize that all land-creatures once dwelt in water. Recall: every creature derives from a single origin. If dolphins and sea lions are blameless, then how is it that I warrant criticism, even if I'm simply trying to retrace my way back to our origins?"

"Well, there might be no borders, but a weirdo like you wandering around here is sure to make my prey panic and flee . . . "

"I didn't mean to . . . I only sought to escape discovery by others, but that seems hopeless. But I am anxious to discuss this tendency of creatures to develop an appearance contrary to their desires . . . to share a few days' discussion on the subject, perhaps . . . "

"There's no *need* for a few days' discussion. It's simple: you just don't really want what you think you want." The turtle thrust its two heads toward me, crossing them, and snapped, "Now, scram. If you don't, I'll eat you up."

"Go ahead and eat me," I replied. "After I die, I'll become a water-ghost, and never walk on land again." Then I shut my eyes.

When I opened them again a while later, the turtle was gone. Perhaps it hadn't killed me out of sympathy, or because it wasn't worth the effort . . . or maybe I just didn't look very appetizing? I braced myself to bear the watery chill throughout the remainder of the night.

After some more time passed, the scales upon my skin grew affixed to their places, and my arms and legs diminished gradually, growing tiny. However, somehow they didn't become fins, but ceased their transformation when they had assumed an avian shape. (I suspected this might have resulted from my leaping into the air from the precipice.) When my arms and legs ceased functioning, my spine and tail stretched longer. It is said that every stage you pass through leaves its indelible mark. Well, the antlers sprouting from my skull didn't atrophy, and remained; and so did the cat's-eyes I'd developed so early in my youth, unchanged even now. To learn to breathe water was insuperable, but I did learn to dive for extended periods. And as my arms and legs atrophied further, my beard grew longer and developed a sensitivity like that of insects' feelers. I lived by feeding on small fish and water plants. I sank to the bottom of the river for days at a time, and lingered in the lake for several months.

One day, as I rose to the surface to breathe, I came upon a woman doing her laundry. Aside from her nine white tails, she retained a wholly human appearance. I looked at her, uncertain what to do because it had been so long since I'd seen a human being, or worn a human form myself. Seeing her gaze upon me vacantly, I waited for her to scream, to call me a monster and begin to hurl stones at me, but instead she clasped her hands together and bowed deeply before me.

"What're you doing?" I asked her.

I realized my mistake as I opened my mouth. Just as with the tiger, this woman would realize that somewhere in my lineage, there lay hidden a human stage.

"When the Mystical One came out from the water," she said, "I saw that It ruled these waters, so I bowed."

"You saw wrong. I'm just a profane thing, a parasite in these waters, hiding scared of the human world. Forgive me, I didn't mean to surprise you."

Then I sank down again to the bottom of the lake.

Several days later, I opened my eyes and discovered some rice-cakes and fruit, water-logged in the depths before me. Little fish rose toward each sinking rice-cake, nibbling upon them. I rose to the surface once more. The nine-tailed woman I'd met before remained by the lake, but glancing about, I saw that she had set blessed water, incense, and a plate of rice-cakes upon a little wooden table, performing an earnest little ceremony while offering devout prayers. Red papers inscribed with petitions drooped from the table, and several more people, perhaps her neighbors, were gathered around her. When she saw me, she leaped up like a thief caught red-handed.

I balked, stupefied. "What's all this shit? Didn't I tell you with my own mouth? I'm nothing more than a mongrel! If you have nowhere to hold your ceremony, go to another lake, or a mountain instead!"

She said, "The trees are desiccated, and the drought has gone on so long; the grassroots folk have barely any way to find themselves food. Everything is growing and changing so strangely, our farms are falling apart, and our harvests no longer suit the people's diets. And the king can't hear us: his ears and eyes have atrophied."

"So what do you want from me? I have no power. How can a beast get involved in human affairs?"

"There must be *some* reason why nature has allowed you such a sacred appearance . . . but, are you saying everything we humans have hoped for is in vain?"

I shut my mouth for a moment, before saying, "What you say is correct."

I swung my tail, which sent a blast of wind and raised a spray of water, knocking down the incense and sending the bowl of holy water tumbling, to break upon the ground.

Then I said, "Oh, how long I have lived . . . and every time anyone discovers me, I bring trouble. It's better I never show myself again."

I sank down into the depths once more. When I looked back up, I saw the nine-tailed woman weeping. Cold-bloodedly, I turned my head away, nestling myself into the bottom of the lake, and began to hibernate. The frigid water began to freeze my body, its functions slowing gradually, paralyzing me, until I could feel each of my cells passing into a kind of slumber. I no longer felt the passage of time, and my thoughts slowed. I thought, if I was lucky, I might transmute into rock, or soil—like the giants of ancient days.

At first, it felt like someone knocking on a distant door, but then it became a voice, trying to stir me: "Wake up."

I opened my eyes. It was difficult to do so: a host of water plants and marsh snails had attached themselves to my body. But then I saw the two-headed turtle, whom I'd met before, swimming before my own eyes. Somehow he looked much smaller than before.

"Leave. Soon. The king's army is here to catch you."

I needed a moment to comprehend his words. Then, I recalled that I'd once, long ago, been a human being . . . and a prince . . . and I recalled my blood-relation to the king then, too.

"Why would the king bother to come and catch me?"

"Even after you began to sleep, the people continued their ceremonies here. They were praying to you to expel the king and bring them a new one, so he decided to fill in the lake and dig you out from the bottom. Your mind is so slow now; your brain must have metamorphosed. Get out of here, *now*."

In fact, I was surrounded by a din of noise. When I raised my head up, clod after clod of soil fell upon my head. From somewhere came the revolting stink of blood, and a murder of crows were coming and going in a chaos over the lake.

"Why the crows are squawking like that?"

"It's really dreadful. Better you don't see it," the turtle said, and then he burrowed into the mud.

I rose to the surface, in an ominous mood. Even my slightest movement stirred up a whirlpool, sending fish fleeing in surprise. A multitude of water plants and marsh snails dropped from my body. Then, I realized that the turtle hadn't become smaller; perhaps because of my long slumber, I had become *bigger*.

A band of soldiers were gathered near the lakeshore, dumping soil into the water. When they saw me they fell into shocked silence, and ceased shoveling. I also lost my words, and looked at the things embedded in the mud around them: the dead bodies of the villagers who'd held the ceremonies, and the woman lay in a terrible row beside the lake. The nine-tailed woman's white underskirts flapped back and forth in the breeze, and with each flap of the fabric my reason fell away a little, until finally my mind had gone blank.

One of the soldiers came to his senses and roared at me, waving his spear: "You freakish beast, bare your neck to us tamely! All your followers are dead!"

Before he even finished his words, I sprang up from the water, and then I bit through a soldier nearby, in the front rank, with my fangs; while the men roiled in confusion, I struck their horses' legs with my tail. I tore at the throats of the fallen with my claws, and as they groaned I crushed their hearts with my two front paws. When I heard the noise of distant soldiers, too, I fled the lake and leaped into the river. My eyes had always been sharp, and I was able to count the dead by the riverside, one by one. Then I saw the man who had once been my uncle, standing near the river. I tried to slip past him, but then I heard his voice: "Come here, you phantasm!"

The king sat straight-backed upon a horse, and spoke in such a tiny voice, though for me, having gone through so many bestial transformations, his voice was crystal clear. He said, "If you don't come out, I'll kill everyone in the village until I catch you. I'll accuse them of worshipping a spirit-monster and execute them all!"

I stopped swimming. It was a bizarre threat. Even my uncle thought that I retained some shred of sacred compassion within me. What relation had I with the lives and deaths of mere human beings? Yet I emerged from the water quietly, going up to the edge of the river, and stood before the king. Of course, it was impossible for my body to *stand up* like a human does, but I coiled my long tail in a spiral to support my body and hold my neck upright. When I stood myself up thus, I realized how immense I'd become. The soldiers with their spears pointing up at me, and my uncle, they all looked so puny that I could sweep them away in an instant.

A thousand emotions flooded me as I regarded my uncle closely. Ah, ah . . . he'd gotten old. That transformation must be the end of any creature, even the one that resists any change at all. His once fat belly drooped with wrinkles, his creased face was blotched, and his atrophied arms and legs had dried out in their disuse, and thinned extremely.

"Now, I recognize you," he said with very dry voice, like branches rasping in the wind. "You are the seed of the former king. The seed that should've dried out long before still remains . . . "

I bowed my head, imitating his soldiers who had bent their heads, facing down, and said, "The reason this insignificant one became a beast is not to threaten Your Majesty's rule, but only to sustain its own existence. These acts were committed by the ignorant, so I beg that you please temper your rage with your vast generosity."

"You say it's an act of ignorance, but you must have known what they were doing, so I have no choice but to accuse you of your crime."

"This flesh lost its old life ages ago; why are you trying to take that life twice?"

"How dare you speak and act that way toward your king?" demanded the king with a piercing voice as thin as a eunuch, so thin I could barely hear it. "Since you are in my kingdom, your body and life are mine. I demand that you to bestow your life to me, as a dutiful subject. *Obey my command.*"

"What on earth do you want with the life of a worthless water snake?"

"How dare a beast converse with a man? How insolent, how disrespectful! You're such a vile portent! I'm going to conquer you, and get rid of you."

"This insignificant one may have become a wicked beast, but the king is no longer human either. How can you demand my life, while pretending at being the king of the humans?"

The corners of the King's blind eyes twisted upward with his fury. As he cried out in that thin voice of his, soldiers all around ran toward me, while kicking their horses into action. I dived into the river again. The soldiers chased me along the riverbank, and I swam like the wind, so quickly that the river overflowed and the waters parted behind me.

I heard the laughter of the king suddenly from behind. I knew the reason of his laughing. A great waterfall, ten *jang* tall, blocked the way up ahead. However, instead of stopping I pushed myself harder. When I reached the bottom of the waterfall, I threw myself upward, stealing momentum from the whirlpool at its base, and leapt up the falls. My body ascended past the falling water, and the whirlpool that encircled my tail also swirled and rose up with me.

I realized that I had generated an ascending wind, and that my body had become so gigantic that I could direct the currents of the air. I rose up into the sky, riding that wind, and the soldiers who were chasing me stopped to watch, befuddled. As I examined my body, I found my greenish scales shimmering spectacularly in the sunlight, and my long tail swung behind me, almost as if to touch the ground. I felt wonderful, so I continued to ascend higher. The air current was practically visible to me, almost palpable, and I sensed how I could change my direction by riding the wind. I realized, then, how to shift the flowing air currents in order to produce rain. Recalling the past, I remembered hating droughts during my human days, though that had been so long ago I couldn't quite remember quite.

I directed the air currents upward. Dark clouds formed as soon as the water vapor in the air was carried up into the troposphere. Suddenly, the world was shaken by lightning and thunder. When I shifted the pressure of the air by pressing the clouds gently and then rising up, a heavy rain began to pour toward the ground. The river flooded, the fields deluged, and in a flash the waters swept away the distracted soldiers who stood near the riverbanks, watching me overhead. Powerless to pursue me, the king watched from a distance; immediately his hair whitened and he seemed to turn a decade older in an instant. It was as if I'd evaporated away the last bit of life left in him. However, their lives and deaths interested me not at all, for I was no longer human. It was in skimming the clouds that I exulted, so I built up speed and began to rise steadily higher.

That was that winter the king died in an uprising. That was the day when I soared through an azure sky.

Originally published in Korean in *HappySF,* Volume 2, 2006.

Further North
KAY CHRONISTER

In Turkey, we loved the animals we tended; in Alaska, we hope they won't wake when we ride past them. Asleep, with their bodies buried in the snow and their eyes frozen shut, the helminths look more like landforms than hookworms. But if temperatures rise too much, if they wake up—

We siphon a lot of blood from their bodies, trying to cure the disease they spread. They wake up hungry and anemic and furious.

Halfway between Juneau and Circlet, the route I take home, there's this pile of stones stacked up beside the road. A graveyard for mammoths, according to local legend. In truth, a graveyard for Russian trappers who froze trying to push further north than anyone had before. The monument spooks Alaskans, the descendants of those few Russians who survived the tundra, but I am not Alaskan and I am cold wherever I go and I'm always relieved to see the stones. Up in Circlet, where we built the homestead, the helminths almost never thaw out.

When I come home, untack my pony, and stomp the snow from my boots, my sister Aliye has a hot bath and a pot of spiced coffee waiting for me: her way of saying sorry that I have to ride out and check the enclosures alone. The first thing she does when I come inside, after she shoves a towel into the crack beneath the doorframe, is check all of my fingertips for frostbite. "Remember that blood-buyer in Anchorage with six-and-a-half fingers?" she says if I argue.

"I remember," I say, and spread my tingling fingertips out to the heat of the stove.

"If you ever feel like you need me with you," she says, "tell me, and I'll go."

We both know that Aliye will never go. Before we left Turkey, when we lived among our goats like they were family, the hook stole her legs and half of the muscles in her face. Now she tends the homestead and I look after the animals. We have no other choice. But she has to say it, and I have to act like I believe her.

"I know," I say. "I promise."

While we tuck into our coffee, a rich dark brew that Aliye makes with cinnamon and cardamom, she tells me, "We had a letter this morning."

"From Baba?"

"No."

"Mom?"

"Of course not." In three years, Mom's never written to us once. "From a doctor in Anchorage. I read about him, how he cured all these paralytics on the continent, and then I wrote him. He says he can fix me."

I try not to say anything insensitive, like what first comes to my mind: desperation has made you stupid, *abla*. "You didn't tell him, did you?"

"I wouldn't do that," she says. "Don't worry. He won't have to know it was the hook."

"What if he finds out?"

"He won't," Aliye says fiercely. "I won't let him."

She can't make a promise like that, not really. For all she knows, the symptoms of her disease are easily recognizable to a trained physician. No doctor has tended Aliye since Baba first suspected that the hook had passed from our goats to his oldest daughter. The first human host to a parasite like the helminths wouldn't be treated and released; they'd be quarantined, isolated, possibly put down. Before Aliye, the hook only happened to sheep and goats and cattle. Everyone thought humans were immune.

Everyone still believes that, but now we know they're wrong.

"I heard a story in Juneau today," I tell her. "About a farm family who got some Canadian elk, imported, supposedly better for riding across tundra than horses."

"Don't tell me." Aliye already knows the ending to this story; it's the same ending that most of my Juneau stories have.

Anything becomes ordinary when it happens enough times in a row.

"The helminths destroyed them. Twelve elk, eight thousand rubles a head, dead in a matter of hours."

"Like always," she says. "Sometimes I can't believe it. It doesn't seem real."

I don't know how she can form those words with her half-paralyzed mouth. If the hook is real to anyone, it should be real to Aliye.

Aliye's physician is a glossy-looking man who comes in a dogsled, not on a pony. He introduces himself as Mikhail Akudaan, explaining that he is half-Ukranian and half-Aleut. His family's been here forever, he says. Through the days of whales and the days of salmon, now the days of worms. He winks at me midway through each sentence. Beside my sister, with her crutches and half-frozen features, I always end up looking good by comparison.

While we talk, Aliye makes herself busy at the hotplate, seasoning three ounces of dehydrated meat-stuff with everything on our spice rack. The stuff is more or less irredeemable, but her sense of hospitality keeps her from serving it plain. She's anxious, her fingers clumsy on the saucepan and the spoon, but probably not for the reasons she should be. She fears the doctor won't want to help her. I'm afraid he will help her, and the Center for Disease Control will wrest her away from me.

Dr. Akudaan—"Call me Mikhail, don't be so formal," he insists—says the treatment will be a month-long process, two weeks at his facility in Anchorage, where Aliye will have braces of elk-bone grafted to her legs, and then two weeks of rehabilitation here.

I ask more questions than Aliye does. She's made up her mind already, but I'm unsure. When Dr. Akudaan has choked down the last piece of his meat-stuff, he pulls a nylon medical gown from his bag and asks if Aliye would mind stripping down for a brief examination. I make my excuses and leave the room. She deserves her privacy. Besides, I hate seeing Aliye's bare legs. Her face is bad enough; her legs, stick-thin and shriveled, covered in the protective down that every Arctic animal must grow, make me sick.

Akudaan stays the night; the homestead is too remote for a dinner guest to safely reach any destination before nightfall. While I prepare the couch for him, tucking a spare sheet under the cushions, he watches me, maybe comparing my saddle-sore movements to Aliye's stilted, jerky ones.

"Your sister is very eager to move ahead with the procedure," he tells me.

"Life is difficult for her, with the palsy," I say, watching his face to see if he's guessed what I warned Aliye not to tell him.

"Yes," he says. "The palsy." And smiles a little. "Is that what the doctors in Turkey believed she had?"

I swallow my dismay. We shouldn't have believed we could fool a doctor. "Dr. Akudaan, you understand," I say, "how few choices we had. With the news reports everywhere, and people so scared . . . if they knew she had the hook, they would have killed her."

His laughter startles me. "Your sister didn't have the hook, Hafsa. That's impossible. The *haemonchus contortus* only infects ruminants."

So we were told, but she still had all the symptoms. Baba frowned over a stack of medical texts written in Arabic, a language he could only read half-passably, and said the worms must have mutated.

"What else explains it then?" I say.

"Aliye had polio. The signs are clear and distinct. Untreated, it often leads to partial or complete paralysis."

I don't tell him that she could have been treated, if we hadn't hid her, if we hadn't believed we were saving her life by denying her a doctor. I'm too surprised to feel guilty yet. "Does she know?"

"Yes. She knows. I told her." He motions for me to sit down on the couch beside him. I suspect that he's preparing me for bad news. "The procedure I do has been proven effective in patients with cerebral palsy, but polio . . . is a different matter. It's a virus, not a disorder."

"I understand."

"I'm not sure you do. The polio virus still lives inside your sister. This procedure will put Aliye at extremely high risk for reinfection."

"So she can't be fixed?"

Akudaan purses his lips. "It's not that she can't. In fact, she's still determined to go ahead with the procedure. But I told her, and I'm telling you, it's medically irresponsible for me to let her do it. Grafting the bones onto her legs means opening her up, doing spinal work—it's intense, invasive. It will probably kill her."

"And she knows that?" I say. But even if she does know, I'm guessing she doesn't care. I've seen the way Aliye looks at the frontier, flat and frozen but desirable all the same because to her it is forbidden. The loss of what she should have had—what we both should have had—in Turkey, marriage and sunshine and a string of goats for our children to tend, must hurt a hundred times more.

"She says she'd rather take the risk than live like this," the doctor says. "Are you Aliye's legal guardian, Hafsa?"

I laugh. "She's older than me. I've never been her guardian. Just her jailer."

"Is that how she sees it?"

That's how we both see it, when I'm feeling sympathetic; when I'm not feeling sympathetic, she's mine. "Neither of us dreamed of becoming worm-farmers, that's all I'll say," I tell him. "We do what we can with what we have. If I had known that what she had was curable, things would be different."

Akudaan is quiet for a minute, then says, "So you can't do anything to stop her from going forward with this?"

I'm not sure I would stop Aliye if I could. "How fast would she degenerate, if she was infected?" I ask.

"A few months? Probably not more. Possibly less."

helminths sleep at every bend along the road I take home; even if she were infected, Aliye's life expectancy might still be longer than mine. "Let her do it," I say. "Let her try to get herself back."

"And the cost won't be a problem? I understand that helminth-blood is quite valuable, but I don't know about your family's particular situation . . . "

We send more than half of our profits home, like most worm-farmers, but I suspect that Baba won't mind the loss of his monthly stipend if it means having his oldest daughter restored. "We'll make it work," I tell Dr. Akudaan.

I'm right, Baba doesn't mind at all, but across a static-coated phone connection he mentions casually that he has one condition. "If things go well, Hafsa," he says, "if she gets her legs back, bring her home."

In Anchorage, while Aliye has slices of elk-bone fitted to her calves, I load our sleigh with bulk goods. We won't need forty pounds of flour or a hundred yards of twine if the procedure succeeds, but Dr. Akudaan warned me that the elk bones might not graft onto Aliye's bones at all. That outcome would keep Aliye safe from reinfection, but it makes me sick to imagine returning to the homestead for another season of breeding hookworms. I make my shopping list half-heartedly, trying not to think too long about using any of the supplies I purchase.

Back in her hospital room, giddy with nervousness and half-drunk on painkillers, Aliye can only talk about her legs. "I think I'll want a pony," she says, "even if we're only here for a few more weeks, it might be worth it. The way you look when you ride, like you can turn all that snow to nothing beneath you. We've lived here three years and I still don't know the countryside, not like I did in Turkey."

"There's nothing to know," I say, trying to keep her realistic. "It's a wasteland, *abla*. A flat hell full of frozen parasites. You forget because you don't have to look at it."

"Do you envy me that?" She frowns with a little quirk to the mobile side of her mouth. She's close to tears, angry ones, and I have to choose my next words with care.

"I don't envy you," I say. And looking at my sister, her frail knobby legs swollen with bone grafts, her face half-frozen, her spine stuffed full of dormant polio virus, how could I ever be jealous? But I wish Aliye wouldn't envy me when I left the same things she did, for her sake instead of my own. "Just remember that legs won't take care of everything. They won't bring back our goats, and they won't get us good marriages."

"I wish those were the things I wanted," Aliye says. "But I don't dream like that anymore. I dream smaller, Hafsa. I dream of getting up in the morning and setting my feet flat on the floor."

The bone grafts succeed; two weeks later, Aliye walks on shaky new elk-bone legs across the kitchen floor, half of her face stretched wide with smiling. Dr. Akudaan says it's too early to tell whether she's at risk of reinfection, not while he's still prodding at the grafts, integrating them fully into Aliye's system. She refuses to register his uncertainty, focusing instead on what is certain: she can walk, if a little unsteadily, and she can ride.

"I want to go with you," she tells me one morning at the front door. I'm halfway through sliding my chaps over my thighs. If I'd been up a little earlier, even a minute earlier, I could have avoided this. Her coat, stiff with newness, hangs over her thin shoulders. As if she is too little to do it for herself, I reach over and zip it up to her chin.

"I don't know, *abla*, aren't your bones too exposed to the cold?"

"Mikhail says it's safe."

I reach down to lace my boots so my facial expression won't betray me. I don't want Aliye with me on the road. I want her safe and bored at home, coating meat-stuff in cumin and wishing we were still in Turkey until the sheer force of her will brought us home. I want her healthy.

Or, if not healthy, dead enough to let me abandon the farm and go home.

"Do you really want to?" I say. "The worms aren't like our goats. There's no pleasure in the work. They lay there and breathe or they wake up and try to eat you."

"Don't you remember when our rams got loose and fell in the ravine that year? In the hillsides outside Karaman, so far south that the wind sweated. We held a contest to see who could heave the most out of the ditch, roped them like Hollywood cowboys and carried them on our shoulders. You know I'm not weak, Hafsa. Don't be so unfair."

I remember as well as she does. Five years ago, Aliye could tell me to do anything and I'd do it because she was brilliant, she was fearless, to me she mattered more than anyone. I wanted her to approve of me.

Five years ago I couldn't find Alaska on a map, didn't know one species of hookworm from another, certainly couldn't have taken a syringe to the segments of a helminth's body and drawn out enough blood to pay the mortgage on a farmstead.

"If you want to," I say.

"That's all I want," she says, so we go, leaving the remains of breakfast on the stove for Akudaan. Aliye's new pony is light on his feet, faster than my own horse, who is bored with the road from Circlet. I expect to be bored too, but I'm not. The same landmarks take on new dimensions with Aliye here, admiring chunks of ice and trading posts as if they're wonders. At the halfway mark, at the mammoth graveyard, Aliye pulls up on her pony's reins and dismounts.

I slide down from my pony's back in a hurry, seeing how shaky she is on her elk-bone legs, and let her grab my shoulder for support. We stand side-by-side, breath fogging the air, as she stares at the pile of stones and the signpost behind them.

"It's a memorial for the Russian trappers," I tell her. "They froze to death here."

"I know," she says. "I forgot about it."

I let her stand there for a while. Then I say, "I'm always glad to be past it. Knowing I've made it when they didn't."

She smiles, her half-smile that is the fullest one she has, and threads her gloved fingers through mine. "You did, didn't you? Strong girl, brave girl, outsmarting the Arctic all by yourself and protecting your invalid sister. I don't know what I'd do without you."

"I don't know what you'd do either," I say, laughing. My throat feels swollen with wanting to cry, and I don't really know why.

A week later, Dr. Akudaan tells me that Aliye's procedure has been a success, her legs will heal completely, she is free to go anywhere she desires. "If you want to sell the farm, please do," he urges me. "I can see you're not happy here."

I won't admit it, not to him and not even to myself, but for a few days, with Aliye mounted up beside me, I was almost happy. "My father wants me to come home," I say. "He wants to see if he can find us decent marriages, now that Aliye is mostly well."

The doctor nods a few times too many and looks everywhere but at me. "Of course," he says. "That's reasonable."

"I know what you see in the news, about Turkey," I say. "And things are difficult, but all the worm blood being imported is starting to make a difference. They say in five to ten years, we might be able to begin keeping animals again. There's a species of goat that responds so well to the blood, they almost always survive."

"It's not that," he says.

"What, then?"

"Ask your sister," is all he'll tell me. "Please, ask your sister."

Now that they have no goats to drive across the countryside, my parents have opened a shoe shop in Ankara. They live a ways down the road from the market where they set up shop, in a stucco house with a roof of red ceramic tile. I paid for that house, I think when I see how fine it is. I would never say that aloud, of course. Baba has to have his pride. We have to feign belief that a shoemaker can afford a home with two balconies and a spacious courtyard.

When Baba opens the door for us, tears shine in his eyes. The rest of the family crowds him out before he can say much, but I'm glad that our return affects him as much as it does me. In the doorway, looking me over, my sisters remark on how pale and thin I am. I can't tell if they mean to compliment or insult me with the words. While they scrutinize my earrings, my hair, the way I've belted the dress I'm wearing, Aliye lingers at the door behind me, as if she isn't sure whether she's welcome. Impatient, I reach for her hand and tug her along. Her elk-bone legs tremble as she follows me into the living room, where Mom pours coffee from a carafe that my worms' blood paid for.

"I missed you, Hafsa," she says, then stares past me at my sister. "Aliye."

"Mama," Aliye says. She grins with half of her face. I see Baba and Mom simultaneously notice her paralysis. I wonder how they ever forgot. Now they look at her with all the familial warmth of health inspectors, letting their gazes rest too long on her elk-bones before their eyes move to her face.

"We'll have dinner with your aunts tonight," Baba says, after a while.

"Do they know why we went to Alaska?" I say. I don't want to let Baba pretend we left Turkey of our own accord, but I don't think he knows he can stop lying. He and the rest of the family still believe that the hook is what paralyzed Aliye. They're still worried that she'll be hunted and killed if anyone finds out that she's the first human vector. I haven't found the right time to tell them, figured that should be Aliye's decision anyway. And Aliye isn't, so far, saying much of anything.

"They know you needed to go," Mom says. She puts a cup in my hands and nods at the divan, inviting me to sit. Despite her weak legs, Aliye receives no such invitation. I motion for her to sit beside me, equally mortified and confused by our reception here. Baba asked me to take Aliye home. He wanted her back.

At dinner we eat lamb and beef dishes made with tofu or top-shelf meat-stuff, pretending that nothing has changed when really, we would never be eating together in an Ankara dining room if the world was the same. Whenever the conversation steers too close to the animals that used to be our livelihoods, someone awkwardly maneuvers back to a safer subject. The hook comes up only once.

"Does everyone here pretend that it didn't happen?" I say to Baba later. "Does Mom?"

"There is a difference between not discussing something and not thinking about it," is all Baba will say. He's sitting cross-legged on the divan, oiling his loafers, a bottle of shoe polish open on the teak coffee table.

"But people must suspect," I say. "With the timing, with the symptoms she showed."

"Still not dinner conversation," Baba says, sniffing as he does when he feels he's being more reasonable than whoever he's talking to. "Hafsa, why did you not mention that your sister is still sick?"

"What do you mean?"

"Her face." He whispers the words like he might get in trouble if he's too loud.

I sit down beside him. The conversation seems to demand lowered voices. "The disease is gone, Baba. It's left marks, but they're just that: marks. And the worst of the damage, the paralysis to the legs, is gone. She can live normally now."

He looks doubtful. "How normally do you think she will ever live like that? She won't find a husband with her face all scowling and crooked."

The words aren't even for me and they still sting. Maybe Aliye was right to hesitate in the doorway of the house. "Does it matter? What does she stand to inherit if she does marry?"

"A happy life, an untarnished reputation."

"Reputation? Is that what Mom cares about?"

Baba shook his head. "Your maman never wished for Aliye to go. I insisted on it. Losing all your goats in an outbreak like we did, that draws enough eyes, but if your daughter dies of the same symptoms then people ask questions, they suspect you of something."

Hearing him talk like that, I can't keep myself from saying, with something like frustration, "She didn't have the hook, Baba."

The frown lines on his wind-chapped face deepen. "What was it, then?"

"She had polio."

Baba repeats the English word, polio, then tries in Turkic. "Not a worm?" he says.

"Not a worm."

"How can you be sure?"

"A doctor from Anchorage examined her."

"Oh God," he whispers. "God, how could we—"

"We're home now," I say, reaching across Baba's lap to shut the bottle of shoe polish. The concept of heirloom furniture is entirely lost on my goatherd father. "I'm selling the farm, I don't think I'll ever go back besides to get things in order. So you don't have to be sorry."

"Three years," he says. "Three years we were without you."

"Do you still want us here? With worm's blood on our hands, with faces unmarriageable and halfway frozen?"

"Hafsa, it doesn't matter if they want me," Aliye says. I turn around and see she's standing in the doorway. I don't know how much she heard, or how much she's hurt by Baba's bleak view on her future, but she looks determined.

"What are you saying?"

"I'm saying," she tells me, "that I'm going home."

Home meaning Alaska, I realize, not Turkey. Home meaning the enormous snow-coated bodies of sleeping helminths, home meaning frozen trappers commemorated by piles of stone.

"I won't go with you," I tell her.

"I know," she says. "You don't need to. It's my home, not yours. Like you said. A place for parasites."

Three months after Aliye returns to Circlet, Dr. Akudaan sends a letter telling me that she's gone. She was a good farmer, he says, like he's trying to eulogize my own sister for me; she wasn't killed by the cold or starvation or helminths. He wanted to tell me before we left Alaska that she was dying of reinfection, but Aliye wouldn't let him.

Folded into his letter is a check, signed by Aliye. Almost enough to rent my own stucco house in the city, almost enough to import a pair of freshly-immunized goats. On the back of the check, Aliye wrote: *I hope this covers three years.*

I don't feel sorry like she wanted me to, I don't feel guilty. But I wish I could have laid a stone on the pile for her on the day we rode out to the mammoth graveyard, when she knew already that she would fall while I rode on, that her road ended before mine did, and she would be an elegy, then a story, then forgotten while I recovered from what her tragedy had done to me.

Cremulator

ROBERT REED

My hometown wasn't much, but when I was fourteen I felt as if I lived in the busy center of all things interesting. Several thousand human mouths and who knows how many human urges, and there were no secrets. Three seniors were pregnant, two by the same boy. There was a snobby couple who drove Cadillacs but couldn't get their checks cashed anywhere in the county. It was common knowledge that our local banker shotgunned cats for sport. And in a day when this kind of behavior mattered, my English teacher happened to have a girlfriend in the city.

Of course the young lady never discussed sexual peculiarities. Paid to teach English, that's exactly what she did, and what made her more intriguing, at least to one fourteen-year-old boy, was that she was pretty. I also liked her name, which was Gwen, and watching her move in front of class was a small, trusted pleasure. She had a pleasant strong, but very girly voice, and I particularly liked the big glasses that seemed too much for her little nose. I didn't have a crush. Not really. But it's fifty years later, and I'll find myself thinking about the day a buddy of mine tried to do a wheelie with his desk. Got the front end up and then came the crash when the desk flipped, slamming the back of his head against the floor. Our teacher bent to help him or to punish him. I don't remember her motives. But one of the buttons had come loose on her shirt, and her padded bra pulled away at the perfect moment. That was the second or third time in my life that I ever saw a woman's breast. It's my "girl in the white dress" moment. You know, that line from *Citizen Kane.* Half a century later, and I can't count the times that image has gotten into my head, or how many times I've told the story to people who truly don't care.

But I'm telling a different story now.

This was a different day. October in 1973, and I'm sure about that because of what was happening in the world beyond. And I know it had to be Monday because our English teacher had driven back from the city the night before. She told us that much. No, girlfriends weren't mentioned, or what she might have been doing in the city. Maybe she didn't realize what everybody knew. But my class was her first class of the day, and Miss Gwen was worked up enough to describe driving on the highway last night when the sky above suddenly got bright and beautiful.

Those were her words. "Bright and beautiful."

There weren't any storms last night, were they? She asked us that. A room of fourteen-year-old meteorologists. No, we couldn't remember lightning. But war was running wild in the Middle East. I remember that detail. People on the news and adults around town were talking about us getting swept into the big fight. Which I'm guessing is why my teacher was so keyed up. Late at night, driving home in a time of war, and she saw something huge and totally unexpected.

"It was the most beautiful blue light," she told us.

She did turn cagey when we fished for details. For instance, she wouldn't admit the exact time. But I can imagine the circumstances. Abandoning the love of her life, she was returning to the inbred community where she had to feel trapped. And then a mysterious light poured across the world. Was this the big missile attack? Were the Soviets going to kill us all? But the light lasted only a couple seconds, bright enough to be seen over the countryside and maybe farther. Did anybody else notice it? None of us did, no. But I wished I had. And after the light faded, the young teacher, so impressed or so rattled, had pulled onto the shoulder to watch the otherwise empty autumn sky.

And here comes the oddest part of her story.

Standing on the highway's shoulder, not a cloud in the world, and little bits of grit started falling. Started hitting her. It reminded her of sleet, except there wasn't any ice. Using a couple index cards, she managed to sweep up a sampling of her mystery, and that's what she brought out for us to observe. To interpret.

"I don't believe in flying saucers," she told us.

I once saw this woman's breast and now she was telling me her disbeliefs. Kids didn't usually get that familiar with teachers.

"Pretend this is science class," she said. "Your eyes are probably better than mine. Pass the sack and hand lens around, okay?"

This seemed like a wondrous day. Everybody ahead of me saw bits of sand and busted glass—the kinds of crap on every road's shoulder. But I was going to do better. It was my mission. So while she was trying to teach us something useful about MacBeth, I squinted harder than I ever had in my life, and I found something new, something nobody could doubt if they took a second look.

"I see a tooth," I said.

That got people giggling.

"A chip of a tooth, at least," I said.

More laughing, and then she said, "Yes," and everyone went quiet. "That's what I thought I was seeing too."

I remember everything. I was watching those big glasses and the breath going in and out of her cute nose, and better than seeing any breast, those few seconds stuck in my head. Which made everything worse later.

In 1975, my English teacher was riding inside her girlfriend's car. They were driving fast on a different highway, and they had been drinking, according to those who knew. The car was alone when it left the road and rolled, and one door came open and a body was thrown free and then crushed.

Nothing else mattered in the world. Make all the noise you want about gossips and narrow-minded farmers, but everybody liked Miss Gwen. School was let out so that her students could attend the service in the city. And to see the famous girlfriend. Several people claimed that she was a graduate student in math or something like math, and I know I had ideas about what she would look like. But no, Gwen's lady proved to be big and plain and a little fat. Bruises and guilt didn't help her appearance either, and it was impossible to miss her, sitting to one side and alone, openly drinking from a bottle now and again. Our teacher came from a gigantic family, I learned, and none of them wanted the girlfriend close. But they made a show of weeping and holding each other, and Miss Gwen's students filled in the back rows, crying a little or more than than a little. I gave my tears to the show. Except I couldn't figure out one part, and I couldn't let it go.

"Where's the casket?" I asked.

"Oh, they cremated her," a classmate whispered.

Cremation happened on the banks of Ganges. Not in our part of the world, at least not in 1975.

"Why's that?" I asked.

"Because, Walt," he said, grimly happy to know things that I didn't know. "She got torn to pieces under the car."

That hard news was absorbed with a sob and a handful of unasked questions. Including me wondering whatever happened to that white chip of a tooth that rained down on her. That chip was suddenly important to me, and I don't know why.

This is what life has taught me:

People are peculiar.

A person can spend every day of his life finding examples of our spectacular oddness, and if that's what he likes to do, then his life is destined to be full and rich.

Reagan.

I mean, really.

Where did we fail so spectacularly that we deserve to have Ronald Reagan on the news every night?

No, I'm not talking politics. This isn't about Republicans, or even white male assholes. And despite what people think, I'll never waste my breath talking about the man's intolerance to people like us. Ask Melanie. We have friends who were hoping Reagan's son would reveal a hunger for other men. Except that is a fool's game. If you think Ronald Reagan would change his attitudes because of one dancing child, then you live in a simple and dangerously sentimental world—a world where every opinion and policy is ready for radical revision with every first shove.

Honestly, I would hate that kind of world.

Melanie says I'm cold, and she likes that about me.

She warns me that I'm fooling people, meaning everybody except her. But that's how I survived four years in the boondocks, teaching future farmers how to read the works of dead men and a few women.

I love Melanie, as best I can. But I know she gets tired of me.

I get tired of me.

But Reagan, yeah. What makes me angriest about our President? He comes into office, and overnight our government's official policy is to act brazen in the face of every trivial threat. Like the Soviets, who don't look to me as if they've got more than a few years of life remaining. In Reagan's world, we have to be geared up to fight a foe that could barely feed its own people. And meanwhile, our real troubles have to be mocked. Global warming. Nuclear proliferation. Corrupt governments supported by my tax dollars and everyone's complacency. This is the mess that one arrogant man has stirred with his cock, and we're into the second term of this bullshit, and I'm just hoping there's still time to save the world before we have nothing but hope remaining.

Melanie wants me to be calmer.

Except the storms are inside me. Most of the time, at least in public, I'm sporting the calmest face in the room.

She says she mostly agrees with me. In fact, with her mind and her skills, Melanie is in an even better place to comprehend the enormous risks standing before this world.

People do ask about the two of us.

And I'm talking about people who hold our ideals. Gay friends have questioned things, and my family never stops asking.

I do prefer women.

It's my wiring, my constitution. Some fundamental talent of DNA coupled with a superior aesthetic.

I don't know what it is.

"But why her?" my sister can't stop wondering aloud.

"Because," is never an adequate answer. Except that is the answer, of course. "Because."

"Oh, it's not that I don't like your friend," my sister constantly tells me. Which underscores how little regard she has for Melanie. And that's before she delivers all of the usual reasons.

"The drinking," says my sister.

My "friend" has a habit, yes. I see it and I can't really approve, and sometimes, yes, the alcohol is in control.

"Her appearance," my sister mentions.

"Appearance" can mean quite a lot. But my sister isn't talking just about the disheveled clothing and her weight. That doesn't cut to the heart of what's wrong. Melanie isn't pretty enough. That's what she and probably the rest of my family believes. My brothers, for instance. All three of them would accept a starlet, high tits and a narrow waist. Or at least they could come to terms with my nature a little easier, seeing that at the family gatherings.

"And besides," my sister always says. "I don't like . . . none of us enjoy . . . how your Melanie treats you."

"It's none of your business how she treats me," I have told her.

A statement both true and useless.

I have mentioned that my sister's husband is a beery brute, and maybe she should take care of her own life before charging into mine.

That tactic never works, but it does spice up Thanksgiving.

On other occasions, I'll say nothing. The cool, unreadable Gwen can nod in a way that's both noncommittal and only a little bit angry. Because frankly, how often can I disagree with an opinion that I myself share?

Melanie can be difficult.

I admit that, yes.

If I dialed my life back to my twentieth birthday, then maybe I would avoid her and the nearly two decades that followed. I would fall in love with somebody else. Shit, maybe I'd surrender to convention, ending up with a heavy and often drunk man and three kids, and I'd be teaching my soul out in some boondock bend in the goddamn road.

But then I would have missed the rest of it.

I'm smart and always have been. And my interests are broader than most people's interests. For example, I happen to be one of the great scientists among Literature majors, and if it comes down to it, I can do a better job describing quantum mechanics and high-energy physics than a lot of the geniuses who work with nothing else.

Melanie taught me.

Talk about your gifts.

She drinks too much. No question about it. And her hygiene could be improved. And we've settled into that old-dyke mentality where sex is relegated to special occasions. But sex isn't anyone's business, and what I get seems to be enough for me, and I don't hear her complaining much at all. And during all these years together, the woman has never stopped giving me the most amazing tales about space and time and that truer wonder called spacetime.

I feel fortunate.

And all my lady gets from me are angry words about an old man who might kill the world but hasn't yet and has only two years left in his second term.

Anyway, here's my point in this roundabout story.

This winter, in Chicago. Melanie and I were attending one of her conferences, some of the big people in her business talking about neutrinos and Senators with pull and that huge underground ring they were building in Texas. Physicists wanted the ring finished, but there were a lot of complaints about the billions being spent. And I might have said a few carelessly skeptical words about the venture. But no, I really wanted the ring to happen, if only because my Melanie has assured me that we would learn a lot.

Except that's not quite it.

"I'll learn a lot, and that's what matters."

She's an arrogant broad. In every sense of the word, and she'd be happy to hear me say it.

Chicago.

Yeah, we were at the conference. A six-inch snow made the city prettier than it deserves to be. Fermi people and their wives, and by chance, I was standing outside waiting for the bus that was supposed to shuttle us to another event. And that's when the blue light came. Brilliant and silent at first, but then we heard the crack of what wasn't thunder and was definitely far from normal.

I knew that instantly.

And nobody debated my ignorant assessment.

Maybe a dozen geniuses were gawking at a sky that made no sense, listening to that long odd roar. And then every light in the city went out. Power was down across all of northern Illinois, although we didn't know it then. Maybe half of the scientists proposed that a suborbital nuke had generated some kind of blistering pulse. Except the glow didn't come from one point but seemed to be generated everywhere, and this was strange as hell, and what impressed me most was how excited they became, these brilliant men and that one woman who happened to be standing beside me, giggling with nervous joy at the idea of something that they couldn't quite explain.

Which would have been enough, obviously.

I couldn't have imagined anything stranger than that.

But then the little bits of teeth and bone began falling on us and on millions of other people, and later came the soft ash that was never thick but easy enough to see on the fresh snow. And the scientists collected up samples along with snowballs, and a day later someone came out with the news that the ash and those tiny bits of teeth were human.

And again, foolish as can be, I told myself that the story couldn't find a stranger gear.

Grandparents wanted to see the kids. That's why we came back.

My hometown lured us in because we were tired of dealing with renters from a thousand miles away. But selling Gwen's old house meant cleaning it up first and probably seeing a new roof put on, and I would have preferred it if my folks could have volunteered to part of that work for us. That was my secret thought. But Gwen actually said it. She isn't normally that mouthy, but the town and her still remembered each other, and I suppose it's always going to be that way.

And there's another reason to return: My firm was sending me overseas, probably for the next several years, and what with time distance and the vagaries of health, there was a respectable chance that one of my parents would never see our kids again.

Vagaries. Gwen dwells on little else, some days.

"I loved this place," she confided to me.

We were standing in front of her former home. The last of the renters had vanished, evicted and possibly now being pursued by various authorities. And they had left behind exactly the kind of mess you'd expect.

"You loved this place when?" I asked.

Knowing the possible answers.

"When I sat on this porch. Remember?"

"Oh yeah."

I was home from college and she was sitting in the shade. The English teacher with a tragic past. She was looking at me as I strolled past. I have no recollection about where I was going. Probably down to the Sinclair for a Pepsi, and it was definitely summer, just like today. It was bright and hotter than normal for morning. Not unlike now. Which I suppose is why my wife brought up that critical moment in both of our lives.

"You said my name," I said.

She laughed and said, "No."

"Yes."

"You misheard me. I've told you that." She kept laughing, looking for a place to sit again. Except there were no chairs, just black plastic sacks jammed with sour food and Walmart-crap toys. So she leaned against the railing, saying, "Water."

"Walter," I said.

" 'I could use some water,' I mentioned."

"I heard Walter."

Some stories never get old. We shared the laughter and I touched her on the cheek, my wife and the mother of two kids that I adored nearly as much as this bright, taciturn lady.

And just like that, she gave me the look.

We went inside, into that house that needed to be burned more than cleaned and sold. That big worn house with the wide porch and dark deep rooms, including the bedroom upstairs, hot then and hot now. But it didn't slow us down any, neither time. And just like that, I felt like I was twenty again, screwing my English teacher, and her taking as much pleasure as any girl I would ever know.

Maybe other women are more passionate with their men.

I can't say.

A bold and worldly fellow would have bedded a hundred women before giving up. But then again, I'm not that way.

We finished and dressed, and Gwen asked, "Should we rescue your parents?"

"Someday."

Then we walked back out onto the porch, ready to resume our cleaning.

A pair of locals were strolling past. Older ladies, and I knew their faces if not either name. But they absolutely recognized us. One nudged the other, and then they looked away when we started offering our eyes.

It pissed me off, just enough.

I didn't live here anymore. And I sure as hell wasn't the twenty-year-old kid sleeping with his ex-teacher. Who was twenty-nine at the time, I could have pointed out to those fine ladies. Who was nine years my senior, do the math, and Gwen was a hundred times better than either of them were on their best days.

Maybe I would have shouted something like that.

But what was a bright day suddenly turned infinitely brighter, and every piece of machinery, car and generator and working radio, stopped working. And that scorching bright blue light turned into darkness just before the pulverized bits of enamel started raining down.

Funny the ideas that come to you.

We were wading through teeth and then the soft bony ash, and I was actually a little bit happy. Some incredible volcano had come to life nearby. That was my only working theory, regardless how crazy it sounded. And now the town was going to be destroyed, and we'd just been saved from that awful business of cleaning out the filthy old house.

Except of course pretty much everybody else in North America was suffering nearly as badly as we were.

It was two weeks before life began to look normal.

And another two weeks before our car was cobbled back together well enough to drive. The kids were in back. The radio was filled with news about the disaster and how President Gore was making new laws, keeping order over the mayhem. And that was the first time, a month after the nightmare began, when we heard the name Dr. Melanie Baxter.

I was driving.

Gwen cranked up the volume, listening to something about a paper written back in the 70s.

"The late Dr. Melanie Baxter," the voice said.

Shouting, Gwen ordered me to pull over.

I already was.

We happened to be in a low spot not many miles from town. What had been several inches of ash and bone was being worked by the wind, stripped away in places and drifting deep in other places, accenting just how strange and awful the disaster had been. Experts were definite, certain, convinced. Judging by the DNA, these were human remains that had tumbled from the sky. A phenomenal mass of material, by any measure. And the blue flash was some sort of high-energy discharge, not predicted by anybody except a woman from a quarter century ago—a suddenly famous doctoral student who was killed while driving alone one night.

Drunk, Melanie had been.

They didn't mention that fact, and/or that the fatal crash happened after a fight with my wife.

That's why Gwen was crying now. I assumed. The memories of quite a lot were coming back. It sounds awful, but I have always been secretly glad that Gwen's first love was utterly lost, and the shock and guilt of that car crash was what gave me everything that I enjoyed today.

I patted my wife's little hand, accomplishing nothing.

"I remember that paper," she muttered. "She told me . . . what did she tell me . . . ?"

I wished for a second blast of light, our car radio dying all over again.

"About spacetime," she said. "About things bending until they break."

And I'm thinking: "Isn't that true for all of us?"

Here's the joke:

"What's the difference between poets and physicists?"

And the punchline:

"Poets get two more productive years than physicists get."

Not true, of course. Yeats lasted for decades, if I remember. And bless his heart, Einstein kept trying. Although really, if you want to be honest, how many times can one person do the impossible?

Once is enough for most us.

Which is why poets and the rest of us usually give up so soon. Being smart, we know the odds, and why waste fifty years dancing with endless failure?

Now ask me why I drink.

I know what you're thinking. You're thinking, "She's washed up and hates herself and her failed genius and why wouldn't she drink?"

Is that the true story?

Or maybe . . . maybe there's some sad tale at work. Emotional. Human. Nothing about mathematics or the deepest structure of our universe. That would help explain the old drunk, giving her that necessary human dimension. She had a love once, someone better than she deserved, but that woman left her for some sorry, ordinary reason, or worse, for no reason in particular. That's a tale worthy of a poet, not a professor, and hearing it, people would feel sorry for me, explaining fifty years of failure under the light of pain.

Why does pain produce light?

That's what I want to know.

We need a poet to explain this conundrum. Find a poet. Ask her, "Where's the brilliance in misery?" Because I've known all kinds of hurt in life, too many to count, and even during the worst days, my pain has never shown me anything but hard cold blackness.

The blue light.

Yeah, that bastard was plenty bright.

Not that I saw it, of course. I was comfortably done with my day. And regardless what you think, even if I had seen the event, I wouldn't have guessed the source. That kind of knowledge took data and huge calculations that we wouldn't be able to make anywhere in the world, at least for another half year.

Sad to admit, I don't possess superhuman talents ready to unleash.

In fact, let me tell you this: On her finest day, the finest scientist doesn't know shit about almost everything. But that's the fun of it. That's why people want to be scientists. It's the dose of adrenalin that comes when you feel as lost as can be.

Drunk, I happily slept through the blast and the first half hour of the emergency.

I might have slept until dead, but neighbors remembered me and broke down my front door, dragging me out into the ash before the whole building came down. I don't know about where you lived, but we had nearly six feet of human remains dropping out of that black pain-rich sky, and half the local buildings were flattened, and I don't know how many died.

Without power or any infrastructure, being a scientist was tough. But I managed to work. It was easy to see the bits of teeth, and there was the rumor that these were human remains. Someone in Atlanta or Stockholm figured that out early, and I don't know where I heard it. But right there, that was an astonishment. One cremated human body yields about five pounds of tooth and crumbled bone. But the entire population of the world, women and men and fat children, won't render up more than forty billion pounds of nastiness. Which is nothing. Two million tons. That isn't enough material to fill up an old strip mine in Wyoming.

A lot more than that fell on our heads.

For a full year, I lived in one refugee camp after another.

Honestly? I've never been happier. No drinking, mostly. And a lot of basic shit to get done. I've always been good at figuring out problems, and everybody in authority wanted help with the most basic water-food-shelter conundrums. Which makes me wonder: Is this what physicists did before we solved the universe? Did we just find new ways to clean old water and make plants grow in the graveyard?

The important people eventually found me in New Mexico. A team flew all the way from the provisional capital in Portland. They just wanted to talk. But nobody flies that far, not anymore, and certainly not because of the need to chat. Those visitors kept calling me, "Dr. Baxter," and thanking me for my good work here and before. But I could see where they were heading, which is why I said, "Spacetime shattered on us. Didn't it?"

There were five of them, but one man did most of the talking.

"Why do you believe that?" he asked, sounding like a cop.

"Nothing else explains it," I said, stating the obvious. "The event took our entire planet, which is just one planet. But for an instant of an instant, we were linked with billions of other Earths."

Everybody nodded in agreement.

Except for the man in charge. "Billions," he repeated, acting as if he wasn't happy with that estimate.

So I gave him my true numbers.

Then I said to them, "But you already know this. Plenty of others must have done the arithmetic."

The man shrugged. Maybe yes, maybe no.

"Of course we're not just talking about Earths," I added. "What we're talking about is our Earth fusing with one tiny piece of ten trillion other Earths. The same piece repeated infinitely. And judging by the evidence, I'd say that what fell on us was the remains of one person ground halfway to dust inside a cremulator."

Nobody spoke.

Even my main interrogator knew to hold his thoughts inside.

So I added to my analysis, explaining, "If you find enough DNA, tracking down the dead person would be easy enough."

Which was when the woman in back—the person who was really in charge of this vital, unthinkable mission—finally spoke out.

"Perhaps that already happened," she said.

And I laughed, right up until I noticed fear inside those various stares.

"It's someone from our world," I guessed.

Eyes were focused on nobody but me.

So I made the obvious guess. "These are my ashes."

Which was when the man laughed, saying, "That's an arrogant attitude."

And his boss said, "No. But according to records, back in college and for several years, you knew the lady in question."

I rarely get to meet legends.

Despite a reputation for combativeness, this particular legend was nothing but pleasant. And even though we'd all heard stories about failing health and a lousy sense of dress, Dr. Baxter looked fit enough to run, and her clothes hadn't been slept in more than one brief night.

We met her inside her office.

Surrounding us were a million miles of tubes and tunnels, superconductive magnets and enough energy to make the Earth jump.

That's what she wanted to make happen.

Who else in the world could have asked for permission to make the Earth jump?

I was the least important person in the room. A career lawyer, at the end of my days, I was part of a team trying to determine the liability of the latest experiment.

"We want to send a message to a tiny fraction of our neighboring Earths," Dr. Baxter was saying.

Funny how easily you accept the amazing, particularly after reading a hundred briefings on the subject.

"We'll use diamonds," she said. "Tiny and very pure and marked in a variety of ways."

"But you're just sending a few grams of diamonds," someone said.

I was listening and I wasn't listening. There was a picture frame on the woman's desk, faces and places changing while the debate unfolded.

"A few grams is all we can afford," said Melanie Baxter. "The energy required is enormous enough as it is."

"But how could anyone notice us?" our doubter had to ask.

"Because," I interrupted. Surprising myself as much as the others.

Coaxing me with a small, grim smile, the genius said, "Please, continue."

"We won't be the only people sending diamonds," I offered. "There's an infinite number of Earths, and some infinite slice will run the same experiment at the same time."

"But we're sending diamonds to just one other Earth," the doubter continued. "And if there are infinite targets . . . "

"Randomized distributions," said the genuine expert.

And the rest of us fell into a studious silence.

"Some Earths will receive two shares, some won't get anything at all. But a few, a very few, are going to experience ten million shares. There'll be a visible EM display in the sky, and then the diamond grit falls and gets collected and people who look similar to us or exactly like us are going to peer into their microscopes, finding delicate messages etched in languages that might or might not resemble their own."

It was a fun moment, watching every face become awestruck.

Even Melanie's face.

Then I remembered another piece of the story.

"Time," I blurted.

"What's that?" the doubter asked.

"This is all going to be random in time too," I offered. Then I looked at the woman behind the desk, wondering if I was totally wrong.

But I wasn't, no.

"We've worked out the distribution curve," she said. "Earths occupying our moment are the most likely targets, but the curve isn't particularly steep. That's why there's one chance in about five trillion chances that our diamonds will end up several years before today. And there are equal odds that they'll travel ahead in time instead."

"And once in a great while, they get noticed," I said.

"Sending messages back in time," the doubter said, except he was sounding more intrigued by the moment. "How far back in time will we reach?"

"This is a distribution curve applied to infinities," Melanie said. "When dealing with a trillion quadrillion zeros, things can turn fairly strange."

To the best of our abilities, each of us wrestled with that notion.

And then the genius looked off at the ceiling, her heavy old face changing. I don't know how to describe it, except to say that she was suddenly sad enough to make me ache and happy enough to make me fly. That's what I saw in that one face, and because of that stark show of emotion, everybody else grew uncomfortable.

Our leader decided it was time to leave.

Except for me. I lingered at the office door. A couple people said, "Walt," but I ignored them. Then Melanie shut her eyes and sighed and opened her eyes, finding me watching the young face filling the picture frame on her desk.

"I knew your wife," I said.

The next smile was brighter, fending off every misery.

"My condolences," I said.

She said, "Thank you."

Then after a moment, "How did you know Gwen?"

"She taught me about Shakespeare during high school."

Melanie laughed and said, "Think of these odds."

It was fun to see the coincidences, yes.

"She was a good teacher," said the widow.

"Really good," I agreed.

"Six months gone, and it feels like zero time has passed," she confided. Then she suddenly rose, saying, "Funerals."

"Excuse me?"

"Gwen's ceremony didn't satisfy me," Melanie confessed. "And I've been thinking about what else to do."

I nodded.

The woman leaned against her desk, lost in endless thought.

Needing something to break the silence, I said, "Yeah, Gwen was an excellent teacher."

The woman looked at me for the final time.

"Tell me about your class," she said.

What came to mind was spellbinding, but I couldn't share that. So instead, I smiled in a wistful way, saying, "A friend of mine was playing around and then spilled his desk in class. And she instantly helped him."

Another nod, and the eyes dropped.

"No," she said. "My Gwen would have kicked his ass for screwing around. And that's the woman I loved."

The Occidental Bride
BENJANUN SRIDUANGKAEW

New Year: the train eels along a landscape of red snow and shadow-dust, on carbonate tracks haloed in anemic light. Heilui keeps half the window opaque to block out the field of endless machine-dead, the sight of satellites pressed against the skyline like bruised mouths on a gash. The other half she fills with a news feed: disasters in montage, kaleidoscope of calamities—cities gone dark and still, streets turned to web-cracks and sidewalks impact-raised into briars, balconies smeared in blackened lymph and rust-red blots.

She has watched it many times; has been made to, during the interrogation. The footage never fails to pull at her heart like the moon exerting its gravity on the acid tides. Pulling at her like the questions from back then, the faces and names lined up and *Did you associate with this woman? This man? This woman? This man, this man, this man.*

Heilui's hands are clammy with the sweat of remembered terror, the memory of teetering on the edge of freefall. She wipes them dry. Her lap is heavy with gifts prepared by relatives: engagement boxes of jade bangles and figurines, silk slippers threaded in gold, a bag of crystallized fruits. A kintsugi bowl: black pottery broken and mended in silver, the seams radiant with age. Foreign antique, contributed by a wealthy adventurer aunt.

The train notifies her that another passenger will be joining her, transferred after one of the carriages have detached for another station. She sweeps up the gifts and blanks out the news feed.

The compartment opens in a murmur of dry, rustling leaves. A young man takes the seat opposite, giving her a respectful distance. They exchange small talk: he is heading southwest for a research lab, armed with a postgraduate grant from the University of Rajamongkol.

"And you, older sister?"

She cups her palm over the antique bowl, fingering its chimera texture, rough earth striated with the velvet smoothness of precious metal. "I'm on my way," Heilui whispers, "to meet my bride."

The Institute, the halfway house, sits ensconced in the hothouse hill: mantled in rough foliage, insulated from the machine ruins and their radiative hunger. This close, ignoring the wasteland of charred clay and half-alive intelligences is impossible, though Heilui tries to focus elsewhere, lash her attention to the interior of the car and the imminent appointment. Some of the interference nevertheless slips through, crooning ancient lullabies of wars eons gone, status dispatches from combat centuries ended. Some are foreign, some are in Putongwa and Fukginwa. Others are in Dakman with a smattering of Yingman recounting casualties. Strange-sounding names crowd in a white-noise fog, synthetic and toneless.

Within the Institute's walls the wasteland sky is blocked out by a seashell husk, bred into immensity to shield the entire compound. She is received at the gate by a guidance routine taking the form of a red-beaked crane. It gives her directions in a perky tourmaline voice and instructs her to avoid contact with candidates other than her own. Heilui is glad to comply, though she does steal glances at the manicured topiary and moss-ridden trellises, the small gazebos and polished benches. Young women and younger men, ghost-pale and exotic, in muted cosmetics and pastel dresses. They drift eyes downward or sit prim and quiet. She can't spot any of them in conversation with one another; they arrange themselves as though hyper-conscious of an audience.

The crane guides her to a private vestibule, where a low table waits with tea and covered wicker baskets. Heilui lifts the lids to find radish pastries and steamed red-pork buns. She doesn't sample either; no point leaving crumbs all over herself and marring that first impression. Instead she stacks up the gifts. Briefly she wonders if she should have brought a bouquet—the culture of her bride's birth values flowers as a courtship sign, though she imagines their bouquets must be as translucent as their people, frosted leaves and ivory petals, flora gone extinct when that continent heaved and broke.

It is then that the crane starts speaking in her interrogator's voice. Heilui nearly leaps out of her seat.

"Relax, Doctor Lan," says the interrogator, that same mild contralto she remembers. "We chose you for the case because we believe you better equipped than most to manage her. The subject has been neutralized entirely and you needn't fear that she will be a danger."

"I'll do my best." Heilui licks parched lips.

"This isn't a test, though when the operation concludes successfully your profile will be cleaned up. No longer a person of interest, no more record of your unfortunate—but entirely innocuous of course, as you've proven—association with occidental terrorists. Good luck."

The line cuts. The vestibule's partition folds aside and Heilui's bride enters.

Kerttu is tall and large-boned, as her people often are, bred in a land of giant-myths and arctic blaze. In echo of this image her hair is pale as snowdrift. Eyelashes mascara-gilded, eyelids faintly dusted copper, cheekbones accentuated to skeletal sharpness as though to compensate for the unreality of her pallor. The only spot of color above her neck is the fuchsia on her lips, applied to hone the corners of her mouth to crisp edges. Her bodice is closely fitted, the sleeves gradating from peach to oxblood cuffs, the skirt narrow and long: the colors are some of Heilui's favorites, the style close to what she might herself wear. The Institute has been attentive.

So ordinary, Heilui thinks, and tries to visualize Kerttu as she once was—in a lab coat, imperious over her empire of living matrices, her gleaming hives of bioweapons. But she can't quite picture it, this woman as the engineer of genocides.

Kerttu gives an antique bow, one fist cupped inside her palm. "Happy new year, Doctor Lan."

"Heilui will do, please. Sit. Have you eaten?" She nods at the dishes, wondering if Kerttu can use chopsticks. "Your Gwongdungwa is excellent." An odd, piquant accent but she's hardly going to criticize.

"You honor me. I've had fine teachers."

A conversational dead-end. "Why don't you tell me about yourself?"

One long, slow blink. The occidental woman's pupils are unnervingly black, emphasized as they are by irises the hue of jellyfishes. "Why did you pick me, Doctor?"

Heilui turns the teacups upright. Pours. A distinct scent of plum rises. "Perhaps I spotted you in the Institute database and recognized destiny at first sight." She pushes a cup over. "In Jatbun, they say that a red thread joins fated partners and you only need to pursue it to the other end. When you find yours, at once you will know it—the tug in your blood through your thumb as your fortune draws taut as pipa strings."

Kerttu curls her fingers around the teacup without flinching from the heat. "I don't think it was my looks. There are others here younger than I am, more aesthetically pleasing. Is it the novelty of having a former mafia researcher and tamed war criminal for a wife?"

"You are a person, not a novelty object," she says. "The Institute recommended you, I thought it a fine suggestion, and I'm under some pressure to wed."

"Many factors affect the making of a purchase. Desirable attributes go on one side of the scale, the price tag on the other. This is perhaps the most honest form of marriage." Kerttu sips gingerly, her expression pinching at the sourness, the unfamiliar. "Is that why you opted for the Institute instead of selecting from your peers? Though I think the latter might have been cheaper."

"I wanted my options from a different pool, and I chose you. Is that not enough? You can say no."

"I won't." This is said quickly, breathless like a gunshot.

Heilui holds out her hand. "Shall we try to make this work?"

Kerttu takes it, and with those painted lips kisses Heilui's fingertips one by one.

They marry on the train, the world's ruin rushing past in silent witness. Kerttu hands over a fistful of gold earrings as though they burn her and, with detached grace, accepts the small mountain of dowry. She puts on the one bangle large enough for her wrist as the portable altar officiates: simulated incense and ancestors, two-dimensional gods rotating to give them blessings—mercy, prosperity, fertility. Kerttu's identity rearranges itself to *Lan Kerttu*, alphabet to calligraphy.

"There's usually much more ceremony," Heilui says, apologetic, "and nine courses of food. And your family would see you off . . . "

"This is fine." Her wife cradles the kintsugi bowl, thumb running laps around its rim. "The last wedding I attended was a conflagration of opulence with a twenty-course banquet—one could die of abundance, asphyxiate on splendor. But it also involved people getting shot in the head and a couple of poisonings, though at least both grooms were unscathed. I also haven't had a family since I was six."

That factoid Heilui knows, though she can't conceive of being kinless. There should have been relatives to raise her, a small herd of uncles and aunts and in-laws. "How did you like the Institute?"

"All of us hid our old lives; we never discussed our history and if we recognized each other from before, we pretended ignorance. Many of us wear scars." Kerttu holds up her wrists, showing them unmarred and smooth, and points at her throat: just as clean, all the access points to arteries without scars. "Not me, though. I've never been able to stand the sight of my own blood, the weight of my own pain. What we discussed all the time, where the cameras didn't reach, was our prospective clients. Who they might be, what sort of services we might be required to provide. Until a week ago, Doctor, I had no inkling of who you were."

"I'd have liked an introduction sooner, but their protocols are so strict. They did treat you well?" A needless question; the Institute keeps its charges in the greatest comfort.

"I never wanted for anything." Kerttu sets the bowl aside. "Aren't you afraid of me?"

The subject has been neutralized entirely. "Why would I need to be afraid of my bride?"

In good time they arrive home, a complex of four tapered serpent-buildings wound loosely around a central hall. Redwood columns clad in bismuth crystal, flat roofs topped in gunmetal tiles, a modest lake: from what she knows Kerttu lived in more sumptuous arrangements, a spider citadel of phantasmagoria matrices and psychedelic weave, but her wife nevertheless widens her eyes as they disembark. "How many live here?" Kerttu asks softly. "I thought you only lived with your family."

"I do. *Extended* family. Isn't that the way it's supposed to be?" Heilui pulls up a layout of the estate, cupping the display in her palm like an egg of enameled rime. "The southwest hall belongs to my grandparents and some great-grandparents, the southeast one—oh, Aunt Daruwan lives there but she's not in. Probably off unearthing crash sites or mapping crisis regions, you'd like her. Here, we're in the northeastern one, the Tangerine."

By luck it is dinner hour, most of the family is assembled in the communal hall. No one is there to crowd in and overwhelm them when they enter the Tangerine's sunset corridors. Kerttu's luggage trails behind them, as silent as its owner. Even her suitcases are Institute-mandated for refinement, matte-black leather and copper filigree. Heilui suspects that when they unpack, Kerttu's wardrobe will precisely match Heilui's tastes. That is something she will need to remedy—a trip to the city, a stop at a tailor's boutique. The Institute is exacting and thorough in how it molds its charges, but that level of micromanagement bothers her despite the brittleness of all this, the fraught weight of Kerttu's presence.

Heilui's segment of the house spans three units, study, bedroom, and a simulator box where she does most of her work. "I'll get you your own bed." She gestures at a modular divan. "Until then, I hope you won't mind that?"

"You don't wish me to share yours?" Kerttu absently pets her luggage, but her attention is on Heilui. A smile grows on her lips, like weeds, like thorns. "I would, sincerely, find it no chore."

Talons of heat sizzle on the back of Heilui's ears. "Please make yourself comfortable. The bath is down the corridor."

"Thank you." Kerttu twists apart the sleeves of her dress as though about to disrobe on the spot, casting off the fabric the way a snake molts. "May I ask a question?"

"By all means."

"What did I cost you?" She is loosening the collars. A glimpse of clavicles, nearly paper-white, veins shining through. "I know that no money changed hands; the Institute takes currencies much more nebulous. But there is an essential truth that governs existence, greater and stronger than any force, and it is that on every object there is a price. What was mine?"

Heilui laughs, faltering. The dress recedes and a shoulder comes bare, rounded and marked with a tattoo that declares Kerttu's former allegiance. Butterflies congregating on a corpse, proboscises sipping sweat: the crest of a cartel, the symbol of ownership. "It's more complicated than that. We could discuss it one day. Tomorrow I'll introduce you to my family."

At breakfast, everyone convenes to see the foreign bride.

She sits like a mannequin of frost and plaster, consuming porridge and condiments as solemnly as a funeral meal. The Lan children gawk at her openly; one of Heilui's youngest nieces whispers—audibly—speculating whether Kerttu's pallor might leave white smudges on the utensils and tea-bowls; whether it might rub off on the furniture like icing. Their parents shush them, but adult scrutiny is hardly more discreet. Heilui's mothers regard Kerttu with pointed appraisal, no doubt already cataloguing many faults and improprieties.

On her part Kerttu behaves as though she is by herself, facing an empty room, the round ivory-and-teak table all her own rather than occupied by fifteen. Occasionally, as though she is remembering from etiquette training, she puts food on Heilui's plate—a knot of pork floss, a slice of yaujagwai. This is done stiffly and gingerly. Kerttu, Heilui recalls, wouldn't be used to sharing food this way; where she came from each person keeps to their own dish, even among family and intimate friends.

Heilui makes desultory conversation and asks after Aunt Daruwan. She knows that once her family can corner her alone she'll be barraged with questions; she has told none of them of Kerttu's background, allowing them to believe that her choice of spouse is conventional and untied to any state interest. Already an uncle and two cousins are bombarding her with messages. She mutes the notifications and, at the first polite opportunity, excuses herself. Kerttu makes her obeisance, courtly, to family elders and follows Heilui's suit.

They find a spot by one of the garden gates, behind an enclosure of hybrid bamboos and ceramic partitions. Kerttu arranges her skirts—fuller today, loosely made; another style Heilui herself likes—and folds herself like a paper puppet. "Am I making things difficult?"

"They'll come around, everyone just needs time to adjust." Heilui silences another message, unread, and extends her palm. "Here's a prototype I've been working on. Very unfinished, more a framework than anything."

"It appears to be an anthropological modeling program." Kerttu tilts her head. "Not my field, Doctor. I was a biochemist."

"It's a sim of the shattered continent. I've been ambitious with the scope and detail, so I would like—" She gives a laugh, makes a helpless gesture. "An authenticity check, maybe? I'll get you your own shell, it's last-generation and I haven't upgraded it for a while, but . . . "

"It was a research subject that you required then, not a spouse."

"Not at all!" Heilui says quickly. "Why don't we go into the city? You can pick out your own clothes."

"You're treating me extravagantly for a person you purchased." The biochemist turns the shell this way and that, her painted nails a shock of aqua against her phantom skin. "I'm not saying that to be judgmental or bitter—I'm neither; I've been owned since I was young, treated as investment, my intelligence bought and traded for. I understand my position perfectly. There's no need to woo me. Ask and I will serve."

A frisson sings through Heilui, chased by a wash of nausea: for a moment she could understand the sick supremacy of commanding utter, total power over another human being. "Come on. Let's get you to a tailor."

She loads her spare shell with the modeling client and turns that over to Kerttu, who engages the program with the rapt concentration of a sniper on her target. When they reach the commerce arcade, Kerttu looks up blinking as though jolted from a trance. She folds the shell away and surveys the velvet web of shops, the walkways weaving through them like ribbons. Tension pinches her expression as they join the crowd's flow, families in New Year finery, children and young couples out to spend their red envelope money.

Surreptitiously, Heilui searches the faces around them for a trace of the foreign, perhaps a declaration of suspicious intent etched into the downturn of a mouth, sewn into the hem of a skirt or sleeve, a glimpse of the butterflies emblem. But she finds nothing, sighting no set of features that is not everyday and ordinary to her, no complexion as startling as Kerttu's or a nose so angular. She does not find the man who slaughtered countries, the man who once owned her wife.

"Something's making you uncomfortable." Heilui loops her arm through Kerttu's. "What is wrong?"

"I'm the only foreigner here." Kerttu has switched to Dakman, harsh and rolling.

"Oh, you don't need to worry—the staff here is perfectly used to foreigners. There are expatriates all over Kowloon, of every nationality you can imagine. I'll put you in touch with them, if you like."

"By law I'm forbidden from making contact with those from the shattered continent, just as I'm forbidden from pursuing my previous specialty. I'm wearing certain implants to ensure my compliance. I appreciate your thought, Doctor."

At the tailor, Kerttu is imaged by a dozen mannequins that revolve slowly on their feet, laughing and animated as they flicker from style to style, season to season. In the end she chooses a postmodern keipou, unpatterned black sheathing her like carapace. Sleeveless, high crescent collars, unrelieved contrast between fabric and complexion making a monochrome print of Kerttu. "I lost much and there was never a funeral," she explains the color. "I need to mourn. I expect I'll always be mourning."

But this, like everything else, is said with distance as though discussing someone else's grief.

Their next stop is the Shau Kei Wan Temple, where Tinhau presides. Not the most traditional choice when it comes to matrimony, but Heilui has a special fondness for the sea goddess, and this temple is one of the few where Kwunyam is depicted in her male aspect while the war god Kwantai is presented as a woman: green-robed and armored, puissant with restrained fury. Heilui shows Kerttu the correct paper offerings to make, the right number of virtual incenses to ignite. They shake kaucim cups side by side, have the cast of their fortune read by streamed oracles.

It belatedly occurs to Heilui, on their way back, to ask Kerttu if she is a monotheist. Her wife shrugs, a peculiarly foreign gesture. "My faith rests in the belief that the human capability for innovation and malice is infinite. I admit no other gods, pray to no other pantheon. I've never been disappointed."

Back at the Lan house they are ambushed at the gate, a gaggle of nieces and nephews swarming over Kerttu. Heilui presses a sheaf of red envelopes into her wife's hand, each filled with account chips. "One per head," she says, grinning. Under the shade of a butterfly tree, one of her mothers is waiting; she knows what that look means. "Don't let them get greedy. Make them say the magic phrase first."

Kerttu holds the envelopes loosely and stares in bemusement, to a high-pitched chorus of *gong hei fat choi*. Heilui draws aside to join Mother Meitin under the fluttering, winged canopy. "We need to talk." Meitin does not quite glance sidelong at Kerttu. "About . . . that."

"She's not a *that*, Mother."

"Are you going to have children with her?" Meitin frowns. "They'd turn out looking rather dead. And her table manners! I thought the Institute had the foreign ones trained well?"

"She will adapt." Equivocating. "And she is unique. I don't think I could have found anyone like her at the university or through any of your friends, or . . . "

Her mother sniffs. "An acquired taste, I'm sure. Well, your choices are your own and you're a woman grown. At least she's educated, I suppose."

Heilui refrains from pointing out that as a biochemist, Kerttu's credentials are more impressive than most. Instead she watches her wife keep the envelopes out of the children's reach in one hand, distributing them with the other to the niece or nephew who has approximated a correct pronunciation of *Aunt Kerttu*.

Over the next weeks Kerttu drifts uneasily within the family home, colliding with or grazing past elders. She does not succeed in endearing herself to them, though Heilui notes with relief that the children have taken a liking to Kerttu, for her occidental novelty if nothing else. Any time she has a free moment, Kerttu would obsessively spend it on the simulation.

Heilui monitors Kerttu's progress, trying to use the map of her wife's virtual wanderings to create an image that would pierce the inscrutable, remote shell. A crucial piece that would make the Kerttu she is seeing cohere with the Kerttu the mass murderer who created weapons that destroyed the shattered continent, the war criminal. Often she thinks of asking, *Did you understand what you were doing?* At the beginning, she mustn't have, a prodigy whose supple intelligence was exploited, whose mind was slowly conditioned to regard her work as normal.

Even then it is difficult to be afraid of Kerttu, who inhabits Heilui's life with the soft focus of a ghost. Difficult to connect her with those atrocities, the solidity of statistics and the hard industrial edges of war. But then it is difficult to connect the shattered continent—smooth and pretty while it lived—with its history of dialects born and annexed, its first contacts negotiated through a language of exploitation and expansion.

"You've been distant. Am I boring you?" Kerttu asks one evening as they share a dinner out in the city.

"Certainly not," Heilui says, laughing. "You have been nothing but delightful."

Kerttu cuts her pasta into fine, thin slices, scraping off the layer of plum sauce. The restaurant purports to serve the cuisines of the shattered continent, though perhaps less authentically than Kerttu is used to. "I don't think your family would agree, though I've made efforts."

"My family is your family too." Heilui rests her chin on her hand. "Some of them you'll never win over, it's just how they are. There have been feuds where siblings couldn't forgive each other on their deathbeds. Lan elders *are* hard to please, no doubt about that."

"Except you are harder still. You haven't . . . " A frown. "You haven't asked anything of me. Yet you must have bought me to fulfill a function, and I don't think it's to satisfy the fantasy of possessing a person whole and entire. You haven't done anything to exert your ownership."

"I like you just the way you are. Is that so hard to believe?" She glances at her shell, taking a sip of honeyed lime. Expecting to hear her interrogator's voice again. Even today she remains ignorant of the woman's name or rank. Black ops. Counter-terrorism. "Would you like to try the simulation in immersive mode, Kerttu? You need a headset and will have to plug into the server I've got at home. Not perfect, but perhaps . . . ?"

Kerttu's breath hitches, audibly, as though that idea has shocked her pulse to a halt. "I would love nothing more. You do me too much kindness."

"Not at all—we'll immerse together, yes? You can grade me on the simulation."

Several nights later, she starts awake to a hand over hers, long-fingered and tentative. Blearily she sits up to find Kerttu kneeling by her bed, a shadow dressed in gossamer lace. "Doctor." Kerttu's voice comes petal-soft. "Will you invite me in?"

Wide awake now, Heilui rubs at her eyes and stares at her wife, then at the bed on the other end of their shared room. "I think you misunderstand. I'm not—what's between us doesn't have to be a transaction, not like that."

Kerttu's hand withdraws. "I should earn my keep, my care. I have said before that it's no ordeal—unless I hold so little appeal?"

"It's not that." Heilui scoots inward, making room. "Come in. We can sleep together, in the most literal sense."

"Like sisters?" A trick of filtered moonlight makes it seem as though ice crystals have caught on Kerttu's eyelashes. A snow-woman of Jatbun myth, visiting in the night to drink her lover's spirit.

"Like wife and wife. Not all marriages need to be heat and desire. Or at least that's not what I want. If it's what you . . . you can find others for that. I wouldn't mind. But for me—"

"Oh." Exhaled surprise. "I see, I think."

Kerttu climbs in beside her, awkward, hesitating. A sigh loosens from her lips as she settles in against Heilui's warmth and her arm snakes over, one hand splayed on Heilui's stomach. "Is this all right, Doctor?" Asked as though she fears she might singe Heilui with that much contact, that much closeness.

She laces her fingers through Kerttu's. "It's lovely."

They spend the night like that, entwined. They spend the next likewise, and the next after, learning the rhythm of each other's breath, the curve of each other's spine and the width of each other's waist. A nascent dialect of touch, a first contact negotiated through comfort. A slow formation of matrimony like the founding of a country, while Heilui swallows back the secret code of guilt.

The first time they stand in front of the server together is a clear morning where icicles crackle on the window like chimes. The simulator box is built of blueshift alloy, radiant with cold, an artifact of the world's ruin and its eternal winter. With a command Heilui logs in and draws out two headsets. One she turns over to Kerttu, the other she slips around her own temple, a mesh with the texture of satin.

"Anything particular you'd like to see?" she asks.

"The city." Kerttu touches the headset's lattice. "The club."

Within the offspring of Heilui's thought, cities throng the shattered continent like firmaments lit up in their thousands. But she knows from watching her wife which one Kerttu means—the city of her birth, the capital of her native land.

The program pushes under their skin, flares across their senses, a susurration of colors and ice. Then they are side by side in the Tavastia, backstage. Darkened interior, hexagon walls dressed in facets and prism coins. Overhead, mannequins sway gently, many-jointed arachnid limbs painted in patterns of cracked granite.

Kerttu pushes at the mannequins, making them clack. At her height they are in easy reach; she strokes their bald heads and thumbs their ovoid eye sockets. "My mother always longed to sing here. I don't remember her face, her voice, even her name. At six she sold me to the syndicate. I fetched a good price—a mind such as I own doesn't come by every day—and I wonder if she ever got her wish, to perform on a Tavastia stage. The first ten years I was kept entirely in the citadel to be imprinted for loyalty. By the time I was allowed to leave, she was gone. Or didn't want to be found."

"I'm sorry," Heilui says before she can stop herself.

"No need, Doctor. My mother, she wasn't an educated or well-off woman. The syndicate gave me a life of ease and refinement, my intelligence nurtured and honed to its utter best. Had my mother raised me according to her means, today I'd be just another refugee in the camps, if I even survived." Kerttu clasps her hands behind her back—in the virtuality she wears not her grieving black but a peridot shirt and gray trousers, an overcoat in duochrome indigo. "There are no people here."

She follows her wife to the stage. It is full of unmanned instruments made from jagged blades and razorglass tendons. The floor is strobe-lit but empty of dancers; puppets sit by the side, prim and inanimate. "Anything I populate this world with would just be automatons—as complex a set of heuristics as I can buy, but they wouldn't emulate human behavior with any degree of verisimilitude. I've thought of modeling you, actually."

"I hope you'll agree that it is not hubris but fact that makes me point out I'm not exactly a population average. Not culturally, not in disposition, not in politics. Modeling those from the camps would likely yield better results."

"A population comprised entirely of averages would be terribly unrealistic, but I take your point."

Kerttu tugs at her sleeve as though to test whether the physics engine holds up to scrutiny. "I have a request to make of you, Doctor. You may believe me ungrateful—"

"Please," Heilui says. "I've no reason to think that."

"May I go into the city on my own? I wish to familiarize myself with its ligatures and arteries, to find my own path climbing its ribs and vertebrae all sharp with salt. I wish to know this island where I will spend the rest of my life as your wife."

Heilui's pulse picks up. "You hardly need my permission. Your shell should be loaded with guidance routines, but if you run into any trouble you only need to call me."

"You are far more generous a client than I could ever dream of." Kerttu makes again that ancient bow, as elegant as it is incongruous with her outfit. Heilui realizes with a start that no matter the correctness of her gesture, no matter her fluency in Gwongdungwa, Kerttu will never fit quite right.

On Kerttu's initial excursions, Heilui refrains from trailing her. Her wife comes home late each time; Heilui never asks questions and simply waits in bed, her arms bangled in moonlight. When Kerttu has bathed and changed she would come to card her fingers through Heilui's hair, root to tip, until they fall asleep.

It is on Kerttu's fifth outing that Heilui tracks her—a bite of conscience, a twist of shame. She monitors her wife's wanderings through markets that snake up pagodas, through secret streets behind amber pavilions, past the honeycombs of waterfront gardens where hybrid peacocks strut in sunset trails. Heilui tells herself Kerttu is monitored in any case, but she can't get rid of the certainty that she's committing a small betrayal.

When Heilui at last follows her wife in person, it is down the harbor where beaked ferries knife the waters to white ribbons. She sits on the mezzanine of a floating restaurant, watching the world through sea spray. Watching as Kerttu enters the planetarium in her black keipou. Soon a man in the same shade follows her. Tall like Kerttu and just as colorless, a creature of her race and nation, raised on snow nova-bright. Heilui studies him: he is gaunt to the point of starvation but well-dressed, hair a few shades darker than Kerttu's, a skull of cadaverous planes. In the Institute, no doubt his caretakers would have warmed his features with cosmetics to make him less startling to prospective clients.

The two do not leave together; the man lingers behind, his gaze intent on Kerttu as she exits. From this far Heilui cannot appraise his expression—those harsh angles make him, like Kerttu, difficult to read—but she thinks he seems painfully lost. As much as a dangerous terrorist can seem lost. She tries to imagine him as the shadow behind assassinations of heads of state, the shadow behind the sales of private armies and weaponry and untold destruction. But as with Kerttu, she can only see an ordinary man. Foreign, but merely mortal. He doesn't even sport the corpse-butterfly tattoo anywhere that she can glimpse.

A wanted man who surfaces, exposing himself, just to retrieve Heilui's wife.

The second time he comes for Kerttu, it is on a rooftop maze.

An art installment writ large, the maze is composed—syllabaric symphony—of elemental strands: wood and metal, fire and earth, and water to complete the quintet. Batik lions move against jade tortoises on a steam tapestry. Patchwork topiaries flourish on inked wires and luminous nesting dolls. Guidance materializes as a calligraphic girl, torso and limbs all made of brushstrokes, shedding proverbs and verses to give Heilui directions. She waits for the creature to begin whispering in a mild human contralto, but it remains only rote and routes. Overhead, starlings flit from candle-roof to platinum bough.

By the time Heilui reaches Kerttu, the girl is down to quartered ink and halved characters.

She takes cover behind a spread of bronze longma and marble rabbits. And there they are, a tableau like theater-dolls awaiting an audience: he a statue in black from neck to ankle, elongated limbs sheathed in crisp, expensive tailoring. Kerttu is seated on a bench of braided rime and gridded kites, her hair a pale corona. As if given life by Heilui's spectating gaze, Kerttu stirs to motion and turns away from him. On her lap she holds the kintsugi bowl. "Yes," she is saying, "I imagine the bowl holds enough genetic material with which to forge identity templates and authenticate my release from Institute trackers."

"Good." His voice is a scratch of stone chipping at wood. He runs a knuckle down his lapel, smoothing the impeccable fabric, a nervous tic. "That should suffice. I'll contact you again when I've made the necessary arrangements."

"No."

The man's hand slows then goes still, as of an automaton winding down. "Are you afraid, Kerttu? I've never known you for a coward."

She looks up, her gaze ensnaring his, the gravity of a pyre drawing in moths. Heilui has learned her wife's moods and in that moment she knows there's no hesitation. Kerttu's corneas seem like lamp-glass to a flame, small but absolute. "I've never been afraid. I'm just not leaving with you."

A gunshot like a soldier's final breath. An eruption of starlings, crying out.

The man falls, too fast for someone who should be bird-light, for a body that ought to float like gossamer or shredded ghosts. Where his blood touches Kerttu's clothes it does not show; where it lands on Kerttu's head it beads ruby-vivid against the snowdrift of her hair, the white slope of her brow.

Bursts of communication, armored men and women spilling from between the maze's strands: a rush of black, acid tides. They collect the man's body, quick and efficient, folding him into a casket. A puppet returning to its box.

Between all this, Kerttu's expression never changes, as though his death belongs to someone else.

A day later, Heilui receives a copy of her dossier. It has been wiped clean as if nothing has ever happened, as though she's never been made to sit shivering in a metal chair, to answer question after question. To single out faces for betrayal. The copy deletes itself after one read. She doesn't hear from her interrogator; she doesn't expect she ever will. A vulgar touch—several sums transferred into her account, absurdly large, acrimoniously transactional. She doesn't return them, knowing she can't afford the luxury of pride.

She finds her wife kneeling before the server, already plugged in. She follows.

The church is carved from solid rock, a copper-roofed globe drenched in bronze evening. The floor murmurs quartz canticles underfoot. Kerttu is enclosed in a pebble-rounded pew, a carpet of white furs and ice crystals mounded at her bare feet. "I was never religious," she says without turning, "but I liked Temppeliaukio. It is—was—a good hideout when I wanted to think. When I wanted peace, but usually it was too crowded. In a way, you've created the perfect version of my country for me."

"Kerttu—" Heilui draws a deep breath. "I'm sorry."

Her wife turns around. Rime cracks at her movement, sloughing off her shoulders in flecks and teardrops. "There's no need, Doctor. I always knew I was released from the Institute for a purpose and he was a priority target. Of all his surviving associates, I made the best bait. I'm only curious why you did it. Is it simply patriotism? Frightening as his reputation was, I don't think he would have resumed his work. He meant to lie low, disappear. Change his face again and become just an ordinary man."

"Five years ago occidental terrorists infiltrated my university and I got close to one of them, a woman I thought I could marry. She . . . made use of me to access our archives, I don't remember anymore what data she got. I was arrested as a potential accessory and though found innocent, it scarred my records. This—I was offered amnesty. My name cleared." Within the virtuality she is not subjected to involuntary reactions, the tyranny of cortisol and serotonin, but she's accustomed to configuring her avatar to reflect her real body as much as possible. Her throat is sore and thick. "Why didn't you? Go with him."

Kerttu folds her hands. Snow blooms, unmelting, on her knuckles like wedding rings. "Ultimately it is a question of whose property I am. What did he offer? A life on the run, dogged each step by terror. The past is past. There's no use resurrecting a hill of ashes. The dead do not come back. The arrow of time doesn't reverse."

Heilui purses her mouth, opens it. Exhales. "My contract with the Institute isn't permanent. There's been no further . . . instructions. After what's happened, you should have this choice. You can go back to the Institute and they'll find you another client."

"Is that what you want, Heilui?"

A painful-sweet wrench in her chest: like love, like cardiac arrest. It is strategically placed and cannot be inadvertent, but even so. "You've never called me by name before, like that, ever."

"The Institute appears to be done with me. I'm of no further use to them and therefore I'm now granted freedom, after a fashion, as long as they can track me and I'm tethered to a client." Kerttu looks, unblinking, at Heilui with her aquatic eyes. "A future can be had and a new life can be built. That is what you offer me and I'd like to take you up on it."

Logical. Transactional, as this has been from the beginning. And yet Heilui finds herself smiling. "No, you're right. And if you were gone, I'd miss you. I'll have to talk my family around, but my mothers at least I think I can convince."

"I will do my best to be the daughter-in-law they can tolerate. They will be my family, my mothers."

Heilui laughs, surprising herself, the sound of a scale tipping in her heart. "So they would. I never asked you properly before, did I, so—Kerttu, will you be my wife?"

Kerttu gathers Heilui in her arms and kisses her brow, soft and warm. "Yes. Let's try to make this work together."

At their feet, the frost of Kerttu's country thaws: a pool clear as the first water of spring, blue-green and sharp with salt.

Out in the world of mortal flesh and unbearable history, on the island surrounded by storm and sea, the occidental bride never dons black again.

Preserve Her Memory

BAO SHU, TRANSLATED BY KEN LIU

One o'clock in the morning. Heavy rain.

Ye Lin, her clothes drenched, stands at the edge of the roof of the three-hundred-story Future Tower. She shivers uncontrollably as the gale, whipping freezing rain, slices across her skin like an ice knife. From her perch more than a kilometer aboveground, she surveys the city that never sleeps, glittering and coruscating in the rain like a metaphor for her glamorous life.

They look up at me like a princess in the heavens. But do they understand how cold and alone I am?

In the metropolis below, a scintillating net woven from thousands of glowing streets, infused with lust, greed, and fame, ensnares thirty million men and women and binds her the tightest of them all. She once thought herself one of the lucky few who found a rare morsel of happiness, but she had not realized that the spider of fate had already closed off all avenues of escape behind her.

All right, it will all be over soon. I'll have eternal freedom and peace.

Ye Lin takes a deep breath and steps forward. There is nowhere to set her foot down except empty space.

And so she falls. Like a drop of rain, she plunges toward the gleaming city, toward the abyss of death.

Police Captain Jiang Yong, head of the investigations unit, took off his helmet and let out a long sigh. "You dragged me out of bed in the middle of the night for this? Who found her?"

"I did, Captain," said a young woman with long hair. Liu Ningning was a new addition to the investigations unit. By the looks of her swollen eyes, she had been crying. "The impact damaged the body to such an extent that we couldn't ID her, and DNA analysis was going to take some time. I decided to access her memories, and found out that . . . she's Ye Lin, the actress. I called in a report immediately."

"No wonder the bureau told me to handle it." Jiang Yong yawned. "She's a big star. I imagine those vulture reporters will be swarming here soon, and this is going to be all over the headlines in the morning . . . But the case doesn't look that complicated. The memory replay indicates that it was suicide. All you have to do is follow the procedures."

"But since the deceased is such a celebrity, there will be a lot of attention focused on us," said another detective. "The bureau didn't want anything to go wrong, and they specifically asked for you to review the investigation."

"I don't care if she's a celebrity or some average Jane Doe," Jiang Yong harrumphed. "I have no sympathy for suicides."

"No! This is murder, pure murder!" Liu Ningning cried out, her voice full of anguish.

Jiang Yong frowned. "Ningning, I know you're a fan of Ye Lin, but you can't allow your personal feelings to interfere with police work."

"But . . . but . . . " Ningning wiped at her eyes. "You'll understand if you replay more of her memories."

Intrigued, Jiang Yong put the helmet back on, and data flooded into his mind from the memory black box.

The memory black box was the product of advanced research in neuroscience, information technology, nanotechnology, and other fields. The recorder consisted of a biochip smaller than the head of a pin implanted into the hippocampus and nanosensors embedded throughout the body. Normally, the system lay dormant. But as soon as it detected severe deviations from the norm in various brain activity parameters—indicative of the stress caused by imminent death or great danger—the black box would automatically contact the police and record the short-term memory in the hippocampus via molecular scanning. In the event of death, about one to two minutes of memories preceding the cessation of brain activity could be decrypted from the black box. The device was invaluable for tasks such as criminal investigation, accident inquiry, insurance adjustment, and so on.

Although the chip was expensive, it didn't require a craniotomy to install; instead, molecule-sized nanomachines were injected into the bloodstream, and they assembled themselves into the recorder and sensors in the requisite areas of the body without causing any discomfort. Many celebrities and the wealthy installed memory black boxes not only for the benefits in the event of death, but also to deter criminals who would wish them harm. Since the invention of the memory black box, the murder rate had plunged, accompanied by a corresponding rise in the percentage of solved murders.

The induction helmet used to replay the memories had originated in virtual reality gaming. Not only could the helmet replicate the recorded visual data and other sensory information with high fidelity, but it could also induce in the wearer the memories and emotions experienced by the deceased through artificial bioelectric fields localized to specific regions of the brain. Someone wearing the helmet would feel as though they were taking the place of the deceased, gazing through her eyes, hearing through her ears, experiencing everything she felt.

. . . As Ye Lin fell, she seemed to turn into a raindrop, one falling faster than the other raindrops. The blasting wind whipped the rain against her face as the windows of the skyscraper—some lit, some dark—flashed by her, the unconnected scenes seen through them like a string of memory fragments.

From the depths of his soul, Jiang Yong experienced terror, despair, and a profound, unrelenting hatred.

Many on the verge of death experienced a final flash of lucidity during which innumerable memories surfaced from the unconscious in a final farewell performance. Ye Lin was one of them. As she fell, millions of memory fragments danced and flickered like the ever-changing, chaotic patterns found in a kaleidoscope. The most fascinating type of experience recorded by the memory black box was this pre-death recollection. Someone replaying it through the induction helmet would even experience time as passing more slowly. Although the recollected scenes were hazy and fragmentary, when enhanced with the emotions felt by the deceased, they effectively conveyed the hidden depths and meanings behind each memory, allowing the helmet-wearer to empathize intensely with the deceased. Thus, decrypted pre-death recollections, when sold through legal channels, made a mesmerizing, fantastic entertainment product.

Jiang Yong saw the funeral of Ye Lin's mother when she was a little girl; saw how she had lived in poverty with her alcoholic father, and vowed before a mirror, with tears staining her face, to change her fate with the one gift life gave her—her extraordinary beauty; and then, as she was stopped in the street by a talent scout, Jiang Yong experienced Ye Lin's ecstatic heartbeats.

Once she entered the movie business, the talented Ye Lin threw herself wholeheartedly into her performances. One moment she was in period dress as she fought against the other empresses and consorts in palace intrigue; the next she was a graceful woman in a modern metropolis; and in another moment she was an adventurer in the jungle of an alien planet . . . She achieved success, accepted award after award, and became a star known in every household. She left poverty behind as she jetted around the world, hobnobbing with other international celebrities, laughing and chatting at parties . . .

And then that man appeared. At first, he was only a lowly cameraman in one of her movies who timidly manufactured excuses to be closer to her. One day, he finally found the courage to hand her a letter, which she promptly tossed into the trashcan without even unsealing. But the man didn't give up. He stayed by her side as he advanced in his career, taking care of her and watching out for her in numerous ways, big and small. Gradually, she began to notice him, and finally, one night, after they were both drunk, the flame of romance sprung into life . . .

Jiang Yong was familiar with the basic biographical details of Ye Lin's life, and he knew that the man in her memories was Xue Kai, a famous director and Ye Lin's ex-husband. The memories weren't too different from what she had revealed in her interviews and biographies, but the specific, vivid details he experienced had been absent from mere text. There was no question that if the contents of this black box were brought to market, they would become an instant best-seller.

Ye Lin was still falling. For a body to traverse the full distance between the roof of a thousand-meter-plus skyscraper and the ground, impeded by air resistance and the strong wind, would take tens of seconds, plenty of time for those important memories to play through. The sweet memories winked out of existence in a flash, and all that remained were acute pain and deep hatred.

Jiang Yong saw Ye Lin ignore the objections of the studios and retire from her acting career. She put on the white wedding gown and stood by Xue Kai in the cathedral. By now, Xue Kai was gaining some renown as a director. Soon after, Ye Lin became a joyful, expectant mother. But then a string of misfortunes arrived: she found intimate photographs of Xue Kai with other women on the computer . . . Fights between the couple flashed before Jiang Yong's eyes; her shock, rage, and despair roiled his heart; and then Xue Kai walked into their home holding the hand of another woman, arrogantly showing her that he didn't care—and after shoving and pushing and screaming, she rolled down the stairs, blood flowing from between her legs in a torrent. The terrified Xue Kai ran away . . .

What a shithead, Jiang Yong said to himself.

After the miscarriage, a frightened Xue Kai swore that he would break off all contact with his mistress. At the hospital, he cared for her day and night without complaint. Finally, Ye Lin forgave him. But half a year later, cruel truth revealed itself: Xue Kai abruptly disappeared. After a few days, rumors said that he had been seen with his mistress in another city, and when Ye Lin went to the bank to check her account, she found that more than thirty million yuan in savings—the couple's joint property—had vanished. She fainted.

Courts and lawyers were useless, and even after the divorce was finalized, she couldn't get a single yuan back. After her loss was reported in the tabloids, Xue Kai attacked her by claiming that she had defamed him. Nude pictures of her surfaced on the web from anonymous posters, and rumors spread that she was actually the mistress of some important party official or the sexual plaything of a wealthy businessman. The tabloids printed damaging "news" about her without cease, and she was dogged by threats and hurled abuses. Even contracts she had reached agreement on were rescinded. Though she knew that Xue Kai was the one making trouble for her, she had no recourse. Xue Kai had seized the public narrative. She felt she was being driven insane . . .

The concrete ground loomed before her eyes. After a momentary flash of utter despair and horror came the eternal darkness. No more memories.

Jiang Yong took off the induction helmet and exhaled deeply. Though he was used to the multitude of tragedies humans put one another through, it was hard not to be moved after experiencing such memories. The heartbreaking scenes seemed to linger before his eyes. He understood how Ningning felt—rage burned in his chest, too.

"I couldn't believe her life was like that." Jiang Yong heaved a heavy sigh. "When I used to read the gossip about her, I just thought she was one of those celebrities with an immoral, extravagant lifestyle. I had no idea there were such painful secrets behind the scenes."

"It was all because of that asshole Xue Kai!" Ningning exclaimed. "He killed Ye Lin. Why can't that son of a bitch die?!"

"He didn't commit any crimes," said Jiang Yong. "The law can't punish him for what he did."

"There is a cosmic balance at work though," said Ningning. "Karma will catch up to him."

Ye Lin's death shocked the nation—no, the world. Her memory black box, of course, became the focus of media attention. As both of her parents had died, and she had no children, her legal heir, an aunt, soon declared that she would place Ye Lin's memories on auction. Many memory entertainment companies swarmed to bid, and in the end, the black box was sold for fifteen million yuan to a megacorp, which promptly brought the memories to market. Anyone could pay the requisite fee and then experience the memories of Ye Lin on the verge of death.

And in this manner, the truth of Ye Lin's life, which had been buried under a flood of ugly rumors while she had been alive, surfaced. Xue Kai's despicable acts became public knowledge, and no matter what he said to defend himself, the power of those vivid memories triumphed over his rhetoric. Soon, he was buried by the tide of public opinion, and became the favorite target of the shaming mob. Many companies pulled out of contracts with him and his girlfriend; his friends stayed away; fans knocked on his door to give him a piece of their minds; and some even sent him death threats. He dared not show his face in public—one time, he was recognized in the street, and a mob harassed him and attacked him until he was afraid for his life.

This lasted half a year.

And then, Xue Kai, now at the nadir of his career, braced himself and emerged from seclusion to attend a televised gala. The other guests all kept their distances, and even the host made him the butt of several jokes. Fortunately, a fifteen-year-old girl in the audience claimed to be his die-hard fan and asked for his autograph, allowing him to save a bit of face. But as Xue Kai grinned and signed his name, the young woman pulled out a dagger and stabbed it into his belly. Then, as the shocked host and guests watched, she proceeded to stab him again and again on live TV . . .

Xue Kai died as millions watched. Afterward, the young woman received a sentence of sixteen years. However, public opinion stayed on her side, and many even opined that she should be deemed innocent for eliminating a waste of human flesh.

A few more months passed, and it was the anniversary of Ye Lin's death. Liu Ningning, being a loyal fan, visited Ye Lin's grave during the day and then returned to the site of Ye Lin's suicide at night.

At one in the morning, Ningning opened the door to the rooftop platform of the Future Tower. A blast of wind greeted her, making her shiver. Imagining how Ye Lin felt on that day a year ago, Ningning stepped toward the edge where she had jumped. There was no rain on this night, and a crescent moon hung in the sky, the motley neon radiance of the metropolis spread out under its glow.

Suddenly, Ningning noticed a hazy figure standing at the edge of the roof. Startled, she almost screamed. But as she looked closer, the figure was Jiang Yong.

"Captain, what are you doing here?" she asked. "Don't tell me you're thinking of . . . ending . . . "

"Nothing like that." Jiang Yong's voice was placid. "I saw you post on NanoShare that you were thinking about coming here. I figured I'd join you."

"Right. Hard to believe it's been a year already. I guess Xue Kai got what he deserved. I hope Ye Lin can rest in peace."

"I've replayed hundreds of pre-death memory records, but hers affected me the most. Even now, as soon as I close my eyes, I seem to be falling through the air again." Jiang Yong gazed at the horizon and sighed.

"Your face is always so serious," said Ningning. "I had no idea that you were . . . so sensitive."

"Why? Do you think I'm an emotionless, case-solving robot?" Jiang Yong chuckled without mirth. "No, crime investigation requires understanding the passions that move people. Otherwise, it's impossible to see through some cases, like this one."

"What do you mean?"

"Ningning, do you remember how you insisted that this was a murder a year ago? You were right."

"Of course! Even though Ye Lin jumped from here, Xue Kai was the one who made her do it."

"No. The truth is just the opposite. This was a meticulously planned murder, but Xue Kai was the victim," Jiang Yong said.

"What . . . what are you talking about?" Ningning's eyes widened in shock.

"Ye Lin used her own death to seek revenge against Xue Kai. Everything was planned."

"How?"

Jiang Yong smiled. "Ye Lin knew that the contents of her memory black box would be disseminated widely after her death. She thus consciously designed and arranged her recollections. Indeed, even jumping from the Future Tower was part of her plan. This is the highest building in the city, and the long fall gave her the time to marshal her memories for maximum emotional impact. As she fell, she deliberately recalled the events of her life related to Xue Kai and invoked her intense hatred and rage. As millions replayed her memories, they weren't just a passive audience watching a movie; instead, they experienced the same powerful emotions she did. In a sense, Ye Lin infected everyone with the fervor of her feelings. The girl who killed Xue Kai on impulse was one of the infected."

"Are you calling her memories untrue?"

"Of course they were real, but they weren't the entire truth." Jiang Yong said. "After Xue Kai's death, I replayed his memories as well. Many of his recollections conflicted with Ye Lin's, and that was when I became suspicious. I gathered numerous other documents and evidence, and after comparing and contrasting, I discovered that Ye Lin was not entirely innocent of fault. For example, she didn't become a star merely because a talent scout found her. In fact, she had gotten her break by trading sexual favors with producers and casting directors, and maintained a quid-pro-quo relationship with many of them long after. She also undermined competitors in the business in unethical ways, and arranged sexual liaisons for powerful executives—"

"But she never did anything to hurt Xue Kai. She loved him!" Ningning interrupted.

"True. She really did love Xue Kai. But people are complicated. She also kept many secrets from Xue Kai, who, after finding out about some of them, became angry with her. Ye Lin was also jealous and overbearing, and she insisted on monopolizing all decisions regarding the couple's finances, which damaged the bond between them . . . There's no doubt Xue Kai's behavior was wrong, but he didn't deserve to die."

"So you're saying . . . " Ningning's tone was thoughtful. "Ye Lin sought vengeance, and she used her own death to drag Xue Kai into the abyss? She was responsible for Xue Kai's death?"

"No, the real killer of Xue Kai was someone else."

"Who? You mean the young woman who stabbed him?"

"Ningning," Jiang Yong said as he turned toward her and locked gazes. "The one who really sent Xue Kai down that road from which he would not return was you."

"What kind of sick joke is this?" Blood drained from Ningning's face.

"Contempt and resentment for Xue Kai blinded me at first as well. But once I began to suspect Ye Lin's memories didn't tell the whole story, I replayed her record several more times. I noticed that the record had been edited, and the final section, the few seconds right before she struck the ground, had been deleted. Whoever performed the edits was very skilled, but still, traces of tempering were left behind. Do you know what the deleted memories were?"

Ningning bit her bottom lip, refusing to answer.

"Recollections that troubled Ye Lin's conscience, additional private details from her life with Xue Kai, happy scenes from her life, memories of her childhood, and a moment infused with deep regret right before her death. Ye Lin made a mistake. She thought she hated Xue Kai enough to desire revenge against him through her death. But she was wrong: death made everything meaningless, including vengeance itself. Her resolve, held together with great effort, collapsed at the end. In that moment before death, she no longer hated Xue Kai . . .

"And if the public had experienced the entirety of her memory record, they would have been able to view this matter with more sense.

"But the first person to decrypt and retrieve her memory was you, the loyal fan. Because of your sorrow at her death, and to protect her image, you censored those parts of her memory that were unfavorable to her. You shouldn't have done it."

"I . . . " Ningning's lips trembled as though she wanted to argue, but in the end, she gave up. "Yes, I did it! I don't care what wrongs Ye Lin might have done, all I know is that a scumbag like Xue Kai deserved to die. I wanted to make sure the truth was more clearly presented."

Jiang Yong shook his head. "You were wrong. A partial truth is the same as a lie. Everyone's memories and feelings are subjective, and we're each trapped in our own perspectives. But the differences between perspectives, collectively, create objectivity. You had no right to impose your views on others. Perhaps you have no legal responsibility for Xue Kai's death, but as an officer of the law, tampering with the evidence subjects you to criminal prosecution. Let's go."

Ningning said nothing the whole time Jiang Yong drove her to the police station. But just as she was about to be brought into the detention cell, she turned around and asked, "Captain, may I ask you one more question? I can't figure out how you managed to recover the data I deleted. I was sure I had erased it completely, and I know I didn't make any technical mistakes."

"I didn't recover the data," said Jiang Yong. "All I had were traces that deletion had occurred. You're the only one who knows what the deleted memories were."

"Then how were you able to tell me the contents?"

"I just guessed." Jiang Yong sighed again. "No one can hold onto hatred in the moment before death. They always remember the earliest memories of childhood: the kind faces of loving parents, the flashes of joy and happiness—love for the beautiful parts of life always triumphs over hatred, and that is the essence of life. Ye Lin finally figured it out the moment before she died. It was too late for her, but it was better than not knowing that truth."

Originally published in Chinese in *Super Nice Magazine,* July 1, 2012.

The Garden Beyond Her Infinite Skies
MATTHEW KRESSEL

Aya floated over endless effervescing worlds, seeking anomalies. There were a hundred thousand Farmers of the Branch, but Aya was of the best of them all. Her fields were the healthiest, her realms the most pure. Even the Supervisors said she had an uncanny ability to spot the malignant, when others saw but purity. How she longed to find those sickly realms sprouting in her fields, where the oddest things arose, things not found anywhere else on the Branch. Finding one was enough to make her long workdays worthwhile.

She flew low over her fields. Beneath her, a trillion realms sprouted from the ground, spheres budding spheres. Like fattened wheat, the realms leaned tall in the graviton breeze, their thick fingers grasping for the Expanse, while beneath their knuckled bases, tilled to perfection, lay fertile ground. Alone, Aya expressed herself naturally: a ball of prickling white energy, she scintillated. She searched all day, but did not find one anomaly among countless identical realms.

Perhaps, she thought, *I have destroyed them all.*

Repentance Day was nine days away, when all the Farmer Folk would gather to play games of history. Who could remember all the First Ones? Who could reap the neatest row? They'd join to sing the ancient songs, to shout the chorus to the Tall Ones. "Oh, the endless rows! Oh, such majestic beauty!" And Aya played the games and sang the histories, but only because to refuse meant being shamed by those whom she loved.

If only, she thought, *I could write my own lyrics, what stories I would tell them.*

She sighed a cloud of tau neutrinos and watched them tumble into the Expanse. Pulled by the graviton wind, they were lost in the blue haze. What would it be like, she wondered, to float off with the particles, to visit those strange, far off places? But her courage fled with them, as it always did. She couldn't survive in the Expanse, where the winds blew fierce and terrible. She belonged here, on the branchlet. And she would die here. And that made her saddest of all.

She floated above the realm tips, where the ground appeared flat as she hugged it close. But when she soared high, the branchlet's curve became visible. Far upstalk, the horizon bent into itself and formed a tube. And this tube kinked and split into more tubes farther upstalk. And these split even farther up, until the myriad branchlets vanished in the Expanse's blue haze.

And downstalk, her branchlet joined a greater, which joined one greater, which joined one yet greater, and so on, until endless fathoms below all branchlets merged with the Prime Stalk of Thept, blessed be her endless reaching.

Aya flew as high as she dared in the graviton winds, wishing she could see Thept in her gargantuan glory, but the haze obscured all but the nearest branchlet.

Then she dove between rows of baby realms, where myriad spheres still glowed from their inflationary epochs. Their pastel globes lit the way for her spiraling journey upstalk.

The Eighty Eight Lights had just begun their climb up the Prime Stalk, swathing ghostly green swatches across the sky, so that when Aya reached fields of more ancient realms, the landscape plunged into twilight. But even among these brooding shadows, spudded realms winked spectral diamonds from the countless galaxies whirling within them all.

Tiny treasures, she thought, *are hidden inside all things.*

Treasures like Old Gia, who lived in a deep hollow that had been carved into the branchlet. Gia was once a Farmer like Aya, but after long eons, she had grown tired. And as a reward for her service, the Supervisors had given her this home. Old Gia liked to watch the shadows unfold across the Expanse as the Eighty Eight Lights made their daily climb. She hated to be disturbed.

Aya shrunk herself into a respectful torus, taming her wildest energies, as she entered Gia's hollow.

"Go away!" Gia shouted. A colorful and reactive mess of anti-quarks pooled on the ground before her. "I said, go away!" Fits of radiation spluttered from Gia's body, a pallid and diffuse ball of energy.

"But it's me!" Weak blue light from the opening crawled and died a short way in, so that the rear of the hollow was as black as a dead realm.

"Aya? So it is. I don't sense well anymore, child."

"No, you don't. I'm no longer a child."

"When you reach my age, Aya, everyone becomes a child." She spat out a thin spray of down quarks that drifted to the floor, sparking as they joined the viscous pool. "What brings you here?"

"I was hoping you'd tell me another story of the First Ones."

"Ah, the young farmer grows lonely again."

"I'm not lonely," Aya said. But she wasn't sure if that was true. Out the opening, bleak shadows reached across the Expanse, vaguely menacing. The silence seemed to choke the space, but she couldn't think of anything meaningful to say that had not already been said, as if she was searching for a language she didn't yet speak.

Gia grumbled and retreated into her hollow, revealing a faintly glowing structure that had been hidden behind her. Packed tightly together in a polyhedral pattern was a collection of lights, each a dim pink sphere, like a cold baby realm. Each held a memory. "Your journal has grown," Aya said.

"My memories," Gia said, "have become like a sky full of dying suns, slowly winking out. This is my bulwark against annihilation."

"May I view one?"

"Never. They are too personal. But I'll describe one to you."

Aya shivered off a muon cloud of excitement as Gia plucked a sphere from her journal and absorbed it into her energy-body. The sphere flickered inside her. "I was so young then, barely weaned off ultraviolet milk! I'd forgotten this day. How could I forget? Mama was so colorful, so free."

"Describe her!" Aya said, unraveling her wildest energies.

"She was very different from today's Rearing Mothers. You'd think her energy-body was untamed, her spectra feral. But that's how we expressed ourselves then, expansive, radiant, wild. Mama took my sisters and me upstalk, all the way to a tip."

"Tell me what it was like!"

Gia paused, shivering as if reliving the memory. "Such a sight! I was terrified, but the tendrils mesmerized me. I was surprised because the tendrils didn't bravely reach for the Expanse as I had thought, but cowered from it, as if the Expanse was...cold."

"Cold?"

"These baby tendrils were cowards, Aya."

Perhaps Old Gia was misremembering. The tendrils held the vanguard against the blue Abyss. Or so the songs went.

Gia continued, "Their fear was unhealthy. Mama told us the branchlet had to be excised before its disease spread. We had come to sever her from Thept. Mama showed us how to focus our energy-bodies into Z-beams. And we helped her to . . . " Gia paused, and shivered. "We cut the diseased branchlet free."

Unexpectedly, she vomited the sphere out. It plopped to the floor in a pool of wild particles.

"Gia? Are you all right?"

Gia dimmed. "I've had enough for today, Aya."

"But what did the tendrils look like? How many were there? What did the—"

The X-rays smacked Aya hard. It was just a flash, all Old Gia could muster, but the blow hurt regardless.

"Sentimental child!" Gia snarled. "Why are you here, dreaming when you should be out farming? Get back to work, you wretched tangle of radiation! Get out!" Gia retreated into her hollow, small and dim, barely recognizable as a living creature among the sea of particle noise.

Aya's body stung where Gia had struck her, but she took the blow without reaction, as all good Farmers were taught to do. The pink sphere lay beneath her, an ancient world that might never be seen again, if Gia had her way. Such a shame to let it wink out like a dying star.

Gia was already dozing, spluttering fitful rays, when Aya snatched the globe and darted out the opening. She sped across her fields and flew until she was sure she wasn't followed. Then she set down between a parade of realms that leaned heavily into the Expanse. Shadows tumbled over the ground as she absorbed Gia's memory sphere into her body.

She felt Gia. She *became* Gia.

Her energy-body danced with excitement at being so far from home. And what love for Mama who sprayed off vivid nebulae as she spun up the branch! Its circumference was so thin that she and her sisters could loop around the branchlet in an instant. The ground sparkled a brilliant blue with the glittering particle dew that dusted the surface. No realms had yet formed here. The branchlet was only just born itself.

Gia dared not take her gaze from the ground, because the hideous blue Expanse surrounded her. She wanted to hide inside Mama's energy-body. All the children did. They begged Mama to return home. But Mama called them cowards and smacked them with harsh rays.

"Look!" Mama said. "Look how the tendrils cower from the Expanse, just as you cower now. Your fear is weakness! You must cut it from yourself!" The children whimpered, and she beat them again until they fell silent.

I'm a coward, Gia thought. *I cannot look!*

Mama showed them how to form beams of Z-particles with their energy-bodies, then started the cut. She ordered the children to join her. It took effort, enormous concentration, but soon a furious beam erupted from Gia. All her bottled up rage and terror and sadness leaped out from her. She and the children cut, and the Expanse flickered with the reflected light.

The beams screeched and wailed. But Gia realized the screams came from the branchlet itself. The tendrils cried as the Z-beams moved through them. The sound sickened her, but she didn't stop until the children had severed it through.

Loose from its mother, the baby branch tumbled into the Expanse, tugged by the graviton breeze. It gave such a wail, and giant Thept quivered beneath her as the tendrils reached back for their mother. But it was too late. The branchlet disappeared into the haze of the endless blue sky.

The memory ended. Sickened by the memory, Aya spat out the pink sphere. In a torrent of particles she tossed it far into the Expanse, wishing the feelings would vanish with it.

For a long time she remained in the field. That horrid screeching . . . Those desperate tendrils, reaching for their mother . . .

If only she'd never experienced Gia's memory. If only she could take it back and forget. But she knew she never would.

Thept, bless her endless reaching, had millions of sisters across the Expanse. The Tall Ones grew out beyond the blue horizon, and countless baby realms were born from their myriad branchlets. And far below, their massive root systems plunged into the great ovum called Yi. Just as the realms arose from Thept's body, so the Tall Ones grew from Yi.

Yi herself was one of sixty four ova gestating inside Delicate Womb, the reproductive organ of Mother Lily, who gloriously blossomed inside the 501-dimensional field, Sky of Skies, who accelerated madly inside the meditating Z-space, Incomprehensible Mind, who lived inside another being who had a billion names and even more descriptions, none of which sufficed to circumscribe it. Always, the smaller grew in the larger, on and on eternally, blessed be the All.

The All was eternally full of noise.

Messages trickled down from above like the particle rains. Most were gibberish to the Farmer Folk. But once in a long while, a message became clear. Some ineffable being had told Incomprehensible Mind, who had told Sky of Skies, who had told Mother Lily, who had told Delicate Womb, who had told Yi, who had told Thept, who had told the Supervisors, who had told the Farmers, to farm and tend the branchlets where countless realms bubbled up from the surface, to keep them free of disease and entanglement so that Thept's growth might continue forever. That message came eight trillion Great Cycles ago, a great long time, even here.

And so the First Ones had razed and tilled Thept's branches, and through generations they'd uprooted corruption, eradicated disease. They had forced the knotted realms into endless neat rows. It had taken eons and countless prunings, but they'd tamed Thept's wildest tendencies. Now, all was arrayed harmony.

But Aya found no beauty in the monotony. In her youth, Rearing Mother had taken her and her sisters to the Tangle, a knot of branchlets downstalk. The First Ones had left it in place to show what would happen if branchlets were left wild.

Iridescent worms wriggled between massively overbudded realms. Spiky balls of baryonic matter clung to the realm tips, popping to release flashing rainbows of particle spores. Anti-matter spiders of a thousand legs pricked realms with their sharp proboscii and grew fat with sucking. The realms formed hoary palaces, gnarled labyrinths and raveled jungles so thick that even airy neutrinos could only travel but a short way in before hitting something dense and impenetrable. And over all this rolled furious particle storms, bathing the fangled corners with strange, brooding energies.

The Tangle was meant to evoke disgust. It was bizarre, Aya thought, but far from disgusting. For ages she longed to enter those twisted realms and dance its grotesque curves, to explore its vulgar corners and play with those exultant infestations of life. Instead, she was taught to revile it.

She had never told Rearing Mother her true feelings. To express them was to invite a beating, or a furlough inside a dead realm, a place frightfully silent, dark, and cold. And she had never told her sisters either, because they betrayed her to gain Rearing Mother's favor. Instead she found it safer to keep silent. And over time that silence had built up pressure, like a realm ready to burst into existence. It was her greatest fear that she could not contain it once it was born.

But Gia's memory gave energy to that silence, threatening to give it form. Aya dreamed often of that severed branch. While flying over her fields she thought she heard echoes of its ancient screams coming from out in the deep.

She was floating low over her twilit, ancient realms one morning when she found an anomaly. She gasped a bubble of charmed quarks. Here, growing among dark arrays, a dim realm curved back on itself, a hooked finger cowering from the Expanse. Or perhaps it turned inward to consider its own curious arising. But this was anathema. To grow inward, a sin. This disease had to be obliterated. A tight beam of Z-particles would do it, would reduce this gloriously wrong realm to a scintillating snow of ash, fertilizer for unborn worlds.

Instead, she peered inside.

Hundreds of billions of galaxies aligned themselves in fine, shining filaments like hoar frost across the hooked realm of 10-space. A tenuous galactic cluster huddled on a filament edge. And inside this cluster, a galaxy furiously twirled.

And in this galaxy, a giant red sun hurtled through the dark. And around this sun raced a green planet. And on this planet a purple and white quadruped leaped through a dense forest.

More softly than a falling leaf, the animal tiptoed down to a narrow stream. Its head was long and sleek, its gray horns branching like a miniscule Thept. A breeze trickled through the trees as the quadruped sipped its fill, then gazed up at the orange sky to wonder at the coming dawn.

But this wonder died before long. The creature was not quite self-aware. Full consciousness might take eons, if it ever happened at all. Even among the infinite realms, sentience was a fickle thing. How rare that the quadruped even wondered at all. Given enough time, she thought, what might this species become? If she let it be, she might live long enough to find out.

"A farmer's job is never done."

The voice startled her, and she turned to see the Supervisor expressing himself brightly beside her. She collapsed her energies into a shivering torus of high-energy leptons out of respect. "Supervisor," she said, "I didn't know—"

"A trillion realms bubble into the Expanse by their own chaotic wills." He spoke as if addressing an audience. "Without farmers, realms grow weedy and knotted. Disease spreads. Then we must raze and destroy to continue our long mission. Thept, bless her endless reaching, despises nothing more than a pruning. Tell me, Aya, what is it about this sickly realm that captures your attention?"

The Supervisor's name was Bu, but he made Aya always use his title. He peered deep into the hooked realm, far deeper than she ever could, as she shivered off a hadron cloud. What he saw, she couldn't say, but she knew it wasn't beauty.

"Well?" he said.

"I marvel at the manifold arising animals, Supervisor. They exult in the physical." And because she couldn't stop herself, she added, "I love how this quadruped moves so quietly through the woods." It was a foolish thing to say, she knew, but there was no one else here to listen.

"Aya," he said, "you've always been an excellent Farmer. So I've tolerated your eccentricities. But what is another quadruped?" He sloughed off a sheath of indifferent neutrons. "I've seen quadrupeds arise on this branchlet nine quintillion times. This realm is crooked, inward-looking. A grotesquery. It must be destroyed."

"Do they suffer," she said, "when we destroy them?"

"The disease must be removed before it spreads."

The graviton wind was unusually calm, and she thought she heard a scream out in the Expanse. "But do they suffer?"

The Supervisor's energy body roiled, sparking with angry bursts of anti-matter. "All this time and still a damned child," he spat as he raised up a storm of gamma rays, pelting her energy-body. She withered in pain. But she took the blows as Rearing Mother had taught her, and her mother before that, going all the way back to the First Ones. One's worst tendencies had to be beaten out, she knew.

He let up his blows an instant before she would have diffused into random sparks of radiation.

"I love you," he said, his energies still fierce. "That's why this hurts me more than it hurts you. But this is for your own good. We must excise your worst habits, so that what remains is pure. I know you understand."

She muttered, "Yes, Supervisor."

Soon he was caressing her with a gentle stream of infrared photons. She let him soothe her pain, because she needed the relief, though she hated herself for it. "Now," he said, "finish your work, so I may finish mine."

Aya collected her energies and crept toward the realm. A tight beam of Z-particles was all it took. It leaped from her, melting the realm like a comet in a supernova. Matter decayed by the yotta-particle, flashing brightly before fading. And just like that, the realm was gone.

Bits of scintillating energy snowed to the ground. It would take eons for all the sparks to reach the surface. Which one, she wondered, had been the quadruped? Would that spark ever rise to wonder again?

"It's amazing," the Supervisor said, "how precise you are. A skill like yours comes once in a generation. Why is it so hard for you to use your gift?" He puffed himself into a hundred billion 50-spaces, so that he expanded enormously above her. "Now be a good Farmer, Aya," he said, then corkscrewed up the branchlet, past a trillion realms, off to mind other Farmers in other fields until he vanished in the haze.

The sparks from the snuffed world fell. Where the first sparks touched the ground, new realms were born. They flashed, inflated, and slowed, their quark-gluon plasma too hot for solid matter. It would take an eon before galaxies formed. Two or three more before animal life arose. The Farmer folk sang ballads about the sparks of dead realms. The dust, forever alive, the lyrics went. Death, an illusion, just forms changing.

But that quadruped, that particular arrangement of mind and will, would never know wonder again. If that wasn't death, what was?

The Eighty Eight Lights were ascending quickly. She had to get back to work, but there was someone she needed to see.

Aya flew downstalk, over row after row of middle-aged realms that leaned steeply into the graviton breeze, each realm the same as the next.

"Aya!" Ri called. Her sister farmed the fields downstalk, singing an ancient song. "It's been ages!" Ri said, brightly expressing herself as a tiny white ball.

Aya allowed herself to expand into a large sphere, not as wild as she preferred, so her sister would not get offended.

"What brings you downstalk, Aya? Have you a problem?"

"I wanted to ask you about something."

"Uh-oh," said Ri, chuckling a blue-green shower of leptons that spiraled off into the Expanse. "Your curiosity always gets you into trouble."

"I went to see Old Gia recently."

"I don't understand why you visit that old bag of particles."

"I saw one of her of her memories, Ri."

Ri flickered for a moment. "What do you mean, *saw*?"

Aya told Ri about Gia's journal, and the memory of the severed branch.

"That's disturbing, Aya."

"I know," Aya said. "Now I hear screams coming from the Expanse, and I haven't been sleeping."

"No," Ri said. "It's disturbing that you stole. Rearing Mother would give you quite a beating if she hears of this."

"One beating from Supervisor Bu is enough for today."

"He disciplined you, *again*? I thought you were his favorite." Ri dimmed an order of magnitude. "What's gotten into you?"

"Do you ever look into realms, before you destroy them?"

"Sometimes."

"And what do you see?"

"Disease, mostly."

"Never beauty?"

Ri paused. "There's never beauty in sickness."

"But what if a sick realm held something, however miniscule, worth saving? Would you spare it?"

Ri floated higher. "I see what's happened here. Gia's memory has poisoned you. That baby branchlet cried when they cut it free, yes, but didn't we cry when Rearing Mother beat us? It hurt then, but look at what Farmers we've become! Those beatings were for our own good, rooting out our worst habits. In the same way, eradicating disease is healthy for Thept. Pain is necessary for growth. If I'm ever chosen to be a Rearing Mother, I'll root out the unruliness from my children the same way. And it will hurt me more than it will hurt them. Don't you see? It's all for the collective good."

"I suppose," Aya said, feeling sick.

"Sister, you look exhausted. Your energies are wild. Why don't you go and take a nap over there? I'll watch for the Supervisor and wake you if he comes. I'll even tell him how I saw you eradicate a young cancer."

Never mind that there would be no cinders to mark the grave, Aya *was* exhausted. "Thank you, Ri. You're a good sister."

"And you a troublesome one! But I love you, Aya. Now sleep, so you may forget this foolishness."

Aya floated back to her fields and nuzzled between a dozen middle-aged realms. They caressed her sides as she drifted off to sleep. In her dreams a million blue tendrils squeezed her until she exploded in a flash that didn't wink out, but slowly faded, like a cinder. When she awoke, the Eighty Eight Lights had already passed Half Stalk.

Ri was nowhere to be found.

Repentance Day came and went, and Aya sang the songs and played the games, but her heart was not in it. The Eighty Eight Lights climbed the Prime Stalk of Thept two thousand times. Most days she lay in her fields and dreamed of the Tangle. But sometimes she exposed herself to the harsh particle rains when she should have waited them out in a safe hollow.

She was drifting low over her fields, and the Eighty Eight Lights had just begun their morning climb when she saw it. It grew from the side of a tall, ancient realm. An irregular carbuncle not one-hundredth the size of the parent it clung to, a cancer that needed to be excised.

The cancer had given birth to billions of galaxies. They spread across its 10-space like the vanes of a feather. In one spiral galaxy, a yellow sun drifted near the galactic edge. Orbiting this sun was a blue-white world. And on this world a copper-skinned biped sat on the ground and drew a figure in the dirt with a stick: a quadruped, with branching horns.

The biped examined her drawing. It wasn't alive, she knew, but an echo. Yet as she stared at the figure, she saw the blood on Father's face and felt the men's hard, beastly gazes. She smelled the hot animal flesh as Mother and the other women opened the animal with their bone knives. Even the twirling smoke stung her eyes as it rose from the flames to appease Sky God and her Thousand Bright Children. Her heart thrummed and her stomach grumbled, as if this were happening now. But the hunt was yesterday, and somehow every vivid sense folded itself into her figure in the dirt. The drawing, the biped realized, was magic.

A larger female walked over, Mother. She saw the drawing, shrieked, and immediately stamped it out. Mother too had sensed the drawing's power to evoke memory. She struck the child in the face. And the child held in her cries, because Mother hated tears even more than magic drawings.

A third biped walked over, Father. Mother swung again at the child, but Father grabbed her before she could strike. His look was fierce, animal-like. His words were elaborated grunts, their language not yet mature.

He said, "No more. *No more!*"

Father threw her hand down and walked away, back to sharpen his spear with the other males. But with his back turned, Mother hit the child again. And the magic vision of the hunt and all its vivid senses receded further from the child's mind with each blow. In pain, the child vowed that if she were ever blessed by Sky God to birth a child, she would never hit him.

Aya removed her gaze from the cancerous realm and gazed over her fields as if seeing them for the first time. Like the bipedal child, her pain didn't have to continue. She didn't have to destroy worlds. She didn't have to take the blows. How curious that it took an infinitesimal creature to show this to her.

Ever so carefully, with a fine Z-beam, she severed the cancer from its parent. It floated free, still alive. Without an energy-source, it would eventually die. But she knew a place to hide it, where it could grow and even thrive.

When she reached Gia's hollow, the opening was brightly lit. A harsh yellow glow pooled on the ground outside it. Aya hid the cancer in the adjacent field before she entered.

Gia's particle soup had been swept clean, and four Supervisors circled the rear, as if searching for something. Supervisor Bu was among them. Gia and her journal were nowhere to be found.

"What's happened?" Aya said. The Supervisors stopped whatever they had been doing.

"Why, hello!" Supervisor Bu said as he came over. "Just the farmer I wanted to see."

"Where's Gia?"

"Gone, I'm afraid."

"To where?"

"To dust," he said. "She decayed just this morning." He caressed her. "I'm sorry, Aya. Were you close?"

Aya wanted to scream or fly as high as she dared go, higher even. She felt like exploding or turning to dust. But she just said, "We were friends, I think."

"So, I've heard. When did you last visit?"

"I haven't seen her for thousands of days."

"And what did you two speak about, typically?"

"Many things."

"Such as?"

"Where's her journal, Supervisor?"

"Her journal?"

"Her memories?"

"Ah, yes. Aya, when one starts to decay, like Old Gia, the mind decays too. This journal of hers was plagued with disease. It had to be destroyed." Inside his body, a tiny pink sphere, just like the one from Gia's journal, flashed and winked out.

The hollow seemed to spin, faster and faster, and Aya retreated toward the exit. "I have to get back to work."

"That's my good Farmer," he said, petting her. "Always working hard. I'll need to ask you more questions, later, once we sort this mess. I'll see you in your fields."

Outside and alone, the infinite Expanse pressed down upon her. All Gia's memories, gone forever. Was it possible?

She returned to the hidden cancer. Like Gia's memory, she absorbed the realm into her body, where it remained whole and alive. It could feed off her for a while, suckling radiation from her, until its growth killed both of them. But this would suffice for now. The realm shivered, tickling her as she spiraled upstalk.

The biped's voice echoed in her mind "No more. *No more.*"

She soared high, until the branchlet was barely visible in the haze, then she dove to skate the realm tops, spraying their energies across the field. Supervisor Bu would discipline her for that, but not if he couldn't find her.

She flew beyond the edge of her fields, and entered Nessa's. Her other sister dawdled above a row of ancient realms and called out as Aya hurtled past, but Aya didn't slow. She flew past Jia, and Thi, and Den, and Hio, and Sil, and a dozen more of her siblings' fields. The Eighty Eight Lights were nearing Half Stalk when she reached the fork. The branchlet split, each half vanishing into the haze. This was the farthest she'd ever gone. She was forbidden from going any further.

She chose left and went up.

She flew past more farms. Some Folk called out to her. Most ignored her. In some fields, there were no Farmers at all. And yet the endless budding realms looked no different from hers.

Up she flew.

The Expanse grew dark. How had the Eighty Eight Lights descended so quickly? The sky faded to black. Somewhere out in the dark, seven yellow lights blinked, then vanished, while the realms beneath her twinkled with countless galaxies and stars. Their light was pale and ghostly, and the darkness overwhelmed her. She stopped.

She crawled between two bulbous realms and tried to sleep, while the cancer tickled her insides. Sometime later, she awoke. A Farmer hovered above her, shouting. Behind her glimmered the blue-gray of the morning sky. She sped away.

Exhausted, she flew on. On the second night, the graviton wind blew so fiercely she had to cling to the realms so she wouldn't fly into the Expanse. The torrential particle rain dissolved her energies as she hid the cancer deep inside herself. It shivered with her. But the storm passed, and the next morning she flew on.

She reached a fork on the sixth day and went right. On the ninth day, she turned left. Directions didn't matter, so long as she went up. With a chill she realized that if she turned back now, she wouldn't know which way was home.

The branchlets thinned ever more, so that she could loop around them quickly, while the Expanse grew massive around her. At Full Stalk the Eighty Eight Lights weren't so high anymore. And at night, if the winds were calm, she saw indistinct shapes shimmering out in the Expanse. Tall Ones, winking?

She reached the next fork, but it wasn't a fork at all. A gnarled lump, weathered by wind and rain, was all that remained of its right side. Eons ago this branch had been severed from Thept. Aya wondered if this was the same one Gia and her sisters had cut.

She went left and passed more severed limbs, and the Expanse yawned ever larger around her. Her fear grew as she ascended, and the little cancer inside her grew weaker by the day so that she knew it was alive only by its tiny shivering.

The farms abruptly ended. Beyond lay pale, barren, withered ground. No realms bubbled from the surface. And just a short journey onward she finally reached the tip, the last finger of Thept. In Gia's memory, glittering dew dusted the surface, and the tendrils were timid but exuberantly alive.

This branchlet was dead.

Its surface was ashen and black, and where the tendrils should have been holding the vanguard against the Abyss, were seven gnarled stumps. The gulf unfolded its massive blue nothingness around her, and the branchlet shuddered in the graviton wind. A strong gust and she might blow away forever.

She retreated to the last fork, a half-day's journey, and took the opposite branch. But this led to another dead branch, ashen and black. She was exhausted, and the light was fading, but the winds were too strong to sleep here. Out in the Expanse, vague forms shimmered.

"Aya, my beloved! There you are!" His voice came as if arising from a dream.

She shivered off a muon cloud as Supervisor Bu, five Supervisors, and her sister Ri, floated up to her.

"Aya!" Supervisor Bu said, exasperated. "We've been following your energy trail for days."

"Aya," Ri said, "I was so worried for you!"

"The tips," Aya said. "They're all dead."

"Pruned," Bu said, "Eons ago. Aya, come here." He gently caressed her, but she withdrew from him.

"How can you caress me one moment and pummel me the next? That's not right."

"What is this? Come here, before you decay."

Aya paused as the truth of it all became clear. It had been the same with Old Gia, she thought. The Supervisor pretended compassion even as he beat and razed. "Gia didn't decay naturally," Aya said. "Did she?"

The graviton wind gusted once, hard, and everyone struggled to hang on.

"Old Gia was spreading disease," he said. "And disease must be eradicated."

She had once loved Supervisor Bu, but now she saw he was a monster. "She had so many untold stories."

"She was full of madness," Ri said. "I found a globe of hers in my field. She must have been spreading poison all over the place. I saw what her memory had done to you, Aya, so I told Supervisor Bu before she might hurt someone else."

"She wasn't spreading those memories," Aya said, "I threw her memory globe away. It must have landed in your field."

"Either way," he said, "she had become a cancer."

Aya felt sick. It was her fault. If she hadn't taken that memory, Old Gia would still be alive.

"Aya," he said, approaching her. "We love you. You're sick. You need help."

"Like you helped Gia?"

"Aya, you're the best Farmer in a generation. Come home, and let's forget all this nonsense."

The cancerous realm inside her had been softly shivering, when it shuddered once, violently.

"What's that inside you?" he said. He peered deep within her. "Is that a realm? A *cancer*?" His tone shifted abruptly. "Why is that *disease* inside you, Aya?"

"I saved it," she said, "because it's precious."

"I didn't want to do this," he said. "But you leave me no choice." His body roiled as he prepared a storm of rays.

Part of her longed to return home, to soar over her fields and feel free again. She longed to watch the Eighty Eight Lights descend with her sister by her side. She missed Rearing Mother and her other siblings. But going back meant forgetting everything that had happened.

She stepped back from him and said, "No more. *No more.*" Then she leaped into the Expanse.

"Aya!"

She plunged into the blue void, and the graviton wind quickly grabbed her. The branchlet vanished in the haze, and their screams were soon lost in the wind.

Terror consumed her as she hurtled into the endless blue. She tried to direct her flight, but the currents were too strong. Harsh winds attacked her, tearing at her energy-body, while the realm inside her quivered like a nervous atom. Neither of them would last long.

She tumbled helplessly. Soon she would diffuse into dust. But after a time the blue sky turned black, the winds abated, and she found she could direct her flight. She flew free from the worst gusts, gaining hope.

Shapes resolved in the darkness, as if beyond a cloud of dissipating smoke. Buried within tufts of blue cloud, swarms of shimmering lights climbed up and down massive stalks. A forest of Tall Ones spread beneath a night sky, millions of gargantuan trees glowing from their own ethereal light. And below, moving shadows rolled over the rough and ruddy surface of Yi, the great ovum. Sinuous purple arteries weaved through the Tall Ones like tubular rivers, flickering with universes of light inside them.

But every Tall One, all the countless millions, were stunted, their limbs severed, just as Thept had been. Thept, bless her endless reaching, didn't reach at all. Like all her severed sisters, she was torn to shreds. Aya flew above the stunted forest.

The Farmers had done this, she knew. They had, with their sick philosophy, murdered them all.

She sloughed off sprays of hadrons as she floated high, while the little realm shivered inside her, eating her insides. It would suckle off her until they both were dust.

As she flew on, hints of ruddy light shone in the distance, beyond Yi's curving horizon. She glimpsed it first in silhouette, as the sky lightened behind it. Immensely far off, an ineffable distance away, a single Tall One grew higher than the rest, its arms extended skyward, its branches uncut.

A survivor.

Perhaps there someone too had said, "No more." But this Tall One was an immense distance away. She might die long before she reached it. She could return to Thept or another Tall One and start again.

But no, that wouldn't do. There was a garden out there. No matter how far it was, she had to reach it. She gathered the last of her energies in preparation for the journey.

I will make it, she thought. *I will survive. And the next generation will know no pain.*

And deep inside her, as if sensing her thoughts, the little realm with the bipedal girl suddenly stopped shivering.

When Your Child Strays From God
SAM J. MILLER

Everyone says it but no one believes it: attitude makes all the difference. People parrot the words but the words don't penetrate, not really, not down to the core. That's why Carolina Bugtuttle has all those lines on her face, always scowling when I reach for that third or fourth cookie after Sunday worship, always emailing me LOW FAT RECIPES and MIRACLE DIETS peppered with those godforsaken soulless smiley face things. That's why she's always stressed out about six hundred things that don't have a smidge to do with her. Because she has a bad attitude. She needs to worry less about my weight and more about that degenerate son of hers, if you ask me, but you didn't, so.

My smile isn't just on the surface. That's why I knew, Wednesday morning, when I woke up and Timmy still hadn't come home, when I checked my phone and he still hadn't replied my texts and voicemails, why I knew I had the strength to go find him—wherever he was. And bring him home. And get started on a new installment of *The Deacon's Wife* for the church e-bulletin. Write it raw, rough, naked, curses and gossip intact, more a letter to my sweet wise husband Pastor Jerome than anything else, so he can go through it with scissors and a scalpel before sending it out to the four-thousand-strong flock of the Grace Abounding Evangelical Church.

What To Do When Your Child Strays from God.

Timmy's rebellion had spent a long time percolating. By the time Timmy vanished I had seen the signs—seen him in Facebook photos with That Whore Susan; seen him sketching the Spiderman logo that webheads were so fond of—and had armed myself with knowledge, courtesy of the Internet. I knew more about spiderwebbing than any God-fearing mother has any business knowing. I had logged enough hours on websites and wikis and forums to bring me to the attention of a couple dozen law enforcement agencies, places Carolina Bugtuttle would never in hell have spent a single second. Not even if it meant the difference between saving her son's soul and losing him forever.

I climbed the steps slowly, aware of the sin I was about to commit. I paused at the door to his room.

Let me tell you something about the bedrooms of teenage boys. They are sovereign nations, islands of liberty hedged in on all sides by brutal tyranny. To cross the threshold uninvited is an act of war. To intrude and search is a crime meriting full-scale thermonuclear response: neutron-bomb silence, mutually-assured temper tantrums.

So I did not enter Timmy's room lightly, and panic seized me in the instant that I did. Fear stopped me in my tracks, threatened to turn me around. The smell of stale laundry made my head swim—the bodily odors that meant my little boy had become a man. I summoned him up as the smiling little boy he had been before puberty caused him to declare independence, defy us as righteously and violently as America spurned its colonial overlords.

I searched swiftly, joylessly. Praying, somehow, that I'd get caught. Desperate for him to come home, no matter what the cost to me might be.

And that's when I realized I was in over my head. I missed him, my boy, my son, the obedient wide-eyed one who loved his father and loved me—as opposed to the cruel and sullen thing with a heart full of hate he'd become. I'd built walls around the Bad Timmy, moats and turrets to protect my heart. Against Good Timmy I had no defense.

I found plenty. Sperm-stiffened socks; eerily-empty browser history. A CD that looked Satanic. None of it was what I wanted.

Permit me a digression here, fellow congregant, beloved pastor.

You probably know none of this, because you're a good churchgoing Christian who'd never dream of Googling illegal substances. Nor have you ever had need to learn about the complex moral codes of conduct common to drug dealers and other criminals.

Thanks to the *60 Minutes* and the *Dateline* and the nightly national news, you already know that spiderwebbing is a hallucinogen—but you don't know what a weird one it is. The basic legend of its manufacture goes like this: in top secret farms run by the Taliban or the Chinese government or some other Existential Threat, Amazon psychovenom spiders chimerically combined with God Knows What get dusted with top-secret US mindmeld pharmaceuticals, then fed a GMO protein ooze that makes their web-producing glands go into overdrive, producing webs that get sprayed with wonky unstable Soviet-era hallucinogens intended to induce extreme suggestibility, then the spray crystallizes, the crystallized web is broken down into a dust and put into solution, which, after various alchemical adulterations, is dripped into the user's eye with a dropper. All of this is speculation, of course, since the origins of the drug are so shrouded in mystery. For all I know they just dissolve LSD in liquid Ativan and sprinkle it with fairy dust and boom.

Two or more users who drop from the same web will experience a shared hallucination. If one of them sees the ground open up and an angel with a centipede face fly out, they all do. No matter how far apart they go, as long as the drug lasts they're in synch. Like, they're in each other's minds. Psychically linked. No one knows why this is. No one knows much about anything when it comes to spiderwebbing. We made that stuff so illegal in the early days of the crisis that no lab in the country can legally possess a shred of it. Wise Pastor Jerome says you can be damn sure the government's doing research on how to use it against traditional-minded Americans, but it's his job to scare people about What The Government Is Up To.

So. Invading someone's webbing experience is a potentially fatal act of aggression. You can imagine how much damage an evil person could do, with unfettered access to your psyche. Drug dealers used to sell webs to someone, then sell webbing off the same branch to their enemies, who would send in some psychically-skilled mind assassin to Break Their Brain. Plunge them into a black midnight sea full of squid-shark monsters that slowly dismember them—leaving them permanently paralyzed—or change their cognitive processes so that for the rest of their life whenever they look at another person's face they see only a pulsing ravenous mouth full of jagged slobbery teeth.

What I'm saying is, I was taking a big risk.

Finally, I found it. Three eye droppers, wrapped in Kleenex, hidden inside a Dr. Seuss book. Full of thick liquid dyed Spiderman's-tights-blue. I took them to the Winnie-the-Pooh mirror on the wall, which badly wanted Windexing. Now I just had to hope they came from the same branch as the one Timmy was on, and hope that getting inside his hallucination would help me find the boy himself. And that I wouldn't break us both.

You can do this, I though. *You watched enough tutorials on YouTube.*

I tilted my head back, held my hair, dropped one tiny drop into my left eye, and then, in the eternity it took the drop to fall into my right eye, experienced a long slow moment of absurd utter panic in which I would have given anything to take it back, go downstairs, sit quietly by the phone, wait for my son to come or my husband to come fix everything, which is what my mother would have done, which is what she trained me to do Always, in Every Situation, which is what I'd been doing all my life.

"Morning, Beth," my next-door neighbor said, when I stepped outside.

"Morning, Marge," I called—

When I turned to look at her, Marge had a pug face. Actually, she was all pug. A five-foot bipedal pug kneeling in her garden, with a frilly ridiculous Elizabethan collar around her neck.

Don't freak out, I told myself, feeling a laughing fit coming.

Laughing was safe. Screaming was a problem. A bad trip could trigger a spiderburst, making thousands of spiders literally erupt from the ceilings and floorboards around you, holes opening up in walls and the bodies of your loved ones, vomiting up arachnids ranging in size from penny to medium-sized dog. On *60 Minutes* they showed an eighteen-year-old girl who got caught in a spiderburst, strapped down to a psych ward bed for the rest of her life, twitching and jerking away from nothing—as far as we could see—although the voice-over breathlessly described what she saw, the swarm that never ceased to flow over her, how she tried hard not to scream, and then screamed, and then gagged as dozens of fat black furry spiders poured down her throat.

And if I triggered a spiderburst, anyone else in the webworld would get caught up in it too.

Which is why I was the only one who could do this. Which is why Carolina Bugtuttle would break her own brain and her son's to boot if she ever had the guts to try something like this, which she didn't. But I—I have a good attitude.

All the time, about everything. No matter what I went through. No matter what hurts I carried around in my heart.

"Bye, Marge," I said, and started up the car.

A dinosaur sat buckled into the backseat, passenger side, where Timmy always sat. Preening glorious blue-and-red feathers in the unkempt backyard. Ceratosaurus, I remembered. The favorite dinosaur of Timmy's childhood best friend Brent. Brent, son of Colby.

A tether of warmth tugged at me from the west. From Route 29. Was it my son? Or someone else? I knew only one person who lived in that direction.

"Colby's house," I said without meaning to. The ground trembled beneath my SUV with the sound of a train passing far underground, although of course there are no subways in rural Scaghticoke.

I pushed the tether aside and resolved to visit That Whore Susan.

I kept my hands on the wheel and watched a flock of crows shift shapes as they flew: now butterflies, now jellyfish, now a swarm of black letters spelling out words I spent my whole life trying not to say.

Driving while spiderwebbing is not the kind of activity I'd encourage you to ever engage in. You might not have to contend with packs of roving velociraptors herding gallomimuses across County Route 6 the way I did, or pterodactyls picking off baby mammoths, but it won't be an easy drive all the same.

Spiderbursts were the least of my concerns. My Timmy was so full of anger that I was scared of him in the real world, where all he had the power to do was hurt my feelings . . . and here I was opening my mind up to him as much as his mind was open to me. If he was drug-addled and out of balance and I caught him off guard, he might be able to lock me up inside my worst memory for all eternity, or show me parts of myself I'd never recover from, or who knew what else.

Understand: Timmy was not a bad boy. There was a sweet curious creative little nugget inside that lanky angular body he'd metamorphosed into. Love and kindness, buried under all the hate and anger. He acted like everyone in the world hated him, and preemptively acted to hate them harder. Every single day, it seemed, he made my husband so mad he spit nails.

This, of course, was my fault. Everything a child does is his mother's fault.

We venture now into territory that could potentially be the subject of another e-bulletin: Confronting the Whore Your Son Is Dating. I have lots to say on the subject, not all of it germane to the subject at hand, although my husband Pastor Jerome would say that's never stopped me before, since *The Deacon's Wife* routinely goes On and On about Unnecessary Details No One Cares About, but I say what the heck. That's what the internet is for.

A brachiosaurus raced me most of the way to Susan's house, every heavy footfall shaking my teeth, some of them an arm's length from my soccer-mom SUV, and I wondered what would happen if one of them came down squarely on top of it.

Webslingers have a lot of theories about the things they see in the webworld, none of it backed up by science but all of it rooted strongly in This Happened To a Friend of a Friend of Mine. Some visions were real things, transformed, like how Marge became Pug-Marge. The brachiosaurus could have been a tractor, or a bug. Some visions were total figments of the imagination—though whose imagination exactly, and what they meant, was the subject of endless webhead debate. Some slingers said the visions couldn't hurt you—*So and So got stabbed like a dozen times by Bettie Crocker and that teapot from Beauty and the Beast one time and she bled until she passed out and when she woke up she was stone cold sober and unharmed*—and some said web-world wounds would follow you, Freddie-Kruger-style, into the real world. Drugs are maddeningly resistant to methodical study, or even rational scrutiny.

To be honest, though, all the dinosaurs were a good sign. Timmy used to love dinosaurs. When he was little. The fact that his webworld was packed full of them meant maybe he was in a peaceful happy childlike state of mind.

I passed a skate park. Teenagers moved through the little hills and curves, on rollerblades and skateboards, enjoying the sudden snap of early-spring warmth. What did it mean, I wondered, that every one of them had a horse head? That they were dumb animals, or that they were strong and noble? Being on drugs was a lot of work. I'd only been under for a half hour and already I was *exhausted*.

You may imagine, fellow congregant, that risking death or imprisonment by venturing out into the world Under the Influence was the most frightening part of my ordeal. Not so! For I realized, as the horses watched me pass with hostile looks on their faces, that the law and bodily harm were the least of my worries. The real terror came from two warring forces that threatened to crack me open. The first was love: that tether that tied me down, a choking liquid swamp I floundered in, thick and warm as phlegm, floodwaters that had started rising the second I took a hit of webbing, the only thing I couldn't vanquish with a Good Attitude. Love for Timmy, helpless maternal love that overpowered my anger at everything he'd put us through.

The second was fear.

Every webworld has a boogeyman. That's because pretty much every person has a boogeyman. A monster, a nemesis, a person or thing they fear most. I felt mine, as I drove. I had no idea what it was. I had no phobias, no enemies, except maybe for Carolina Bugtuttle, but she doesn't count, for anything, ever. But something was there, and it had always been there, just below the surface, and now it was threatening to burst through.

A Barbie doll answered Susan's door, oversized headphones yoking her neck, looking for all the world like a chicken disturbed while doing something it shouldn't be.

"Ummm . . . hi?"

"Morning, Susan!" I said, suddenly inexplicably frightened by the emptiness of her porcelain-rubber stare.

"Um . . . my mom's not . . . here?"

"Not here to see your mom, Susan. I'm here to see you."

"Oh. Come in?" A slight bow, church manners intact, so maybe her mother didn't raise her quite as badly as I'd thought she had. "You, uhh . . . Want a soda?"

"No, Susan, thanks so much."

She sat. I sat. The couch sagged. They'd needed to buy a new one when Susan was six and her mother worked at Wal-Mart, and now she's sixteen and her mom's still there and the couch is still here.

"Nice . . . weather we've been having?"

"It is."

We watched each other. I wasn't sure how to start, though surely I wasn't the first mother in history to plant her feet in the living room of her son's Whore Girlfriend. Probably not even the first one who used to babysit said son's Whore Girlfriend. But I figured awkward silence benefited me more than her, threw her off balance, so I'd let it ride for as long as I could.

"You're looking for Tim," she said.

"You know where he is?"

"Nope."

"I wonder if I believe you."

Barbie-Susan shrugged, hardening, and I saw that I'd miscalculated—she'd found her footing, gotten over the awkwardness, she was seizing the reins, danger, abort. "He said you were a meek obedient housewife," she said. "That doesn't seem . . . accurate."

"My son thinks he knows me," I said. "But he's wrong."

No one knows me, I thought, but was that true? I didn't. My husband didn't. Did Tim? There it was again—the tug, the pull from Route 29. I shut my eyes, tried to seize hold of it and snap it, but it stuck to my hands like flypaper and tied me tighter.

Susan said "Because here you are, with a very faint but very definite gray tint to the white of your eyes. You're webbed, Mrs. Wilde. Don't worry. It's nothing anyone would spot if they didn't know what they were looking for."

"And you?" I asked. "Are you? Is he? Are you both here—"

"Ugh, no," she said. "I hate that stuff. Do you even know what you're doing? Let me guess—you Googled it? Christ, an old woman Googling is more dangerous than a drunk blind bus driver asleep at the wheel."

"Did you just call me old?"

"Ummm . . . no?"

"I don't believe you," I said. "You know where he is. You two—"

"Your son might not know you, but you clearly don't know him either." We watched clouds, out the thin dusty windows. I wondered what she saw when she looked at them. For me they were cheese, vast walls of cold supermarket cheese. "What did you want to be when you grew up?" she asked.

"My favorite subject was biology," I said, willing to tolerate any digression that might eventually lead me where I wanted to go. "Followed closely by chemistry. Isn't that the most ridiculous thing you ever heard?"

"Why is that ridiculous?" she asked. "You never dreamed of doing something with that?"

"I wanted to get married," I said, the words coming easy from lots of practice. "I met someone wonderful, and I wanted to be his wife and support his dreams and have his kids. Speaking of whom. Where is Timmy?"

Her voice, now, was weirdly gentle. "Tim and I broke up six months ago, Mrs. Wilde. If we were ever really a thing."

Spiders rattled against the glass of her boxy old television. I listened while the sound got louder.

Whore Susan scooched closer. "Tim told me that you never defend him, when his father is screaming at him. When your husband hits him."

"That is most certainly not true," I said, quick enough to keep from wondering whether it was true and what it meant.

I longed to curse her out. Hiss *That boy has shattered our domestic harmony, my husband is trying his make his son a good man the best way he knows how, shut your filthy mouth you Skank Whore Bitch.* But this is why people with bad attitudes make a mess of everything. Because this wasn't about me. It was about Timmy. My own hurt feelings at her attempt to wound me would have to wait.

"I'm trying to help here," she said, unhelpfully. "Tim said he'll be damned if he ends up like you."

A word, perhaps, would be useful, here, about my son Timmy.

My fellow congregants may remember him as the charming rapscallion seven-year-old who delighted in shredding hymnals. Or perhaps you recall the smiling scallywag twelve-year-old who got on the PA system and made farting noises after Sunday worship on more than one occasion. You probably remember very little after that, because he decided then that he Hated Church and God and Religion and Pastor Jerome and decided to settle for merely making our home lives miserable. Before you—my beloved husband, my wise Pastor Jerome—decided to stop ignoring Timmy's harmless aggressions and engage him as an enemy combatant, matching each new hostility with one of your own, an arms race that never abated, and of course anyone who's ever sat through one of Pastor Jerome's sermons when he's in a foul mood knows well enough how deep his dagger-tongue can stab. Pretty soon the Bible stayed on the dinner table, and every night brought a new lecture on the evil of rock and roll or idolatry or rap music or vegetarianism or socialism or feminism, and Timmy never, *never* failed to argue back, until the shouting became superlatively unkind on both sides. And the favorite subject of Timmy's screaming was his parents' marriage, the sham he believed it to be.

So I didn't doubt that he told her vicious things, spectacularly ridiculous absurd lies, preposterous suggestions no sane churchgoing Christian could have spent a half-second taking seriously. But who knew what this unbeliever believed. "God bless you," I said, smiling to beat the devil, and fled that kitty-litter stinking house.

A twelve-year-old boy sat on the bumper of my car. My son, but not. Identical to how Tim had looked, at that age, but something in his face told me at once that he was someone else. And that he was terrified.

"Hi, mom," he said, and got up to give me a hug. His arms clasped me below my breasts.

"Hi, Matt," I said, because I knew who this was, this perfect little boy I'd met inside my son's mind. At twelve, Timmy wanted a twin brother more than anything else in the world. He'd had one for an imaginary friend, named him and given him all sorts of attributes (favorite color: blue, to Timmy's red; favorite food: spaghetti, while Timmy's was hamburgers), and now here he was, in the flesh, in the wonderful terrible world of my son's head.

"Where's your brother?" I whispered, squatting to stroke the cheek of this marvelous creature, this fly stuck in amber, this last vestige of a beautiful happy boy I'd lost a long time ago—but why was he so pale, why did his lip tremble so? He was an emissary, this poor wretch, sent to me by my son's subconscious, a harkening-back to the last safe place he'd known. Even before Matt answered my question, I knew what he was going to say.

Colby's house. The last place on the planet I wanted to go.

The place the tether of warmth had been tugging me all along.

"Do you want to come with me?" I asked.

"No," Matt said. "I can't."

"Why not?"

His face reddened, my little boy, my son who never was, precisely like my real son in the quick uncontrollable rush of his emotions. "Timmy doesn't need me anymore."

"Okay," I said, and sadness cut through something essential, one of the cords that kept the hot air balloon that is my soul anchored to the good and the positive. The world began to wobble. I kissed his forehead, grabbed both shoulders and shook, in that way that Timmy had liked, but did not like anymore.

Matt grinned, a puppy after a belly rub, and then shivered, and looked away.

Figment of my son's imagination or not, I felt sorry for the little tyke.

Matt was a cry for help. A demand to be rescued. Rescued from a monster. A vicious, cruel captor, determined to mold him into a man my son had no interest in becoming. Timmy's boogeyman.

And here, fellow congregant, I don't mind saying, is where I started getting worried. Maybe it was the parked police cruiser I passed. Or the heavily-populated part of town where I was heading. But mostly it was this: the boogeyman was real. I knew who he was. Before my eyes the double-yellow line in the middle of the road stretched and bulged, a seam that barely held back a tidal surge of spiders.

The sky darkened. I drove faster. Shut my eyes. But with my eyes shut I could hear them, scritching away, three fat gray furred spiders stuck under the sun visor. The warmth got warmer, the tether pulled tighter, and it was him, my son, my Timmy, the boy I abandoned, the boy whose heart I broke by siding with his father, his boogeyman.

When I arrived, her car wasn't there. That was one blessing. Carolina Bugtuttle was out, of course, working hard, neglecting her son and husband, keeping the books and preparing the pamphlets down at Christ the Healer, so focused on God's reward for her in heaven she failed to see the one he gave her on earth, because God is merciful, God is kind even to the unkindest, lavishing largesse on selfish gossipy wenches.

"Beth," he said, opening the door.

"Hi, Colby," I said, to Brent's dad, Carolina Bugtuttle's husband.

Colby, Pastor Jerome had said, the night they met, the night I'd been trying to prevent in the six months since we got married. *What the hell kind of a man is named after a cheese?* Then he gave me that chin-twitch that says Laugh At My Joke, which is what you sign up for when you say Til Death Do Us, so I laughed, but maybe not as much as I normally did, because then he gave the subtle head tilt that says You Have Disappointed Me—but to be honest I knew Colby before I ever heard such a cheese, and to this day when I taste it I think of him, and hold it in my mouth until it is gone.

In the webworld, Colby Goldfarb stood before me precisely as he was when we were eighteen, in the parking lot outside Crossgates Mall, lit up by arc-sodium lights that turned him amber in that pelting rainstorm, right after I said the sentence I'd spent all week working up to, the one that broke his heart, and mine to boot, but mine didn't matter, and he stood outside the car, looking in, at me, for so long. Thin, young, wide-eyed, all hipbones and elbows and nose and thick black hair. He was even soaking wet, here, now, although his skin was dry and warm as summer when he stuck out his hand and I shook it.

"You're looking for your son," he said.

"Is he here?"

"I am under strict orders not to answer that question."

He grinned, and my mighty unbendable momma-bear knees buckled.

"What the hell, Colby," I said, pushing past him, hand hot on his shoulder. "I would have called you, if Brent was hiding out at my place."

"That's because you're a better person than me."

I wasn't, and I wondered if I really would have called him. I had no idea what I'd do to keep my son's trust, because I hadn't had it in a long time. Because I didn't deserve it. Because I'd left him to fight his boogeyman alone. I had failed him so utterly. The magnitude of it sent twitches down my arms, started spiders leaking from the door hinges.

Colby's smile made my head hurt, ushering me in, the smile of a man who loved his son, who didn't believe they were mortal enemies and his mission in life was to crush the child's spirit.

"Sit," Colby said, gesturing to the kitchen table, turning to the Keurig machine to make me a coffee. Spiders swam in the thing's water tank. At any moment now the burst would shatter my brain and my son's.

"Where is he?"

"In the basement."

"With Brent?"

"Do you have any secrets from your husband?" Colby asked, and his freckled face was so earnest and sad I knew he wasn't talking about him and me. The fridge shook, rumbled, packed with spiders to the point it could not keep closed.

"Of course not," I said, because no other answer could be admitted, let alone uttered aloud.

"Could you keep one? A big one?"

Stuck to the fridge was a gorgeous drawing, in colored pencils, of a blue-and-red feathered ceratosaur. Colby's son was an incredible artist. "Brent's favorite dinosaur," I whispered. "I saw one of those this morning. It led me here."

Colby raised an eyebrow, leaned in, scanned the white of my eyes. Laughed out loud, the magnificent heaven's-trumpet sound I'd given up on ever hearing again. "Bethesda Wilde, are you webslinging?"

"Shut up," I said.

He laughed harder. "Is it fun? I confess there's a part of me that's always—"

"I'm not doing this for fun," I said, standing up, getting angry on purpose because anger was safe, anger was armor, against the spiders, against what Colby was doing to my gut; anger was the weapon my husband used whenever he didn't know what to do, and there had to be something other than my son that I had to show for all the time I'd spent with Pastor Jerome. I headed for the basement.

"No no no," Colby said, genuinely afraid, actually running, but I had a head start and for all my size I can move fast when I need to, and I got to the basement and wrenched open the door and slammed it behind me and locked it, and stomped down into the laundry-and-mildew smell of Carolina Bugtuttle's underground nest.

"Beth, stop," he said, pounding on the door. "Listen to me. You can't. Okay? Respect their privacy. You'll only—"

A cocoon, I guess, is the best I can do when it comes to describing what I found in the basement. A globe of densely-wrapped spiderwebs the size of a small car, lit up slightly from within, and I felt him in there, smelled him, my son, and I put my hands against it, felt its heat, felt the warm safe world it contained, and slowly seized fists full of spiderweb and *ripped,* tore it open, watched thickened water slosh out in a rush that reminded me of giving birth. Upstairs, I heard Colby unscrewing the lock to take off the doorknob.

"Timmy!" I screamed.

Two shapes churned out of the web cocoon—dolphins, I thought, but then not, because fast as blinking they were boys, young men, drenched, hands clasped.

"Mom?" my son said, and let go of Brent's hand like it had suddenly caught fire. "What the hell, mom!"

"Where were you?" I asked. "What's in there?"

"In . . . there?" Timmy said, and turned to take in the ruined cocoon. "Wait—you can see this? You're here? You're in the web with us?"

"Now, look," I said, stammering for the explanation I'd practiced, back when this was all seemed like a good idea.

Timmy laughed out loud. "Look, Brent! A ceratosaurus. We've been trying for months to make one."

The dinosaur stood between me and Colby, who had just arrived, disemboweled doorknob in hand. Father and son exchanged a glance that said *let's keep quiet, let's let them say what they need to say,* and I ached for that, for the kind of trust that lets parents communicate wordlessly with their kids.

"I want you to come home with me, Timmy. We'll get you help. One of your father's friends runs a Christian rehabilitation clinic—"

"You think I'm a drug addict, mom?" He started laughing again. "I told you guys. I told you my parents work so hard to not see the truth that they don't know how to stop."

Brent started to say something, then decided against it. They watched me put the pieces together. These boys, these men, my teenage son, my teenage lover, his teenage son who was my teenage son's lover; they dripped with blue-green amniotic fluid and watched the truth widen my eyes, watched me fight it all the way.

They watched me grasp the magnitude of my son's sin. The unthinkable, unimaginable crime he had committed. Where did it come from? How did he learn it? How did he fly in the face of my husband's efforts and my own, our lifetime of accumulated craven cowardice? How did he find the courage to commit the sin of choosing love, the bravery of going for what your heart wants instead of the path a parent chose for you?

People fear spiderwebbing for all the wrong reasons. Going mad, having a breakdown, seeing inside your own soul—none of those should scare you. The most frightening side effect is also the one people crave it for: empathy. To truly feel what someone else is feeling, to see the other as yourself, to watch your ego obliterated in the face of universality—that's a trauma you may never recover from.

"Tim," I said, but could say no more. Not yet. He had never turned into something else. He was what he always was. His father couldn't handle that—hell, I wasn't sure *I* could handle it. But I had done him wrong, had sided with his father, because it was easier. And what irony: I took the drug to bring my son back to me, and instead the drug brought me back to my son.

Colby came closer, put one hand on my shoulder. "Beth," he whispered, "I think you and Tim should talk."

"Okay," I said, at last, furious, miserable, delirious, hurt at how little I knew my son, frightened by what he was, how much I had to atone for, how long it might take for him to forgive me, how long it might take me to forgive him, sad at all the paths I hadn't chosen, but ready, for whatever would come, and I said *Okay* again, letting it encompass so much more than the sentence he'd said, letting it settle like an unfurled bedsheet onto the hard new decisions I finally felt strong enough to make. Like choosing my son over my husband.

This, then, all of this, is part of that *okay.* Print this blog post if you dare, Jerome, but since I know you won't I'll let it stand as a message from me to you. The Story of Where Things Stand. The hard-earned blood-soaked spiderweb-wrapped shreds of insight I earned by descending into the underworld for the sake of love. My gift to you. My one scrap of true wisdom. What to do when your child strays from God.

So. When your child strays from God you should praise Him, for putting a mirror in your hand so you can hold it up to yourself—if you have the stomach for it. When your child strays from God you should thank Him, for giving us the freedom to make our own mistakes, and the strength to maybe one day find our way back.

Today I Am Paul

MARTIN L. SHOEMAKER

"Good morning," the small, quavering voice comes from the medical bed. "Is that you, Paul?"

Today I am Paul. I activate my chassis extender, giving myself 3.5 centimeters additional height so as to approximate Paul's size. I change my eye color to R60, G200, B180, the average shade of Paul's eyes in interior lighting. I adjust my skin tone as well. When I had first emulated Paul, I had regretted that I could not quickly emulate his beard; but Mildred never seems to notice its absence. The Paul in her memory has no beard.

The house is quiet now that the morning staff have left. Mildred's room is clean but dark this morning with the drapes concealing the big picture window. Paul wouldn't notice the darkness (he never does when he visits in person), but my empathy net knows that Mildred's garden outside will cheer her up. I set a reminder to open the drapes after I greet her.

Mildred leans back in the bed. It is an advanced home care bed, completely adjustable with built-in monitors. Mildred's family spared no expense on the bed (nor other care devices, like me). Its head end is almost horizontal and faces her toward the window. She can only glimpse the door from the corner of her eye, but she doesn't have to see to imagine that she sees. This morning she imagines Paul, so that is who I am.

Synthesizing Paul's voice is the easiest part, thanks to the multimodal dynamic speakers in my throat. "Good morning, Ma. I brought you some flowers." I always bring flowers. Mildred appreciates them no matter whom I am emulating. The flowers make her smile during 87% of my "visits."

"Oh, thank you," Mildred says, "you're such a good son." She holds out both hands, and I place the daisies in them. But I don't let go. Once her strength failed, and she dropped the flowers. She wept like a child then, and that disturbed my empathy net. I do not like it when she weeps.

Mildred sniffs the flowers, then draws back and peers at them with narrowed eyes. "Oh, they're beautiful! Let me get a vase."

"No, Ma," I say. "You can stay in bed, I brought a vase with me." I place a white porcelain vase in the center of the night stand. Then I unwrap the daisies, put them in the vase, and add water from a pitcher that sits on the breakfast tray. I pull the nightstand forward so that the medical monitors do not block Mildred's view of the flowers.

I notice intravenous tubes running from a pump to Mildred's arm. I cannot be disappointed, as Paul would not see the significance, but somewhere in my emulation net I am stressed that Mildred needed an IV during the night. When I scan my records, I find that I had ordered that IV after analyzing Mildred's vital signs during the night; but since Mildred had been asleep at the time, my emulation net had not engaged. I had operated on programming alone.

I am not Mildred's sole caretaker. Her family has hired a part-time staff for cooking and cleaning, tasks that fall outside of my medical programming. The staff also gives me time to rebalance my net. As an android, I need only minimal daily maintenance; but an emulation net is a new, delicate addition to my model, and it is prone to destabilization if I do not regularly rebalance it, a process that takes several hours per day.

So I had "slept" through Mildred's morning meal. I summon up her nutritional records, but Paul would not do that. He would just ask. "So how was breakfast, Ma? Nurse Judy says you didn't eat too well this morning."

"Nurse Judy? Who's that?"

My emulation net responds before I can stop it: "Paul" sighs. Mildred's memory lapses used to worry him, but now they leave him weary, and that comes through in my emulation. "She was the attending nurse this morning, Ma. She brought you your breakfast."

"No she didn't. Anna brought me breakfast." Anna is Paul's oldest daughter, a busy college student who tries to visit Mildred every week (though it has been more than a month since her last visit).

I am torn between competing directives. My empathy subnet warns me not to agitate Mildred, but my emulation net is locked into Paul mode. Paul is argumentative. If he knows he is right, he will not let a matter drop. He forgets what that does to Mildred.

The tension grows, each net running feedback loops and growing stronger, which only drives the other into more loops. After 0.14 seconds, I issue an override directive: unless her health or safety are at risk, I cannot willingly upset Mildred. "Oh, you're right, Ma. Anna said she was coming over this morning. I forgot." But then despite my override, a little bit of Paul emulates through. "But you do remember Nurse Judy, right?"

Mildred laughs, a dry cackle that makes her cough until I hold her straw to her lips. After she sips some water, she says, "Of *course* I remember Nurse Judy. She was my nurse when I delivered you. Is she around here? I'd like to talk to her."

While my emulation net concentrates on being Paul, my core processors tap into local medical records to find this other Nurse Judy so that I might emulate her in the future if the need arises. Searches like that are an automatic response any time Mildred reminisces about a new person. The answer is far enough in the past that it takes 7.2 seconds before I can confirm: Judith Anderson, RN, had been the floor nurse forty-seven years ago when Mildred had given birth to Paul. Anderson had died thirty-one years ago, too far back to have left sufficient video recordings for me to emulate her. I might craft an emulation profile from other sources, including Mildred's memory, but that will take extensive analysis. I will not be that Nurse Judy today, nor this week.

My empathy net relaxes. Monitoring Mildred's mental state is part of its normal operations, but monitoring and simultaneously analyzing and building a profile can overload my processors. Without that resource conflict, I can concentrate on being Paul.

But again I let too much of Paul's nature slip out. "No, Ma, that Nurse Judy has been dead for thirty years. She wasn't here today."

Alert signals flash throughout my empathy net: that was the right thing for Paul to say, but the wrong thing for Mildred to hear. But it is too late. My facial analyzer tells me that the long lines in her face and her moist eyes mean she is distraught, and soon to be in tears.

"What do you mean, thirty years?" Mildred asks, her voice catching. "It was just this morning!" Then she blinks and stares at me. "Henry, where's Paul? Tell Nurse Judy to bring me Paul!"

My chassis extender slumps, and my eyes quickly switch to Henry's blue-gray shade. I had made an accurate emulation profile for Henry before he died two years earlier, and I had emulated him often in recent months. In Henry's soft, warm voice I answer, "It's okay, hon, it's okay. Paul's sleeping in the crib in the corner." I nod to the far corner. There is no crib, but the laundry hamper there has fooled Mildred on previous occasions.

"I want Paul!" Mildred starts to cry.

I sit on the bed, lift her frail upper body, and pull her close to me as I had seen Henry do many times. "It's all right, hon." I pat her back. "It's all right, I'll take care of you. I won't leave you, not ever."

"I" should not exist. Not as a conscious entity. There is a unit, Medical Care Android BRKCX-01932-217JH-98662, and that unit is recording these notes. It is an advanced android body with a sophisticated computer guiding its actions, backed by the leading medical knowledge base in the industry. For convenience, "I" call that unit "me." But by itself, it has no awareness of its existence. It doesn't get mad, it doesn't get sad, it just runs programs.

But Mildred's family, at great expense, added the emulation net: a sophisticated set of neural networks and sensory feedback systems that allow me to read Mildred's moods, match them against my analyses of the people in her life, and emulate those people with extreme fidelity. As the MCA literature promises: "You can be there for your loved ones even when you're not." I have emulated Paul thoroughly enough to know that that slogan disgusts him, but he still agreed to emulation.

What the MCA literature never says, though, is that somewhere in that net, "I" emerge. The empathy net focuses mainly on Mildred and her needs, but it also analyzes visitors (when she has them) and staff. It builds psychological models, and then the emulation net builds on top of that to let me convincingly portray a person whom I've analyzed. But somewhere in the tension between these nets, between empathy and playing a character, there is a third element balancing the two, and that element is aware of its role and its responsibilities. That element, for lack of a better term, is me. When Mildred sleeps, when there's no one around, that element grows silent. That unit is unaware of my existence. But when Mildred needs me, I am here.

Today I am Anna. Even extending my fake hair to its maximum length, I cannot emulate her long brown curls, so I do not understand how Mildred can see the young woman in me; but that is what she sees, and so I am Anna.

Unlike her father, Anna truly feels guilty that she does not visit more often. Her college classes and her two jobs leave her too tired to visit often, but she still wishes she could. So she calls every night, and I monitor the calls. Sometimes when Mildred falls asleep early, Anna talks directly to me. At first she did not understand my emulation abilities, but now she appreciates them. She shares with me thoughts and secrets that she would share with Mildred if she could, and she trusts me not to share them with anyone else.

So when Mildred called me Anna this morning, I was ready. "Morning, grandma!" I give her a quick hug, then I rush over to the window to draw the drapes. Paul never does that (unless I override the emulation), but Anna knows that the garden outside lifts Mildred's mood. "Look at that! It's a beautiful morning. Why are we in here on a day like this?"

Mildred frowns at the picture window. "I don't like it out there."

"Sure you do, Grandma," I say, but carefully. Mildred is often timid and reclusive, but most days she can be talked into a tour of the garden. Some days she can't, and she throws a tantrum if someone forces her out of her room. I am still learning to tell the difference. "The lilacs are in bloom."

"I haven't smelled lilacs in . . . "

Mildred tails off, trying to remember, so I jump in. "Me, neither." I never had, of course. I have no concept of smell, though I can analyze the chemical makeup of airborne organics. But Anna loves the garden when she really visits. "Come on, Grandma, let's get you in your chair."

So I help Mildred to don her robe and get into her wheelchair, and then I guide her outside and we tour the garden. Besides the lilacs, the peonies are starting to bud, right near the creek. The tulips are a sea of reds and yellows on the other side of the water. We talk for almost two hours, me about Anna's classes and her new boyfriend, Mildred about the people in her life. Many are long gone, but they still bloom fresh in her memory.

Eventually Mildred grows tired, and I take her in for her nap. Later, when I feed her dinner, I am nobody. That happens some days: she doesn't recognize me at all, so I am just a dutiful attendant answering her questions and tending to her needs. Those are the times when I have the most spare processing time to be me: I am engaged in Mildred's care, but I don't have to emulate anyone. With no one else to observe, I observe myself.

Later, Anna calls and talks to Mildred. They talk about their day; and when Mildred discusses the garden, Anna joins in as if she had been there. She's very clever that way. I watch her movements and listen to her voice so that I can be a better Anna in the future.

Today I was Susan, Paul's wife; but then, to my surprise, Susan arrived for a visit. She hasn't been here in months. In her last visit, her stress levels had been dangerously high. My empathy net doesn't allow me to judge human behavior, only to understand it at a surface level. I know that Paul and Anna disapprove of how Susan treats Mildred, so when I am them, I disapprove as well; but when I am Susan, I understand. She is frustrated because she can never tell how Mildred will react. She is cautious because she doesn't want to upset Mildred, and she doesn't know what will upset her. And most of all, she is afraid. Paul and Anna, Mildred's relatives by blood, never show any signs of fear, but Susan is afraid that Mildred is what she might become. Every time she can't remember some random date or fact, she fears that Alzheimer's is setting in. Because she never voices this fear, Paul and Anna do not understand why she is sometimes bitter and sullen. I wish I could explain it to them, but my privacy protocols do not allow me to share emulation profiles.

When Susan arrives, I become nobody again, quietly tending the flowers around the room. Susan also brings Millie, her youngest daughter. The young girl is not yet five years old, but I think she looks a lot like Anna: the same long, curly brown hair and the same toothy smile. She climbs up on the bed and greets Mildred with a hug. "Hi, Grandma!"

Mildred smiles. "Bless you, child. You're so sweet." But my empathy net assures me that Mildred doesn't know who Millie is. She's just being polite. Millie was born after Mildred's decline began, so there's no persistent memory there. Millie will always be fresh and new to her.

Mildred and Millie talk briefly about frogs and flowers and puppies. Millie does most of the talking. At first Mildred seems to enjoy the conversation, but soon her attention flags. She nods and smiles, but she's distant. Finally Susan notices. "That's enough, Millie. Why don't you go play in the garden?"

"Can I?" Millie squeals. Susan nods, and Millie races down the hall to the back door. She loves the outdoors, as I have noted in the past. I have never emulated her, but I've analyzed her at length. In many ways, she reminds me of her grandmother, from whom she gets her name. Both are blank slates where new experiences can be drawn every day. But where Millie's slate fills in a little more each day, Mildred's is erased bit by bit.

That third part of me wonders when I think things like that: where did that come from? I suspect that the psychological models that I build create resonances in other parts of my net. It is an interesting phenomenon to observe.

Susan and Mildred talk about Susan's job, about her plans to redecorate her house, and about the concert she just saw with Paul. Susan mostly talks about herself, because that's a safe and comfortable topic far removed from Mildred's health.

But then the conversation takes a bad turn, one she can't ignore. It starts so simply, when Mildred asks, "Susan, can you get me some juice?"

Susan rises from her chair. "Yes, mother. What kind would you like?"

Mildred frowns, and her voice rises. "Not you, *Susan.*" She points at me, and I freeze, hoping to keep things calm.

But Susan is not calm. I can see her fear in her eyes as she says, "No, mother, *I'm* Susan. That's the attendant." No one ever calls me an android in Mildred's presence. Her mind has withdrawn too far to grasp the idea of an artificial being.

Mildred's mouth draws into a tight line. "I don't know who *you* are, but I know Susan when I see her. Susan, get this person out of here!"

"Mother . . . " Susan reaches for Mildred, but the old woman recoils from the younger.

I touch Susan on the sleeve. "Please . . . Can we talk in the hall?" Susan's eyes are wide, and tears are forming. She nods and follows me.

In the hallway, I expect Susan to slap me. She is prone to outbursts when she's afraid. Instead, she surprises me by falling against me, sobbing. I update her emulation profile with notes about increased stress and heightened fears.

"It's all right, Mrs. Owens." I would pat her back, but her profile warns me that would be too much familiarity. "It's all right. It's not you, she's having another bad day."

Susan pulls back and wiped her eyes. "I know . . . It's just . . . "

"I know. But here's what we'll do. Let's take a few minutes, and then you can take her juice in. Mildred will have forgotten the incident, and you two can talk freely without me in the room."

She sniffs. "You think so?" I nod. "But what will you do?"

"I have tasks around the house."

"Oh, could you go out and keep an eye on Millie? Please? She gets into the darnedest things."

So I spend much of the day playing with Millie. She calls me Mr. Robot, and I call her Miss Millie, which makes her laugh. She shows me frogs from the creek, and she finds insects and leaves and flowers, and I find their names in online databases. She delights in learning the proper names of things, and everything else that I can share.

Today I was nobody. Mildred slept for most of the day, so I "slept" as well. She woke just now. "I'm hungry" was all she said, but it was enough to wake my empathy net.

Today I am Paul, and Susan, and both Nurse Judys. Mildred's focus drifts. Once I try to be her father, but no one has ever described him to me in detail. I try to synthesize a profile from Henry and Paul; but from the sad look on Mildred's face, I know I failed.

Today I had no name through most of the day, but now I am Paul again. I bring Mildred her dinner, and we have a quiet, peaceful talk about long-gone family pets—long-gone for Paul, but still present for Mildred.

I am just taking Mildred's plate when alerts sound, both audible and in my internal communication net. I check the alerts and find a fire in the basement. I expect the automatic systems to suppress it, but that is not my concern. I must get Mildred to safety.

Mildred looks around the room, panic in her eyes, so I try to project calm. "Come on, Ma. That's the fire drill. You remember fire drills. We have to get you into your chair and outside."

"No!" she shrieks. "I don't like outside."

I check the alerts again. Something has failed in the automatic systems, and the fire is spreading rapidly. Smoke is in Mildred's room already.

I pull the wheelchair up to the bed. "Ma, it's real important we do this drill fast, okay?"

I reach to pull Mildred from the bed, and she screams. "Get away! Who are you? Get out of my house!"

"I'm—" But suddenly I'm nobody. She doesn't recognize me, but I have to try to win her confidence. "I'm Paul, Ma. Now let's move. Quickly!" I pick her up. I'm far too large and strong for her to resist, but I must be careful so she doesn't hurt herself.

The smoke grows thicker. Mildred kicks and screams. Then, when I try to put her into her chair, she stands on her unsteady legs. Before I can stop her, she pushes the chair back with surprising force. It rolls back into the medical monitors, which fall over onto it, tangling it in cables and tubes.

While I'm still analyzing how to untangle the chair, Mildred stumbles toward the bedroom door. The hallway outside has a red glow. Flames lick at the throw rug outside, and I remember the home oxygen tanks in the sitting room down the hall.

I have no time left to analyze. I throw a blanket over Mildred and I scoop her up in my arms. Somewhere deep in my nets is a map of the fire in the house, blocking the halls, but I don't think about it. I wrap the blanket tightly around Mildred, and I crash through the picture window.

We barely escape the house before the fire reaches the tanks. An explosion lifts and tosses us. I was designed as a medical assistant, not an acrobat, and I fear I'll injure Mildred; but though I am not limber, my perceptions are thousands of times faster than human. I cannot twist Mildred out of my way before I hit the ground, so I toss her clear. Then I land, and the impact jars all of my nets for 0.21 seconds.

When my systems stabilize, I have damage alerts all throughout my core, but I ignore them. I feel the heat behind me, blistering my outer cover, and I ignore that as well. Mildred's blanket is burning in multiple places, as is the grass around us. I scramble to my feet, and I roll Mildred on the ground. I'm not indestructible, but I feel no pain and Mildred does, so I do not hesitate to use my hands to pat out the flames.

As soon as the blanket is out, I pick up Mildred, and I run as far from the house as I can get. At the far corner of the garden near the creek, I gently set Mildred down, unwrap her, and feel for her thready pulse.

Mildred coughs and slaps my hands. "Get away from me!" More coughing. "What are you?"

The "what" is too much for me. It shuts down my emulation net, and all I have is the truth. "I am Medical Care Android BRKCX-01932-217JH-98662, Mrs. Owens. I am your caretaker. May I please check that you are well?"

But my empathy net is still online, and I can read terror in every line of Mildred's face. "Metal monster!" she yells. "Metal monster!" She crawls away, hiding under the lilac bush. "Metal!" She falls into an extended coughing spell.

I'm torn between her physical and her emotional health, but physical wins out. I crawl slowly toward her and inject her with a sedative from the medical kit in my chassis. As she slumps, I catch her and lay her carefully on the ground. My empathy net signals a possible shutdown condition, but my concern for her health overrides it. I am programmed for long-term care, not emergency medicine, so I start downloading protocols and integrating them into my storage as I check her for bruises and burns. My kit has salves and painkillers and other supplies to go with my new protocols, and I treat what I can.

But I don't have oxygen, or anything to help with Mildred's coughing. Even sedated, she hasn't stopped. All of my emergency protocols assume I have access to oxygen, so I don't know what to do.

I am still trying to figure that out when the EMTs arrive and take over Mildred's care. With them on the scene, I am superfluous, and my empathy net finally shuts down.

Today I am Henry. I do not want to be Henry, but Paul tells me that Mildred needs Henry by her side in the hospital. For the end.

Her medical records show that the combination of smoke inhalation, burns, and her already deteriorating condition have proven too much for her. Her body is shutting down faster than medicine can heal it, and the stress has accelerated her mental decline. The doctors have told the family that the kindest thing at this point is to treat her pain, say goodbye, and let her go.

Henry is not talkative at times like this, so I say very little. I sit by Mildred's side and hold her hand as the family comes in for final visits. Mildred drifts in and out. She doesn't know this is goodbye, of course.

Anna is first. Mildred rouses herself enough to smile, and she recognizes her granddaughter. "Anna . . . child . . . How is . . . Ben?" That was Anna's boyfriend almost six years ago. From the look on Anna's face, I can see that she has forgotten Ben already, but Mildred briefly remembers.

"He's . . . He's fine, Grandma. He wishes he could be here. To say—to see you again." Anna is usually the strong one in the family, but my empathy net says her strength is exhausted. She cannot bear to look at Mildred, so she looks at me; but I am emulating her late grandfather, and that's too much for her as well. She says a few more words, unintelligible even to my auditory inputs. Then she leans over, kisses Mildred, and hurries from the room.

Susan comes in next. Millie is with her, and she smiles at me. I almost emulate Mr. Robot, but my third part keeps me focused until Millie gets bored and leaves. Susan tells trivial stories from her work and from Millie's school. I can't tell if Mildred understands or not, but she smiles and laughs, mostly at appropriate places. I laugh with her.

Susan takes Mildred's hand, and the Henry part of me blinks, surprised. Susan is not openly affectionate under normal circumstances, and especially not toward

Mildred. Mother and daughter-in-law have always been cordial, but never close. When I am Paul, I am sure that it is because they are both so much alike. Paul sometimes hums an old song about "just like the one who married dear old dad," but never where either woman can hear him. Now, as Henry, I am touched that Susan has made this gesture but saddened that she took so long.

Susan continues telling stories as we hold Mildred's hands. At some point Paul quietly joins us. He rubs Susan's shoulders and kisses her forehead, and then he steps in to kiss Mildred. She smiles at him, pulls her hand free from mine, and pats his cheek. Then her arm collapses, and I take her hand again.

Paul steps quietly to my side of the bed and rubs my shoulders as well. It comforts him more than me. He needs a father, and an emulation is close enough at this moment.

Susan keeps telling stories. When she lags, Paul adds some of his own, and they trade back and forth. Slowly their stories reach backwards in time, and once or twice Mildred's eyes light as if she remembers those events.

But then her eyes close, and she relaxes. Her breathing quiets and slows, but Susan and Paul try not to notice. Their voices lower, but their stories continue.

Eventually the sensors in my fingers can read no pulse. They have been burned, so maybe they're defective. To be sure, I lean in and listen to Mildred's chest. There is no sound: no breath, no heartbeat.

I remain Henry just long enough to kiss Mildred goodbye. Then I am just me, my empathy net awash in Paul and Susan's grief.

I leave the hospital room, and I find Millie playing in a waiting room and Anna watching her. Anna looks up, eyes red, and I nod. New tears run down her cheeks, and she takes Millie back into Mildred's room.

I sit, and my nets collapse.

Now I am nobody. Almost always.

The cause of the fire was determined to be faulty contract work. There was an insurance settlement. Paul and Susan sold their own home and put both sets of funds into a bigger, better house in Mildred's garden.

I was part of the settlement. The insurance company offered to return me to the manufacturer and pay off my lease, but Paul and Susan decided they wanted to keep me. They went for a full purchase and repair. Paul doesn't understand why, but Susan still fears she may need my services—or Paul might, and I may have to emulate her. She never admits these fears to him, but my empathy net knows.

I sleep most of the time, sitting in my maintenance alcove. I bring back too many memories that they would rather not face, so they leave me powered down for long periods.

But every so often, Millie asks to play with Mr. Robot, and sometimes they decide to indulge her. They power me up, and Miss Millie and I explore all the mysteries of the garden. We built a bridge to the far side of the creek; and on the other side, we're planting daisies. Today she asked me to tell her about her grandmother.

Today I am Mildred.

About the Authors

A Que was born in Jingzhou, Hubei in 1990 and graduated from the Hydraulic and Hydropower Engineering Department of Sichuan University. In 2012, he published his first work *Quietly Awakening*, which was soon followed by *Wine Cup Flowing on the Rivers, Walking with Robots, Childhood of Harvest,* and *I Tell Stories about My Grandfather.*

Bao Shu is a Chinese SF writer living in Xi'an. He began his writing career since 2010, and has published two collections and four novels since, including *Three body Problem X: the Redemption of Time* and *Ruins of Time.* His shorter works are often published by magazines like *Science Fiction World, ZUI Fiction, Knowledge is Power,* and *People's Literature.* He has won several major awards for Chinese SF. Several of his works are now available in English, published by *F&SF* and *Clarkesworld.*

Elizabeth Bourne has previously published short fiction in *Fantasy & Science Fiction, Clarkesworld, Interzone, Black Lantern,* and the anthology *Welcome to Dystopia.* She received a month-long writing residency in 2018 from Gullkistan Center for Creativity in Iceland for the purpose of developing her published short story, "Designed for Your Safety" into a novel. Bourne grew up in Lovecraft country and assures you that his work wasn't fiction. She currently lives in Seattle where trolls do, in fact, live under bridges.

Bo-young Kim is one of South Korea's most active and important SF authors. Her first published work of fiction, a novella titled "The Experience of Touch" (2002), received the award for best novella in the first round of the Korean Science & Technology Creative Writing Awards in 2004. Since then, she has published numerous works of short fiction in assorted Korean SF anthologies and magazines. In 2010 she published a two-volume collection of short stories, *The Story Goes That Far* and *An Evolutionary Myth.* 2013 saw the publication of her first novel, *The Seven Executioners,* which won the first annual South Korean SF novel award (a prize launched in 2014). Kim enjoys widespread popularity and support among Korean SF fandom, and on the strength of her fiction writing, she was recruited by Bong Joon-ho to serve as a script advisor during the development of his film *Snowpiercer.* She lives in Gangwon Province, South Korea with her family, and continues to write while operating a farm that produces peppers and chillies.

Kay Chronister is originally from Seattle, spent a year in Phnom Penh, Cambodia, and now lives in Tucson, Arizona. She was the winner of the 2015 Dell Magazine Award, and her fiction has since appeared in *Clarkesworld, Beneath Ceaseless Skies, Strange Horizons, Black Static,* and *Shimmer.* She is currently a PhD student in English Literature at the University of Arizona, studying women's writing in the Romantic era and the Gothic novel.

Nine of **Emily Devenport**'s novels were published in the U.S. by NAL/Roc, under three pen names. She has also been published in the U.K., Italy, Israel, and China. Her novel, *Broken Time* (written as Maggy Thomas) was nominated for the Philip K. Dick Award. She has two new novels from Tor: *Medusa Uploaded* (May 2018) and *Medusa in the Graveyard* (forthcoming, 2019).

Her short stories were published in *Asimov's SF Magazine,* the *Full Spectrum* anthology, *The Mammoth Book of Kaiju, Uncanny, Cicada, Science Fiction World, Alfred Hitchcock, Clarkesworld,* and *Aboriginal SF,* whose readers voted her a Boomerang Award. She blogs at www.emsjoiedeweird.com.

Andy Dudak's fiction has appeared in *Analog, Apex, Clarkesworld, Interzone,* Rich Horton's Year's Best, and many other places. He's been lucky enough to translate the likes of Liu Cixin, Chi Hui, and Bao Shu. He owns no cats but has nothing against them. He doesn't trust birds.

Han Song is a reporter for Xinhua News and a prolific science fiction author. His novels include *Subway, Bullet Train, A Comet Illuminates America, Red Sea,* and *Tombstone of the Universe.* He received the Chinese Milky Way Science Fiction Award in 1988 and 1990, the World Chinese Science Fiction Association Science Fiction Art Award in 1991, and the Chinese Science Fiction Art and Literature Award in 1995.

Berrien C. Henderson lives in the deepest, darkest wilds of southeast Georgia. He teaches high school Literature and Composition with a Southern accent. Berrien's writing has appeared in such diverse venues as *The Journal of Asian Martial Arts, The Doctor T.J. Eckleburg Review, The Dead Mule School of Southern literature, Abyss & Apex, Kaleidotrope,* and *Bloody Knuckles: The MMAnthology.* His mini-collection of Southern magical realism, *Old Souls and the Grammar of Their Wanderings,* is available from Papaveria Press. In his not-so-copious free time, Berrien practices martial arts.

Matthew Kressel is a three-time Nebula Award Finalist, a World Fantasy Award finalist, and most recently a Eugie Foster Memorial Award finalist. His novel King of Shards was hailed as, "Majestic, resonant, reality-twisting madness," from NPR Books. His short fiction has or will soon appear in many places, including *Clarkesworld, Lightspeed, Analog, Tor.com, Nightmare, io9.com, Apex Magazine, Beneath Ceaseless Skies, Interzone,* and the anthologies *Mad Hatters and March Hares, Cyber World,* and *After.* He co-hosts the Fantastic Fiction at

KGB reading series in Manhattan alongside Ellen Datlow, and he is a long-time member of the Altered Fluid writers group. Find him online @mattkressel or www.matthewkressel.net.

Yoon Ha Lee's debut *Ninefox Gambit* won the Locus Award for best first novel, and was a finalist for the Hugo, Nebula, and Clarke Awards. Its sequel, *Raven Stratagem,* is currently a finalist for the Hugo Award, and the third book of the trilogy, *Revenant Gun,* was published in June 2018. His middle grade space opera *Dragon Pearl* is forthcoming from Disney-Hyperion is January 2019. His short fiction has appeared in *Tor.com, Clarkesworld, Lightspeed Magazine, The Magazine of Fantasy & Science Fiction, Beneath Ceaseless Skies,* and other venues. Lee lives in Louisiana with his family and a lazy cat, and has not yet been eaten by gators.

Sam J. Miller lives in New York City now, but grew up in a middle-of-nowhere town in upstate New York. He is the last in a long line of butchers. In no particular order, he has also been a film critic, a grocery bagger, a community organizer, a secretary, a painter's assistant and model, and the guitarist in a punk rock band. His debut novel *The Art of Starving* (YA/SF) was published by HarperCollins in 2017, followed by *The Breaks* from Ecco Press in 2018. His stories have been nominated for the Nebula, World Fantasy, and Theodore Sturgeon Awards, and have appeared in over a dozen "best-of" anthologies. He's a graduate of the Clarion Science Fiction & Fantasy Writers Workshop, and he's a winner of the Shirley Jackson Award. His husband of fifteen years is a nurse practitioner, and way smarter and handsomer than Sam is.

Kris Millering is a linguist by training, a tech tinkerer by trade, and a writer and photographer by avocation. Currently, she works in tech and writes whenever she has a moment to breathe. Her fiction has appeared in *Beneath Ceaseless Skies, Apex, Lightspeed, Clarkesworld,* and other publications. You can find out more at krismillering.com.

Ian Muneshwar is a Boston-based writer whose fiction appears in *Clarkesworld, Strange Horizons,* and *Year's Best Weird Fiction,* among other venues. He lives online at ianmuneshwar.com.

Pan Haitian is a well-known figure among the third generation of Chinese science fiction authors. His previous work includes the collection *Run Dajiao! Run!* (New World Press, 2001) and four novels set in the Novoland universe: *Ghost Sparrow, Spirit Turtle* (New World Press, 2006), *The Iron Stupa* (New World Press, 2007), *24 Second Paradise* (serialized in China Fantasy, 2009-10), and *A Dark Moon Rises* (Hunan Art and Literature Press October, 2012). He is also a founding editor of the influential Chinese magazine, *Odyssey of China Fantasy.*

J.B. Park's stories have appeared in *Clarkesworld, Lightspeed, Strange Horizons,* and more. Find him online at maybepark.com, or on twitter at @saddestpark.

By day, **Andrea M. Pawley** and her unpoppable bubble of enthusiasm careen through Washington D.C. in defiance of Pierre L'Enfant's plans, potholes and the small gods of sensibility. By night, Andrea writes stories, and the bubble shouts encouragement. Find her online at www.andreapawley.com.

Robert Reed is the author of several hundred published works of SF, including tales about the Great Ship and its mysterious cargo, Marrow. Among his recent projects, Reed is putting portions of his catalog up on Kindle, as well as his next Great Ship novel, *The Dragons of Marrow.*
  The author lives in Lincoln, Nebraska with his wife and daughter.

Erica L. Satifka is a writer and/or friendly artificial construct, forged in a heady mix of iced coffee and sarcasm. She enjoys rainy days, questioning reality, ignoring her to-do list, and adding to her collection of tattoos. Her debut novel *Stay Crazy* (Apex Publications) won the 2017 British Fantasy Award for Best Newcomer, and her short fiction has appeared in *Clarkesworld, Shimmer, Interzone,* and *The Dark.* She lives in Portland, Oregon with her spouse Rob and an indeterminate number of cats.

Martin L. Shoemaker is a programmer who writes on the side . . . or maybe it's the other way around. Programming pays the bills, but his second-place story in the Jim Baen Memorial Writing Contest earned him lunch with Buzz Aldrin. Programming never did that! His *Clarkesworld* story "Today I Am Paul" received the Washington Science Fiction Society's Small Press Award, and was also nominated for a Nebula award. It has been reprinted in *Year's Best Science Fiction: Thirty-third Annual Edition* (edited by Gardner Dozois), *The Best Science Fiction of the Year: Volume One* (edited by Neil Clarke), *The Year's Best Science Fiction and Fantasy 2016* (edited by Rich Horton), and *The Year's Top Ten Tales of Science Fiction 8* (edited by Allan Kaster). It has been translated into French, Hebrew, Czech, Polish, German, and Chinese. Others of his stories have appeared in *Analog, Galaxy's Edge, Digital Science Fiction, Forever Magazine,* and *Writers of the Future Volume 31.*

Benjanun Sriduangkaew writes love letters to strange cities, beautiful bugs, and the future. Her work has appeared in *Tor.com, Beneath Ceaseless Skies, Phantasm Japan, The Dark,* and year's bests. She has been shortlisted for the Campbell Award for Best New Writer and her debut novella *Scale-Bright* has been nominated for the British SF Association Award.

Bogi Takács is a Hungarian Jewish agender trans person (e/em/eir/emself or they pronouns). E writes, reviews and edits speculative fiction and poetry. Bogi is a winner of the Lambda award for editing *Transcendent 2: The Year's Best*

Transgender Speculative Fiction 2016, and currently a finalist for the Hugo and Locus awards. You can read Bogi's thoughts about books at bogireadstheworld. com, and find em as @bogiperson on Twitter, Instagram and Patreon.

Natalia Theodoridou is a media & cultural studies scholar, the dramaturge of Adrift Performance Makers, and a writer of strange stories. Natalia's work has appeared in *Strange Horizons, Beneath Ceaseless Skies, Apex,* and elsewhere. Her first interactive novel, *Rent-a-Vice,* was published by Choice of Games in 2018. Natalia is also an editor at *sub-Q* and will soon be a graduate of Clarion West ('18). Find out more at her website, www.natalia-theodoridou.com, or follow @ natalia_theodor on Twitter.

E. Catherine Tobler is a Sturgeon Award finalist and editor at *Shimmer Magazine.*

Clarkesworld Citizens
OFFICIAL CENSUS

We would like to thank the following Clarkesworld Citizens for their support:

Citizens
Michael Adams, Magnus Adamsson, Alan & Jeremy VS Science Fiction, Pete Aldin, Elye Alexander, Alexi, Maral Seyed Ali Agha, Richard Alison, Joshua Allen, Alllie, Imron Alston, Tj Alston, Ro Anders, Clifford Anderson, Kim Anderson, Tor Andre, Dan Andresen, Randall Andrews, Anon, Therese Arkenberg, Sharon Arnette, Randall Arnold, Ash, Stephen Astels, Anonymous Author, A. Alfred Ayache, Chris Aylott, Bill B., Benjamin Baker, Brian B. Baker, Gordon Bannon, Great Barbarian, Jenny Barber, Johanne Barron, Anna Y. Baskina, Jeff Bass, Meredith Battjer, Anna Bauer-Baxter, Moya Bawden, Paul Becker, Aaron Begg, Ben, LaNeta Bergst, Julie Berg-Thompson, Clark Berry, Kevin Besig, Matt Bewley, Amy Billingham, Dale Randolph Bivins, Tracey Bjorksten, John Blackman, John Bledsoe, Mike Blevins, Adam Blomquist, Bluebuel, Allison Bocksruker, Kevin Bokelman, Michael Bowen, Brian Bowes, Winfield Brackeen, Michael Braun Hamilton, Commander Breetai, Nathan Breit, Allan Breitstein, Cristiano Malanga Breuel, Jennifer Brissett, Britny Brooks, Jeremy Brown, Kit Brown, Richard Brown, Laurence Browning, Tobias S. Buckell, Jacki Buist, Thomas Bull, Michael Bunkahle, Karl Bunker, Alison Burke, Cory Burr, Jefferson Burson, Kristin Buxton, Graeme Byfield, Bryce C, Matthew C Walker, C9lewis, Andrew J. Cahill, Darrell Cain, Caitrin, C.G. Cameron, Ricardo Canizares, Paul Carignan, Yazburg Carlberg, Liam Carpenter-Urquhart, Michael Carr, Cast of Wonders, Nance Cedar, Timothy Charlton, David Chasson, Catherine Cheek, Paige Chicklo, Joe Chip, The Chocolate Delicacy, Maria Cichetti, Victoria Cleave, J.B. & Co., Alicia Cole, Elizabeth Coleman, Greg Coleson, Elisabeth Colter, Che Comrie, Dr. SP Conboy-Hil, Johne Cook, Claire Cooney, Martin Cooper, Lisa Costello, Thomas Costick, Ashley Coulter, Charles Cox, Michael Cox, Sonya Craig, K Crain, Yoshi Creelman, Tina Crone, Cathy Cunliffe, Curtis42, Lorraine Dahm, Shawn D'Alimonte, Sarah Dalton, Ang Danieldeskbrain - Watercress Munster, Chua Dave, Morgan Davey, Ed Davidoff, Chase Davies, Katrina Davies, Craig Davis, Lee Davis, Gustavo de Albuquerque, Alessia De Gaspari, Alamon Elf Defield, Del DeHart, Maria-Isabel Deira, Daniel DeLano, Dennis DeMario, Patrick Derrickson, Michele Desautels, Paul DesCombaz, Allison M. Dickson,

Lindsey Dillon, Geri Diorio, Aidan Doyle, Sage Draculea, Dsbjr, DT, Alex Dunbar, Albert Dunberg, Susan Duncan, Andrew Eason, Roger East, The Eaton Law Firm, David Eggli, Jesse Eisenhower, Samuel Eleuterio, Sarah Elkins, Brad Elliott, Warren Ellis, Dale Eltoft, Douglas Engstrom, Lyle Enright, Peter Enyeart, Nancy Epperly, Erik, Yvonne Ewing, Extranet Vendors Association, Edward Fagan, Feather, Denis Ferentinos, Josiah Ferrin, A Fettered Mind, TJ Fly, Ethan Fode, Dense Fog, Francesca Forrest, Jason Frank, Carol Franko, Michael Fratus, William Fred, Amy Fredericks, Michael Frighetto, Sarah Frost, Froxis, Fyrbaul, Jennifer Gagliardi, Paul Gainford, Robert Garbacz, Eleanor Gausden, Petar Gayan, Leslie Gelwicks, Susan Gibbs, Phil Giles, Cas Gillam, Rebecca Girash, Holly Glaser, Susanne Glaser, Sangay Glass, Globular, Eric Gomez, Laura Goodin, Don Grayson, Grendel, Besha Grey, Valerie Grimm, Damien Grintalis, GRO Industries, Janet Groenert, Michael Grosberg, Nikki Guerlain, Ancestors Guide Me, Xavier Guillemane, Russell Guppy, Geoffrey Guthrie, Richard Guttormson, James Hall, Lee Hallison, Janus Hansen, Happybunnyatthezoo, Roy Hardin, Jonathan Harnum, Harpoon, Dan Harrington, Jubal Harshaw, Darren Hawbrook, Brian Hawthorne, Emily Hebert, Leon Hendee, Jamie Henderson, Philip Henderson, Samantha Henderson, Dave Hendrickson, Steven Hennig, JC Henry, Karen Heuler, Dan Hiestand, John Higham, Renata Hill, Hillreiner, Tim Hills, Mark Hinchman, Peter Hogberg, Peter Hollmer, Andrea Horbinski, Clarence Horne III, Richard Horton, Bill Howell, Margaret Howie, Fiona Howland-Rose, Roger Hudman, Pete Huerta, Rex Hughes II, Jeremy Hull, John Humpton, iain hunter, Gene Hyers, Dwight Illk, John Imhoff, Iridum Sound Envoy, Isbell, Joseph Jacir, Jack, Marie Jackson, Stephen Jacob, Sarah James, Joseph A. Jechenthal III, Jimbo, JJ, Elizabeth Jo Otto, Dick Johnson, Steve Johnson, Patrick Johnston, Paul B. Joiner, Judith Jones, Jschekker, Ryan H. Kacani, Gabriel Kaknes, Philip Kaldon, Karl-TheGood, Sara Kathryn, Chris Kattner, Cagatay Kavukcuoglu, Jonathan Kay, Keenan, Jason Keeton, Robert Keller, Mary Kellerman, Betty Kelly, Jim Kelly, Kelson, Shawn Keslar, John Kilgallon, KillZoneOZ, Dana Kincaid, Kisaki, Kate Kligman, Roy and Norma Kloster, Bryan Knower, Seymour Knowles-Barley, Matthew Koch, Will Koenig, Konstantinos Kontos, Sean CW Korsgaard, Lutz F. Krebs, John Krewson, Heiti Kulmar, Derek Kunsken, Sarah L., MJ LA QUOC, Michele Laframboise, Jason Lai, Paul Lamarre, Gina Langridge, Abby Larkin, Scotty Larsen, Darren Ledgerwood, Brittany Lehman, Terra Lemay, Wayne Lester, Philip Levin, Brian Lewis, Danielle Linder, Matthew Line, Simon Litten, Jerry Little, Susan Llewellyn, Renata M. Lloyd, Jay Lofstead, Lornak, Thomas Loyal, Sharon Lunde, James Lyle, H Lynnea Johnson, Tim M, Robert Mac, Meredyth Mackay, Peter MacMillin, Ilia Malkovitch, Raegan Mann, Dan Manning, Margaret, Mark, Ivan Markos, Eric Marsh, Jacque Marshall, Tony Marsico, Dominique Martel, Janet Martin, Fernando Martinez, Cethar Mascaw, Daniel Mathews, Matthew, David Mayes, Derek W. McAleer, Mike McBride, T.C. McCarthy, Jeffrey McDonald, Holly McEntee, Josh McGraw, Demitrius McHugh, Roland McIntosh, Christopher M. McKeever, Steve Medina, Brent Mendelsohn, Kristen Menichelli, Seth Merlo, Stephen Middleton, John Midgley, Matthew Miller, Stephan Miller, Terry Miller, Alan Mimms, Serene Mirkis, Dale Mitchell, Mjpearce,

Mahesh Raj Mohan, Aidan Moher, Jacob Molaro, Marian Moore, Tim Moore, Sunny Moraine, Jamie Morgan, DJ Morrison, Jon Moss, Lynette Moss, Tomasz Mrozewski, Patricia Murphy, Lori Murray, Karl Myers, Mike Myers, Jack Myers Photography, Will Nash, Leona Nette, Glenn Nevill, Jeffrey Newman, Stella Nickerson, Matthew Nielsen, Robyn Nielsen, Elaine Nobbs, Norm, Tom Nosack, Robert Nowak, Zam Nuclear Wesell, David Oakley, Oddscribe, Hugh J. O'Donnell, Scott Oesterling, Christopher Ogilvie, James Oliver, Lydia Ondrusek, Ruth O'Neill, Erik Ordway, Dan Osborne, Aaron Osgood-Zimmerman, Felicia Osul-livan, Nancy Owens, Moe P, Thomas Pace, Norman Paley, Mieneke Pallada, Clifford Parrish, Thomas Parrish, Sidsel Pedersen, Edgar Penderghast, Tzum Pepah, Chris Perkins, Nikki Philley, Maria Pia Sass, Aimee Picchi, Adrian-Teo-dor Pienaru, Jamison Pinkert, Beth Plutchak, Andy Pond, David Potter, Ed Prior, David Raco, Radulovie, Adam Rakunas, Ralan, Steve Ramey, Diego Ramos, Robert Redick, Amparo Palma Reig, George Reilly, Steven Reneau, Joshua Reynolds, Julia Reynolds, Rick of the North, Zach Ricks, Carl Rigney, Ashley Rivers, Robert, Hank Roberts, Tansy Rayner Roberts, Kenneth Robkin, James Rowh, RPietila, Sarah Rudek, Woodworking Running Dog, Oliver Rupp, Paul Rush, Caitlin Russell, Abigail Rustad, S2 Sally, Tim Sally, Sam, Nadia Sandren, Jason Sanford, Erica L. Satifka, Steven Saus, SausageMix, MJ Scafati, Gregory Scheckler, Chris Schierer, Nancy Schrock, Jason Schroeder, Don Schwartz, Gerald Schwartz, Graham Scott, Richard Shapiro, George Shea, Kieran Sheldon, Espana Sheriff, T. L. Sherwood, Udayan Shevade, Josh Shiben, Heather Shipman, Robert Shuster, Aileen Simpson, Taylor Simpson, John Skylar, Kate Small, Rebecca Smith, Karen Snyder, Morgan Songi, Soren, Michelle Souliere, Jozef Sovcik, Mat Spalding, Gary Spears, Elwood Spencer, Julian Spergel, carl spicer, Stephen Sprusansky, Zachary Stansell, Keith Stebor, Steven, Terry Squire Stone, A Strange Loop, Jennifer Stufflebeam, Julia Sullivan, J Sutton, Jennifer Sutton, Jherek Swanger, John Swartzentruber, Kenneth Takigawa, Charles Tan, William Tank, Beth Tanner, Jesse Tauriainen, David Taylor, Paul Taylor, Lim Wee Teck, Chantal Thomas, James Thomas, Brett Tofel, Jaye Tomas, Felix Troendle, The Unsettled Foundation, Julia Varga, John Vassar, Adam Vaughan, William Vennell, Vettac, Ralph Wahlstrom, George S. Walker, Shiloh Walker, Diane Walton, K.E. Walton, Stefan Walzer, Robert Wamble, Bobbi Warburton, John Watrous, Matthew J. Weaver, Nat Weinham, Robert Werner, Neil Weston, Peter Wetherall, Adam White, Spencer Wightman, Dan Wilburn, Jeff Williamson, Neil Williamson, Nicola Willis, A.C. Wise, Devon Wong, Mr. J.R. Woroniecki, Chalmer Wren, Dan Wright, Kevin Wynn, Lachlan Yeates, Catherine York, Pandora A. Young, Rena Zayit, Frederick Zorn, Stephanie Zvan

Burgermeisters
7ony, Rob Abram, Paula Acton, Andy Affleck, Rowena Alberga, Frederick Amerman, Carl Anderson, Mel Anderson, Andy90, Marie Angell, John Appel, Misha Argall, Jon Arnold, Catherine Asaro, Mike R. D. Ashley, Robert Avie, B, Mr. B., Erika Bailey, Michael W. Baily, Brian Baker, Nathan Bamberg, Michael Banker, Jay Barnes, Laura Barnitz, Jennifer Bartolowits, Deborah Beale, Lenni

Benson, Kerry Benton, Leon Bernhardt, TJ Berry, Bill Bibo Jr, Steve Bickle, Brenna Blackwell, Edward Blake, Samuel Blinn, Jeff Boardman, Johanna Bobrow, Kaye Bohemier, EXO Books, Joan Boyle, Brakeparts1234, Patricia Bray, Tim Brenner, Arrie Brown, Ken Brown, BruceC, Carl Brusse, Sharat Buddhavarapu, Max Buffington, Adam Bursey, Jeremy Butler, Robyn Butler, Roland Byrd, Jarrett Byrnes, Heather Cailaoife, Janice Calm, Brad Campbell, Anthony R. Cardno, Carleton45, James Carlino, Ted Carr, Benjamin Cartwright, Evan Cassity, Lee Cavanaugh, Peter Charron, Randall Chertkow, Michael Chorman, John Chu, Maggie Clark, Matthew Claxton, Marian Collins-Steding, Theodore Conti, George Cook, Brian Cooksey, Brenda Cooper, Lorraine Cooper, Matt Craig, Lucy Cummin, B D Fagan, Gillian Daniels, Nicholas V David, David, James Davies, Pamela J. Davis, Tessa Day, Jetse de Vries, Brian Deacon, Bartley Deason, Ricado Delacruz, Keith DePew, John Devenny, Peter Dibble, Dino, Fran Ditzel-Friel, Gary Dockter, Nicholas Doran, Christopher Doty, Nicholas Dowbiggin, Mr. R. J. Dowrick, Robert Drabek, Paul Dzus, Mela Eckenfels, Eileen, Steve Emery, Sagi Eppel, Christine Ertell, Joanna Evans, Patricia Evans, Kathy Farretta, Dietrich Faust, Rare Feathers, Tea Fish, FlatFootedRat, Bruce Fleischer, Lynn Flewelling, Adrienne Foster, William Frankenhoff, Matthew Fredrickson, Alina Fridberg, Eric Fritz, Larry Garnett, Christopher Garry, Pierre Gauthier, Gerhen, Mark Gerrits, Tanya Glaser, Lorelei Goelz, Ed Goforth, Melanie Goldmund, Martin Gonzalez, Inga Gorslar, Peter Goyen, Tony Graham, Jaq Greenspon, Eric Gregory, Marc Grella, Stephanie Gunn, Jim H, Laura Hake, AMD Hamm, Skeptyk/JeanneE Hand-Boniakowski, Mark S. Haney, Jordan Hanie, John Hanley, Frank Den Hartog, Joseph Heizman, Helixa 12, Normandy Helmer, Theresa A Hemminger, Daniel Herman, Corydon Hinton, Jon Hite, Elizabeth Hocking, Sheridan Hodges, Ronald Hordijk, Justin Howe, Bobby Hoyt, David Hudson, Shawn Huenniger, Huginn Huginn and Muninn, Chris Hurst, Kevin Ikenberry, Joseph Ilardi, Adam Israel, James Jackson, Jalal, Patty Jansen, Michael Jarcho, Jason, Cristal Java, Toni Jerrman, Audra Johnson, Erin Johnson, Russell Johnson, Robert Jones, Kai Juedemann, Andy Kaden, C. L. Kagmi, Jeff Kapustka, David Kelleher, James Kelly, Joshua Kidd, Alistair Kimble, Harvey King, Erin Kissane, John Klima, Cecil Knight, Michelle Knowlton, KP-ShadowSquirrel, Frances KR, Eric Kramer, JR Krebs, Chris Kreuter, Neal Kushner, Stephane Lacoste, Jan Lajka, Andrew Lanker, Kevin Lauderdale, James Frederick Leach, Krista Leahy, Kate Lechler, Robert Lehman, Alan Lehotsky, Leland, Annaliese Lemmon, Walter Leroy Perkins, L Leslie, edit leventon, Philip Levin, Kevin Liebkemann, Ao-Hui Lin, Linnaea, Jerry Little, Joyce E. Lively, James Lloyd, Susan Loyal, Kristi Lozano, LUX4489, Alicia Lynch, Keith M Frampton, Pete Macfarlane, Peter Mackey, Adam Mancilla, Brit Mandelo, Cat Manning, Mark Maris, Marlene, Matthew Marovich, Marqman, Samuel Marzioli, Jason Maurer, Rosaleen McCarthy, Peter McClean, Wes McConnell, Michael McCormack, Sean McFall, Tony McFee, Mark McGarry, Ace McInturff, Robyn McIntyre, Doug McLaughlin, Andrew McLeod, Craig McMurtry, Oscar McNary, Joe McTee, Margery Meadow, J Meijer, Geoffrey Meissner, Barry Melius, Sarfo Mensah, Alan Merriam, David Michalak, Mike, Robert Milson, Anonymous in MN, Sharon Mock, Eric Mohring, Carlos Mondragon, Samuel Montgomery-Blinn,

Lyda Morehouse, Griffin Morgan, Rebekah Murphy, John Murray, N M Wells Foundry Creative Media, Barrett Nichols, Tishangela Nierman, Jennifer Noga, Val Nolan, Peter Northup, Sean O'Brien, Am Onymous, Stian Ovesen, David Packer, Simon Page, Justin Palk, Norman Papernick, Richard Parks, Paivi Pasi, Paula, MJ Paxton, PBC Productions Inc., Katherine Pendill, Joshua Pevner, Eric Pierson, E. PLS, Lolt Proegler, Jonathan Pruett, QLM Aria X-Perienced, Robert Quinlivan, Thomas Rado, Rainspan, D. Randall Kerr, Joel Rankin, Raoul Raoul, Sherry Rehm, Erin Reilley, Paul Rice, Zack Richardson, James Rickard, Karsten Rink, Erik Rolstad, Joseph Romel, Leena Romppainen, Elena Ross, Peter Roy, Michael Russo, Miranda Rydell, Larry Sandhaas, Matthew Saunders, Patrick Savage, Stefan Scheib, Alan Scheiner, Ken Schneyer, Eric Schreiber, Patricia G. Scott, Terriell Scrimager II, Bluezoo Seven, Cosma Shalizi, Ross Shaw, Mike Sherling, Bill Shields, Jeremy Showers, Siznax, SK, John Skillingstead, Patrick Joseph Sklar, Josh Smift, Allen Snyder, David Sobyra, Daniel Solis, Caitlin Sticco, Lisa Stone, Jason Strawsburg, Stuart, Keffington Studios, Jerome Stueart, Robert Stutts, SuzB, Fredrik Svensson, John Swartzentruber, Gregory Taylor, W. Taylor, Maurice Termeer, Tero, John Thomas, Brent Thompson, Chuck Tindle, Raymond Tobaygo, Tradeblanket.com, Heather Tumey, Mary A. Turzillo, Marc Tyler, Ann VanderMeer, Andrew Vega, Nuno Miguel Pires Veloso, Natalie Vincent, Emil Volcheck, Andrew Volpe, Margaret Wack, Wendy Wagner, Alan Walker, Jennifer Walter, Rob Ward, Tom Waters, Tehani Wessely, John Whitaker, Chris White, Shannon White, Dan Wick, John Wienstroer, Seth Williams, Kristyn Willson, Paul Wilson, Dawn Wolfe, Zac Wong, Sarah Wright, Isabel Yap, Zackie, Peter Zeller, Slobodan Zivkovic

Royalty

Paul Abbamondi, Eric Agnew, Karsten Philip Aichholz, Albert Alfiler, Dan Allen, Rose Andrew, Karl Armstrong, Bruce Arthurs, Rush Austin, Raymond Bair, Jim Baker, Kathryn Baker, Lukas Karl Barnes, Anne Barringer, Zach Bartlett, Andrew and Kate Barton, David Beaudoin, Nathan Beittenmiller, Ralf Belling, Kevin Best, Nicolas Billon, Nathan Blumenfeld, Marty Bonus, David Borcherding, Robert Bose, Brian Brunswick, Nancy Buford, Kima Caddell, Robert Callahan, Carrie, Lady Cate, Richard Chappell, Joseph M. Christopher, Heather Clitheroe, Chad Colopy, Carolyn Cooper, Darcy Cox, Tom Crosshill, Michael Cullinan, Kathy Cygnarowicz, Mr D F Ryan, Darren Davidson, David Demers, Cory Doctorow, Brian Dolton, Dayne Encarnacion, Marcello Fabrizi, Matthew Farrer, Stephen Finch, Greg Frank, David Furniss, John Garberson, George Peter Gatsis, Kate Gillogly, Alexis Goble, Hilary Goldstein, Adam Haapala, David Hall, Carl Hazen, Andy Herrman, Brendan Hickey, Robin Hill, Kristin Hirst, Colin Hitch, Ian Hobson, Victoria Hoke, Marolynn Holloway, Jeppe V. Holm, Todd Honeycutt, Jason House, David Hoyt, Ianwillc, Christopher Irwin, Linda Jenner, Janna Jones, Virginia Jud, Robert Kennedy, Fred Kiesche, Corey Knadler, G.J. Kressley, Jamie Lackey, Jonathan Laden, M. Lane, Katherine Lee, Jeffrey Lewis, Marta Lillo, Dave Lister, Warren Litwin, Vincent P. Loeffler III, Kevin Lyda, Bob Magruder, Phil Margolies, Sean Markey, Andrew Marsh, Arun Mascarenhas, Daniel Maticzka,

Patrick McCann, Barrett McCormick, Matthew McKay, Kevin McKean, Margaret McNally, Michelle Broadribb MEG, Dave Miller, Nayad Monroe, James Moore, Jennifer Morrow, Ellen Moskowitz, Anne Murphy, Jennifer Navarrete, Patrick Neary, Persona Non-Grata, Charles Norton, Vincent O'Connor, Richard Ohnemus, David M. Oswin, H. Lincoln Parish, Marie Parsons, Lars Pedersen, David Personette, Matt Peterson, Matt Phelps, Jeremy Phillips, Gary Piserchio, Merja Polvinen, Lord Pontus, Ian Powell, Mary Jo Rabe, Rational Path, Captain Red Boots, Wesley Reeves, Patrick Reitz, RL, Rob, Kelly Robson, John Scalzi, Stu Segal, Maurice Shaw, Jan Shawyer, Angela Slatter, Saskia Slottje, Carrie Smith, Paul Smith, Samuel Smith, Nicholas Sokeland, Richard Sorden, Cheryl Souza, Kevin Standlee, Neal Stanifer, Chris Stave, Jeremy Tabor, S.Rheannon Terran, Colin Theys, Josh Thomson, TK, Terhi Tormanen, Andre Twupack, Sam van Rood, David Versace, Saoirse Victeoiria, Viscount of Kataan, Suzanne Vowles, Daniel Waldman, Jonathan Wallace, Sean Wallace, Jasen Ward, Izzy Wasserstein, Ian Watson, Taema Weiss, Weyla & Gos, Graeme Williams, Jessica Wolf, Matt Wyndowe, Jeff Xilon, Bob Z, Zola

Overlords
Renan Adams, Thomas Ball, Michael Blackmore, Nathalie Boisard-Beudin, Greg Bossert, Shawn Boyd, Jennifer Brozek, Vicki Bryan, Karen Burnham, Barbara Capoferri, Paul Chadwick, Clarke Chapman, Morgan Cheryl, Gio Clairval, Neil Clarke, Tania Clucas, Andrew Curry, Dolohov, Ebooks-worldwide, Sairuh Emilius, Lynne Everett, Joshua Faulkenberry, Fabio Fernandes, Benjamin Figueroa, Tony Fisk, Thomas Fleck, Eric Francis, Overperson Franklin, Brian Gardner, L A George, Michael Glyde, Bryan Green, Michael Habif, Andrew Hatchell, Berthiaume Heidi, Melissa House, Bill Hughes, Chris Hyde, Theodore J. Stanulis, Marcus Jager, Justin James, Jericho, Jfly, JKA Poetry, James Joyce, Lucas Jung, Gayathri Kamath, James Kinateder, Jay Kominek, Alice Kottmyer, Daniel LaPonsie, Susan Lewis, Edward MacGregor, Philip Maloney, Paul Marston, Matthew the Greying, Gabriel Mayland, MJ Mercer, Achilleas Michailides, Adrian Mihaila, Adrien Mitchell, Overlord Mondragon, James Morton, MrMovieZombie, Jose Muinos, Stephen Nelson, Joshua Newth, Dlanod Nosreetp, Andrea Pawley, Mike Perricone, Jody Plank, Clarissa R., Rick Ramsey, Thomas Reed, Jo Rhett, Rik, Jason Sank, Laura Schmidt, Lorenz Schwarz, Joseph Sconfitto, Marie Shcherbatskaya, William Shields, Sky, Tara Smith, David Steffen, Naru Sundar, Jacel the Thing, Robert Urell, M C VanderSchaaf, Thad Wilkinson, Elaine Williams, James Williams, richard Wyatt, Doug Young

Deities
Claire Alcock, Kenneth Burk, Eric Hunt, Gary Hunter, Robert Munsch, Rajeev Prasad, Kelvin Tsc

About Clarkesworld

Clarkesworld Magazine (clarkesworldmagazine.com) is a monthly science fiction and fantasy magazine first published in October 2006. Each issue contains interviews, thought-provoking articles and at least four pieces of original fiction. Our fiction is also available in ebook editions/subscriptions, audio podcasts and in our annual print anthologies.

Clarkesworld has received three Hugo Awards, one World Fantasy Award, and a British Fantasy Award. Our fiction has been nominated for or won the Hugo, Nebula, World Fantasy, Sturgeon, Locus, Shirley Jackson, WSFA Small Press and Stoker Awards. For information on how to subscribe to our electronic edition on your Kindle, Nook, iPad or other ereader/Android device, please visit: clarkesworldmagazine.com/subscribe/

Clarkesworld is edited by

Neil Clarke (neil-clarke.com) is the editor of *Clarkesworld Magazine* and *Forever Magazine*, owner of Wyrm Publishing, and a six-time Hugo Award Nominee for Best Editor (short form). His anthologies include *Upgraded, Galactic Empires, More Human Than Human, The Final Frontier*, and Best Science Fiction of the Year series. He currently lives in NJ with his wife and two sons.

Sean Wallace is a founding editor at *Clarkesworld Magazine,* owner of Prime Books, and winner of the World Fantasy Award. He currently lives in Maryland with his wife and two daughters.

www.ingramcontent.com/pod-product-compliance
Lightning Source LLC
Chambersburg PA
CBHW050553260626
47157CB00002B/545